DAZZLING REVIEWS FOR
SUE-ELLEN WELFONDER
AND HER NOVELS

SEDUCING A SCOTTISH BRIDE

"4½ Stars! Welfonder sweeps readers into a tale brimming with witty banter between a feisty heroine and a stalwart hero . . . The added paranormal elements and sensuality turn this into an intriguing page-turner that fans of Scottish romance will adore."
—*Romantic Times BOOKreviews Magazine*

"Extraordinary . . . a rare gift to savor."
—**SingleTitles.com**

"A great paranormal historical romance . . . Fans will read this in one delightful sitting, so set aside the time."
—*Midwest Book Review*

"Marvelous . . . Welfonder writes wonderful Scottish tales . . . This one is filled with danger, love, lust, and intrigue."
—**RomanceReviewsMag.com**

"A fabulous author . . . Gelis is a spirited heroine . . . and Ronan is a lovely Scottish hero . . . Does it get any better?"
—**BellaOnline.com**

more . . .

"Enchanting . . . Scotland is one of the most magical lands in history, and Sue-Ellen Welfonder brings it alive in this tale . . . You'll fall in love with Ronan and Gelis, and if you haven't read the rest of the MacKenzies' stories, you'll be chomping at the bit to get them after reading *Seducing a Scottish Bride*."

—RomRevToday.com

"A remarkable Scottish tale . . . Enchanting . . . [Welfonder's] words are so real we can almost hear the warriors' swords clashing, see the mist on the moors, and smell the moss gathered on trees and clinging to rocks . . . *Seducing a Scottish Bride* is the latest in a long line of Scottish stories by Ms. Welfonder that will charm you."

—FreshFiction.com

"One of a kind. The sensuality abounds . . . An astounding and worthy read . . . Welfonder continues her penchant for penning romances that touch the heart."

—MyShelf.com

"I love a good Highland novel and this book did not disappoint. If you're a member of the kilt-o-holic club like I am, then I think you've found a book to read."

—OnceUponaRomance.net

BRIDE FOR A KNIGHT

"[Welfonder] skillfully draws you into a suspenseful mystery with wonderful atmosphere."
—Romantic Times BOOKreviews Magazine

"Once again, Welfonder's careful scholarship and attention to detail vividly re-create the lusty, brawling days of medieval Scotland with larger-than-life chivalrous heroes and the dainty but spirited maidens chosen by the old gods and blessed by the saints to partner them."
—Booklist

"The paranormal and mystery elements blend nicely into the story line as those segues enhance a fine historical romance."
—Midwest Book Review

"This is not just a love story, but one of mystery as well. Sue-Ellen Welfonder has a beautiful way of spinning a story."
—FreshFiction.com

"Again Sue-Ellen Welfonder uses surprises and special twists and turns as she tells a poignant love story."
—NovelTalk.com

more . . .

UNTIL THE KNIGHT COMES

"To lovers of all things Scottish, [Welfonder] writes great tales of passion and adventure. There's magic included along with the various ghosts and legends only Scotland could produce. It's almost better than a trip there in person."
—RomanceReviewsMag.com

"Welfonder's storytelling skill and medieval scholarship shine in her latest Kintail-based Scottish romance with magical elements."
—*Booklist*

ONLY FOR A KNIGHT

"Captivating . . . fast-moving . . . steamy, sensual, and utterly breathtaking . . . will win your heart."
—FreshFiction.com

"4½ Stars! Enthralling . . . Welfonder brings the Highlands to life with her vibrant characters, impassioned stories, and vivid description."
—*Romantic Times BOOKreviews Magazine*

"A book I highly recommend for those who enjoy sexy Scotsmen. A wonderful tale of love."
—TheRomanceReadersConnection.com

WEDDING FOR A KNIGHT

"With history and beautiful details of Scotland, this book provides romance, spunk, mystery, and courtship . . . a must-read!"

—*Rendezvous*

"A very romantic story . . . extremely sexy. I recommend this book to anyone who loves the era and Scotland."

—TheBestReviews.com

MASTER OF THE HIGHLANDS

"Welfonder does it again, bringing readers another powerful, emotional, highly romantic medieval that steals your heart and keeps you turning the pages."

—*Romantic Times BOOKreviews Magazine*

"Yet another bonny Scottish romance to snuggle up with and inspire pleasantly sinful dreams."

—*Heartstrings*

BRIDE OF THE BEAST

"Larger-than-life characters and a scenic setting . . . Welfonder pens some steamy scenes."

—*Publishers Weekly*

"4½ Stars! . . . A top pick . . . powerful emotions, strong and believable characters, snappy dialogue, and some humorous moments add depth to the plotline and make this a nonstop read."

—*Romantic Times BOOKreviews Magazine*

more . . .

KNIGHT IN MY BED

"Exciting, action-packed . . . a strong tale that thoroughly entertains."
—*Midwest Book Review*

"Steamy . . . sensual."
—*Booklist*

DEVIL IN A KILT

"A lovely gem of a book. Wonderful characters and a true sense of place make this a keeper."
—Patricia Potter, author of *The Heart Queen*

"As captivating as a spider's web, and the reader can't get free until the last word . . . tense, fast-moving."
—*Rendezvous*

A HIGHLANDER'S
TEMPTATION

BOOKS BY SUE-ELLEN WELFONDER

Devil in a Kilt
Knight in My Bed
Bride of the Beast
Master of the Highlands
Wedding for a Knight
Only for a Knight
Until the Knight Comes
Bride for a Knight
Seducing a Scottish Bride
A Highlander's Temptation

ATTENTION CORPORATIONS AND ORGANIZATIONS:
Most HACHETTE BOOK GROUP books are available
at quantity discounts with bulk purchase for educational,
business, or sales promotional use. For information,
please call or write:

Special Markets Department, Hachette Book Group
237 Park Avenue, New York, NY 10017
Telephone: 1-800-222-6747 Fax: 1-800-477-5925

A HIGHLANDER'S
TEMPTATION

SUE-ELLEN WELFONDER

FOREVER

NEW YORK   BOSTON

If you purchase this book without a cover you should be aware
that this book may have been stolen property and reported
as "unsold and destroyed" to the publisher. In such case
neither the author nor the publisher has received any payment
for this "stripped book."

This book is a work of fiction. Names, characters, places, and
incidents are the product of the author's imagination or are used
fictitiously. Any resemblance to actual events, locales, or persons,
living or dead, is coincidental.

Copyright © 2009 by Sue-Ellen Welfonder
All rights reserved. Except as permitted under the U.S. Copyright
Act of 1976, no part of this publication may be reproduced,
distributed, or transmitted in any form or by any means, or stored
in a database or retrieval system, without the prior written
permission of the publisher.

Cover illustration by Alan Ayers
Book design by Stratford, A TexTech business

Forever
Hachette Book Group
237 Park Avenue
New York, NY 10017
Visit our website at www.HachetteBookGroup.com.

Forever is an imprint of Grand Central Publishing.
The Forever name and logo is a
trademark of Hachette Book Group, Inc.

Printed in the United States of America

First Printing: October 2009

10 9 8 7 6 5 4 3 2 1

This one is for Catherine Abernathy.

A very special friend and one of the most caring souls I know, she is living proof that great-hearted people exist outside medieval Scotland.

Like many of my longtime readers, she's especially fond of Duncan MacKenzie, hero of *Devil in a Kilt*. If it were possible, I know he'd give her a tremendous hug. He might even shout *Cuidich 'N' Righ!* in her honor. As it is, I hope these words express how much I love and appreciate her.

Acknowledgments

Scotland is my greatest passion and the heartbeat of every book I write. Most of my MacKenzie tales are set in Kintail, a truly magnificent part of the Highlands. It was there, many years ago, that Duncan MacKenzie strode into my imagination, demanding that I write his story, which became *Devil in a Kilt*. With each new book and every successive visit to Kintail, I've come to think of these rocky shores and mist-hung hills as Duncan's own and likely always will.

In *A Highlander's Temptation*, I gave his daughter Arabella an adventure, letting her visit another part of Scotland that I love. I chose a place of family ties and old history, basing MacConachers' Isle on my own ancestral isle of Colonsay. Only a few square miles of windswept wildness, jagged cliffs, and sandy bays, this tiny Hebridean isle is a place of unforgettable beauty.

Many special corners of Colonsay can be glimpsed in this book. Kiloran Bay, with its sweeping crescent of golden sand and towering cliffs, made the ideal setting for Castle Bane. These crags are riddled with caves, and readers will spot where I've used this feature. The Seal Isles actually exist and lie close by. Rich Viking tradition also thrives on Colonsay, with traces of the distant Norse past visible everywhere. Olaf Big Nose, Asa Long-Legs, and others were a nod to my own fascination with Viking lore.

My interest also stems from cherished visits to Shetland, where Viking heritage is greatly honored. I have a favorite restaurant on Scalloway Bay where it isn't unusual to glance out the window and see a replica longship sail by. Excavations of Viking Age settlements dot the landscape, and I thrill to explore such places. These remnants of the past, both on Colonsay and in Shetland, provided the creative sparks that became Arabella's adventure.

Four special women also helped me: Roberta M. Brown, my agent and dearest friend. She is a true *skörungur*. Karen Kosztolnyik, my much appreciated editor. A pleasure to work with, her insightful suggestions are always spot on. Celia Johnson, for being so helpful and sweet. And a grateful nod to copyeditor Lynne Cannon Menges for making sure all i's were dotted and all t's properly crossed. She has a fabulous eye!

As ever, thanks and love to my very handsome husband, Manfred, who tolerates my daily jaunts to medieval Scotland with the patience of a saint and grumbles only slightly when I visit modern-day Scotland. I couldn't do this without him. And my little dog, Em, who graciously decides when I need walks and cuddle time. He rules my world with tail wags and sloppy wet kisses. I hope he knows how much I love him.

Extra special thanks to the many readers who support my books. I love hearing from you. You make writing all worthwhile.

The Legacy of the
Thunder Rod

❧

Along the west coast of Scotland lies a chain of islands of such beauty and grandeur even the most ardent romantic is hard-pressed to describe their majesty. Curving bays of glistening white sand and glittering seas of every hue vie to catch one's breath while jagged, spray-strewn skerries and sheer, impossibly steep cliffs compete with gentle, grass-grown dunes and long-tumbled ruins to stir the soul.

Ruled for centuries by the pagan Norse, the Hebrides are a place of legend, each isle steeped in ancient lore and tradition. Sea gods, merfolk, and fabled Celtic heroes abound, their mythic tales spun with relish by silver-tongued bards in the long, dark cold of deep winter nights.

But not all such tales are widely known.

Indeed, some are kept secret.

And one of the most intriguing secrets to be found in the vast Sea of the Hebrides belongs to the once proud Clan MacConacher.

Broken, small in number, and ill-favored with the Scottish crown, the MacConachers dwell far from their erstwhile seat in Argyll; their straight-backed, long-suffering ranks reduced to scratching out a living on a rocky, windswept isle surrounded by reefs and rough seas.

An isle they cherish because it is all that remains left to them, and, above all, because MacConacher's Isle lies well beyond the reach of the dread MacKenzies, the powerful clan responsible for their ruin.

Not that the MacConachers wish to forget their doombringing foes.

Far from it. The present chieftain is young, bold, and of fiery spirit. Keen to throw off his clan's mantle of shame and sorrow, he has only two burning ambitions. He lives to restore his family's good name and fortune. He also plans for the day he can wreak vengeance on Clan MacKenzie.

His least concern is his clan's most precious possession, the Thunder Rod.

Given to an ancestor by a Norse nobleman, the relic is a polished length of fossilized wood, intricately carved with runes and still bearing bits of brilliant color. Clan elders claim the rod was either a piece of wood torn from the prow of Thor's own longboat or, perhaps, crafted by a great Viking lord for his lady to keep in his remembrance when he is at sea.

Roughly the size of a man's forearm and rumored to hold great magic, its particular powers do not interest the braw MacConacher chieftain.

Until the stormy morning when the black winds of fate present him with an irresistible opportunity to settle a long-simmering score.

Now, at last, he can use the Thunder Rod.

If he dares.

Chapter One

❖

THE GREAT HALL AT MORNING

AUTUMN 1350

What do you mean you wish to see the Seal Isles?"

Duncan MacKenzie, the indomitable Black Stag of Kintail, slapped down his ale cup and stared across the well-laden high table at his eldest daughter, Lady Arabella. His good humor of moments before vanished as he narrowed his eyes on her, his gaze piercing.

Arabella struggled for composure. Years of doing so helped her not to squirm. But she wasn't sure she could keep her cheeks from flaming. Already the back of her neck burned as if it'd caught fire.

So she moistened her lips and tried to pretend her father wasn't pinning her with a look that said he could see right into her soul, maybe even knew how her belly churned and that her palms were damp.

Or that all her hopes and dreams hung on this moment.

"Well?" He raised one dark brow.

Arabella plucked at a thread on her sleeve, then, realizing what she was doing, stopped at once. She looked up, somehow resisting the urge to slip a finger beneath the neckline of her gown or perhaps even loosen her bodice ties. Faith, but she needed air. Her chest felt so constricted, she could hardly draw a breath.

She did manage to hold her father's stare. Hot and bold MacKenzie blood flowed in her veins, too. And even if she'd spent her life quashing any urges to heed her clan's more passionate nature, this was one time she meant to do her name proud.

So she angled her chin and firmed up her jaw with just a touch of stubbornness.

"You heard what I said." She spoke as calmly as she could, her daring making her heart skitter. "The seals..."

She let the words trail off, the excuse sounding ridiculous even to her own ears.

Her father huffed, clearly agreeing.

"We've plenty of such beasties in our own waters." He made a dismissive gesture, his tone final. "You've no need to journey to the ends of nowhere to see them."

At once, a deafening silence fell around the hall's torchlit dais. Somewhere a castle dog cracked a bone, his gnawing all the more loud for the sudden quiet. Everywhere kinsmen and friends swiveled heads in their puissant chieftain's direction, though some discreetly glanced aside. Whatever their reaction, no one appeared surprised by the outburst. Those who called Eilean Creag their home were well used to the Black Stag's occasional bouts of temper.

"If it is such creatures you wish to study, I saw one just

yestere'en." He sat back in his carved oaken laird's chair, looking pleased. "A fine dog seal sunning himself on a rock down by the boat strand."

Arabella doubted every word. She did tighten her fingers on the handle of her spoon.

This wasn't about seals and she suspected her father knew it. His continued stare, narrow-eyed and penetrating, was more than proof.

She started to lower her own gaze, but caught herself and frowned instead. And rather than returning her attention to her wooden bowl of slaked oats as she would have done just a few days ago, she sat up straighter and squared her shoulders.

She only hoped that no one else heard the thundering of her heart.

It wasn't every day that she dared defy her fierce-eyed, hot-tempered father.

Indeed, this was the first time she meant to try.

Her contentment in life—she couldn't bring herself to use the word *happiness*—depended on her being strong.

Firm, resolute, and unbending.

"I'm not interested in Kintail seals, Father." She cleared her throat, careful to keep her chin raised. "And there *is* a need. Besides that, I want to make this journey. The Seal Isles are mine now. You gave them to me."

"I added them to your bride price!"

"Which makes them my own." She persisted, unable to stop. "It's only natural I should wish to see them. I can make a halt at the Isle of Doon on the way, bringing your felicitations to your friends the MacLeans and the cailleach, Devorgilla. You can't deny that they would welcome me. After that, I could perhaps call at—"

"Ho! What's this?" Her father's gaze snapped to a quiet, scar-faced man half-hidden in shadow at the end of the table. "Can it be a certain long-nosed loon of a Sassunach has been putting such mummery in your head?"

Arabella bit her lip. She wasn't about to admit that her head had been fine until a courier had arrived from her younger sister's home a few days before, announcing that Gelis had at last quickened with child.

A pang shot through her again, remembering. Hot, sharp, and twisting, her bitterness wound tight. Just recalling how the messenger's eyes had danced with merriment as he'd shared the long-awaited news that had upturned her world.

It'd been too much.

The whole sad truth of the empty days stretching before her had come crashing down around her like so much hurled and shattered crockery.

She refused to think about the cold and lonely nights, warmed only by the peats tossed on the hearth fire and the snoring, furry bulk of whichever of her father's dogs chose to scramble onto her bed.

Setting down her spoon, she fisted her hands on the cool linen of the table covering and swallowed against the heat in her throat.

To be sure, she loved her sister dearly. She certainly begrudged her naught. But her heart wept upon the surety that such joyous tidings would likely never be her own.

"Faugh!" Her father's voice boomed again. "Whoe'er heard of a lassie wanting to sail clear to the edge of the sea? 'Tis beyond—"

"Hush, you, Duncan." Stepping up to the high table,

her mother, Lady Linnet, placed a warning hand on his shoulder. "Bluster is—"

"The only way I ken to deal with such foolery!" Her father frowned up at his wife and, for a moment, all the fury drained from his face.

Linnet, the mirror image of Gelis, only older, flicked back her hip-length, red-gold braid and leaned down to circle loving arms around her husband's broad shoulders. Blessed with the sight—another gift she shared with her youngest daughter—Linnet's ability to soothe her husband's worst moods wasn't something Arabella needed to see at the moment.

The obvious love between the two only served to remind her of the intimacies she'd never know.

Burning to call such closeness her own, she winced at the sudden image of herself as a withered, spindle-legged crone humbly serving wine and sweetmeats to her parents and her sister and her sister's husband as they reposed before her on cushioned bedding, oblivious to aught but their blazing passion.

Arabella frowned and blinked back the dastardly heat pricking her eyes.

Her mother's voice, clearly admonishing her father, helped banish the disturbing vision. "Ach, Duncan." Linnet smoothed a hand through his thick, shoulder-length black hair, sleek as Arabella's own and scarce touched by but a few strands of silver. "Perhaps you should—"

"Pshaw!" He made a derisive sound, breaking free of her embrace. "Dinna tell me what I should and shouldn't do. I'd rather hear what that meddling lout who calls himself a friend has—"

"Uncle Marmaduke has nothing to do with it." Arabella

spoke before he could finish. "He is a better friend to you than you could wish. Though he did mention that he's here because a southbound trading ship—"

"A vessel said to be captained by an Orkneyman you know and trust." Her uncle sipped slowly from his ale cup, his calm giving her hope. "Word is that the trader is large enough to take on your girl and an escort in all comfort."

"Hah! So speaks a meddler!" Her father smacked his hand on the table. "Did I no' just say you were the cause of this?" He roared the words, glaring round. "Aye, there's a merchant ship set to call at Kyleakin. Could be, the captain is known to me. I ken most traders who ply these waters!"

"And I *ken* when you are about to make a bleeding arse of yourself." Sir Marmaduke set down his empty cup and leaned back in his chair, arms casually folded. "A pity you do not know when to heed those who care about you."

Duncan scowled. "And I say it's a greater pity that you dinna ken when to hold your flapping tongue!"

He flashed another look at Arabella. "I'll take you to see what wares the merchant ship carries. There are sure to be bolts of fine cloth and baubles, perhaps a few exquisite rarities. Maybe even a gem-set comb for your shiny black tresses."

Pausing, he raised a wagging finger. "But know this. When the ship sails away, you will no' be on board!"

Arabella struggled against tightening her lips.

The last thing she wanted was to look like a shrew.

Even so, she couldn't help feeling a spurt of annoyance. "I have coffers filled with raiments and I've more jewels than I can wear in a lifetime. There is little of interest such a ship can offer me. Not in way of the goods it carries."

She took a deep breath, knowing she needed to speak her heart. "What I want is an adventure."

"*A what*?" Her father's brows shot higher than she'd ever seen.

He also leapt to his feet, almost toppling his chair.

Out in the main hall, several of his men guffawed. On the dais, one or two coughed. Even the castle dogs eyed him reproachfully.

Duncan's scowl turned fierce.

"A little time away is all I ask." Arabella ignored them all. "I'm weary of waiting for another suitor to make his bid. The last one who dared approached you over a year ago—"

"The bastard was a MacLeod!" Her father's face ran purple. "Dinna tell me you'd have gone happily to the bed of a sprig of that ilk! We've clashed with their fork-tongued, cloven-footed kind since before the first lick o' dew touched a sprig of heather!"

"Then what of the Clanranald heir who came before him?" Arabella uncurled her fists, no longer caring if anyone saw how her hands trembled. "You can't deny the MacDonalds are good allies and friends."

Her father spluttered.

Lifting her chin a notch higher, she rushed on. "He was a bonny man. His words were smooth and his blue eyes kind and welcoming. I would have—"

"All MacDonalds are glib-tongued and bonny! And you would have been miserable before a fortnight passed." Her father gripped the back of his chair, his knuckles white. "There isn't a race in the land more irresistible to women. Even if the lad meant you well, sooner or later, his blood would have told. He would've succumbed, damning himself and you."

Arabella flushed. "Perhaps I would rather have chanced such a hurt than to face each new day knowing there won't be any further offers for me."

Mortification sweeping her, she clapped a hand over her mouth, horror stricken by her words.

Openly admitting her frustration was one thing.

Announcing to the world that she ached inside was a pain too private for other ears.

"Why do you think I ceded you the Seal Isles?" Her father's voice railed somewhere just outside the embarrassment whipping through her. "Soon, new offers will roll in, young nobles eager to lay claim to our Hebrides will beat a path to—"

"Nae, they will not." She pushed back from the table, standing. "You've frightened them away with your black stares and denials! There isn't a man in all these hills and isles who doesn't know it. No one will come. Not now, not after all they've seen and heard—"

She broke off, choking back her words as she caught glimpses of the pity-filled glances some of her father's men were aiming her way.

She could stomach anything but pity.

Heart pounding and vision blurring, she spun on her heel and fled the dais, pushing past startled kinsmen and serving laddies to reach the tight, winding stairs that led up to the battlements and the fresh, brisk air she craved.

Running now, she burst into the shadow-drenched stair tower and raced up the curving stone treads, not stopping until she reached the final landing. Hurrying, she threw open the oak-planked door to the parapets and plunged out into the chill wind of a bright October morning.

"Ach, dia!" She bent forward to brace her hands on her thighs and breathe deeply. "What have I done...."

Shame scalded her, sucking the air from her lungs and sending waves of hot, humiliating fire licking up and down her spine.

Never had she made a greater fool of herself.

And never had she felt such a fiery, all-consuming need to be loved.

Wanted and desired.

Cherished.

Nearly blinded by tears she refused to acknowledge, she straightened and shook out her skirts. Then she tossed back her hair and blinked until her vision cleared. When it did, she went to the battlements' notched walling and leaned against the cold, unmoving stone.

Across the glittering waters of Loch Duich, the great hills of Kintail stretched as far as the eye could see, the nearer peaks dressed in brilliant swatches of scarlet and gold while those more distant faded into an indistinct smudge of blue and purple, just rimming the horizon. It was a familiar, well-loved sight that made her breath catch but did absolutely nothing to soothe her.

She'd lied about her reasons for wanting to journey to the Seal Isles. But she wished to keep her reasons secret. Even so, she'd never before lied to her family. And the weight of her falsehoods bore down on her, blotting everything but the words she couldn't forget.

Words her sister had spoken when last they'd visited.

Innocently shared accountings of the wonders of marital bliss and how splendorous it was to lie naked with a man each night, intimately entwined and knowing that he lived only to please you.

Exactly how that pleasing was done had also been revealed, and thinking of such things now caused such a brittle aching in her breast that she feared she'd break if she drew in too deep a breath.

Worst of all were her sister's repeated assurances that Arabella, too, would soon be swept into such a floodtide of heated, uninhibited passion.

Everyone, Gelis insisted, was fated to meet a certain someone. She'd been adamant that Arabella would be no different.

It was only a matter of time.

Then she, too, would know tempestuous embraces and hot, devouring kisses the likes of which she couldn't begin to imagine.

As for the rest... it boggled the mind.

And ignited a blaze of yearning inside her that she feared would never be quenched.

Frowning, she flattened her hands against the cold, gritty stone of the wall and turned her gaze away from her beloved Kintail hills and imagined she could stare past the Isle of Skye far out into the sea.

But still she heard her sister's chatter.

Her insistence that the feel of a man's hands sliding up and down one's body, his fingers questing knowingly into dark, hidden places, brought a more intoxicating pleasure than the headiest Gascon wine.

Arabella bit down on her lip, sure she didn't believe a word.

What she did believe was that she had to be on the merchant trader when it set sail from Kyleakin.

And what she *knew* was that—if she made it—her life would be forever changed.

Many leagues distant, across the vast stretch of sea Arabella imagined her gaze to stray, a sleek, newly built birlinn that swept around a headland of tall, thrusting cliffs and sped into the deepest, most sheltered bay of a remote Hebridean island, known to those who dwelt there as MacConacher's Isle.

Oars flashing and gong beating, the high-prowed galley shot forward in a cloud of spray, its bold race for the bay's curving, white-sanded shore churning the water and drenching the oarsmen with plume. On the stern platform, Darroc MacConacher's heart swelled with pride.

This was why he lived.

Never before had his plans for avenging the MacConacher name seemed a greater possibility. For years— nearly a lifetime—he'd burned to redeem their honor. The MacKenzies might not expect vengeance now, so long after their dark deeds, but the surprise on their hated faces would only serve to sweeten Clan MacConacher's triumph.

Almost tasting the glory, Darroc grinned.

The day's victory set fire to his soul. It'd been overlong since a chieftain of his name could claim such elation, and the headiness was almost too sweet to bear.

And he wasn't going to let his sour-faced seneschal's presence on the strand spoil his triumph.

Still grinning, he waited until his oarsmen raised the long, dripping sweeps, then he leapt down into the boiling surf. He splashed ashore even as the birlinn surged up onto the sloping, wet-sanded beach.

"Ho, Mungo!" He made straight for his dark-frowning seneschal. "Have you filled your eyes with the seafaring skill of MacConacher men?" he greeted, careful to keep his grin in place.

"I have only one eye, if you've forgotten!" The seneschal's bushy gray brows lowered over the eye in question and he put back his twisted, somewhat hunched shoulders. "And you needn't mind me of the sea prowess of our men. There's ne'er been a MacConacher born who wasn't nursed on seawater along with his mother's good, sweet milk."

"Then why meet us with scowls?" Darroc slung an arm around Mungo's shoulders, using camaraderie to disguise his attempt to keep the older man's feet from slipping on the slick, weed-strewn shingle.

He also bit back a frown of his own, furious that he hadn't spoken with greater tact.

Everyone on MacConacher's Isle knew that the once tall and straight seneschal had never come to grips with the battle injuries that disfigured him.

Darroc also knew what was plaguing the man.

Mungo didn't share his faith in the battered clan's ability to best their foes. And he resented the coin needed to build such a splendid warship.

Coin the seneschal would rather have seen spent on a bride who would bring them new blood and, perhaps through her dowry, a garrison of strong and bold warriors.

"Scowls, you say?" Mungo glowered indeed. "I was only scrunching my good eye to see how many men I'd have to help climb the cliff path back to the keep!"

"Nary a one." Darroc laughed. "They are as fit now as when we pushed off this morn."

"Humph!" Mungo looked sullen.

Releasing him, Darroc tossed back his spray-dampened hair and flashed his brightest glance to where his men crowded around the birlinn. With luck, their enthusiasm would soften the seneschal's humor.

Unfortunately, Mungo's face remained as set as hard-boiled leather.

Darroc's grin almost slipped.

Determined not to let it, he tried another tactic. "The birlinn gave a fine flourish, eh?" He hooked his thumbs in his belt. "She is nimble, I say you! I'd set her against any full-manned, sixty-four-oared dragonship to sail the Hebrides."

Mungo snorted. "You could build a fleet of such sixteen-oared demons o' agility and it'd matter naught without the men to sail them! Yon birlinn might well be a fishing coble for what little she will serve us."

"She is a beginning." Darroc refused to be daunted. "Our men handled her well."

"The only men we have who are able." Mungo's lips tightened. He threw a glance down the strand to where the newly tested seamen cavorted about the little galley like giddy-headed loons, slapping backs and laughing.

Turning again to Darroc, he jammed his hands against his hips. "There's no' a man amongst those leaping fools what could hold his own against a MacKenzie. No' on land, as well we ken, and no' by sea, either."

Darroc breathed out hard, unable to deny Mungo's words. It was true that each man who'd handled the birlinn with such flourish bore some kind of physical imperfection—faults visited upon them by the MacKenzies—and couldn't be expected to stand well against that powerful race.

As for the few stalwarts without battle scars, or who didn't miss an ear or a digit, their greater age gave them a distinct disadvantage.

Darroc struggled against looking pained. His gaze stretched past the cliff-guarded bay to the reefs that circled his isle. Black, jagged, and menacing, some ledges rose sharply above the crashing waves while others, even more dangerous, lurked unseen beneath the seething foam.

It'd been nothing short of a miracle that his men had sent the birlinn dancing in and out of the bay's narrow opening with such dash and flair.

Seawater in their veins or nae, they were limited. But that only made the day's triumph all the more sweet.

And just as he greeted their victory as a turning point for the clan, so did his men need the burst of pride he'd seen light their eyes when they'd raised the oars with such aplomb, their gleeful shouts ringing as the fine little warship slid to a halt on the shore.

It'd been a moment of hope the likes of which Mac-Conacher's Isle hadn't seen in centuries.

Hope he meant to kindle until it blazed brighter than the sun.

He flashed another glance at the excited men. "They'll no' face our enemy alone. The birlinn will stand them by as well as a score of good fighting men. Nor will we challenge anyone until we have several more such warships. Then," he grinned, "we beat north and harry their shores. When they give chase, we attack and harass like fleas to a dog. We'll use our birlinns' greater maneuverability and fighting decks to chase the MacKenzies low-sided longships from the seas."

Mungo remained unimpressed.

"The MacKenzies are bog trotters." Darroc sought to sway him. "Their strength lies in fighting on land."

Sure of it, he allowed himself another grin. "At sea, we can best them."

"No' with graybeards and war-blighted manning our galleys." Mungo spat onto the sand. "Or will you be taking down the keep stone by stone and"—he cast a sulky glare at the stark, square tower of Castle Bane, perched on the edge of a soaring sea cliff on the far side of the bay—"calling on the Auld Ones to turn each brick into a man?"

"Pride will be magic enough for us." Darroc's glance flicked again to his men. "And,"—he tossed back a fold of his plaid—"we aren't the only clan with a taste for MacKenzie blood. Once we have a few more birlinns and word spreads, others will join us."

"Salting the MacKenzie's tail is all you'll be doing." Mungo jutted his bearded chin. "Kintail has the luck o' the devil. Any word that spreads will reach him first and he'd swoop down here to smash this isle as soundly as his father chased us from Argyll."

"Then he'd meet a surprise, for I am no' my grandsire or my father, rest their souls." Darroc patted his sword hilt and gave Mungo a hard smile. "I say it is time he learns the true measure of the name MacCon—"

"And I say our race will disappear as fast as the tide if you won't be seeding it soon!" Mungo set his jaw, his good eye flashing hotly.

Darroc gritted his teeth.

What he wanted to do was throw back his head and laugh.

He did plenty of *seeding* each time he sailed to

Glasgow for supplies. And if such an urge plagued him betwixt journeys, his good friend Olaf Big Nose and his camp was only a day's sail away. The little Norse settlement provided more free-spirited, well-made wenches than a hot-blooded man could savor in a fortnight.

Fine, big-bosomed lasses as willing to flip up their skirts as they were to flash a smile. Wonderfully skilled Valkyries, capable of milking seed from any man, sometimes with just a single heated look.

Darroc curled his hands around his sword belt, certain he could feel a flush creeping into his cheeks.

Unfortunately, he was also certain Mungo didn't mean that kind of seeding. He meant the kind that would see Darroc with a parcel of bawling, squirming bairns.

Feeling trapped, he looked up at the scudding clouds, hoping the seneschal would drop the matter.

A thick finger jabbed into his chest proved how futile that hope was. "For the price of that birlinn yonder, you could have sailed to Orkney or Shetland and fetched a fine bride."

"Perhaps I do not want an Orkney or Shetland bride?" Darroc circled Mungo's wrist with a firm but gentle hand, removing the prodding finger from his breast.

That Mungo didn't suggest a Highland bride bit deep. The unspoken admission that there wasn't a clan who'd welcome such a union pierced Darroc's pride.

"I will seek a wife when the time is fortuitous." He turned back to the sea, not wanting Mungo to see any pain that might flicker across his face.

"And when might that be?" Mungo placed himself between Darroc and the bay. "There's some of us might no' live long enough to celebrate the day."

Darroc frowned.

The old man knew how to parry.

"I will consider the matter once we've dealt with the MacKenzies." Darroc folded his arms, his gaze set on the distant horizon. "Then and no' a day before."

But when the seneschal gave another snort and stomped off down the strand toward the steep track that wound up to the cliff-top castle, Darroc rammed both hands through his hair and blew out a hot breath.

Mungo wasn't the only one who knew how empty his words had been.

Albeit not for the reason the seneschal might guess.

It was true that he'd not seek a bride until he'd won back his family's honor and avenged himself on those responsible for blackening it. But it was also true that he loved this rocky, wind-blasted isle his people now called home.

Even if he were able to return to the lost MacConacher lands in Argyll, he knew in his heart he'd never go.

Just as he knew he'd never bring a bride here.

MacConacher's Isle wasn't made for women.

Much as he wished otherwise.

Saints pity him.

Chapter Two

❖

T ry again."

Duncan didn't bother to temper his tone. Nor did he care if his wife or his ale-sipping Sassunach friend saw the heat stealing up his face. Truth was he didn't feel a twinge of guilt. It was his daughter's life that was at stake, after all. So he thrust a hand through his hair and forced himself to push Linnet one more time.

"Perhaps if you gaze into the fire or look down at the loch?" The suggestions sounded brilliant to him. Both methods had worked in the past.

But Linnet only shook her head.

"Duncan...my heart." Her tone was quiet and sad. "You know I cannot summon my gift at will. Were we meant to know such things, the answer would appear. As is"—she looked up, her eyes troubled—"I see only blackness."

"She's also freezing." Sir Marmaduke set down his ale cup and took a folded plaid from the top of a coffer near the door. Then he crossed the room to where Linnet sat on a low, three-legged stool. He settled the tartaned cloth around her shoulders with a careful exactness surely designed to bedevil less placid souls.

"To be sure, she's cold!" Feeling most *un*-placid, Duncan whirled to the window and closed the shutters with a bang. "It is autumn if you've forgotten."

Turning back to the room, he dusted his hands. "I was about to fetch a plaid for her myself." He glared at his friend, not about to admit that he hadn't noticed her shivering.

He was chilled, too.

Though it was fear for his daughter that jellied his knees and iced his blood. If his wife and Sir Marmaduke—the meddler—Strongbow chose to ignore certain dire travelers' tales they'd heard of late, he knew better. And he wasn't taking any chances. Not with word that the dread plague fumes, long believed to be a God-sent damnation of the English, were slowly creeping into Scotland.

It didn't matter that the malaise had only been reported in St. Andrews, a corner of the land as remote from Kintail as the moon.

Such a noxious cloud could drift anywhere.

That a distant scattering of seal-infested isles on the outermost edges of the Hebridean Sea might prove a better refuge than Eilean Creag's own walls was something he chose not to consider.

So he crossed his arms and summoned his best scowl. "If you see only blackness," he reasoned, pinning his stare on his wife, "then we know naught will come of Arabella's fool notion. She's intended to stay here."

Behind him, Sir Marmaduke snorted.

Linnet peered up at him, her teeth chattering in a way that raised the hairs on his nape. "You're hearing what you want me to say." She drew the plaid more snugly around her shoulders, her gaze not leaving his. "The darkness means that I cannot see into her future, not the path it will take."

A muscle began to twitch in Duncan's jaw. To be sure, he was hearing what he wished. Such was a chief's due. But for the sake of domestic harmony, he decided to keep the thought to himself.

"I can tell you that no harm will come to her." Linnet pushed to her feet and came forward to uncross his arms. "Not here, nor if she leaves us for a time," she said, reaching for his hand and twining their fingers. "That surety I can give you."

"Hah!" Triumph surged through Duncan. "So you have seen something."

The look on Linnet's face crushed his hope. "Nae, though I would that it were so. I know it here." She released his hand to place her own over her breast. "As would any mother who loves."

"Humph." Duncan refolded his arms. "That tells me nothing."

She lifted her chin. "Then you know less of a woman's heart than I would have credited."

Duncan clamped his mouth shut before he said something he'd surely regret.

Sir Marmaduke strode all too casually to a table and refilled his ale cup. Duncan stared daggers into his back, knowing what was to come. He braced himself, aware that he wasn't going to like it.

"And I say," the lout began, his English voice annoyingly sage, "that you know absolutely naught of a daughter's heart. Arabella is your eldest. She has seen her younger sister wed and now she's learned that Gelis—"

"The lass is no' jealous of her sister!" Duncan stared at his friend, gall sweeping him. "A more docile, sweet-natured maid ne'er walked these hills. She—"

"She is a woman now." Sir Marmaduke retained his usual calm. "A woman overripe and aware of wants and needs you're keeping from her."

"*Overripe*?" Duncan could feel his eyes bulging, the veins throbbing at his temples. "You're her uncle, by God's hallowed bones! How dare you—"

"I do because it must be said." Sir Marmaduke took a sip of ale. "Without doubt, Arabella has a kindly disposition. But she is also stubborn even if she seldom shows it. She's a strong young woman and"—he glanced at Linnet as if seeking agreement—"the truth is if you disregard her wishes now, you do so at your peril."

Duncan's brows shot heavenward.

Words failed him.

A red haze blurred his vision and he started to blast his interfering friend with every curse he knew. Sadly, he only spluttered like the village idiot.

He'd caught soft footfalls outside the solar door. It wouldn't do for someone to hear his bellowing and alert the whole castle that he was having another rant.

It'd been bad enough seeing glimmers of sympathy cross his men's faces in the hall earlier. Barely veiled flashes of support meant for Arabella and not him, their chief and the man with whom they ought to be commiserating.

Their lack of loyalty sat like a hot, iron ball in his gut.

And promptly let him forget his wish not to shout.

"The only peril about to visit us is my fist when it crashes into your nose!" he roared, glaring at Sir Marmaduke.

Outside the door, Arabella took a deep breath and tried to back away. Unfortunately, she couldn't move. Her legs had somehow turned to lead and her feet appeared nailed to the floor. So she stood frozen, certain she had but an eyeblink before her father found her on the threshold, listening.

She knew he'd heard her.

His ire rolled at her in great, angry waves that penetrated the thick oaken planks of the door. Even so, she strained her ears. A rustle of linen, combined with her mother's sigh, promptly rewarded her.

"Leave be, Duncan." The softly spoken words came as balm to her soul. "You know Arabella is not a maid to have her head turned lightly if that's the reason you'd begrudge her such a journey."

"I'd deny her nothing!" her father snapped, his deep voice making the door tremble. "Arabella is no lass to lose her heart to a man unworthy. She's no' the sort to fall for a glib-tongued oarsman on a merchant ship. No' with my own best men guarding her!"

"You say so?" Sir Marmaduke again, clearly readying for a verbal strike. "If you are sure she won't succumb to temptation, you can have no objections to letting her go."

Her father made a sound in his throat that could've been a growl. Arabella could almost see him scowling at the ceiling, his gaze black enough to scorch the rafters. She also imagined he'd blow out an agitated breath and ram his fingers through his hair.

She knew him well.

And she knew he was livid.

Sir Marmaduke sounded anything but. "You've as much as admitted that your men would guard her fiercely."

Another garbled *humph* proved her father's only reply.

"He's right, Duncan." Her mother's support made her heart soar. "There isn't a man in your garrison who wouldn't give his life to protect her. There can be no harm in—"

"No harm?" Her father's outburst shook the door again. "'Tis no' roving-eyed Orkney merchantman I'm fashed about! Or have you forgotten the pestiferous darkness sweeping our fair land?"

Arabella's eyes widened, comprehension flooding her.

The pest.

He could mean naught else. Several nights ago at the high table, he'd railed against the tales brought to them by a traveling minstrel. He'd insisted the malaise known to have cut a devastating swath through England was God's own damning of the Sassunachs. He'd closed his ears to the bard's claims that the pox had crept into Scotland.

When the bard then named several notable men who'd fallen to the scourge, her father brought his fist down on the table. He'd glared around, loudly declaring that the mighty hills of Kintail would turn away any clouds of doom long before they reached his walls.

And if such a terror dared, he'd added, his deep voice ringing, he'd simply send his loved ones to an even more secure hideaway.

A place distant and remote.

On recalling his words, Arabella drew a tight breath.

There wasn't a place in the world more far-flung than the Seal Isles.

Her father didn't know it yet, but he'd blustered himself into a corner.

Arabella's heart began to pound again, this time hard and slow. She agreed with her father that the pestilence wouldn't cross the Highland line. And she doubted even more that such vileness could taint the Hebrides.

Still pressed against the door, she glanced at an arrow slit in the opposite wall. Afternoon sun filled the narrow opening, the soft light turning the stone splay a lovely shade of deep gold.

A good portent, Gelis would say.

Arabella shivered.

Any other time, she would have clucked her tongue at such fancy.

As it was, she allowed herself a glimmer of hope. She could feel it growing inside her, a sweet rush sweeping up to warm her cheeks and make her pulse quicken.

Then she heard another swish of linen. Soft steps she knew were her mother's, the sound immediately followed by a deep and heaving sigh. A masculine sigh steeped in resignation and—to those who knew her father—the first sign he ever gave of his pending capitulation.

Her mother's voice floated through the door. "Ah, well." There was a trace of victory in her tone. "If the minstrel's gloom and doom is what's bothering you, perhaps we really should send Arabella on a voyage through the Hebrides."

"Indeed." Sir Marmaduke sounded almost jovial. "Did the bard not say that the only surety against the plague was flight? I seem to recall him telling us that Lowland worthies were fleeing, running away to the most remote corners they—"

"You recall stories your wet nurse told as she suckled you!"

Arabella started at her father's bellow.

Sir Marmaduke continued as if he hadn't heard. "Be glad I have such a fine memory as yours is obviously lacking. Or will you deny your own words? How you stood in the great hall earlier, declaring that such ills as are ravaging the south will never reach these hills?"

"I ken what I said!"

"And so does everyone who heard you." Sir Marmaduke won again.

Arabella held her breath.

Her father paced. She felt frustration in his hurried footsteps. It throbbed in the air, thick, hot, and agitated, even through the door's heavy oak planking.

"Whatever you do now, my friend, you have little choice but to let the girl go." Sir Marmaduke's voice rose above the angry footfalls. "You've backed yourself into a corner."

Her father stopped his stomping at once. "Did I ever tell you I like you better when you hold your flapping English tongue?"

Silence answered him.

Quiet in which Arabella was sure her uncle either shrugged or flicked a speck of lint off his sleeve. Such was the usual pattern of their bickering.

"My daughter," her father groused, "will go with me to Kyleakin and she'll have her choice of whate'er goods the merchant ship can offer. As for anything else"—he almost choked on the words—"I will think on it."

Nae, he'd see her off, even if he did so sourly.

He couldn't do anything else.

And knowing it sent a jolt of excitement whipping through Arabella.

Already feeling the brisk Hebridean wind stinging her cheeks, she eased away from the door. She imagined the thrilling roll of the large merchant ship. How it would cut the waves, its bold path sending up salt spray to mist her face. Heart pounding, she thought, too, of night skies filled with stars and air sweet with the tang of the sea. Almost trembling in anticipation, she closed her eyes and said a hushed prayer of thanks.

Then, smiling for the first time in days, she hitched up her skirts and slipped back down the corridor, making for the great hall and dinner.

Not surprisingly, her appetite had returned.

And with it, a sense of joy and purpose such as she'd never known.

The worst was behind her.

Now she just had to hope nothing else went wrong.

MacConacher's Isle wasn't made for women.

Darroc's own words circled back to haunt him as he stood at one of the four tall windows of the bleak chamber he thought of as the notch room. Fully bare except for a tiny hearth and the windows, one gracing each blank, cold-stoned wall, the room didn't even offer the comfort of strewn rushes, though Darroc made certain that the floor's sturdy wooden planks stayed well scrubbed.

For all that, the room did have two redeeming features.

It held pride of place as the topmost chamber in Castle

Bane's tower. And the four windows offered magnificent views of the sea in every direction.

Indeed, the room could have been quite grand if its history weren't so grim.

Pushing that particular darkness from his mind, he reached for the special mallet and chisel he kept on the window ledge. Then, with the ease of much practice, he set to work adding another notch to the long row of nicks in the side of the window arch.

He took great pleasure in each tiny chip of stone that flew away beneath his tapping, the gritty dust that rose around him like a gray-white cloud.

He ignored the baleful stare of his dog, Frang, who sat just inside the doorway. An enormous, fierce-looking beast, the dog had only entered the notch room once. And that was years ago when Darroc first brought his people, or what remained of them, to MacConacher's Isle.

On exploring Castle Bane's long-empty tower, and knowing its past, he'd been intrigued by the notches filling one of the window arches. Little more than faint scratches, it wasn't difficult to discern their significance.

Frang, tagging along beside him, took one sniff of the notched window and shot from the room with his tail between his legs.

Darroc frowned.

Then he set down his mallet and chisel, his task finished.

His notches were celebrations.

Each one marked another day in his quest for vengeance. Every rising and setting of the sun brought Clan MacConacher closer to regaining their former glory. Not that any one of them strove for riches. They knew better than most that a good man carried his wealth inside him. It was clan pride and honor that mattered.

He let out a long breath, remembering the light in his men's eyes earlier that day. From below, he could hear their excited banter in the great hall. Laughter, a few good-natured roars, and lots of pounding on the trestles under-scored that they were still in high fettle.

Tantalizing dinner smells reached him, too. Thin drifts of cook smoke carrying the aroma of rich meats and even richer sauces. If he weren't mistaken, the mouth-watering scent of fresh-baked bread. He also caught a distinct waft of heather ale, so tempting with its honeyed sweetness.

Feast goods and, he knew, portions generous enough to sate the hungriest amongst them.

His heart seized.

There'd been times when his noble sea warriors had filled their bellies on limpet broth and seabird stew.

Years when even watered ale and the most rancid wine went down like nectar.

And not a man had complained.

At once, the burn of a long-simmering anger blazed hot in his blood and he fisted his hands. But he unclenched them almost as quickly and stepped forward to trace the newly cut window notch with the fingertips of his right hand.

Unchecked fury was for fools.

He knew better. So he took a deep breath and stilled his fingers on the small, perfectly edged notch. Satisfaction began to pulse through him, replacing his rage. More scenes from the afternoon's accomplishments flashed across his mind and his joy in his men's burgeoning self-respect rose inside him, tightening his chest.

They were making splendid progress.

Soon they'd teach their foes the worth of Clan MacConacher.

Until then—

"Ho—Darroc!" A jovial voice boomed in his ear. "The seals are singing. Can you hear them?"

Darroc jumped and swung around. His cousin, Conall, stood behind him. The only other soul at Castle Bane anywhere close to his age, the lad's copper-red hair shone bright in the flames of a handheld torch and his blue eyes sparkled with mischief.

"Sakes!" Darroc glared at him. "Can you no' make a bit of noise next time you come looking for me? A clanking sword or some foot stomping would serve. Better yet, the slamming of a door?"

"Caught you off guard, didn't I?" Conall grinned.

"Only because I let you." Darroc's mouth quirked on the lie.

"Say you!" Conall hooted. "Did you truly no' hear the seals?"

"Banshees could be screaming and I wouldn't hear them above your bellows."

"I do have a good set o' lungs, eh?"

"The finest." Darroc cuffed him on the shoulder, secretly pleased the strapping young man could move so quietly. Such a skill might come in use someday.

"So everyone says." Conall's laugh rang out again. "I'm light on my feet, too. Or"—he cocked a brow—"will you be denying it?"

"Nae, I willna." Darroc gave the answer he knew the lad wanted.

Dusting the stone grit from his hands, he refrained

from reminding Conall that he'd issued orders that he wasn't to be disturbed when he spent time in the notch room. Nor would he reprimand Conall for laughing at him. Even if some chiefs might take high offense at a kinsman allowing himself that kind of liberty.

Such rigidity wasn't practiced at Castle Bane.

Each man for the clan and the clan for every man was their motto.

Just as keeping up spirits was his own personal creed.

So he matched the younger man's grin and ignored the pity that almost choked him each time he caught a glimpse of Conall's burn-scarred hands. Long healed and of no bother, or so Conall swore, the damage was just another reason Darroc made his daily climb to the notch room.

Beneath his jollity, Darroc's gut clenched.

He forced his smile not to slip.

He'd make a notch in every rock on the island if doing so would repair Conall's scars.

As it was, he just hoped the lad had erred about the seals.

At the door, Frang pushed to his feet and stood looking at some invisible spot in the room, his eyes wary. Then he dropped back onto his haunches, tilted his head toward the ceiling, and howled.

Darroc's eyes narrowed.

Frang didn't howl without reason.

The fine hairs on Darroc's nape lifted but he ignored the sensation. "Come, you." He gripped Conall's elbow and steered him toward the door. "Enough of this cold chamber. I'm for the hall and—"

He got no further, for a long, haunting cry echoed

beyond the room's tall shuttered windows. Worse, before the first lonely plaint faded away, other wails rose in answer. Wild, eerie, and undeniably musical, there could be no mistaking their source.

Darroc froze. A chill sped down his spine.

"There they are again!" Conall jerked free of Darroc's grasp and ran to the nearest window. "The seals," he cried, flinging open the shutters. "Wait till you see. They're everywhere!"

And they were.

Joining Conall at the window, Darroc gave a low whistle. "There must be hundreds, perhaps thousands, of them." He didn't like admitting it. "The herring must be running, something the like."

Conall scoffed. "The clan elders believe they're celebrating our success with the birlinn." He leaned farther out the window, his eyes round as he stared down at the night-silvered sea. "Soon as we heard them, everyone agreed, some claiming seals always know—"

"They know where and how to best catch their next meal."

Conall straightened, some of his excitement fading.

Darroc frowned.

He'd regretted his shortness as soon as he spoke, but already he could feel the blood draining from his face, his heart thudding with dread.

Seals reminded him of the MacKenzies.

The dastards did hold an ancient claim to the nearby Seal Isles, though as far as he knew it'd been hundreds of years since any one of their race had bothered to set foot on the wee islets, if ever.

Like as not, they'd forgotten the Seal Isles existed.

Darroc certainly had no trouble ignoring them, even if a few of the bays and beaches were right bonny.

Seal-infested or no.

Unfortunately, the seals beneath his tower were too many and too loud to pretend they weren't there.

Their song, as men who lived by the sea called such keening, filled the notch room. Mournful and chilling, the sound even welled up inside Darroc, pouring through him until he couldn't deny its power.

Conall felt it, too. The lad's eyes were alight again, his face wreathed in wonder.

Darroc shoved a hand through his hair, feeling like an ox.

"Mayhap they are celebrating us," he belatedly agreed, certain they weren't. "God kens they have reason to be impressed if they saw our men's flourish."

That, at least, was true.

"We were grand, weren't we?" The brag in Conall's voice brought a lift to Darroc's heart.

"We were the best." Another truth, if slightly embroidered.

Conall shot him a glance. "Better than those born sea hounds, the MacDonalds?"

"Well..." Darroc folded his arms, not wanting to exaggerate too greatly.

"The MacDougalls?"

Darroc arched a brow, letting silence be answer enough.

"Then what of the MacLeods?" Conall persisted. "Surely we were better than them?"

Darroc snorted. "A galley manned by wart-nosed, hunchbacked crones could outdo that cloven-footed race."

Conall looked pleased.

Darroc slung an arm around the lad's shoulders, giving a quick squeeze. "Even so, we shall leave Clan MacLeod to be challenged by others. Our purpose is to tread on the MacKenzies' heels."

"Their heels?" Conall slapped the stone of the window ledge. " 'Tis their arses what'll be feeling my tread! And I say you this"—his face split in another grin—"yon seals know it, too. That's another reason they're here, singing."

"For sure, they've come to tell us something." It was the best Darroc could do.

Life was too precarious to tempt the gods with yet another lie.

Indeed, he did believe the seals' song had meaning.

He just didn't like it.

Looking down at them now, he knew they bode ill. Some of them were hidden by the night's drifting mist, but the sea was flat and smooth as a polished mirror, its stillness letting him see enough of their dark, round heads to know they'd come in multitudes.

They bobbed in the sleek, gleaming water, their brown bodies rolling and tumbling, while others clustered on jagged tidal rocks. Some had dragged themselves onto the shingle of the boat strand, including several huge silver-gray ones with dappled coats.

All sang.

And, Darroc was sure, every last one of them had fixed their soulful, doglike stares on Castle Bane.

He shuddered.

Someone whose ties to the sea went far deeper than his own had once sworn that though beautiful, the song of the seals warned of coming disaster.

And that was something he couldn't, wouldn't accept.

So he reached around his oblivious cousin and grabbed the shutter latches, closing them with a bit more force than was necessary.

"Come now." Again he snagged Conall's elbow, this time gripping harder as he pulled him toward the door. "There's a fine joint of roasted meat waiting for us in the great hall," he said, laying on his jauntiest tone. "I, for one, am famished!"

"Saints, Darroc, the seals—"

"Will also be heard belowstairs." Darroc marched on, wishing it weren't so.

Conall threw a last, frustrated glance at the closed shutters.

Darroc didn't break stride.

It was good that the lad believed the seals were celebrating them.

With luck—which they so rightly deserved—there'd be no reason for any of them to think otherwise.

He would make sure of it.

Chapter Three

❧

A fortnight later, Arabella stood at the edge of Kyleakin's curving road and wondered how a fishing village she'd known all her life could feel so daunting. Behind her, the same row of thatched cottages crowded the muddy foreshore, the peat smoke from their cook fires as familiar as her name. Across the bay, Dunakin's tower loomed atop its knoll, imposing as always. Directly in front of her, the little harbor proved a hive of activity.

There was nothing to account for the queasiness churning inside her.

Late afternoon sun sparkled on the water and the reek of dried fish and eel tickled her nose, letting her know the contents of a pile of barrels on the quayside. Huge wine casks were there, too. And great stacks of iron-bound coffer chests, some protected by thick canvas covering. Men, children, and dogs scrambled everywhere, the ruckus almost hurting her ears. But neither the smells nor such bustle was new to her.

Damp from the muddied road seeped into her shoes and a brisk sea wind sliced through her cloak, but that, too, didn't faze her.

She ignored the chill just as she refused to acknowledge her father's fierce expression as he surveyed the chaos. He held her arm in a bruising grip and scowled at every seaman that dared glance their way.

Despite his vows that he wouldn't shame her.

As if to prove it, he cleared his throat. "Are you hungry?" He looked to where a young boy stirred a steaming cauldron of fish stew. Beside the lad, a wizened old man had skewered conger eel steaks onto sharp green sticks and was preparing to broil them on a bed of fired stones. Crisp, fresh-off-the-griddle oatcakes rounded up the pair's offerings.

The smells were tantalizing.

Arabella's mouth watered.

But she shook her head, declining. "I'll eat later… after you've gone."

Her father's jaw tightened. "You only ate half a bannock this morn."

He looked at her, his eyes narrowing.

She stood her ground. "I'm not hungry."

"Humph!" He dismissed her excuse. "Dinna think Cook ne'er told me who raids the kitchen stores late of an e'en, after everyone else is asleep!"

He leaned close, not bothering to lower his voice. "You have a greater appetite than some men. I'll fetch you something." His gaze flicked back to the fishmonger's stall. "You'll no' be spending your first night away from home with naught but a few bannock crumbs in your belly."

Tightening his grip on her arm, he frowned. "You need to eat."

Arabella blinked.

She thought she'd seen a man staring down at her from one of Dunakin's upper windows. But when she scrunched her eyes to make sure, he was gone. His outline—if he'd been there at all—had appeared decidedly well-muscled and powerful. Too bad he'd only been a shadow.

She straightened, annoyed by her fancies.

Everyone knew the MacKinnon who lairded it at Dunakin was an old done man, looked after by his equally aged wife and a handful of loyal servitors.

No bold Highland warriors dwelt there.

She shivered and drew her cloak tighter, the man's image still branded on her mind.

"You're cold!" Her father pounced. "A bowl of hot fish stew and—"

"Nae." Arabella stopped him before he could stalk over to the fishmonger.

I may never eat again if my stomach doesn't stop feeling as if it's filled with lead.

The unspoken words echoed in her head, making her doubt everything she'd started to believe about her strength and daring. Her father's words squeezed her heart, his gruff tone saying so much more than his scowls.

He could summon all the dark looks he wished. She knew how to see behind them, always catching his true feelings before he could shield them. Recognizing them now, she blinked against the heat pricking her eyes.

She bit her lip, the truth scalding her.

It wasn't her father. It was her.

She was shaming herself.

Her palms were damp and a cold lump of fear sat fast in her throat. Her guard—twelve of her father's best archers and swordsmen—stood in a nearby cluster, their watchful eyes and glinting steel reminding her of the perils that might be before her.

She tried to squash all thoughts of danger and took a painful breath.

If Arnkel Arneborg, shipmaster of the *Merry Dancer*, the merchant cog, approached them now, she wouldn't be able to offer more than a raspy croak in greeting.

Keeping her chin raised, she clenched her fingers into the folds of her cloak and hoped no one would notice the whiteness of her knuckles. She forced herself to smile at the men her father blasted with his stares. She ignored the stony-faced guardsmen. Standing proud, she dug deep for the calm that had always come so easily.

Unfortunately, it remained elusive.

An old woman hawking a basket of roasted-in-their-shell oysters paused to cast a narrow-eyed glance at her, as if she sensed her apprehension.

At once, Arabella released her grapple hold on her mantle.

If her jitters showed, she'd die.

Gelis, she knew, would have set the day ablaze, making it into a high-flown celebration. Laughing, batting her lashes, and perhaps even clapping in glee. For sure, she'd turn heads and capture hearts.

Seafarer or oyster woman, all would have flocked around her, succumbing to her charm.

Arabella swallowed.

The thickness in her throat didn't lessen.

Far from it; the swelling worsened until she could

barely draw in breath. The din around her increased. Screeching seabirds made it difficult to think. Their piercing cries were giving her an aching head. And although she knew the tide hadn't yet turned, the water slapping the quay's wooden pilings sounded so loud she'd have sworn the sea surge had roared into the harbor.

In truth, the roar was the blood pounding in her ears.

For a beat, she considered tossing her head and letting her eyes spark. A flashed smile of dazzling brilliance and, if she dared, a slight adjustment to her cloak so that its drape emphasized the swell of her breasts. No one would guess her misery.

All she had to do was pretend she was Gelis. An artful blush and fiery, snapping eyes worked wonders. She'd certainly observed her sister's ploys often enough to mimic them.

She could do it.

Her brows snapped together at the very idea.

She wasn't her sister.

And this was *her* dream.

So she stood a bit taller, making sure to keep her back straight. And instead of flaunting her beauty—and there were many who said she was pleasing to the eye—she took several deep breaths to compose herself.

Unfortunately, her father appeared to have caught her brow snapping.

"We can leave now." He misunderstood her frown. "No one will blame you for changing your mind. If we make haste, you can look over the vendors' offerings, choose some baubles and cloth, and we can be home before—"

"Nae . . . ." Arabella let her voice trail off, her attention snagged by a small wooden crate near one of the canvas-covered strongboxes.

Something was moving inside the crate, and as she looked the top shifted, revealing the tufted head of a tiny red and white puppy. All silky ears and bright, round eyes, the wee creature won her heart with a single high-pitched squeak.

Arabella stared at him, a warm glow spreading all through her.

She had to have him.

"O-o-oh!" She shook free of her father's grasp, starting forward. "There *is* something I want. That puppy—"

"Is no' for you." Her father sounded horrified. He caught her before she'd gone two paces. "You can't take a dog—"

"Ho, Kintail!" A tall blond-bearded man broke through the crowd, his sea-weathered face split in a grin. "Just arrived on the quay and already your girl is keen to test her sea legs!"

Arabella's cheeks flamed. "I—"

"She was making for yon wee dog." Her father answered for her.

"Dog?" Arnkel Arneborg scratched his beard, looking around.

His gaze lit on a shaggy black mongrel sniffing near the fishmonger's stall.

"No' that one." Her father flung out an arm, indicating the crate with the puppy. "She'd have that bit of fluff yonder," he said, surprising her. "Name your price and I'll keep the beastie here until her return."

"Ah, well...." The shipmaster rubbed the back of his neck. "That's a fine puppy for sure. Mina's her name. But she isn't to be had for any coin." He looked uncomfortable, slid a sympathetic glance at Arabella. "She's a sleeve dog I'm to deliver to one of the Manx princesses. I picked her up in Flanders and there'd be hell to pay if I arrive in Man without her."

"Oh." Arabella bit back her disappointment.

Her father assumed his most belligerent look. "I'll make it worth your trouble, Arneborg. What say you to double what Manx is offering?"

Arabella caught her breath. "Father!"

He only grinned, sure of his triumph.

"I gave my word, sir." Arnkel Arneborg turned to gaze at his ship. "But I know the breeder in Flanders. I can pick up another puppy next time I'm there. For the now, perhaps Lady Arabella will care for Mina during the voyage?"

Arabella's heart sank.

She didn't want another dog. She wanted this one.

She also knew that honor was the one thing no MacKenzie would argue against.

A word given was sacred.

"My lady?" The shipmaster was looking at her, awaiting her answer. "You know my own cabin has been prepared for you. It's not large, but there's more than enough room for yourself and Mina."

Arabella shifted her feet.

Her stomach was rolling again and the throbbing in her temples was worse than ever. The little dog—Mina—was still watching her. She could feel her piercing stare even without looking.

"Well?" Arnkel Arneborg persisted.

Despair wrapped around her, squeezing hard and tight.

Getting attached to Mina would only make it harder to let her go. But she could see the puppy's tail wagging through the slats of the crate. She also saw the excitement in Mina's eyes, the quick flashes of her tiny pink tongue.

Arabella's father glanced at her, one brow arcing.

When she didn't answer, he frowned and returned his attention to the shipmaster.

"We expected you weeks ago." His gaze followed Arnkel's to the *Merry Dancer*. The high-sided cog with its fore-and-aft-castles looked large and bulky riding anchor so close to the sleek, low-slung galleys.

Another chill slid down Arabella's spine.

Now that the time was nigh, she wasn't sure it was a good idea to spend a settle-in night on the ship before they left Kyleakin in the morning.

Her father slid an arm around her, drawing her close. "Your cog looks sound." He eyed the other man. "I trust you didn't run into difficulties?"

"Only great basking sharks!" Arneborg laughed. "Leaping clean out of the water they were, scores of them. Any seaman will tell you that they only do that when a fierce storm is brewing. So-o-o"—he looked around, drawing nods of agreement from passersby—"we changed course and lost a few days in the offing."

Arabella glanced at her father.

He was nodding. Sagely, as if he agreed with every word.

Yet she knew he'd never heard the like.

Arnkel Arneborg hooked his thumbs in his belt. "Last time I didn't heed jumping baskers we sailed into a storm so wicked the wind blew off my beard!" he boasted, rocking back on his heels. "Better to make port a few days late than risk life and limb, eh?"

Arabella saw her father conceal a grimace.

She knew from experience that his patience only went so far.

Quickly, before he could change his mind about letting her go—or before the shipmaster could be persuaded to deny her passage—she reached inside her cloak and retrieved a small leather satchel.

If she wasn't as strong and daring as she'd hoped, she had come prepared.

"See here!" She untied the bag's strings to retrieve a square of well-stitched linen. "Should anything happen onboard, I will be of use to you." She thrust the patch in the shipmaster's hands, pride in her work making her bold. "You can see how fine I ply my needle. So, too, can I mend flesh if such needs arise."

She lifted her chin, not stopping now. "I'm also well versed in medicinal herbing." She indicated her pouch, stuffed with cures and remedies. "My mother is a skilled healer and I've worked at her side since I was young."

"By thunder!" Arneborg peered at the cloth, then her. "Did I not want to frighten the good folk of this village I'd raise my sword to you. As is"—he turned to her father— "I'll commend you on having a fine daughter! Not only is she a woman of beauty and spirit, but she's of a practical mind."

Her father's eyes darkened. "She is . . . everything."

Arabella felt his arm tighten around her. His words caught in her throat.

"That I know!" Returning the linen to her, the shipmaster grasped her father's hands with both of his. "I'll look after her as if she were my own, never you worry," he assured, pumping hard. "See her on board whenever you're ready."

Stepping back, he planted his hands on his hips. "I've a hold full of French bay salt to see unloaded." He winked. "Barrels for yourself, Dunvegan, and even old Dunakin if he's still got the breath in him to pay me!"

And then he was gone, striding off down the quay as quickly as he'd appeared.

Arabella stared after him, some of her earlier exhilaration returning.

Her adventure was about to begin. Already, she'd taken her farewells at Eilean Creag, bidding her mother and others to stay behind when she'd left with her father for Kyleakin.

Now he, too, would be leaving her.

He'd give her into the care of twelve MacKenzie stalwarts and a sea captain that he knew well but that she'd never seen in her life.

Arabella smoothed her cloak and tried to look brave. "Did he truly say I can have his cabin?"

"He said it'd been prepared for you." Her father shot a glance at the man's retreating back. "What he should have said is that I've bought his cabin for you. Truth be told"—he threw back his plaid and patted the money pouch at his hip—"after all the silver I poured o'er his palm he ought to have strewn the cabin's floor with rose petals and painted the walls with liquid gold."

Arabella's heart filled on seeing her father's black scowl return.

Faith, but she'd miss him!

But first she had a mission . . . a secret one.

And she could only see it accomplished if she reached the Seal Isles.

So she cleared her throat, eager to be on her way. "I have one question before you go," she began, not missing how his brows flew together on hearing her dismissal. "Are you sure the MacLeans of Doon know I'll be coming?"

Her father snorted. "You ask?"

Snatching up her travel bag, he signaled to her guards to fetch it and her coffer chests. They'd agreed he wouldn't go with her onboard.

As soon as the men gathered her goods and set off for the *Merry Dancer*, he turned to her, placing his hands on her shoulders.

"To be sure, the MacLeans know." He wrapped his arms around her, pulling her close. "You ken their cailleach, old Devorgilla, is likely peering at us even now! That one doesn't miss anything. She sees the path of every raindrop to fall from a Highland leaf."

"But—"

"But is a word MacKenzies don't speak." He crushed her to him, letting his fierce hug say the words she knew would break him if spoken aloud. "Devorgilla will ensure the MacLeans know you're on the way. Just you return safe in the spring...."

"I will!" Arabella drew back to kiss his cheek, her world spinning when she found it damp as her own. His dark blue eyes, so like hers, glittering with the same brightness. "Oh, Father! I love you so—"

But like the shipmaster, he, too, was suddenly gone. Only the four guardsmen who'd stayed behind to escort her onto the *Merry Dancer* remained.

She hoped that Devorgilla really did know she meant to call at Doon on her way south.

Such magic wasn't easy to believe.

Not because it didn't happen.

She'd seen enough proof of the crone's powers to never doubt her. But this time the magic would involve her. She was the one MacKenzie not born under a charmed star.

And that changed everything.

Unless—she flashed one last look at Dunakin's empty tower windows—she took matters into her own hands.

Which was exactly what she meant to do.

"She saw him!" Devorgilla of Doon, the most far-famed cailleach in all the land, rubbed her hands together in satisfaction. Scudding mists swirled around her, dark and mysterious. Night wind, thick with damp and the tang of the sea, whistled past her. And a bright full moon rode high above the towering cliffs, its silvery light giving the strand an eerie, luminous glow.

Almost as if the Auld Ones were smiling.

As they should be.

She served them well.

"Great is our magic," she cackled, looking down at the little red dog fox standing so quietly beside her at the rock pool.

The fox didn't blink.

Devorgilla laughed with glee, not bothered by his solemn stare.

"A mere wriggle of these fingers"—she held out her hand and admired each knotty-knuckled digit—"and there he was in Dunakin's tower window!"

Her old bones warmed with the glory of it.

Her pulse quickened.

Of all the tidal pools dotting the narrow stretch of beach beneath Doon's cliffs, she'd chosen rightly. Its smooth surface understood her need, allowing her to peer into its secrets, conjuring as she wished. The most powerful spelling words she could've mumbled wouldn't have mattered if the water wasn't obliging.

Even a newt-brain knew that.

Her own knowledge was vast.

Throughout the land, paeans were sung of her skills. Those who loved her threw open their doors in welcome. Anyone fool enough to shun her was wise to hide in shadow, quaking in their fear.

Devorgilla patted her grizzled hair, pleased with her reputation.

Soon, this very night, she'd demonstrate that greatness.

But first she'd celebrate having shown the doubtful one a glimpse of her future.

So she took a small silver flask from her belt and treated herself to a sip of her own prized heather ale. Then, after wiping her mouth with the back of her gnarled hand, she rummaged in her skirts until she found a little bag filled with twists of dried meat.

From this she selected a particularly large strip and handed it to the fox.

He, too, played a role in her success and deserved his due reward.

"Did you see her eyes widen?" She relived the moment, victory still sweet. "How her breath caught as she stared up at him?"

Somerled, her pet fox and helpmate, continued to eat in silence.

He didn't seem to appreciate their accomplishment.

With a disdain worthy of the most high-browed noble, he ignored the two keeps that were only now beginning to fade from the dark, mirrorlike surface of the tide pool. Instead, he turned a deliberate gaze on the steep stone steps carved into the cliff face.

As he'd done again and again, ever since they'd picked their way down the harrowing path with its many heart-stopping twists and plunges.

Indeed, if she hadn't nudged him with her black-booted foot, he might have missed the grand moment when she'd caused the young warrior's silhouette to disappear from his own window and reappear at Dunakin.

And even then—as soon as the wonder happened—a single swish of the fox's plush, white-tipped tail was the only indication he'd noticed.

The cliff path fascinated him more.

A fixation that annoyed Devorgilla until he returned his attention to her and she saw the worried look clouding his deep golden eyes.

Understanding, she laughed. Then she hitched up her skirts, displaying ankles surprisingly well-turned for someone of her untold years.

"These feet are as sure as your own, my little friend. Even if I hobble, I made it down yon slippery track. The climb back up will be no bother! Now come"—she dropped her skirts and began peering along the strand—"help me find a curl of mist thick enough for our purpose."

At once, Somerled dipped his paw into the rock pool, rippling the surface until the fading outlines of the two keeps vanished completely. The deed done, he lifted his foot and shook off the water droplets.

They fell to the sand, cold sparkles lit by moonglow and—Devorgilla beamed—caught up by a sudden gust of wind and turned into a lovely, whirling twist of blue-white haze.

"O-o-oh!" Devorgilla trilled her approval.

Somerled nodded acknowledgment.

Then, as the mist pulsed and thickened, she wiggled her fingers again, this time procuring a length of thin, knotted rope.

Thrusting her hands into the spinning mist, she caressed each of the four knots—one for each direction of the wind—before untying two...the knots representing the north and the west, the direction from which a certain merchant cog would approach Doon.

"North wind, so cold and mighty," she chanted, lifting her voice as the mist whirled even faster, "carry this fog to where I will it. West wind, so strong and honored, keep it there so long as needed. Old Ones, you who rule all days that have passed and all those yet to come,"—the cording vanished from her hands—"hear my plea and bless what has begun."

The spell released, she took a deep breath.

No longer a tight, fast-spinning vortex, the mist now shimmered and grew, spreading and thickening as it drifted seaward, moving slowly toward the horizon.

There, she knew, the creamy white fog would remain until she recalled it.

An impassable barrier, dense and impenetrable, its eastern edges shaded in black.

Devorgilla's eyes flew wide.

She clapped a hand to her breast, her jaw dropping.

But there could be no mistake.

Even Somerled saw the unholy blackness. His hackles on end, the little fox ran to the water's edge, snarling. Not that his growls and agitation or Devorgilla's own dread could change what was done.

They could only look on in horror, watching as the blackness spread.

A terrible darkness such as Devorgilla had never seen.

And that she knew meant grave danger.

All her earlier elation evaporated. Her mouth went dry and her stomach dropped.

Unknown evil was almost impossible to challenge.

Shuddering, she grabbed up her skirts again and hastened for the cliff path, leaving Somerled to trot after her. If they hurried, they might be able to avert disaster.

So much was at stake.

Perhaps even Lady Arabella's life.

Chapter Four

❧

You should be in your cabin, my lady."

The MacKenzie guardsman gave Arabella a look that said he wasn't making pleasantries. And even if his eyes held concern rather than fierceness, she recognized the iron will her father prized in those who served him.

"Not just yet." She tried a smile.

The guardsman's face didn't crack. "I don't like these seas." He glanced at the thick drift of mist just beginning to swirl around them. "If you ask me, it's worsening faster than a wink."

She hadn't asked him, but she refrained from saying so.

She understood why he didn't want her on deck. The endless blue-green of the Hebridean Sea had turned murky and dark, the waters churning and white-capped. Nor did she need anyone to tell her that the tides ran with ever increasing speed. She could taste the salt tang on her tongue and inhaled it with each breath. Almost as if the sea was claiming the air. And that wasn't all. The winds no longer simply blew but shrieked through the rigging, the wildest gusts they'd seen since leaving Kyleakin a sennight before.

Seven days of calm, barely rippled water. Only an oddly persistent bank of fog had broken the monotony.

This was different.

And the cold, flying spray and heavy swells excited her.

The guardsman narrowed his eyes as if he knew. "This is no place for you."

When he took a step toward her, she flashed a glance at her aft-castle cabin with its sturdy door and security. A tiny coal-burning brazier waited within, spending warmth, and a small table and chair and a snug berth lent an air of coziness. She'd even taken a few curls of cinnamon bark and dried heather from her herb pouch, using them to scent the air.

But at the moment, such comfort didn't interest her.

Looking away from the cabin, she eyed the tossing seas. Huge breaking seas that tested her mettle, as did the darkening sky. Never had she seen such heavens. Seething black clouds blotted the moon and stars, leaving only angry, rumbling masses that boiled like an upturned cauldron.

Arabella shivered.

But beneath that one wee quiver, her heart soared. Frightening or not, the roll of the ship exhilarated her. The leaping waves were a delight, absolutely fascinating. And the racing wind, so sharp and brisk, made her feel more alive than ever before.

Just days ago she might have hidden in her cabin's

bunk, the covers to her chin, and curled into a cold ball of fear and dread.

Now...

She tossed back her hair. "I came on deck to fetch a meat bone for Mina," she lied. The little dog was asleep in her padded crate, her belly filled with tidbits and broth. "As soon as—"

"I'll see to the dog bone." The guardsman dismissed her excuse.

She started to argue, but just then a plume of spray arced over the side, wetting them both. An irresistible urge to laugh welled inside her. She burned to give into it and savor the night's fury. Revel in the icy prickles of the sea misting her skin. Instead, she blinked and lifted a hand to slick the damp from her face.

Her father's man was only doing his duty.

A bit longer and she'd return to Mina.

Even so, she shifted her feet on the slick deck, made sure she was standing ramrod straight.

The guardsman came closer. "See here, lady. Your father would know you safe."

"I'm not afraid." Arabella scooted down the railing, secretly relieved by how strong and solid it felt beneath her fingers. The rise and fall of the sea suddenly made that so important.

"I'll go inside shortly." She lifted her voice above the wind, her bravura making her pulse quicken. "For now"— she pressed against the rail and hoped he wouldn't notice how tightly her hands gripped the slippery wet wood— "I will stay here."

The guardsman frowned.

She pretended not to notice.

"Come, lass." He tried a different tone, but his eyes still glinted like steel. " 'Tis fell dangerous, such pitching and rolling. It isn't natural for a good, God-fearing soul to have naught between hisself and the deep, dark depths than a thin plank o' wood!"

"Captain Arneborg said cogs are the safest ships afloat." She held fast to the rail as the cog lifted, then plunged into a trough. "Nigh unsinkable."

The guardsman's scowl deepened.

Arabella smiled sweetly.

It was new for her to be so bold.

Having none of it, the guardsman snorted. "If he believes that, then why does he have bells hanging everywhere to ward off sea dragons?" He grabbed the rail, his knuckles whiter than hers. "That proves he's fearful of capsizing!"

"Faugh!" The shipmaster strode up to them, laughing. "It proves you've let my crew fill your ears with nonsense. The bells"—he reached out to set a cluster of them clanking—"are *plague bells*. They have naught to do with sea beasties. They—"

"There isn't any pest in these waters." The guardsman swelled his chest, ready to argue. "Latest word put the malaise many leagues from here, in England and—"

"Then who's to say it isn't my bells that's keeping us safe?" Arneborg jutted his chin. "Everyone knows the scourge travels on the wind. A medical man in Hamburg told me jangling bells break up the air, scattering the pest. As I've not been bothered anywhere I've journeyed since tying the bells to my ship's timbers, I believe him."

"I've ne'er heard the like." The guardsman remained doubtful.

Arnkel Arneborg shrugged. "Be that as it may"—he flashed a bearded smile—"the bells serve me well."

"Ah..." Arabella's heart stuttered.

She'd forgotten the bells. Even though their clanging had rung in her ears since she'd boarded the *Merry Dancer.* The rising tempest drowned their clatter and that could only mean one thing.

The storm was worse than she'd realized.

"Er..." Once again, the words stuck in her throat.

"Eh, lass?" Arneborg looked at her, one bushy blond brow raised in query.

She swallowed. "Do the bells help against storms?"

There.

She'd blurted her dread.

Heat flamed her face and she glanced aside, letting the spray cool her cheeks. Across the deck, several men rushed about lashing together the huge herring barrels. Only the barrels had already been tied in place. The portent of the men's preparations made her stomach clench.

There'd be no need to secure the barrels with extra lines if they weren't in danger of being swept away.

Arabella's eyes widened.

The shipmaster followed her gaze. "Yon's but a wee precaution. And, nae, the bells aren't storm charms."

He stepped closer, taking her elbow in a firm, fatherly grip. "Such things aren't needed on the *Merry Dancer.* There isn't a gale that can take her or a breaking sea she can't ride." He sounded sure of it. "We'll wait out the storm here and sail on when the fury's past us."

Arabella bit her lip, unconvinced.

If only the guardsman hadn't spoiled her brief moments

on deck. She'd done so well before his arrival—and his voiced concern—reminded her of the dangers.

"Have you already forgotten the fog bank?" Arneborg looked down at her, his smile still flashing. "Such impenetrable mist could have brought ill to a lesser ship. Yet here we are"—he started leading her across the deck, toward her cabin—"and nary a wood splinter out of place."

Arabella nodded.

She wanted to believe him.

Her guardsman caught up to them, blocking the way. "We avoided the fog by not sailing into it. This storm"—he shot a glance at the living seas—"is all around us. Wouldn't it be better to seek shelter in the bay of some islet? The saints know we've passed enough of them!"

"All the more reason to stay put!" The shipmaster stepped around him and reached for the cabin door. "Were you a seaman, you'd know anywhere near land is the worst place to be in a gale. If that land is a lee shore..."

He shot a glance at the guardsman, letting his expression explain the unspoken words.

"I am thinking of Lady Arabella." The young man flushed. "Her safety—"

"Will be assured in my cabin"—Arnkel flung open the door and ushered Arabella inside—"well away from breaking swells and jagged rocks and ledges that could rip the bottom out of us were we to approach land."

Releasing her, he crossed the cabin and lit two horn-held candles bracketed in the wall. "In such weathers, it only takes one strong gust to hurl a ship to her doom. Here, at sea, we have naught to fear but greensickness!"

The guardsman frowned, looking a bit queasy already.

Arabella started feeling better. Now she knew why her father had trusted her to Captain Arneborg's care.

But hours later, when a great thump in the hold jerked her from her sleep, she couldn't help but wish that his bells did work against storms.

Apparently Mina felt the same, for the little dog had burrowed beneath the covers and was snuggled tight against the backs of her knees, trembling.

Arabella reached down for her, gathering the dog into her arms. She bundled her into a fold of the bedclothes, then stroked her silky, warm fur until her shaking and whimpering lessened.

"Shush, Mina." She cradled the dog to her breast, holding her close. "It will be over soon."

She wished she believed it.

She didn't want to be afraid.

But the cog rocked crazily. And the timbers screeched louder each time a new swell crashed into them. Arabella stifled a shudder and tried to ignore the noises. She knew the ship was straining. Scariest of all, at some point while she'd slept, the candles in the two horn lanterns had gutted, leaving her in cold, inky darkness.

The cabin had but one small porthole and she could barely see its outline, dimly lit by the silvery gleam of the moon. She heard the clanging of the bells and the shouts of men as the thuds and bangs in the hold increased.

She sat up and felt for her cloak, swirling its warmth around her shoulders. Unfortunately, it didn't do much to ease her chill.

Something was different.

The air in her cabin felt wet. Even more alarming was the strange—surely imagined—sensation that spume swirled around her, lashing her with tiny, needle-sharp pellets of icy sea water.

Inside her cloak, Mina squirmed, whining.

"Shhhh..." Arabella tried to soothe her. "It's only the cargo wine casks and strongboxes. I'm sure they've just broken loose. There's nothing—*agggh!*"

The cog lurched violently, flinging her from the bunk. Somewhere in the darkness, Mina yelped. But before Arabella could scramble to her feet and look for her, one of her iron-bound coffers shot across the slanting floor and slammed into her.

"Owww!" She ignored the blaze of pain in her shoulder and pushed up on her knees, clutching the bunk with one hand and using the other to grab Mina who—praise be—was scrabbling at her legs.

"Ach, dia!" She scrambled onto the bunk, the little dog clasped in her arms.

Mina trembled uncontrollably.

Arabella sat frozen.

For some ridiculous reason, she thought of the man she'd imagined in one of Dunakin's windows. If such a warrior's arms were now holding her, she knew she'd fear nothing. As it was, she found herself alone, dread tightening her chest as the thumps and thuds in the hold erupted into a series of ear-splitting crashes.

Thunderous bangs that shook the cabin, threatening to splinter its walls. Furious poundings too close to come from the cog's well-laden belly.

"Lady!" The door burst open. "Make haste!"

Arabella jerked, the command putting a cold lump in her stomach.

"What...?" She couldn't get the words out, couldn't stand because her legs had turned to jelly.

Bobbing torchlight spilled into the cabin, revealing her most persistent guardsman. He rushed in, terror in his eyes and his face ashen.

"Come now!" He seized her, yanking her to her feet. "They're lowering the spare boat. You must be on it—you and four of us to guard you."

"Dear God!" Her heart stopped. "We're sinking?"

"Nae, but—"

"Then why?" Hope surged. "If we aren't—"

"We're no' sinking yet." His words chilled her. "But we soon will be—or worse!"

"*Worse?*" The shrill voice surely wasn't hers.

"Just come, my lady. We must go while there's time." He started pulling her to the door.

It was then that she noticed he'd strapped on more steel than her father kept in his armory. Nor did she miss how his gaze kept darting to the porthole. Feeling sick, she twisted away from him and ran across the cabin. Not wanting to look, but unable not to, she peered out into the darkness.

What she saw iced her blood.

A great Norse dragon ship was flying straight at them, its long sweeps sending up clouds of spume as it sped across the water.

"Mercy!" Her eyes rounded. "They're pirates. Vikings!"

"They're demons from hell." The guardsman reached for her again, taking her arm in a bone-crushing grip. "We'll get you away before they reach us. The fog will hide—"

"They're almost upon us now!" She couldn't look away.

Horror drenching her, she watched as the galley closed the distance between them with incredible ease. Sail, hull, and even the shields lining its sides gleamed black as pitch. Most terrifying of all was the steel-headed ramming lance projecting from the tall dragon-headed prow.

She whirled from the porthole. "They're going to pierce us!"

The guard didn't deny it.

Instead he swept her up in his arms and ran with her from the cabin. He raced to the other side of the cog where Captain Arneborg and several of his men were heaving the spare boat over the side.

It didn't look any larger than a skiff.

Arabella stared in disbelief.

It was a cockle shell!

But before she could object, they were at the rail. Three of her father's men leapt overboard, each one landing in the tossing, bobbing craft. The crewmen closed around her, lifting her over the side. Clearly, they meant to drop her into the outstretched arms of the men already in the little boat.

Arabella closed her eyes and screamed.

Then she was falling.

But the men never caught her.

She plunged into the icy, surging sea. Down and down she plummeted, the cold shocking her. Her lungs burned like fire. But she kept her mouth clamped shut, knowing she didn't dare gulp seawater.

Frantic, she kicked and thrashed, fighting her way to the surface. A near impossible task with one arm clasped like iron across her breast. But at last she broke free, choking and gasping.

Her men and the cockle shell were nowhere to be seen.

Nor was the *Merry Dancer*.

She splashed about in the darkness, alone save the towering seas. Everywhere water swirled around her, pulling her into troughs, then sweeping her up again, tossing her over foaming crests. Fear almost lamed her and her heavy cloak tangled around her legs, dragging her down. Each time a new swell crashed over her, it was more difficult to claw her way out again.

She didn't want to die.

Terrified, she blinked hard, straining to see. But waves kept slapping into her and the stinging sea spray blinded her. If her men and the spare boat were near, they would have found her by now.

There was no one to save her.

Above the shrieking wind and the roar of the seas, she caught sounds of battle. Though distant, the angry shouts of men came to her. As did the screech of steel on steel, then—most horrifying of all—the unmistakable cracking and splintering of wood.

The *Merry Dancer* was breaking apart.

She heard screams and knew men had been thrown into the water and were drowning. The raucous hoots and jeers of the sea raiders proved it. As did the abrupt silencing of Arnkel Arneborg's plague bells.

Arabella shuddered.

A terrible sadness flooded the place where her heart should have been. It spread through her, numbing her worse than the frigid water.

She thanked the saints she couldn't see.

Strangely, the burning in her eyes suddenly lessened

and her vision cleared. Only it wasn't the smashed cog that loomed before her, spelling her demise. It was the near-vertical wall of the most enormous wave she'd yet seen.

And it was rushing right at her.

Arabella screamed.

Then the monstrous black wave reached her and she knew no more.

Deep in the silent hour before sunrise, Darroc frowned in his sleep. His heart thundered and a strange urgency pulsed inside him. Not quite dreaming yet not awake, he flipped onto his back, barely aware of the damp, twisted bed sheets. Except for the muted roar of the sea, the quiet should have been absolute. But something else slipped in through his bedchamber's shuttered windows.

Something more than thin gray light and chill air.

It was the song of the seals.

He groaned and flung an arm over his eyes.

Cold sweat beaded his brow and—causing his scowl—desire throbbed hot and needy at his groin. The raven-haired beauty who'd haunted his dreams of late had returned to tempt him. Only this time, instead of enticing him with the sleek glide of her silky thighs and lush curves, she used her mouth, wet and delicious, to slide kisses up and down the hard, aching length of him.

Yet each time he reached for her, she immediately ceased her wondrous ministrations and an icy, black emptiness swirled around him. He cursed under his breath and rolled back onto his stomach.

He'd seldom endured a worse night.

Even the seals invaded his sorely needed rest. Some

half-awake part of him knew they weren't really there. He was dreaming them. But he heard them all the same. Their music teased and taunted, first hauntingly beautiful, then so terror-filled that the cries chilled his marrow.

"Damnation!" He dragged a pillow over his head.

Someone yanked it away.

"By all the powers!" He jerked upright, somehow not surprised to find Mungo clutching the pillow. The old goat wore a look fearsome enough to blast the frost off a witch's behind.

Darroc glared at him. "What are you doing here?"

"Waking you." Mungo eyed him as if he were a simpleton.

"That I know!" Darroc leapt to his feet, naked as he was. "I also know I've been waking myself fine ever since I can remember," he snapped, scowling at the shadows, still thick in the room's corners.

The ungodliness of the hour soured his mood.

Unable to summon his usual good humor, he jammed his hands on his hips. "Tell me the keep's caught fire—or leave me be so I can go back to sleep."

At the foot of his bed, Frang stretched and opened one eye, pinning them both with an accusatory canine stare. Like his master, Frang enjoyed his leisure.

"Well?" Darroc waited.

He did take malicious pleasure in the cloud of tainted fumes Frang used to show his displeasure.

Mungo grimaced, his nose wrinkling.

Then he tossed aside the pillow and cleared his throat. "The keep's fine, but there's a wreck on the beach."

Darroc's eyebrows shot up. "You're sure?"

He could scarce believe it.

Remote as MacConacher's Isle was, galleys rarely came anywhere near them and those that did were his own or belonged to his friend, Olaf Big Nose. And both of them knew the treacheries of these waters well enough to keep their boats away from rogue currents and blade-sharp rocks.

But Mungo was bobbing his head. "Mad Moraig roused the men in the hall. 'Twas her what saw the little red fox and heard the ruckus. She—"

Darroc snorted.

Now he knew this was folly.

"There aren't any foxes on this isle." He dropped back onto his bed, annoyed anew. "If Mad Moraig has anything to do with this—"

"She wasn't just blethering this time." Mungo defended the clan's well-meaning but slightly addled hen wife. "I saw the fox myself. He was harrying the broody hens in the bailey, causing them to squawk and make a racket." He paused to scratch his beard. "Strange thing is he didn't touch a feather on any of them. Just chased them about until I ran out and shooed him away."

That did it.

Darroc pressed his fingers to his temples. His clan had gone daft.

"The fox had queer eyes." Mungo kept pulling on his beard. "I swear he looked at me as if he knew me."

"And what does all this have to do with a wreck?" Darroc's head was beginning to pound.

He didn't believe a word he was hearing.

"A wrecked cog." The seneschal surprised him. "For some reason I can't explain, I followed the fox after shushing him out of the bailey. He trotted right down to the boat strand then just disappeared. That's when I saw—"

"*A cog?*" Darroc jumped to his feet, not caring about vanishing foxes. If Mungo could specify the kind of ship that had foundered, this was serious.

Wide awake now, he started snatching his clothes off the floor. "You saw the wreckage?"

"That's what I've been trying to tell you."

Darroc stared at him, his blood icing. "Were there survivors?"

Frang barked then, suddenly alert.

But the seneschal shook his head. "Six bodies so far, all ripped and slashed by the rocks. Conall and some of the others are down on the strand now, burying them."

"We'll have to search for men." Darroc threw on his plaid, dressing with all speed. "There could still be—"

"We needn't bother." Mungo sounded sure. "There's none left alive. 'Tis the wood what's the reason I came to fetch you."

Darroc looked up, his foot halfway into a *cuaran*. "The wood?"

"Aye, just!" Mungo tossed Frang another angry look when the dog flew off the bed, almost knocking him down. "The beach is covered with broken spars and pieces of the hull and deck. Some barrels and casks, and there's more in the water. To my way of thinking, we can profit from the refuse. Salvage what's no' too damaged and turn a good coin."

Darroc stared at him.

Mungo grinned.

"You're mad." Darroc finished lacing his shoes and strode for the door. "MacConachers don't line their purses with another man's loss."

Mungo hurried after him. "Then what'll you do?" He

kept pace, following Darroc into the darkened stair tower. "Let valuable wood rot on the strand?"

"To be sure, nae." Darroc took the steps two at a time, Mungo and Frang close on his heels. And with each downward-winding spiral, the horror-filled cries of his dreams rushed back to him. Now he knew it hadn't been the seals. Or even his imaginings. He'd heard the death throes of drowning men and the thought split him.

"We'll no' be wasting the wreck goods?" Mungo grabbed his arm as they reached the bottom of the stairs. "We don't even know what's in the barrels and casks. Could be fine Rhenish wine or—"

"We'll burn it all, whate'er." Darroc jerked free, his mind set. "But first we'll say prayers over every stick of wood, blessing the lost cog and pleading mercy for the souls who went down with her."

"You could use some of the wood to build a second birlinn." Mungo hurried after him as he sprinted across the hall. "We all know you want—"

"What I want isn't important." Darroc's voice hardened. "It's about honor. Respect."

Quickening his pace, he reached the hall door in a flash, flinging it wide. "Aught else is a betrayal of our name. What matters"—he threw Mungo a glance before he dashed down the outer stairs—"is making sure there's no' some poor soul out there who needs our help."

"Humph." Mungo sounded skeptical. "We can search the seas till the sun goes down and rises again and we'll be finding naught but wind and cold!"

But a few moments later, as Darroc tore down the cliff path to the strand, he knew Mungo was wrong. For sure, the beach was awash with wreckage. And the morning was cold, the wind sharp and biting.

Yet there was something else.

Something uncanny.

Bells clanged from the deadly tidal rocks that rimmed the bay.

Hundreds by the sound of them and their ringing chilled him to the core. The clanging was horrible, the eerie noise branding itself into him just like the anguished cries he'd heard in the night.

Those screams, too, wouldn't leave him. The memory burned inside him like a white-hot blaze.

"Ho, Darroc!" Conall ran up to him, the shovel in his hand revealing what he'd been about. "Belike yon bells are caught on the rocks, eh?"

"No' for long they won't be." Darroc frowned at his cousin, then turned away to scan the choppy seas.

The very idea of allowing the bells to remain on the skerries curdled his blood.

The sound was unholy.

Wasting no time, he strode over to one of the smaller boats beached in the shallows. "Conall—grab a few extra oars or a pole we can use to unhook them and come!" He flung the order over his shoulder as he splashed into the water. "While we're out there, we search for survivors."

Conall tossed aside the shovel and wheeled to do his bidding. Darroc vaulted over the side of the bobbing skiff. Not to be left behind, Frang bounded into the water and launched himself into the little boat before anyone could stop him. Once settled, the dog's expression said there'd be no point in trying to send him back to the beach.

As if to make that clear, Frang placed a possessive forepaw on one of the thwarts.

He wasn't going anywhere.

Knowing it, Darroc reached to rub his ears. "You think there's someone out there, don't you, old boy?"

Frang's quick bark said he did.

Darroc thought so, too. The surety of it tightened his chest and rode his shoulders like a sack of stones. Heart racing, he grabbed the oars and pushed off. Conall plunged through the surf, two oars and a hook-ended pole tucked under his arm. Racing, he took a sailing dive and landed—albeit somewhat clumsily—in the boat.

"Whew!" He righted himself at once, his copper red hair glowing in the first glints of morning sun.

"Away!" Darroc claimed the stern bench and began rowing.

Conall joined in, his muscles bunching as he plied his oars. He matched his strokes to Darroc's and they gained speed, soon approaching the narrows of the bay and the black glistening rocks beyond.

Moving fast, they shot past the bay's enclosing cliffs and into open water. The wind caught them at once and they had to stay hard at the oars to swing the skiff toward the first of the looming skerries. Huge rollers crashed into the jagged rocks, the creaming waves leaving plumes of foam and froth in their wake.

Lashing spray drenched them, but they drove on, using the tidal flow to get as close as they dared. For the benefit of Conall, Darroc pulled with all his might, wrenching the little boat away from the sharp, seaweed-covered rocks and into the deep roll of a trough-like wave.

"Are you run mad?" Conall nearly fell off his thwart.

Frang barked excitedly.

The skiff bobbed in the rough seas, blessedly a safe distance from the death-bringing rocks. Darroc glanced round at the huge troughs, his relief so thick he could taste it on the back of his tongue. All around them, the wretched bells tolled. Had he been alone, he would have risked putting an end to the infernal ringing.

But with Conall and Frang onboard...

His throat closed on thinking how near to unnecessary danger he'd brought them.

"And now?" Conall huffed.

"Just pull with me." Darroc gripped the oars tighter as the skiff plunged into a cresting wave. "It was a fool notion to try and get the bells. Yon skerries"—he flashed a glance at them—"are half submerged just now. At flood tide, only their tips will break the surface. I'm thinking the seas will wash away the bells—"

Someone on the shore yelled.

"Heigh-ho!" Conall glanced at the boat strand. "What are they going on about?"

Men dashed along the water's edge, gesticulating. Dark figures limned against the high open hills rising behind the strand. Darroc understood their agitation, feeling it in his bones.

"There's someone out here." He shot to his feet, causing the skiff to tilt and dip. He twisted around, trying to see behind them, over the tossing waves.

But nothing stirred.

Only what looked to be a great number of bobbing wine casks or barrels.

Disappointed, he dropped back onto the thwart. "They'll

be hoping we pull in a few of those casks," he said, flashing another glance at the men on the shore.

"Pah!" Conall rolled his eyes. "The tide will bring 'em in, sure enough. I'm for—"

It was then that Frang turned his head into the wind, nose high and quivering.

He barked madly, his stare fixed on the barrels.

Darroc looked again, shock slamming into him when he saw what appeared to be a clump of wet cloth spread across some of the barrels. Large cargo barrels that—he could see now—were lashed together like a raft.

"God be good—that's a man!" He stared, horror stopping his breath.

"Nae." Conall leaned forward, his eyes narrowing as they rowed furiously. "No' unless he has breasts. I say that's a woman!"

Darroc scarce heard him, so intent was he on reaching the barrel raft. Even before they bumped up against it, he saw what his cousin meant. A young raven-haired woman lay on her back across the barrels, her face turned away from them, her long hair trailing in the water.

"Saints o' mercy!" Darroc's eyes rounded. "You're right—it is a woman. Pray God she's alive!"

Frang barked wildly, not even waiting for Darroc to grab the bow line and secure them to the odd raft. In a flash, he jumped onto the barrels, tail wagging.

As soon as he did, a tiny red-and-white dog crawled from beneath the edge of the woman's sodden cloak. Shivering and bedraggled, the wee creature collapsed at Frang's feet. Obviously female, the little dog gave a whimper and lifted her head to peer up at him, her liquid eyes adoring.

Frang threw a triumphant glance at the skiff and then turned a moony-eyed look on the smaller dog.

He was clearly in love.

Ignoring him, Darroc scrambled onto the raft and dropped to his knees beside the woman. His heart thundered, too, but for an entirely different reason. Was there a man living who could look on such a tragedy and not have his guts twist?

The woman was too still.

She wasn't breathing.

Darroc reached for her, lifting her against him. She was cold, so cold. But the moment he touched her, something clenched inside him. Though near frozen—to him—she felt warm and vibrant, her pliant body molding to his. She'd been made for his arms. That surety filled him with dread. If she was dead, he knew a part of him would die, too.

Crazy as that was.

He looked down at her, everything in his world contracting until he only saw her beautiful limp form. Her breasts pressed against him and he willed his warmth to flow into her. This couldn't be the end for her. But she didn't respond at all. Her head only lolled to the side, the silky mass of her raven hair spilling across her face.

"*Lass.*" He held her gently, fearing of hurting her as he slicked back her long, tangled tresses. Sooty lashes rested against her smooth, white cheeks and her lips were sweetly curved and full. She was lovely. More perfect in her beauty than a living soul had a right to be.

Darroc's heart seized, the thought chilling him.

Surely the gods wouldn't damn her because of her exquisiteness?

Praying it wasn't so, he felt along her throat, hoping for a pulse.

Blessedly, there was one.

"Conall!" He flashed a glance at his cousin, still in the skiff. "Toss me your spirit costrel!"

But even as Conall unfastened the flask from his sword belt and sent it arcing through the air, the woman stirred in Darroc's arms, moaning.

Her eyes fluttered open. Deep blue eyes, dark as the sea, and filling with panic as she glanced about, trying to focus. *"Mina…"*

Darroc stared down at her and a wild, whirling sense of inevitability seized him. He fell into those haunted, sapphire eyes, losing himself. Heat, blazing hot, whipped through him, searing his soul.

Heart pounding, he snatched up the costrel from where it'd landed and, unstopping it, tipped the flask to the woman's lips. He forced the life-spending *uisge beatha* down her throat, willing the fiery spirits to revive her.

He knew who she was, though he couldn't explain such a wonder.

Now that he'd found her, he wasn't about to let her go.

He absolutely wasn't going to let her die.

Not in a thousand lifetimes.

Chapter Five

❖

"Her name is Mina."

Darroc let the words hang in the air, a shimmering statement.

Not that he thought Mad Moraig was paying him any heed. Lost in her own world, she'd occupy herself with Mina for days and nights to come. As he'd known she would even before he'd swept into the hall and raced up the tower stairs with the mysterious beauty.

Seeing him rush past, the hen wife had cried out and hobbled after them, climbing the stairs as quickly as her bent legs allowed.

Mad Moraig had a need to care for people.

Understanding her, Darroc always let her have her say. Even if sometimes, that meant undoing her *goodness* as soon as time and discretion allowed.

This was one of those times. So he stood in the center of his room, taking care—as the old woman had admonished him—to keep his back to the bed. Lady Mina lay

there, no mere slip of a girl, but wondrously made and
with her glorious hair now combed and spilling about
her shoulders like a lustrous skein of firelit ebony. How
he burned to smooth back those silky tresses and touch
her gently, perhaps even kiss the sensitive hollow of her
throat.

Truth was he ached to do a lot more.

But he was certain she was of gentle birth. Her elegant, unmarred hands bespoke her station. As did the
fine weave of her ruined cloak and the delicate silk of her
tattered night rail. The graceful lines of her face and her
milky smooth skin were equally telling.

With surety, she was a lady.

She was also naked.

Gloriously so and—because of her condition—she was
draped across the bed in a way that wasn't good for him,
her most intimate secrets fully exposed. His loins tightened and he bit back a groan. He couldn't risk another
look. He'd seen more than enough helping Mad Moraig
undress her.

Mad Moraig fussed and fretted over her still. Clucking
her tongue, applying her salves, and muttering words he
didn't attempt to understand.

"Did you hear, lambie?" Her reedy voice addressed
her charge. "He's for calling you Mina."

Across the room, the little red and white dog gave an
excited yip.

Darroc looked her way, his eyes widening to see her
enthroned on Frang's hearthside bed of ancient plaids.
Frang sprawled on the floor rushes beside her, his head
resting on his paws.

Thing was, Frang never laid on the rushes.

As a chiefly dog, Frang considered rush-lounging beneath his dignity. He had a pallet in every chamber and fiercely defended them all.

Darroc's lips twitched.

How was it possible that one female—albeit a beauty— and a tiny dog not much larger than a squirrel could turn his world upside down so quickly?

He cast a glance at the room's one opened window, pleased to see thick, rain-laden clouds scudding across the sky. A good steady downpour or even a bit of sleet would suit him well. With luck, the day's increasing chill would temper the heat simmering inside him.

He almost threw back his head and laughed. There wasn't anything simmer*ish* about what was happening to him.

It felt more like a sunburst.

His brows snapped together. If he wasn't careful, he'd turn into a poet.

At least the bells had stopped ringing.

He shuddered, relieved that the horrible sound no longer filled his ears.

From behind him, he did hear Mad Moraig *tsk-tsk*'ing as she rummaged importantly in her healing basket. "This lassie willna be caring what we call her," she trilled in her singsong voice, now dipping a cloth into a basin from the sound of splashing water. "The poor bittie be out o' her head for the now. Eh, Mina?"

"*Lady Mina*." Darroc knew the distinction wouldn't mean anything to Mad Moraig. But he liked the feel of her name on his tongue. Saying it aloud also seemed to give life to her. Much as the *uisge beatha* in Conall's costrel had put a spot of color into her cheeks.

Or so he told himself.

Unfortunately, the spirit-induced flush had faded quickly. And before he'd even moved her off the barrel raft and into the skiff, she'd once again slipped into darkness. Now she'd also been given a dose of Mad Moraig's sleeping draught. And even though he knew the tincture caused a good part of her slumber, she looked way too lifeless.

Almost like the beautifully serene marble effigies on the tombs of great ones and other worthies.

The comparison squeezed his heart, especially now that he'd not just seen the perfection of her firm, round bosom and the voluptuous curve of her hips, but held her in his arms. His hands splayed across her smooth and shapely thighs and—saints help him—catching that one fleeting glimpse of the silky black triangle of her female curls.

Darroc's need flamed anew.

Furious, he looked up at the ceiling and clenched his fists.

He'd found her just hours ago and already his honor had flown out the window.

He frowned.

Only the lowest dredge would think of such things now. But how sweetly those glossy raven curls had beckoned. Until—with a sharpness that surprised him—Mad Moraig caught him staring and slapped a drying cloth across Mina's naked hips, hiding her enticements.

Not that any length of linen could banish such sweetness from his mind.

Even now, two full candle notches later, awareness sizzled inside him, heating his blood and almost splitting him with sheer, unreasonable desire.

Her eyes also haunted him. Beautiful, and of the deepest blue he'd ever seen, unusually thick lashes and tiny flecks of gold made them even more remarkable.

He knew they'd stolen his soul.

Blowing out a hot breath, he tried to conjure the buxom nakedness of the last Norse wench he'd tumbled at Olaf Big Nose's encampment. But the image wouldn't come. He could only summon a blur of white limbs and flowing, flaxen hair. A flash of large, bouncing breasts and a face that was even more difficult to distinguish.

Mina blazed bright.

He saw her as clearly as if he still stood staring down at her. As if it were only moments ago when she'd moved so sinuously against him, hotly entwined and firing his dreams in ways no other woman had ever done.

She was a born siren.

She lay naked in his bed.

Darroc shoved a hand through his hair, frowning.

A man so long without a woman shouldn't be presented with such temptation.

A Highlander never.

Knowing himself lost, he began to pace. Stalking about, perhaps counting his steps, would keep him from giving in to the urge to return to the bedside. There were other reasons for staying away.

He couldn't bear to see the ugly gash just above her left knee.

Surely caused by the skerries or floating wreckage, the wound gaped deep and stretched up the inside of her thigh. And much as it had grieved him to discover the injury, the prospect of watching Mad Moraig's shaky fingers probe and stitch the torn flesh was even worse.

But there was no one else at Castle Bane capable of

doing the deed. His own hands would have made an even greater mess of it. Even so, his gut clenched and a taste like cold, soured ash flooded his mouth.

He cleared his throat. "Have a care with those stitches. I'd no' want—"

"Aieee!" Mad Moraig shrieked.

Darroc winced.

He didn't have to look to know she'd clapped her hands over her ears. He also knew that she'd be staring at something no one else saw, her eyes turned more inward than ever. And that they'd fill with a glistening brightness that had nothing to do with age.

He was a dolt!

His face heated and he whirled to make amends. "You misheard me," he lied, crossing the room to pry her hands from her head.

A task he'd done often enough over the years.

"Good on you, Moraig." He put all the admiration he could into his voice. "I meant have a care no' to rush. Lady Mina is sleeping soundly enough for you to take time to do your best work."

"Hech, hech! They do be fine stitches." Her face wreathed in a smile as she took the bait. "There'll be nary a mark to show where I've sewn her up."

"For sure, she'll be grateful." Darroc dreaded the moment when the lass saw the crooked stitching. The bunched and gathered flesh that a more able leech master would have fitted together as carefully as possible before setting his needle to the wound.

Mad Moraig beamed. "Aye, she'll be pleased."

Darroc doubted it.

He did rest a hand on the old woman's shoulder. He

could feel her bones, fragile as a bird's. Her age-spotted hands were stitching furiously again. And as far as he could tell, she was nearly finished.

Knowing what an unsightly scar the jabbing needle would leave had him clenching his jaw so hard he wondered it didn't break. At least Mad Moraig's herb-washings and sphagnum moss dressings would keep the flesh from fevering. Still, sweat began to bead his brow and stinging droplets rolled into his eyes, making him blink.

It was then that Mina moaned.

Only she hadn't stirred.

Her beautiful body looked as cold and still as chiseled marble. The pale oval of her face remained white as death. Her lips were unmoving. Or so he thought until the sound came again. Low-pitched, sleep-blurred, and utterly feminine, it was a sound that couldn't be ignored.

It definitely wasn't Mad Moraig.

Indeed, she'd finished her task and had already tottered away from the bed. Ever particular, she stood at a nearby table and busied herself with carefully returning her bone needle and horsehair thread to their proper places inside her wicker healing basket.

"She's waking!" Darroc grabbed her arm, relief sluicing him.

"Ahhh, so she is!" Mad Moraig wrinkled her brow and peered at her.

She trilled with delight.

Arabella heard the skirling and knew true terror.

She'd been floating in a void of cushioning blackness. Soft, warm, and silent, the stillness soothed her. Now she felt again the icy embrace of the sea. The comforting darkness was receding, letting her hear men's screams and the frightening howls of the wind, the roar of tumbling, crashing waves.

Worst of all they'd found her.

The sea raiders.

They'd almost seized her once before. She remembered the broad width of a man's shoulders looming above her, then his arms reaching for her, sweeping her up against his iron hard chest. At first she'd thought he might be the warrior hero she'd imagined in Dunakin's tower window.

His dark outline certainly reminded her of him.

When he'd touched her, she'd even felt a faint fluttering deep in her belly and her heart skittered. It was a wild and giddy sensation, much as her sister Gelis insisted happened when a woman first met the man she was destined to love.

But then a horrible, oddly furred sea serpent—all fangs and glowing red eyes—had risen behind Mina and she'd known the end was near.

If she'd had any doubt, the outlaw Norseman she'd mistaken for the Dunakin warrior swiftly abandoned her to a second Viking. A denizen straight from the edge of hell, that raider stared at her with fierce blue eyes, hot as Nordic ice and equally terrifying. Most alarming of all, he'd reached for her with arms covered in flames.

Then she'd known no more until they attacked her.

Though they appeared to have stopped, she could still feel them stabbing her. Again and again, they'd wielded fiery hot blades against her tender flesh. And she'd been helpless against their assault. Her protests came to nothing more than a painful welling in her throat. When she tried to move, to flee their evil, her entire body felt so leaden that she couldn't even lift her smallest finger.

She only wanted to sleep.

But the blessed darkness was slipping away and her foes were celebrating her wakening. No doubt such fiends took more pleasure skewering a lucid victim.

They just hadn't reckoned with her being a Mac-Kenzie.

Proud of her blood—and taking strength from it—she cracked her eyes ever so slightly.

To her surprise, she wasn't on the deck of the black-painted Norse dragon-ship. She didn't even seem to be at sea. Far from it, she appeared to be in the four-postered bed of a modest tower room. A room too dark to see clearly, for only one window had its shutters opened and the day outside looked gloomy. But she could make out the shapes of a strongbox and a table with two matching chairs.

A tapestry—its colors faded and the edges worn—graced the opposite wall, and there were several iron-bracketed torches though none were lit. The rest of the chamber swam in deep, silent shadow. Someone had pulled a linen coverlet over her, though she couldn't imagine why they'd show her such consideration.

Nowhere did she see any Vikings.

She tried to push up on her elbows, but she couldn't muster the strength. The effort also sent sharp jolts of pain knifing through her shoulder. Her leg hurt even worse, throbbing maddeningly. But she did manage to summon her courage. If her tormentors meant to start attacking her again, they were in for a surprise.

MacKenzies didn't cringe in fear.

So she took a deep breath and opened her eyes fully.

"I know you're here!" She ignored the hoarseness of her voice and put all her outrage in the words. "Do what you will. I won't cower before Vikings so spineless they dress their ships black!"

"Vikings?" A bent old woman with a whirr of iron-gray hair appeared from the shadows. "Here be no Vikings. We—"

"We mean you no harm, lady." A man spoke from the gloom behind the woman. His voice was deep, rich, and wonderfully soothing.

Her pulse leapt and some of the distress in her heart began to ease.

"Moraig, go belowstairs and make our guest one of your wine caudles. And"—the man came forward to put a hand on the crone's shoulder—"be sure to add extra egg yolks. The lady needs the strength."

The old woman sniffed. " 'Tis sleep she needs, just!"

But she hitched up her skirts and went dutifully to the door. Arabella scarcely noticed. She kept her attention on the man. The room's dimness shadowed his face, but not so much that her breath didn't catch just looking at him.

Her heart slammed against her ribs.

His presence surrounded her, something about him sending deliciously hot shivers rippling through her. She had vague recollections of his arms encircling her, carrying her. The memory made her breath catch. If she were standing, she was sure her knees would turn to water.

As it was, she could only stare.

Tall and powerfully built, he looked dark as she was, if not more so. His long, silky black hair gleamed with the same midnight sheen, but there the similarity ended. While she prided herself on her femininity, he was surely the most manly man she'd ever seen.

He was certainly the most beautiful.

In a bold, savage kind of way.

Cold wind pouring in through the window tossed glossy strands of his hair about his face, but rather than lift a hand to push them aside, he appeared amused. As if he enjoyed the wind and courted its wildness. A wide gold armband clamped around the bulging muscles of his right upper arm and a large Celtic brooch winked at his shoulder, the bright glint of its red center stone paling by comparison when he stepped closer and flashed a smile.

Arabella gulped.

She was lost in the dazzle of him.

"So-o-o!" He tossed back his plaid and flourished a bow. "I am MacConacher. Darroc MacConacher, chief to my people and keeper of Castle Bane. I welcome you to my home, Lady Mina. Be assured you are safe—"

"Mina!" Arabella's heart stopped. "I am not Mina. She's Captain Arn—" She broke off, horror washing through her. Again she heard the screams, the bells, and the awful cracking of wood. Blinking back tears, she dashed a hand across her cheek and tried again.

"I am Arabella of Kintail," she managed, pushing the words past the dryness in her throat. "Mina is my dog." She lifted her chin, hoping Arnkel Arneborg wouldn't mind the lie. "Please tell me she—"

A frantic yipping erupted and Mina burst out of the shadows. She streaked across the rushes, tiny legs pumping as she flew at the bed and then sailed into Arabella's arms.

"Mina—my sweet!" Arabella seized her, crushing the dog's wriggling little body to her breast, half-crying and half-laughing as Mina squirmed and wagged and used her quick pink tongue to smother her face with kisses.

Until the MacConacher plucked Mina from her hands and settled her onto the covers beside her. "She might hurt you, my lady." His deep voice had lost some of its warmth, but he rested a large, calming hand on Mina's wiggling body, quieting her. "You've been injured and must lie still."

Arabella peered up at him, something about his name—and him—dancing about the fringes of her mind. She tried to think, to remember, but the remaining drifts of darkness made it so hard to concentrate.

She frowned, trying anyway.

Her efforts only made her head pound. A memory was there, she was sure. But it was distant and blurred by years. Even so, she felt a strange prickling on her nape and a chill slid through her. She inhaled a shaky breath, wishing she knew what was gnawing at her. Sadly, whatever caused the ill-ease remained hidden deep inside her, inaccessible.

The MacConacher was watching her closely. Almost as if he, too, had questions on the edge of his mind.

"Your name..." Arabella peered at him. "Can it be I know you? There's something—"

"There is nothing." He seemed to stiffen. "I assure you we've never met."

The words spoken, he stepped back so that he was limned by the cold gray light of the window. Arabella's eyes widened, recognition slamming into her. Looming above her and with his broad shoulders silhouetted so clearly, there could be no doubt that he was the man who'd rescued her.

When a massive shaggy-coated *monster* appeared at his side and leaned heavily into him, she was sure. The ferocious-looking beast could only be the creature she'd seen with Mina and mistaken for a furred sea serpent.

The only one missing was the man with arms of flame.

Arabella swallowed.

She was still so weary and it was difficult to keep her eyes open.

"You were there—in the water. I remember now." She paused, the thickness in her voice slurring her words. "Another man was with you. He had fiery-red hair and"— she drew a breath before rushing on, embarrassed—"I thought his arms were made of flame."

A muscle jerked in the MacConacher's jaw. "You mean Conall, my cousin. His arms are burned. The scars may have looked like flames in the light of the rising sun."

He studied her a moment, his eyes narrowing as if he expected some reaction other than the pity that swept her on hearing his words.

Arabella felt herself flush.

She now suspected her travails at sea were responsible for the chills that had just swept her. Worse, she'd insulted her rescuer's kinsman.

Uncomfortable, she curled one hand into the linen coverlet and slid the other around Mina. The little dog nudged her with a cold wet nose. Arabella glanced at her, grateful. She needed Mina's warmth.

The MacConacher continued to look at her, his expression unreadable. "Conall held you, my lady. He cradled you in his arms as I rowed us to shore."

"There aren't words to thank you." Arabella knew he didn't believe her. "I am indebted to you both. Especially"—she looked down at Mina, snuggled so tightly against her—"for rescuing Mina."

"Frang is responsible." The words were clipped. But

when he glanced at the dog, his face softened. "He knew you were there before Conall and I saw you."

As if in agreement, the huge dog's tongue lolled out and he wagged his tail.

"Then Mina and I will consider him our champion." Mina tilted her head and laid a paw against Arabella's arm as if she agreed. Arabella looked on as the MacConacher dropped a hand to rub his own dog's ears.

"He is a hero." Arabella saw the MacConacher's face harden again.

"All MacConachers honor life, my lady." He gave her another strange, almost piercing look. "There isn't a one of us who would stand idle when a ship founders in our waters. We—"

"The *Merry Dancer* didn't founder." Arabella shuddered just remembering. "There was a storm, yes, but the shipmaster swore the cog could ride it out. I believed him. What happened was"—she glanced aside, tears burning her eyes again. "We were attacked. A black-painted dragon-ship sank us."

"The Vikings you mentioned?" Darroc stared at her, horror freezing his blood.

He'd so hoped he'd misheard.

Or that she'd dreamt such a nightmare.

But she was nodding and the terror in her eyes told him she spoke true. "They came out of the mist, shooting straight at us with a long steel-headed ramming lance projecting from the prow. They pierced the cog and—"

"You fell overboard?" Darroc could hardly speak past the bile in his throat.

"No." She pressed trembling fingers to her lips. "The

shipmaster and his men lowered the spare boat, but when they dropped me over the side the men in it didn't catch me. I don't remember much after that."

Darroc rubbed the back of his neck. "You were on a raft of cargo barrels when we found you."

"I don't know how I got there." She dashed away the tears dampening her cheeks. "The seas were high. Perhaps I was washed onto it?"

Darroc considered.

He didn't like any of this.

Least of all her name.

"You say the dragon-ship was painted black?" He posed the question that troubled him almost as much.

Again she nodded and Darroc's heart sank.

The certainty on her face gave substance to a myth most folk in these remote isles told around the fireside to frighten children into behaving.

If they weren't good, the Black Vikings would get them.

Darroc glanced aside, his gaze going to the window arch. The sky was even darker now and the first spatters of rain were just beginning to pelt the tower. From below, the crashing of the waves was louder, too, the familiar sound filling the little room.

When he looked back at Lady Arabella, he saw the day's bleakness all over her. "My regrets, lady"—he hated having to push her, even if she was a MacKenzie—"but can you tell me of them? The Black Vikings?"

"I..." She trailed off, shuddering. Then she pulled the little dog—Mina—onto her chest and dug her fingers in the dog's long, silky fur. "I only caught a glance at them, but it was enough. Everything about them was black, the hull and shields, the sail, and even the sweeps."

She looked up from stroking the dog, her eyes glistening. "I'm not certain, but I think even the men were clad in black jerkins."

Darroc released a grim breath. "You cannot have been mistaken? There were thick drifts of fog last night. Perhaps you—"

"I know what I saw." Her chin set with a stubbornness that would have amused him under different circumstances. "Would that I were mistaken! But"—She held his gaze, her expression determined. "I must ask...I would know if..."

Her voice cracked and her bravura faded. "If anyone else...if there were—"

"My sorrow, lady." Darroc spared her the question. "You were the only living soul we found."

She bit her lip and glanced aside, her entire body shaking. Darroc clenched his fists. He didn't want to feel sympathy for a MacKenzie. But when she finally looked back at him something had changed. Her eyes still glittered and her cheeks remained damp, but her gaze was steady and she no longer trembled. He could almost see the steel flowing in her veins.

"You said I was injured." She didn't make it a question. "It must be my leg, for it pains me the greatest."

Darroc nodded, unable to lie.

But he wished she hadn't mentioned it. He'd hoped for her to recover before she saw Mad Moraig's handiwork.

And now...

He cleared his throat. "There was a gash in your left leg. It was bad and needed immediate care. Old Moraig, our clan hen wife, cleaned and stitched it for you. She'll make certain the wound doesn't fever and heals well. Until then, I advise you no' to look—"

But it was too late.

She'd already lifted the coverlet's edge to peek beneath.

Darroc braced himself for her screams, but she only stared down at bunched and sewn flesh. Her eyes did widen and the blood drained from her face, but she didn't dissolve into panic.

"Please thank Moraig for her kindness." She looked up from the clumsy stitching. Her pallor was the only indication that the sight unsettled her. "If you swear not to tell her, I would be grateful for a small knife, a needle, and stitching-thread. I can undo her work and re-sew the wound myself."

"Lady, I do not believe that is wise." Darroc stared at her, his own insides quivering at her proposal.

Everyone knew her race had hearts of stone and cold iron for backbones, but she *was* a lass. Even if being in the same room with her cost him dearly, he wouldn't have it on his conscience to allow such foolery.

He shook his head. "You do not know what you're saying. The wound is—"

"I have tended more grievous injuries." She set Mina aside and clasped her hands, linking her fingers with purpose. "Now it would seem I must see to my own."

Darroc frowned.

She angled her head, unbending.

"Is that Moraig's healing basket?" Her gaze went to the table where the hen wife had left her leeching goods.

Darroc clamped his jaw.

"I will not shame the woman." She looked back at him,

misunderstanding his silence. "She will think the work is her own."

"I am thinking of you, my lady." Darroc's heart galloped at the notion of her cutting into her own flesh.

The image tied his guts in a knot.

"Then please bring me the stitching tools." Her voice held an edge of iron.

"As you wish." He bit out the words.

Then he went to do her bidding, silently vowing to snatch the blade from her if she so much as flinched. But when he returned to the bed and handed her the basket, he saw by the hard set of her face that she could likely slice off her entire leg and sew it back on without cringing.

He had a sinking feeling as to why.

"You are a bold-hearted woman, Lady Arabella." He spoke before he could stop himself, needing to know. "There are many MacKenzies in Kintail. Which family of that race do you call your own?"

"My family is Kintail." She looked up from the basket, the pride on her face as damning as her words. "I am the eldest daughter of Duncan MacKenzie. He is the Black Stag of Kintail, chief of our clan."

Darroc nodded, his worst dread confirmed.

Something inside him clenched and twisted until he was sure he couldn't draw another breath.

His hated enemy's daughter returned her attention to Mad Moraig's healing basket, oblivious. "Do you mind leaving me now?" The words were sweet, even calm. "I would be alone when I tend myself."

He still couldn't speak.

She glanced up at him, waiting.

"I will leave you, aye." He found his voice at last, the

words emerging in a strange, hollow tone he didn't recognize as his own.

He crossed the room, glad to be gone from her. A thousand screaming demons buzzed in his head and he only wanted to get away.

He needed air.

A hefty swig of mind-numbing *uisge beatha*.

But he paused at the door to glance back at her. "I will look in on you later," he said, honor demanding the courtesy. "I'll keep Moraig occupied the while."

To his horror, she smiled. "You are kind, my lord. I thank you."

He almost choked.

She simply nodded, dismissing him.

And looking as serene as if she were about to sit down to a meal of honeyed cakes and mead and not preparing herself to begin her grisly task.

Chills spiking through him, he escaped onto the landing and closed the door. Not that such a flimsy barrier made a difference. He could still feel her all around him, see her sapphire eyes watching him so innocently, so totally unaware of the storm she'd unleashed.

He shoved a hand through his hair, striving to gather his wits.

The saints knew he needed them.

But as he hurried down the tower stairs, he knew things were going to go badly for him. Arabella MacKenzie had stolen more than his ability to think clearly.

She'd dug her fine Kintail-born talons into him and he wasn't sure how to break free.

He just knew he had to.

Anything else was unthinkable.

Chapter Six

❖

Days later, across the glittering expanse of the Hebridean Sea, Linnet stood before the window of her herbarium, breathing deeply. She loved the little stone workshop set against her herb garden's seaward wall. Ever sensitive to still and gentle places, she'd claimed the garden and its workshop as her own almost immediately upon arriving at Eilean Creag as a young bride so many years ago.

Thick-walled, low-ceilinged, and brimming with treasures for those with a hand for herbs and healing, the dimly lit herbarium soon became her sanctuary.

It was here that she spent her sweetest hours.

She found peace inside the herbarium, beneath the smoke-blackened rafters, each beam crowded with bundles of dried herbs and flowers.

Someone—Duncan himself, she suspected—made certain that a small brazier always crackled in a corner, the brazier's few lumps of burning peat taking off the worst of a day's chill. Equally pleasing, the single, deep-set window where she now stood let in just the right amount of tangy sea air to keep her alert when she worked on her medicinal tinctures, poultices, and salves.

Though, in truth, she didn't always come here to work.

Sometimes she just appreciated the pungent, homey smells. The comforting blend of dried herbs, peat smoke, the sea, and—she couldn't deny—the earthy richness of the hard-packed dirt floor.

Other times she simply let the quiet surround her. The well-filled shelves and work tables were her friends. Each flagon, jar, or earthenware pot held a memory. As did her carefully tended pestles, mortars, and wooden mixing bowls. They all told stories that warmed her heart. Even the precious set of metal scales, dented and grimed when she'd first discovered it in a corner cupboard. Now the scale set gleamed bright and never bore a speck of dust.

Then there were times this place embraced her, softly.

Today was one of those days.

So she flattened her hands against the smooth surface of her work table, enjoying the connection to all the MacKenzie women before her who might have stood in this very spot.

They, too, would have used their skill and knowledge to the good of the clan. Women like her who toiled daily, making their own cures, creams, and powders. Perhaps they also used their time here to savor the silence and solitude.

Linnet hoped it was so.

"*Beannachd leat.*" She spoke the words with a smile, as she always did. "Blessings be with you."

She never failed to offer the greeting to those long-ago kinswomen. She was certain they heard and it was important that they knew she wished them well.

Unfortunately—for she was a bit tired this day—it was also important that she do some work.

But not before she treated herself to a glimpse out the window. For once, no soft mists floated across the loch, hiding the great hills and turning the water a deep, slate-colored gray.

The sky was high and blue, without a trace of cloud. And although a freshening wind stirred up little white-caps, the sun shone brilliantly. The whole glory of Kintail stretched before her, ancient and magnificent.

Her breath caught, the beauty piercing her.

For a beat, she felt quite spoiled and indulged, so blessed to call this place her home.

"Ah, well..."—she spoke to the view, not feeling a bit ridiculous doing so—"I see I shouldn't have praised you so lavishly."

On the far side of Loch Duich, where the hills rose so stark and rugged, a dark bank of heavy rain clouds gathered and swirling mist already wreathed the highest peaks. Linnet frowned, at first thinking she'd imagined the swift change in weather.

The day had been so cold and sunny.

But as she stared, long swells began rolling across the loch, chased by rainy squalls until they crashed against the rocky base of the cliffs. Even at a distance, she could see how each new wave sent up spumes of glistening white spray.

She almost laughed.

She should have known the sun-bathed afternoon wouldn't last.

Not that she really cared.

She loved Kintail in all weathers. As did every soul

she knew who dwelled here. A fierce love of land was a Highland tradition, unspoiled. And she was no different from any other of her race.

Though at times, she'd swear she loved these hills even more.

So with her heart full, she reached for an earthenware bowl and tipped its contents—freshly harvested sphagnum moss—onto her work table.

Outside the window, the branches of her crabapple tree rattled in the rising wind. Already the bright sky she'd so admired was darkening and she could hear the higher waves smacking against the garden's seaward wall, just behind the herbarium.

Well used to such sudden Highland storms, she puffed a strand of hair off her face and began sorting her bog mosses. First she divided the moist, springy clumps by color. This batch—collected by one of her husband's youngest squires—proved particularly varied, including fine mosses of bright green, deep brown, and rich blood-red.

She pressed a finger into a plump bit of the blood-red moss, pleased by its bounce and rich color.

Long experience told her that the red sphagnum, when boiled and steeped in water, made a wonderful soak for weary feet. Her lips twitched on the thought. As a certain ill-humored someone had been prowling the battlements of late, oftentimes even missing his dinner, she considered the possibility that a surprise late-night foot bath might improve his mood. So she set these mosses aside and concentrated first on the green and brown ones.

These more common varieties would make excellent wound dressings once she'd picked away all the embedded bits of dirt, leaves, and twigs. A task she always saw to herself, not trusting anyone else to clean the precious medicinal moss as thoroughly as she did.

Even so, she'd let the squire carry the prepared mosses up to the workshop's drying loft. Much as she tried to ignore the discomfort, her knees weren't the best in recent years. She knew better than to scramble up a ladder in the darkest corner of the herbarium.

And it *was* dark.

A glance out the window proved it.

Shimmering curtains of rain now obscured the view. Her beloved hills were gone, the awe-inspiring peaks and corries hidden by gloom. Even the air had chilled, turning so icy she wouldn't have been surprised to see her breath emerge as white puffs.

"Ah, well..." She tightened her shawl around her shoulders and picked up another wet clump of red sphagnum, adding it to her pile.

She also fought back a smile.

The rushing wind and rain would drive Duncan down from the battlements. Unlike her—she did enjoy a good storm—her formidable husband preferred the comfort of his hearthside in such wild weathers.

Knowing he'd deny any such hint of softness, her smile deepened and she reached for the one remaining bit of red moss. But before her fingers could grasp it, the color changed. No longer the deep blood-crimson of wine, the sphagnum shone with an emerald brilliance she was certain hadn't been in the squire's gathered assortment.

The green peat mosses spread across her work table were a lighter, less rich shade.

At least, they had been.

Now each clump of sphagnum winked back at her,

dark green and unfamiliar. Her little pile of red sphagnum had vanished completely.

Linnet blinked. She pressed a hand to her breast as the work table also disappeared and a smaller table loomed in its place.

This table, too, held peat mosses.

But these were dried and filled a wicker creel.

Linnet's heart began a fast, frantic hammering. Somewhere—too close to her ears to be outside—the shrieking wind and hissing rain became a high-pitched, deafening buzz.

It was a sound she knew well.

Even as she recognized the familiar herald of her visions, Arabella's face and shoulders appeared, hovering above the wicker creel. More beautiful than Linnet had ever seen her, Arabella's remarkable eyes glistened and her lips were curved in the sweetest smile.

But a strange luminosity surrounded her and her skin was whiter than milk.

Deathly white.

Linnet's chest squeezed as whirling gray mist swept in through the window to whip around and disperse the image. The fast-spinning mist quickly blotted everything but the little oaken table set with a single wax candle and the basket of dried moss.

Wound dressing moss.

The basket began to glow, the innocent clumps of healing sphagnum getting brighter and brighter until their meaning burst through the darkness swirling around her.

Arabella was in danger.

Injured or . . . worse.

"No-o-o!" Linnet's legs buckled and she sagged to her

knees, some always coherent part of her making her grab
for the edge of the work table.

She clung tight, grateful the sturdy table was there
even though she couldn't see it. The buzzing in her ears
reached a fever pitch and she gripped the table harder. But
it wasn't her own work table that she held so fiercely.

It was the little oaken table.

And, she could see now, the hands clutching its edge
weren't her own.

They were age-spotted and knotty, the fingers thin and
withered as claws.

Linnet's breath froze.

Chills sped up and down her spine. She began to
tremble and the fine hairs on her nape lifted. Though she
knew she was kneeling, she could no longer feel the cold,
earthen floor beneath her.

Nothing around her existed.

The ancient hands intensified in clarity.

She could see them clearly. The mottled, papery skin
shone so brightly there could be no question that the hands
were of great significance.

Linnet shook her head, trying to break the *taibh*—the
frightful vision she didn't want to see—but even as she
squeezed shut her eyes, rebelling, a deeper part of her soul
knew she couldn't banish the image.

As a *taibhsear* blessed—or cursed—with second sight,
trying to deny what her gift wanted her to see could spell
terrible disaster.

But when the hands moved to dip clawlike fingers into
the glowing basket of wound dressing moss, pure dread
flooded Linnet's heart. The swirling darkness lightened
a bit, giving her a look at the owner of the hands. It was a

bent-legged old woman, garbed in black and with a whirr of iron-gray hair.

Devorgilla.

Relief shot through Linnet until the crone turned and hobbled right past her to vanish into the swirling mist.

The old woman wasn't Devorgilla.

She was a stranger. But her watery blue eyes had been kind. And her ancient hands, though shaky, had clutched great masses of dried sphagnum. Wound dressing she wouldn't have needed if Arabella were...

Linnet couldn't finish the thought.

The buzzing in her ears was growing even louder, the whirling mist darker. The little oaken table was gone now, though the single candle remained, its golden flame flickering and dancing.

Linnet bit her lip, tasting blood.

Something sharp and hard dug into her knee—perhaps a pebble she'd fished out of her peat mosses—and she gasped, though she couldn't hear her own cry.

She did hear the crackle and hiss of the candle flame.

Almost a roar now, the noise rose above the horrible buzzing, getting louder and louder as the golden flames grew and spread into a large and glowing heart.

Linnet's own heart stopped and then slammed against her ribs.

Arabella was inside the golden heart.

Whole, beaming, and naked save for a swath of unknown plaid.

Linnet stared.

Arabella was so close she could almost touch her. And she looked so blissfully happy.

So in love.

At once, the terrible buzzing stopped, replaced by the loud and joyous ringing of bells. The sound filled Linnet's ears and welled inside her. Then the pealing rose to a crescendo when a tall, powerfully built man stepped into the flaming heart. He took Arabella in his arms, pulling her close with such fierce protectiveness that Linnet's own tears kept her from seeing the man's face.

Then the bell ringing stopped and the image vanished as if it'd never been. The dark mists glittered brightly and then spiraled away, leaving Linnet slumped against her work table.

She took several long, deep breaths and lifted a hand to knuckle her eyes.

Slowly her world came back into focus.

Then from somewhere behind her she heard a loud bang and a crash.

"Saints, Maria, and Joseph!" The roared curse could only be Duncan.

Linnet tightened her grip on the table—she was still too weak to stand—and twisted around, not surprised to see him towering just inside the threshold.

There was only Duncan.

Her heart's mate and father to her girls.

Fists clenched at his sides, he stared at her, horror all over him. His face was grim, blacker even than the storm that was no more.

Behind him, the workshop door swung on its hinges, testimony to his furious entrance. A three-legged stool lay toppled on its side, the large earthenware pot it'd held smashed in jagged, irreparable shards.

Linnet sighed.

She'd planned to steep the red sphagnum in that pot.

"By the Rood!" Duncan kicked aside the stool and strode across the pot shards toward her. "You've been seized by your *taibhsearachd* again! And"—his brows snapped together—"you've been crying! Are you unwell?"

"I am fine. But—" Linnet's voice cracked. Her throat was still too thick for words.

Before she could swallow and try again, Duncan was upon her.

"What did you see?" He pulled her to her feet, dragging her against his iron-hard chest. His heart thundered so loudly she could hear every hammering beat.

He drew back to look at her, his midnight blue eyes almost black with worry. "Was it Arabella?"

The dread in his voice cut to her soul.

"Yes." Linnet couldn't lie. "She's been...she is—"

"What?" The blood drained from Duncan's face. "What has happened to her?"

"She is well...now. But—"

"*Now*?" Duncan turned even whiter. "What do you mean *now*?"

Linnet leaned into him, not knowing where to begin.

Searching for the right words, she stared past his shoulder out the window. The world was still now, windless and quiet. Mist still clung to the hills, but the sky was once again a dazzling, cloudless blue and the low evening sun turned the loch's smooth, gleaming waters to a mirror of pure molten gold.

Once again she saw the flaming golden heart.

She drew a deep breath, encouraged.

It was now or never.

Duncan had stepped back and was glaring at her, a muscle twitching beneath his left eye.

The MacKenzie eye tic.

A terrible sign if ever there was one.

Linnet smoothed a hand down the front of her gown, seeking calm.

Then she lifted her chin.

"Our daughter has been injured." She spoke quickly, needing to finish before Duncan started yelling too loud to hear. "I do not know how or what happened, but I did see that she's well tended. There's an old woman with her. And a man—"

"*A man?*" Duncan's bellow shook the herb bundles hanging from the rafters.

"A man!" He roared again, his face turning scarlet.

The tic beneath his eye went wild.

Linnet stepped toward him, one hand extended. But he leapt backward, waving his arms. Doing her best not to frown, Linnet kept on, wanting to soothe him.

"He's a good man." The surety of it filled her, giving her confidence. "He is—"

"He's a dead man if he touches her!" Duncan grabbed his sword hilt, whipping out the blade with an ear-splitting screech. "As for Captain Arneborg and the fools I sent along to protect her"—he waved his sword in the air, cutting down three bunches of dried mint—"I'll have their heads on spits!"

"My love." Linnet started forward again, heedless of his weaving steel. "It isn't as you think. Let me think on what I saw before you rile yourself."

"*Rile myself?*" His eyes rounded. "I will do more than that! Wait until I rally my men. We'll sail on the morrow, at first light!"

He jammed his sword back in its sheath, his face livid.

"I'll find our girl if I must scour every living rock in the Hebrides!"

"Duncan, please." Linnet pleaded. "I'm sure she is well. If her injury—"

"I'll kill the bastard who hurt her!" He grabbed his sword hilt again. "Did you see his face? His name?"

"Nae." Linnet shook her head, wishing she had.

But not for Duncan's reasons.

She twisted her hands in her skirts, his terror breaking her heart. "My dearest . . . ." She tried so hard to reach him. "The man I saw had nothing to do with Arabella's injury. I'd know if that were so. But I do think he—"

She broke off when he spun around and shot through the door, leaving her to stare after him as he tore through her garden and then pounded across the bailey. Not looking back, he ran for the keep and, she knew, the unsuspecting men who'd be gathering in the great hall for the evening meal.

It would be a night like no other.

Linnet sighed.

Determined to do what she could, she hitched up her skirts and hastened after her husband. Already, she could hear his shouts and rants echoing from the keep.

He was in a dreadful state.

So she quickened her pace, her feet flying across the cobbles. If the gods were kind, she'd reach him before he made a fool of himself.

And—she hoped—before he cost Arabella the love of a lifetime.

"Father's gone mad!"

Lady Gelis, Linnet's youngest daughter, burst from the

shadows of the hall's entry arch just as Linnet reached for the door's heavy iron latch. Home to celebrate her pregnancy before travel became too difficult, her cheeks were flushed and her bright red-gold braids askew. In truth, she was radiant, more beautiful than ever before. But she also looked agitated, rushing forward to grab Linnet's arm, preventing her from opening the door.

She tightened her grip on Linnet, panting. "If I didn't know him, I'd be trembling in fear. I swear he has fire coming out his eyes. He's raving about Arabella and some man—"

"I know he is, dear." Linnet softened her voice. Gelis shouldn't be distressing herself. "I was visited by a *taibh* a short while ago. Arabella has been injured, yes. I believe something happened on the merchant cog. But she's in caring hands. I am sure of it and I told your father as much. Sadly, he only heard—"

"Nae." Gelis flicked at her skirts. "It's more. Much more! He says Arabella is being held by a band of scale-backed hell-fiends. He means to catch the man responsible and"—she pressed a hand to her middle, already thickening with child—"have him ... err, ah ... unmanned."

"Scale-backed hell-fiends?" Linnet's eyes rounded. "Unmanned?"

Gelis's head bobbed. "That was just the beginning of his rant."

Linnet frowned.

Duncan had taken it worse than she'd thought.

"We must calm him. I told him nothing that should have upset him so."

"It wasn't what you told him."

"Then what was it?"

"A courier rode in while you were in the herbarium."
Gelis glanced over her shoulder as if she expected to see
the man there, mud-splattered and tense. "He came from
Doon, not stopping until he reached us. The MacLeans
sent him. Arabella's ship went down at sea. Word is she's
safe, as you saw, but"—she spoke fast in her agitation—
"everyone else was lost."

"Dear saints…" Linnet closed her eyes. The steps
seemed to dip beneath her feet. She'd hoped it hadn't been
so bad.

"Father is vowing vengeance." Gelis rushed on, her
voice blending with the angry cries from within the hall.
Grumbles and shouting filled the stone archway and
echoed across the bailey. "He's leapt up on one of the
trestle tables and is waving his sword over his head, yelling for blood. I've never seen him so—"

"Ah, but I have, my dear." Linnet sighed, remembering the time. It was many years ago, when she was still a
young bride. Kinsmen who worked outlying MacKenzie
lands had been attacked and slaughtered. Innocent farm-
ers who'd had only scythes, rakes, and shovels to wield in
their defense. Duncan's wrath had been terrible. His retri-
bution was worse, swift and merciless.

Now it wasn't cottars he meant to avenge.

It was his daughter.

This time his fury would sear the heavens.

And—Linnet was certain—it would scald a man unde-
serving. Perhaps even an entire clan if the roars from the
hall were any indication.

Feeling ill, she pulled free of Gelis's grip, determined
not to let that happen. "He wouldn't heed me last time,"
she said, reaching again for the door latch. "Now, when

we both march in there, he'll have no choice but to see reason. Arabella must be our only concern. We need to sail to Doon and see to her comfort. Not wave steel against longtime friends and allies. The MacLeans—"

"She isn't with the MacLeans." Gelis almost wailed the words. "They only sent the messenger when they learned of the cog sinking. Father is riled because Arabella was picked up at sea by the MacConachers. It is there, on their isle, where she's—"

"*The MacConachers*?" Linnet's blood chilled.

Now she understood.

Gelis was bobbing her head again, the terror in her eyes only making Linnet's heart clench tighter. "I heard some of the garrison men saying they will use her and pass her around until she—"

"They will not." Linnet wished she believed it.

Almost, she could.

The old woman she'd seen tending Arabella had been kindly. And the braw warrior who'd gathered Arabella into his arms, cradling and protecting her, the golden heart that had blazed so brilliantly around them...

Such were portents of truest, brightest love.

Even now, Linnet's pulse quickened just remembering the devotion in the man's eyes. She suspected he'd cut down anyone who so much as laid a finger against Arabella. Linnet bit her lip, tasting blood. Never had her gift told her wrong, a truth that welled in her now, demanding acceptance.

But a MacConacher...

She shuddered and pulled her shawl more closely about her shoulders. "All Highlanders have honor. If Arabella is in MacConacher keeping, we must trust in theirs."

"But you do not believe in it."

"I am *hoping* for it." Linnet hooked her arm through her daughter's and threw open the hall door. "That is all we can do," she owned, pulling Gelis with her into the crowded, smoke-hazed hall. "Now come, we must speak with your father."

"*Cuidich 'N' Righ!* Save the king!" The clan war cry greeted them, every man shouting with fullest lung power so that their roars filled the cavernous space.

Linnet froze, transported back in time.

As then, Duncan stood on a table in the center of the hall, legs arrogantly wide and holding his great, two-handed sword high above his head. Only now her beloved warrior looked even more fierce, more magnificent, and without doubt more deadly. His eyes did spark flames and the naked steel of his blade gleamed blood-red in the torchlight.

He'd donned his old black mail hauberk—not worn for years, but still polished bright—and just as so many years before, his proud mane of raven hair was tangled and wild, seeming to whip about his shoulders as if he stood in the face of the devil's own wind.

It was as if all the years between now and then were no more.

Linnet began to tremble. Hot and cold chills raced through her. The threads of silver in Duncan's hair seemed to have vanished and he looked taller, broader, and more muscled than he had that morn when they'd risen. Even the lines that crinkled his eyes and bracketed his mouth were gone.

He looked young again.

And so like the Duncan she'd fallen in love with that she almost forgot to breathe.

"*Cuidich 'N' Righ*!" He thrust his brand higher in the air, his head thrown back as he roared the slogan. "*Arabella*!"

"Arabella!" His men shouted back, rage in their voices. Stomping feet or leaping onto benches, they shook their own swords in the air, following Duncan's lead. "Hail the Maid of Kintail!"

"Death to MacConachers!" Someone bellowed near Linnet and Gelis.

"Aye!" Another agreed. "Their heads on spikes!"

"See!" Gelis grabbed Linnet's elbow, shaking. "It isn't just Father. They've all turned blood-mad."

"Not for long." Linnet blinked, the horror in her daughter's voice bringing her back to the present. "Take heed," she urged, summoning all the courage of her years. Then she grabbed two large metal ewers off a table and started clanging them together.

"Hear me, men of Kintail!" She scrambled onto a bench, lifting her voice and banging the jugs until the hall fell silent.

"I am Lady of Kintail!" She looked around, letting her gaze challenge. "And I say MacKenzies and MacConachers have spilt enough of each others' blood. We have heard my daughter is safe. I have seen that it is so."

She waited for the men to comprehend and then tossed down the two dented ewers. "I say we sail for MacConacher's Isle, aye. But we must go in caution and without rattling swords until we've seen—"

"*We*, my lady?" The voice was deep, husky, and right behind her.

Duncan.

Two strong hands seized her waist and lifted her off

the bench and into the air. Effortlessly, he turned her to face him, his well-loved scent of sandalwood, musk, and a hint of wood smoke swirling around her as he swung her back down on the rushes.

Linnet tried not to notice, but her heart made a little, capitulating roll.

"We are no' going anywhere." He spoke with finality.

But the confident, up-tilted corner of his mouth made her stubborn.

"You"—the corner-tilt deepened—"will stay here as is fitting. I'll no' have you—"

"You'll have me at your side." Linnet lifted her chin, unbending. "If you do not take me, I shall hire someone who will. We shall dog your every move, sail after you in your wake."

She folded her arms, pleased by the shock on his face.

He glanced round. "Where is that blundering Sassunach? He put you up to this! I'll—"

"Sir Marmaduke is in his own keep just now—as well you know." Linnet smiled sweetly.

Her husband glared. "Then who—"

"No one." She flashed a look at Gelis, delighted to see approval on her daughter's face. "Arabella is not just *your* daughter. She is ours. And we shall make this journey together."

Duncan compressed his lips.

His men were equally silent.

Avoiding his eyes, they began sheathing swords and otherwise occupying themselves. Some shuffled their feet. Many took sudden interest in their fingernails, and a few brushed or tugged at their plaids.

"Spineless bairns!" Duncan glowered at them.

Linnet leaned forward and kissed his cheek. "*Cuidich
'N' Righ*!" she whispered, for his ears alone. "All will be
well, I promise you."

"Aye, I've no doubt." His eyes flashed as he patted his
sword hilt, his meaning clear.

Then the indomitable Black Stag of Kintail strode
from his hall, slamming the great iron-studded door
behind him.

Hours later, as a fulling moon dipped low in the night sky,
Darroc tossed and turned in his bed. Leastways, the bed
he'd claimed since Arabella of Kintail had been using his
own. Not that it mattered just now. Caught in the gray dark
between sleep and waking, he splayed his hands across
the borrowed bedcovers, feeling not the mussed linens
but the sweet curve of smooth, warm flesh.

Sleek, silky thighs and, he was sure, the tempting
rounds of a plump and well-formed bottom. Full lush
breasts, firm and wonderful, with—he could feel them—
hot, tight nipples that begged tasting.

A spill of cool, satiny hair brushed against him. Luxu-
rious tresses, loose and free-flowing in a sensual cascade
meant to bewitch him. A beguiling scent surrounded him,
rich, dark, and just a bit exotic.

Darroc's blood flamed.

Desire flashed through him, swift and demanding.

His breathing stopped.

He ran hard, need consuming him. It didn't matter that
he burned for the daughter of his worst enemy. He wanted
the lass and he wanted her now. A groan rose deep in
his throat, proving it, and he slid his hands up and down
the vixen's nakedness, seeking her slippery wet heat. He

opened his eyes, wanting to see her face as he claimed her, knowing the triumph would be sweet.

But instead of Lady Arabella the sleep-stealing siren, a sword-wielding, glowing-eyed she-demon glared at him from the shadows.

Naked save a narrow swath of MacKenzie tartan knotted low around her hips, she had the same silky smooth skin and glorious tresses of the object of his desire. But this Arabella of Kintail, with her talon nails and blood-red lips, was the stuff of a fearing dream.

She glided toward him, hatred glinting in her eyes as she came.

"You think you've waited long for vengeance, Mac-Conacher." The words hissed from lips that didn't move. "In truth"—she raised her sword, testing its edge with her thumb—"we have waited longer. Now you will learn what happens when MacKenzies are wronged."

She flew at him then, swinging the blade in a vicious arc, her feet not touching the floor.

Darroc's heart froze.

His protest lodged in his throat, choking him. He stared, waiting for the stinging bite of steel, but the sword—and the she-demon—vanished into thin air, leaving him alone in the room.

A room that was empty save its single, threadbare tapestry and two long-gutted wall torches.

"Saints!" Darroc's pulse thundered in his ears.

Shaken, he flung off the bedcovers and leapt to his feet. That would teach him to let Mungo hover around him before he sought his bed. The cantankerous old goat couldn't string two words together without harping about how much Darroc needed a bride.

If he knew who Arabella was, he'd be full of ways they could use her to bring down her hated clan.

Darroc blew out a quick, hot breath.

He wouldn't—couldn't—use a woman to serve vengeance.

He did stride across the room and throw open the shutters to glare out at the moon-silvered sea. Something he'd done repeatedly throughout the night, though he couldn't explain why he felt such a need.

Nothing but the moon and a few pale stars peered back at him. In the distance, the outline of his friend Olaf Big Nose's isle showed as a low, dark smudge against the horizon. And he could see that a strong swell was running. The jagged rocks rimming his bay gleamed blackly, their edges frothed white with foam.

From beneath the tower, he could hear the crash of good-sized rollers hitting the cliffs. The seals that had so unsettled him weeks ago were nowhere to be seen.

But someone strongly connected to them now slept in his bed.

Darroc frowned.

The thought galled him.

Furious, he glanced over his shoulder at the bed across the room. Borrowed or not, its comforts beckoned. He was so tired. But he remained where he was, his hands braced on the cold stone splay of the window, the chill air welcome.

A good night's rest wouldn't be his this night.

Indeed, it wouldn't surprise him if he never slept well again.

Chapter Seven

✦

"Black Vikings?"

Mungo nearly choked on the words. He did spew the ale he'd just tipped down his throat. "Pshaw, I say!" He tossed aside his empty cup and drew his sword. "I'd sooner believe this cold steel"—he brandished the blade with relish—"will turn into a wriggling, two-headed snake!"

Several kinsmen nodded agreement.

One snickered.

Only Conall took a slow sip of his own ale, his expression guarded.

"Mayhap a three-headed snake." Mungo rammed his sword back into its sheath. "If Black Vikings were more than myth, we'd have seen them by now. I say they're naught but a bunch o' belly wind. Isles chieftains have more pride than is good for them. I'm for thinking some find it easier to blame disaster on rogue Norsemen than admit their own galley men ran a ship onto the rocks!"

"So say we all!" Geordie Dhu slapped his thigh.

Named for the dark mane that had once crowned his now shiny pate, he flashed a gap-toothed smile.

More head bobbing, a hoot, and a bit of hearty foot stomping showed that most of the clan's esteemed elders were of a like mind.

Conall held his silence and stooped to retrieve Mungo's discarded ale cup. He placed it on a table discreetly. In a household where few tread nimbly, such carelessness could be hazardous.

If Conall hadn't retrieved the cup, Darroc would have done so himself.

As it was, he continued to ignore the bickering and kept pacing the little room where they'd gathered. Cozily warm thanks to a well-laid peat fire no one ever let extinguish, the chamber boasted a fine groin-vaulted ceiling and was ringed with cushioned settles, providing sitting comfort for the clan's least hardy warriors.

It was a place good men could seek quiet when nights in the hall turned a bit raucous.

But Darroc thought of the chamber as his thinking room.

His best ideas came to him here.

Unfortunately, none appeared just now.

Too many conflicting emotions whirled inside him. Shock, frustration, and anger were only three. He didn't have room for more.

Least of all Lady Arabella.

Even if he was honest enough to admit that she was the reason he'd been wearing a track in the floor rushes. Or that because of her he needed all his willpower to keep from clenching and unclenching his hands as he paced.

Regrettably, she wasn't just the spark that set his world to collapsing around him.

She was the purpose of this meeting.

She was his greatest foe.

It scarce mattered that she was a woman. She carried tainted blood and the weight of deeds so foul their darkness could never be erased.

Or forgiven.

Truth was, he'd sooner cut off his sword arm.

So he willed himself to stop imagining her lush nakedness or how badly his fingers itched to glide along every curve and dip of her creamy, satiny smooth skin. He certainly didn't need to think about her flowing raven tresses. What it would be like to bury his face in those silken skeins. To nuzzle deep, breathe in the heady scent of her.

Darroc frowned.

His blood iced with fury.

Stomach clenching, he hitched his hip on the room's sole table and crossed his arms. "Good men, hear me! This is a serious matter." He closed his eyes for a moment, hoping no one would notice. But he could feel the back of his neck burning like fire, hated how closely entwined the she-demon was with his clan's privy affairs.

But that was the sad way of it, so he took a deep breath and plunged on. "God alone knows the truth of the Black Vikings. Whate'er, we must consider well. The lady's tellings give us no other choice."

"Bless me!" Mungo waved his hands. "The poor lassie doesn't know what she saw. Mad Moraig said she's been in and out o' her heid for days."

"Aye, just! And here's proof!" Geordie Dhu flung out an arm. "Has anyone seen the day?" he demanded, pointing at the nearest window.

Little more than a narrow oblong and fairly high-set,

the window's unshuttered opening revealed inky black clouds, thick, heavy, and rumbling.

They sailed past at impressive speed.

And it was at them that he stabbed a finger. "Yon are the maid's sea raiders. *Cloud galleys*! The storm that doomed her cog was a tempest. When the ship hit our skerries and started to break apart, she saw demons where there were none."

Swelling his chest, he glanced around. "I'd wager my beard on it."

"That wouldn't be wise." Darroc looked at him, the once doughty warrior and now Castle Bane's cook. Geordie Dhu's mastery in the kitchen—and his magnificent black curling beard—was all that remained of his pride.

Able to make the most savory pottages out of ground fishbone meal when times were lean and delighting even jaded palates with his egg batter fritters and custard tarts on feast days, he was well-loved by all.

And when he accompanied Darroc to Glasgow-town, the dock-and-tavern lassies never failed to succumb to his charms.

His beard was a true lady lodestone.

Grinning, he pulled on that beard now. "I wait! Who'll take my wager?"

"No one because we all ken you'd lose against the lass's claims." It galled Darroc to take her side. "She came to her wits soon after Moraig dressed her leg. And"—he shot a glance at Mungo—"she isn't the fearing sort. Nor do I think she's inclined to fancies. I believe she spoke true."

Six slack-jawed faces stared at him.

Then one of the men glanced back at the window, his face deeply troubled. "I'm with Mungo and Geordie Dhu. The maid was terrified for her life. She—"

"She may be the only living soul to survive a Black Viking attack." Conall pushed away from the settle he'd been leaning against. "We've heard tales of them for years. Nor"—he looked round, his gaze challenging—"is there anyone in this room who won't agree that a cog is damty hard to sink. Without a bit of help, that is."

"Bah!" Mungo jammed his hands on his hips. "Are you saying the wrath of the sea wasn't enough?"

Conall shrugged. "I'd sooner think the sea saved the lass. We all know that the sea takes what the sea wants. Some might say her life wasn't meant to end yestere'en. As for the lost men..."

He looked down at his feet. "Who knows what burdens they carried? Perhaps the sea didn't want them crossing its deeps? Or"—his bright head snapped up—"the Black Vikings gave them no choice?"

Mungo snorted. "I ne'er heard such twaddle."

Darroc shuddered.

He'd heard the like often enough.

If the cog carried MacKenzie men as well as Lady Arabella, he could well imagine the sea's displeasure in knowing such murderers rode the waves.

Still...

"We cannot ignore the lady's accounting." There he was defending her again. "Her story might seem as far-fetched as a little red fox causing a stir in the bailey"—he cut a look at Mungo—"but we still need to run the possibility to earth. If such marauders are plying our seas, we must find and banish them."

Several of his men's faces whitened.

One or two jutted chins.

Darroc held his course. "Need be... we destroy them."

"Pah!" Mungo bristled. "That's folly."

"The only folly would be allowing another ship to be attacked." Darroc stood. "We can't challenge such foes with a single birlinn and a few fishing cobles, but I will soon visit Olaf Big Nose."

He hooked his thumbs in his swordbelt and assumed the kind of fierce mien he usually strove to avoid. "'Tis true that Olaf scoffs when tongue waggers speak of such predators, but we can now persuade him otherwise. If he rallies his men and will engage his longboats, we have a good chance of chasing the fiends from our waters."

Geordie Dhu stepped forward. "Olaf Big Nose is a Viking. Why should he—"

"Olaf is a Norseman and our friend. He's been the like in times when no other soul would even glance at us. He is a man of honor who only wants to live in peace on his isle. He will—" Darroc broke off, an idea coming at last.

It was a great one.

So brilliant he almost whooped.

He did grin, causing his men to stare in bewilderment.

"Olaf will join us because we now have sure word that there are Black Vikings and"—he raised his arms above his head and cracked his knuckles—"because doing so is an opportunity he will no' want to miss."

"You're for giving him the cog's cargo barrels?" Mungo cocked a shaggy brow. "We opened a few. They're full o' wine and salted herring."

"We burn the lot—as ordered." Darroc's smile slipped a bit. "Olaf will be keen to help because if we succeed in vanquishing the sea raiders, the Scottish crown might be so pleased as to grant him the right to finally call his little isle his own."

His men's eyes rounded.

Darroc waited until the thinking room worked its magic and they comprehended.

It didn't take long.

"By glory!" Mungo's jaw slipped. "Such a feat—if there are Black Vikings and we besiege them—would put us back in the crown's good graces!"

"Our honor restored," another agreed, his face alight with wonder.

"That is my hope, aye." Darroc could scarce contain his own pleasure.

The possibilities were tremendous.

A master stroke of fate.

But then—as was the way with such marvels—his thinking room intruded beyond what was good for him. One by one, glints of an entirely different nature entered the eyes of his men and he braced himself as they exchanged telling glances.

The back of his neck started to heat again and the air around him turned cold and seemed to recede, making it difficult to breathe.

He gritted his teeth, waiting.

He knew what was coming.

As did Conall if his twitching lips and high color were any indication.

Mungo spoke first, his gaze shrewd. "The crown might even reward us."

"They might." Darroc nodded.

It was thinkable.

He just hoped his men left it at that.

But Geordie Dhu grabbed his arm, proving they wouldn't. "You could wed yon lassie abovestairs! She'd make a meet bride, comely as she is. And"—he chortled, his eyes dancing—"she's already in your bed!"

Merry laughter filled the room.

Darroc winced.

His men didn't notice.

All around him, they hooted and guffawed, slapping each other on the back or using scarred and age-worn hands to sketch a woman's voluptuous form in the air. Even Conall joined in, hastily filling two ale cups and thrusting one into Darroc's hands.

He set it aside untouched.

This was the moment he'd been dreading.

He cleared his throat, wishing he didn't have to dash their high spirits. It wasn't often that the men of Castle Bane found themselves in such fine fettle. Indeed, they were so busy cavorting, no one looked his way until he whipped out his dirk and used its handle to bang on the table.

The gabble stopped at once.

"MacConachers!" He spoke strongly. "What you suggest would land us in a greater broil than we've e'er seen. There can be no pairing between myself and the maid. Neither with God's blessing or otherwise."

He shuddered at the thought.

His men gaped, clearly disappointed.

Conall's shoulders slumped. "She's already wed?"

"She is Arabella of Kintail." Darroc kept his voice firm, making sure everyone heard. "Lady Arabella, eldest daughter of the Black Stag, Duncan MacKenzie."

"*MacKenzie*?" His men spoke together, their voices aghast.

Darroc nodded.

He wasn't surprised to see them blanch. He'd felt his own blood drain when he'd learned.

But then Mungo brightened. "Heigh-ho!" He jumped as if someone pricked him with a pin. "That does change things. Now we needn't worry where we'll get the coin to search for the Black Vikings. We—"

Geordie Dhu elbowed him.

Mungo didn't care. "We ransom the lass!"

Darroc gave him a look that would have fried another man's gizzard. "She stays here—as our guest—until it is safe to transport her. Then we see her home without a word of thanks or a siller expected."

Mungo's brows snapped together. "But—"

"MacConachers do not make war on women." Darroc's words were final.

"I'm no' saying we throw her in the dungeon." Mungo remained belligerent. "Just that—"

"There will be no *just that* or aught else." Darroc raised his hand when the seneschal started to argue. "Anyone who even looks at her sideways will find themselves in the pit. No matter."

The edict spoken, he folded his arms, waiting.

An awkward silence followed. A bit of foot shuffling and knitted brows, some glances at the window where the storm now raged in all fury.

Conall went to the hearth, where he stood staring at the glowing peats.

No one said anything.

Then finally they nodded, each in turn.

Including Mungo.

But the set of his hunched shoulders said he wasn't ready to concede. "I'd be hearing where we'll get a fat enough purse to fund such a crazy venture as you're proposing?" He thrust out his chin, eyes flashing. "Olaf Big Nose may be a friend, but he likes his palm well-greased. By my last reckoning, we scraped the coffers to build the new birlinn."

He hooked his thumbs in his belt, letting his stance announce his displeasure with the cost of the flashy little galley.

"I'll think of something." Darroc forced a light tone.

The new birlinn had beggared them.

But he wasn't about to tell the seneschal why it'd been so dear. Only Conall knew and Darroc trusted his cousin with his life.

As for the others...

Some things were best kept secret.

So he turned to retrieve the ale cup Conall had given him, this time downing its contents in one great gulp. Feeling better, he reached to pour himself another measure when Mungo appeared at his elbow.

"I know how we can refill our coffers." He leaned close, his tone conspiratorial.

Darroc inhaled. "I've spoken my last. The maid—"

"This has naught to do with her." Mungo's voice dipped low. "We can sell the Thunder Rod. There are men who would empty a king's treasury for—"

The ale jug slipped from Darroc's hands, landing on the floor with a thump. Ale splashed onto his legs and spilled across the rushes. Bending, he snatched the ewer and plunked it back on the table.

"Are you mad?" He stared at the seneschal, not caring that all eyes were on them.

Or what they heard.

Every man in the room knew the powers of the clan's fabled Thunder Rod.

It hung in this very room, the nature of its magic

demanding easy access to any MacConacher who wished its services. In the clan's possession since the laying of Castle Bane's first cornerstone, the gleaming length of fossilized wood claimed pride of place above the hearth.

Beautifully etched with intricate Nordic runes and still bearing traces of dazzling red, yellow, and blue paint, there were many legends as to the rod's origins. Some believed it was a piece of wood wrested from the prow of Thor's own dragon-ship. Others insisted a besotted Norse nobleman crafted it for his lady, presenting it to her as a reminder of his love when he was away at sea.

It was the clan's most prized possession.

And despite its dark history—the rod was responsible for much sorrow—no MacConacher had ever dared suggest they use it to gain riches.

Darroc frowned.

He could almost feel the Thunder Rod glaring at him, highly affronted.

Mungo had the gall to grin.

"So far as I know, no one's used the rod in ages." He slid a sly-eyed glance in the relic's direction. "Belike there are some limp-plagued men in the realm who'd pay handsomely to see their woes ended. A deep-pursed noble or"—he roared—"a Campbell! Those wily dastards are born schemers but word is they lack steel in their swords!"

A chorus of laughter filled the room.

One man choked on his ale. Conall grinned broadly and Geordie Dhu's guffaws were so great that he bent double, beard jigging and belly shaking.

"Aye, the Campbells are our men!" Mungo rocked back on his heels, triumphant. "They're also easily found, the cloven-footed buggers. There be more o' that race in Argyll than dew on the grass. Their wealth—"

"Shall remain their own!" Darroc looked hard at his men. "If the Campbells are *soft*, it is no concern of ours. The Thunder Rod remains at Castle Bane. No matter its worth. Or"—his voice was stern—"have you forgotten what happened the last time the rod changed hands?"

The laughter died.

All around the thinking room, men shifted uncomfortably. One or two dropped onto settles, looking morose.

Even Mungo clamped his jaw, then glanced down and busied himself brushing at his plaid.

Dark flushes stained the faces of every man.

No one spoke.

"I see you do remember." Darroc spoke the obvious.

A desirable young woman left alone to meet her fate on a remote isle, with an empty, echoing tower her only shelter, wasn't something easily put from one's mind.

And her death wasn't the only one.

Others had paid dearly when the Thunder Rod passed into MacConacher possession.

Darroc flinched.

He looked to where the peats glowed so quietly on the hearthstone and tried not to think of certain cliffs where the wind sometimes held fragments of men's screams. Nor was it good for him to dwell on the scratches in the stone of the *other* window in his notch room.

Faint marks etched by a feminine hand.

Just as strong male hands—those of his own ancestor, Rhun MacConacher—were believed to have done with the men who'd so loyally served him, vowing silence as they'd toiled to do his bidding.

Had they guessed what would happen when they completed their task? Did they sense that the bold Hebridean chieftain had his own plans for ensuring secrecy? That he meant for no living soul save himself and his nigh-abducted concubine to know of Castle Bane's existence?

Had Rhun known that his hastily built love nest would become a death trap for the very young woman he supposedly loved so obsessively?

Darroc's heart seemed to stop.

Feeling cold, he went to stand by the hearth, needing its warmth. The thinking room had grown dark and still, his men—he'd make amends with them later—having somehow slipped out beneath his brooding nose.

"That was in very old times." Mungo spoke from the shadows near the door.

Darroc started, then whirled to face him.

"As you saw"—the old man gestured at the empty room—"the men do remember, even if Rhun and Asa are now naught but moldered bones."

A shiver sped down Darroc's spine, but he ignored it and held the seneschal's stare. "Then they'll understand why we mustn't part with the relic. Its powers go deeper than helping a man be a man! It holds a darker magic and I'll no' spread that kind of—"

"Faugh!" Mungo snorted. "I won't be naming names, but there be some beneath this roof who feel differently. They think the rod's magic is good. Very good, if"—he winked—"you ken what I mean."

Darroc kept his face blank. To be sure, he knew.

He just didn't care to admit it.

Not that there was a need because the seneschal flipped

his plaid back over his shoulder and sailed out the door, leaving him alone.

Except, of course, for the chill of the cold, rain-damp air blowing in the window, the familiar earthy-sweet scent of the room's ever-burning peat fire, and the Thunder Rod that—he'd swear—appeared to be glowing as brightly as the orange-red bricks of peat.

Darroc studied the rod, hanging so innocently above the hearth. With surety, the strange glow was nothing more than firelight glinting off the bits of brilliant color that speckled parts of the relic.

Even so, he stepped away from the hearth fire and placed a hand on his sword hilt, letting his fingers curl loosely around the worn, leather-wrapped grip.

For some odd reason, he felt watched.

Almost as if Rhun was in the room with him. Perhaps even Gunnar the Strong, the wealthy Shetland trader who'd presented the Thunder Rod to Rhun, never guessing that doing so would forever damn his beautiful daughter, Asa Long-Legs.

Darroc tightened his grip on his sword hilt, half expecting the two men to spring from the shadows. He imagined them whipping out their steel and glaring at him, each one for a different reason.

But the little room was completely silent around him.

Nothing stirred but the rain-dampened wind. No hot-eyed, sword-swinging ancients assailed him.

Only a single thought.

And as so often happened when he was in the thinking room, the notion rang in his ears. Loud and penetrating as if the walls had come alive and were shouting the idea at him.

It was a terrible idea.

A possibility that shamed him even as images of himself and Arabella of Kintail flashed across his mind, stirring his blood and tightening his loins. Bold, brazen images, heated and intense, that showed her naked on the soft wet earth, knees bent and with her arms reaching up to him. Her eyes pleaded and her lips beckoned, passion beating between them like a living, scalding blaze.

Then he was throwing off his plaid to join her, the two of them hotly entangled and rolling on the ground, kissing and kissing as they coupled wildly on a sweet, fragrant bed of grass and heather.

"Damnation!" He squeezed shut his eyes. Unfortunately, his closed lids only intensified the sordid images. Dreadful visions of him besotted and consorting with the devil's own spawn, fetching as she was.

Darroc opened his eyes at once, scowling.

There were certain aspects of the rod's magic no honorable man would employ. No matter what notions the thinking room put in his head.

He wouldn't do it.

Turning on his heel, he pretended cold sweat wasn't misting his brow and marched for the door. But he paused on the threshold, some inexplicable feeling freezing him in place. Heart pounding, he was unable to keep from glancing back at the hoary relic.

Only it no longer hung from its ribbon on the wall.

He held the length of tartan silk in his hands, the magical rod dangling from his fingers.

Darroc stared, horror washing through him.

He was sure he hadn't retrieved it. And he was even more certain that his fate was now sealed. His most burning ambition loomed before him, bright and beckoning.

He could bring the MacKenzies to their knees.

Slay the hated Black Stag of Kintail without a single sword strike.

If he dared use the rod's most despicable powers.

Darroc's mouth went dry.

Blood roared in his ears and his palms turned cold, slick with damp. But his fingers continued to grip the ribbon and his gaze fixed on the Thunder Rod, its mysterious runes seeming to stare right back at him.

Reminding him of the past and the debt he owed his slain kinsmen.

He inhaled deeply.

He was tempted . . . sorely tempted.

High above the thinking room, Asa Long-Legs glimmered before her window in Castle Bane's topmost chamber. Once—in her short and distant life—she'd scratched markings in the stone of the window arch. Each nick, however faint, had given her hope. She'd believed that soon enough time would pass and *he* would return to her.

Rhun MacConacher.

The bold and lusty Hebridean chieftain who'd swept into her father's hall so many centuries before, conquering her heart with his laughing eyes and silvered tongue. A giant of a man, all golden and magnificent, he'd scorched her with his fierce embrace and white-hot kisses. Ruining her for all others with the way he looked at her, his heated gazes setting her aflame until passion and need consumed her.

How she'd loved him.

And what a fool she'd been to trust him.

Because of him, she was a ghost. Earthbound and lonely, trapped in a place where she'd expected to find only joy and happiness . . . .

Asa touched a shimmering finger to one of her notches, her pain as deep as if she'd made the mark only yesterday. Perhaps it was well that, at the time, she hadn't known he was forever gone to her.

Or what dark deeds hid behind his twinkling blue eyes.

Instead, she'd made her mark each day, ever certain that his raging desire for her would keep him from abandoning her on his cold and rocky isle.

Then the day came when she was no more.

But she still had her rituals....

Floating closer to the window, she lifted the hem of her luminous white gown, so different from the gaily colored raiments she loved in life. She peered at her legs, less substantial than a breath of cobwebs, then let the gown's air-light folds drop back down to cover them.

As a child, her legs had been spindle thin. And according to her beloved father, they'd stretched to her ears, hence her name, Asa Long-Legs.

When she'd reached womanhood, they'd been sleek and shapely. The loveliest legs Rhun had ever seen. Or so he'd claimed when she'd first stood naked before him.

No other man had ever seen her unclothed.

And now none ever would.

She looked at her legs once a day, the shocking transparency proving what she'd become.

It was so hard to believe otherwise.

She still felt so alive.

But she wasn't, so she stared out her window at the heavily falling rain and did her best to think of other things. In particular the young chief, Darroc, the only soul who visited her, though she knew he came to make his own window notches and not to see her.

Of course, he didn't even know she was there.

Even so, she liked him.

Though it pained her to see the anger inside him.

Every time he picked up his special mallet and chisel she could look into his heart and see how it heated, glowing red with fury.

She wished he burned with such passion for a woman.

Seeing love—pure and true—bloom at Castle Bane would do so much to ease the sorrow in her own heart. The keep had been built for love, or so she'd believed at the time. Now she knew differently, and the truth burdened her as cruelly as if she wore weighted chains rather than a gown lighter than the sea mist that so often slid past her window.

Now, at last, she could hope again.

Excitement was stirring at Castle Bane and the young chief was in the thick of it.

The maid, regardless of her name, was beautiful and alluring.

Above all, her heart was innocent.

Asa rested her hands on the stone of the window splay and leaned out as far as she dared. The rain didn't bother her and she enjoyed the sea wind, so cold and invigorating. Better yet, she suspected the night's wildness would send Darroc to look in on Lady Arabella.

He was like that, she knew.

Asa sighed, the possibilities making her soul tingle. She turned her face upward, letting the rain spatter her and the wind toss and tangle her hair.

Then she did something else.

Something she hadn't done in centuries.

She smiled.

Chapter Eight

❖

Darroc's thinking room had made a grievous error.

Surprisingly, he'd reached his bedchamber before the realization hit him with the force of an almighty blow. He froze where he stood, one hand on the door latch, the other gripping the ribbon of the Thunder Rod. His every muscle clenched with revulsion and hot bile rose in his throat. Ruining Arabella of Kintail was a great temptation. It would be no hardship to seduce her. The deed would shatter her prideful clan and bring her father lower than the grass he walked on.

Darroc's pulse quickened just imagining the Black Stag's horror. Unfortunately, he also knew that the shame of such an act would damage him more.

The stain on his honor would follow him to the grave.

That he'd hardened at the mere thought of having Arabella naked in his arms was already a damning smudge. Yet he couldn't deny that it stirred him to think of her hot, writhing, and wildly insatiable for him.

Hell's inferno!

He was no better than his roving-eyed ancestor, Rhun.

He'd defiled himself without even touching the lass. Most damning of all, his strong pull to her hadn't lessened on learning her name. That alone was enough to scald his soul and condemn him before his men. Yet she continued to consume him as much as when he'd first looked on her. Perhaps even more because he found her strength of spirit as irresistible as the curves and lines of her sinuous body.

Darroc swallowed a groan.

Boiling rage swept him and only his desire to get away quickly—and undetected—kept him from cursing aloud. He needed to return the Thunder Rod to the thinking room and never touch the benighted relic again.

But for some inexplicable reason he couldn't move.

He held the door latch in a white-knuckled death grip and couldn't let go. He did drag in a furious breath. Regrettably, the rapid intake of air caused him to jerk and the Thunder Rod swung forward to knock against the door.

Darroc's heart stopped.

The Thunder Rod glittered brightly . . . and bumped the door again.

"God's curse!" He forgot himself and swore.

"Eh?" Mad Moraig's voice trilled from within. "Be that you, Darroc?"

He cringed.

The door swung open.

Mad Moraig beamed at him. "Come away in." She indicated the dimly lit room behind her. "I told the wee lambie you'd be along."

Darroc almost choked. "I . . ." he spluttered, tripping over his own tongue.

A *wee lambie*, his bluidy big toe.

There wasn't anything wee about Lady Arabella. She was as well-made and robust as a Valkyrie. And devil blast Mad Moraig for saying something—however innocently meant—that reminded him.

"She was cold. Shivering something fierce and with her teeth all a-chatter." Mad Moraig clamped a clawlike hand on his arm. "So I—"

"I see what you did." Darroc stared past her to where Arabella rested in his bed. She was propped most proprietarily against his pillows and—he could scarce believe it—with one of his spare plaids wrapped snugly around her shoulders.

MacKenzie shoulders!

The sight tied his gut in a knot and behind his back, his fingers tightened on the Thunder Rod's ribbon. He didn't need to see the rod to know it'd be glowing madly. He could feel its infernal heat licking at his hand.

He blinked, casting about for something to say that wouldn't make him sound like a cold-hearted dastard.

The lass couldn't, after all, stay naked.

Her own clothes were ruined. Her shredded camise and cloak already burned. The ancient code of Highland hospitality demanded he see to her comfort. He had to clothe her. But his plaid wasn't the means to do so.

It was too personal.

"That won't do." He extracted his arm from Mad Moraig's grip and stepped into the room. "My spare plaids are old, the wool too scratchy for a woman's tender flesh," he declared, still eyeing his unwanted guest.

Not missing how beautiful she looked with her hair flowing around her, lustrous and gleaming against the folds of his plaid. Equally damning, Frang sprawled beside her, his huge shaggy body taking up nearly half the bed. The beast's head rested near her feet and the expression on his furry face could only be called an affront.

The brute looked besotted.

Though—Darroc hoped—that could be because Mina snuggled tight against him. Frang had definitely lost his heart to the tiny red and white she-dog.

Too bad she belonged to a MacKenzie.

Darroc frowned.

Next time he was in Glasgow-town, he'd pick up a more suitable mate for Frang. For now, he stared at the spectacle on his bed, half certain some power beyond his kenning was bent on torturing him.

He raised a brow, striving to appear in command of the situation.

Lady Arabella held his gaze, watching him steadily. Her deep sapphire stare made him feel like a bug pinned to the wall.

He was sure she could see into his heart.

That she knew he and all his people believed there wasn't a crack of hell vile enough to hold her father. And that some sickening gut feeling told him that she, of all women, might be the only one with a stout enough heart to embrace life on MacConacher's Isle.

Worst of all that she might guess he wished that could be so.

Darroc stifled a groan, miserable.

She *was* extraordinary.

Something about her made him believe she could walk the isle's wild moorland and see more than stunted heather strewn with stones. She'd laugh in the face of drenching rain and keep him warm on the coldest winter night. She was the heroine of every Gael's deepest romantic fancy. A woman—he was certain—who would stand on Castle Bane's bleak battlements, listening to the roar of the wind and the crash of the sea and be filled with awe and wonder.

She'd turn his blighted home into a place of peace and sanctuary.

If only she weren't a MacKenzie.

Darroc took a deep breath, amazed that he could.

Then he focused on the plaid draped so fetchingly around her. Seeing it there helped him harden his features. "She can wear one of my shirts." He jerked his head to where several hung from a peg on the wall. "They are worn, but the linen is soft and—"

"What are you hiding?" Her eyes narrowed.

Sapphire shards, piercing him as she lowered her gaze to stare at his left arm.

The one he still held behind him.

He opened his mouth to spew some excuse—anything—but before he could, the Thunder Rod's ribbon somehow slipped from his fingers and the magical relic dropped to the floor.

It landed with a clatter at his feet.

From somewhere, he thought he heard the tinkle of a woman's delighted laugh. But Lady Arabella was only staring, wide-eyed and silent. And Mad Moraig hovered at his elbow.

For sure, she hadn't laughed.

She did look horrified.

"O-o-oh!" She clapped her hands to her face. "It be the Thunder Rod!"

Darroc flushed.

"The what?" Arabella pushed up on her elbows and leaned forward to peer at the brightly shining rod. "I've never heard of a thunder rod."

"Be glad you haven't!" Moraig shot forward with amazing speed and snatched up the glittering piece of wood, holding it by a length of tartan ribbon. "It's not something fit for your gentle ears."

"I'd like to see it." Arabella strained to get a better look.

Roughly the size of a man's forearm, the rod's age-blackened wood was highly polished and appeared to be covered with intricate runes. Speckles of red, yellow, and blue paint caught her eye, the colors brilliant as gemstones.

It was the kind of thing Gelis would insist had to be enchanted.

She suspected it was a family heirloom.

Nothing more, nothing less.

She fell back against the pillows, the effort of leaning forward wearying her. As did the strange way her pulse leapt with awareness beneath the MacConacher's dark-eyed stare. She knew it was fancy, but his nearness also made her skin tingle. Even the shadowy room shifted and changed around him, the stark contours of its few embellishments seeming to soften and glow, almost glittering.

A transformation she was sure had nothing to do with his thunder rod.

It was him.

She pulled in a shaky breath. Astonishment seared her, hot and sweeping. But if he felt it—the invisible something that crackled and hummed between them—he gave no sign. He stood as if hewn of granite, fists clenched at his sides and his expression hard-set.

Everything about him took her breath.

She clearly irritated him.

Not sure why, she lifted a hand to brush a few wisps of hair off her face. "The thunder rod must be very old." She peered at it again, pretending more interest than she felt.

Anything to break the odd spell he cast over her.

"The rod is older than time and"—he gritted the words—"it is dangerous."

Arabella kept her attention on the relic. "It's quite beautiful."

"So be the devil—or so some say!" Moraig flashed a testy look at Darroc. "I'm after hearing what you were doing with it?" She poked him with a bony finger. "Here in the maid's room, of all hallowed places!"

To his credit, he didn't bark at her.

Arabella watched them, curious.

Her father would have taken off the head of anyone who'd dare speak to him thusly.

But except for her host's high color—his face had run scarlet when he'd dropped the rod—he only stepped forward to take the relic from Moraig's hands. Like her, he held it by the ribbon, seeming careful not to touch the actual wood as he set it on a coffer near the door.

"The rod went missing." He spoke to the old woman, not to her.

He was also lying, she was certain.

A muscle jumped in his jaw, always a sure sign.

"Geordie Dhu or one of the others must've borrowed it and forgot to return it to the thinking room." He went to stand by the hearth, one arm braced against the mantelpiece. "I was just taking it belowstairs."

Moraig clucked her tongue. "Fie, you were!"

Her gaze sharpened, then snapped to Arabella before she hobbled across the room and once again jabbed him with a finger. "I'll be keeping my eye on you, laddie," she *tsk*ed, shaking her gray head.

"There is no need." The words were surprisingly cold.

His tone was chillier and much more harsh than he would have wished, especially when he'd directed the terse reply to poor old Moraig.

She stood before him now, wringing her hands and shuffling her black-booted feet. Her sporting show of bravura vanished like a snuffed candlewick; her downcast eyes made his innards churn with shame and regret.

Arabella of Kintail brought out the worst in him.

She was turning him into an ogre.

He thrust his hands through his hair and looked her way, wondering if she knew the turmoil she was causing in his household.

But she merely met his stare, her expression cool as spring rain.

Three of Mad Moraig's special wine caudle cups also stared back at him. Large, wooden, and clearly empty, they bespoke how busy the old woman had been.

It took time to make her secret strengthening concoction.

A blend of wine and beaten egg yolks, laced with costly sugar and spices, then thickened with the hen wife's own mix of breadcrumbs and the saints knew what else. Served warm, one cup of the caudle was enough to put iron back in the blood of the most battle-wearied warrior.

Some claimed it caused chest hair to grow on men's backs.

Others swore it could rouse the dead.

Darroc stared at the cups. A sense of foreboding welled

in his chest. What three servings of the caudle would do to the virago in his bed didn't bear consideration.

"It's true enough—my caudles have mended her!" Mad Moraig followed his gaze. "She's slept well and her leg stitches be healing finely."

Darroc nodded.

He was too concerned about the sprouting of unwanted chest hair to do aught else.

Mad Moraig took no heed.

Tottering past him, she crossed the room and—shooing Frang and Mina from the bed—whipped back the covers to reveal her handiwork.

"Tell me," she twittered, "be this not my best work?"

"Aye, well…" Darroc stepped closer, bracing himself. But when he looked down, he saw there was no need.

Beneath the herbal-and-sphagnum moss compress Moraig gently lifted, it was startlingly clear that Arabella of Kintail had indeed plied her own needle to the wound.

Although darkly bruised, the sleek flesh of her upper thigh was no longer swollen and red. Gone, too, was the crooked line of Moraig's stitching. Lady Arabella's sure hand had also smoothed the bunched and gathered folds of skin that would have marred her for life.

Darroc cleared his throat. "For truth, you've done yourself proud, Moraig."

It wasn't a lie.

He just didn't say what it was that he was praising.

"She has cared for me well." Lady Arabella's voice was strong, the look she gave him almost challenging.

As if she expected him to stomp on Moraig's glory and meant to warn him before he said something to wipe the glow off the old woman's face.

"When I am healed, there will hardly be a scar." That pert MacKenzie chin lifted.

The sapphire eyes flashed.

Darroc made sure his own remained neutral. "God be praised, it is so."

It stunned him that he spoke true.

But the mastery of the maid's healing craft couldn't be denied. Nor his own relief in knowing her smooth, white skin would be spared harm by Moraig's disastrous if well-meant ministrations.

Truth be told, if it weren't for the neat seam running from just above her knee to where Moraig clutched the bedclothes, he'd almost doubt her leg had been so badly injured.

The stitches were nearly invisible.

The barely there smile curving Lady Arabella's lips said she knew it. "I am grateful for your healer's skill. There are many leech-women in the hills around my home who could learn much from her."

She spoke the words without an eye blink.

Mad Moraig drank them in, her thin chest swelling.

She preened. "I was taught by my mother and she by her mother before her." She slid a look at Darroc, eyes bright with pride. "There be some who say MacConacher women were always so gifted."

Darroc did his best not to let his jaw slip.

He'd never heard the like.

Nor had he ever met a woman with so smooth a tongue as Lady Arabella.

Or—and this he was loath to admit—one who was kinder to those less blessed.

Above all, her bravery humbled him. He knew men—

fierce and true warriors, not his stalwart graybeards—who would've fainted dead away at the prospect of unstitching and then re-sewing their own wound.

Arabella of Kintail inspired awe.

Clearly, she also knew something about winning hearts. There could be no doubt that Mad Moraig had heard her name. The kitchens would be rife with such tidings. Geordie Dhu wasn't one to hold his tongue.

The hen wife had to know.

Yet she gave no indication of being repelled.

Far from it, she clucked, fretted, and crooned, patting her compresses into place again and then gently drawing down the coverlet.

Darroc eyed her narrowly.

Mad Moraig wasn't concerned. "I'll be away to the kitchens now." She stepped back from the bed, dusting her hands. "Geordie Dhu promised he'd be making one of his fine meaty pottages for the lass."

"Geordie Dhu?" Darroc couldn't believe it.

More like he'd use granite slivers to make his pottage rather than tender morsels of stewed beef.

But Mad Moraig was bobbing her head.

"So I said, aye. Geordie Dhu and no other." Her voice rang with triumph. "He's baking his best wheaten bread to make sops for the pottage."

This time Darroc's jaw did drop.

Geordie Dhu hoarded his finest flour as if it were gold dust. Heavy bran loaves and oatcakes were the daily fare at Castle Bane. Only on the greatest of feast days could the bearded warrior-turned-cook be persuaded to dip into his prized stores.

Until now, it would seem.

Sensing doom, Darroc narrowed his eyes at Mad Moraig who—he shouldn't have been surprised—went scooting out the door. Black skirts crisply rustling, with the Thunder Rod clasped tightly in one hand, she moved at a pace that would have put many young girls to shame.

Darroc's brows snapped together.

His world was crashing down around him.

Frowning blackly, he flashed a glance at Lady Arabella. "Stay there!" He blurted the ridiculous command before he could stop himself. Well-stitched leg or no, she wasn't going anywhere for a while.

He doubted she could even stand.

Feeling foolish, he jerked a nod at her. "I'll be back anon."

Then he whirled and sprinted for the door, catching Mad Moraig just as she hitched up her skirts to descend the tower stairs.

A dark stairwell that—his nose twitched in recognition—held the distinct aroma of freshly baked bread.

Darroc's head began to ache.

But he did manage to thrust out a hand and latch onto Mad Moraig's elbow, gripping gently but firmly.

"Eh?" She turned to peer up at him, the image of innocence.

Darroc glared down at her, not missing how she'd whipped the Thunder Rod behind her back. "Do what you will with the rod." He released her elbow and folded his arms. "I didn't come after you to fetch the wretched thing."

Mad Moraig's expression turned mulish. "Then why make such a stir?"

Darroc drew a steadying breath. Behind Mad Moraig,

angry storm clouds raced past an arrow slit in the turn-pike stair and—at the moment—he wouldn't have been surprised if the black roiling masses poured their teeming rain right down onto his head.

"You'll be keeping the lass from her healing with your dark looks and bluster." Mad Moraig's bristly chin jutted. "Dinna think she doesn't see how you glare and fume at her. She—"

"She is a MacKenzie." The ache in Darroc's head became a fierce pounding. "*MacKenzie*, I said. Though"—he unfolded his arms and jammed his hands on his hips—"I'm certain you've already heard."

Mad Moraig compressed her lips.

Her silence spoke volumes.

"You do not care?" Darroc hands clenched. He couldn't help it. "Her father is the Black Stag of Kintail. He—"

"I ken well enough who he be." Moraig's voice sharpened with disapproval. "But"—her face softened—"the lassie now, she be her own self."

"She's bespelled you." Darroc looked at her. "Is that no' the way of it? She—"

"She calls me Moraig. Only Moraig, just!" The old woman met his stare, her eyes defiant. "I am no' so daft-headed that I'm no' aware o' what the others whisper behind my back, calling me mad and worse."

She wagged a finger. "If I do think too much on darker days, there be naught wrong with my ears."

Darroc nodded. "I see."

And he did.

He was doomed.

Geordie Dhu. Mad Moraig. Soon his entire clan would be enchanted. To a man, they'd fall prey to Lady Arabella's charms. They'd make mooney eyes at her like Frang and eat out of her slender, aristocratic hands.

Hands he'd love to feel sliding around his neck or perhaps sweeping down his naked back only to then dip lower and glide around to grasp...

He frowned.

Somewhere in the shadows of the landing he again thought he heard a woman's silvery laugh. But when he glanced back at the open bedchamber door, it loomed quiet. Though he did imagine he caught a fleeting glimpse of a tall, voluptuous woman in a clinging white gown.

He blinked.

Outside the tower, thunder cracked and boomed. Then—praise God—a bright flash of lightning explained his folly. He shoved a hand through his hair, more frustrated than ever. Floating maidens in white, indeed! Soon he'd be as befuddled as Mad Moraig.

He cleared his throat. "Lady Arabella does not need you to champion her."

That, at least, was true.

He'd never seen a stronger maid.

Mad Moraig tilted her head. "You will treat her kindly?"

"I would hear how she bewitched Geordie Dhu." He posed his own question, refusing to answer hers.

"Well?" He waited.

Mad Moraig once again assumed her look of studied innocence. "Could be"—she couldn't quite keep the smugness out of her voice—"that someone told Geordie Dhu the lassie saw him in the hall when you carried her in."

"Geordie Dhu was in his kitchens at the time."

"Be that as it may—"

"What did you tell him?" Darroc's frown returned.

The hen wife's eyes danced with mischief. "Only what would please him most."

"And what was that?" Darroc was sure he didn't want to know.

Mad Moraig chuckled. "Could be I told him the lady admired his beard, claiming there wasn't a man in all Kintail able to grow one so fine."

"I don't believe you." Darroc eyed her suspiciously.

"'Tis true as I'm standing here." Mad Moraig hitched up her skirts again, turning back to the downward-winding stairs. "Geordie Dhu struts about like a crowing cock, always boasting there isn't a woman living who can resist his beard. He forgot all about the lassie's name when he heard she was soft on him."

"Pah!" Darroc waved a hand. "Geordie Dhu might be fond of his beard, but he hates MacKenzies. He'd have the lass chained in the pit below his kitchens before he'd serve up delicacies for her."

"Say you." Mad Moraig winked, looking mightily pleased. "Could be someone also told him I'd no' be making any more healing ointment for his toenail what's growing wrongly lest he treat the maid goodly."

"So that was the way of it." Darroc looked at the old woman, surprised by her wit.

"Could be …." She started down the stairs, stepping sprightly. "Now I'll just be for seeing if the black-bearded cockerel has made his meaty pottage to go with the fine wheaten bread I be smelling!"

Darroc watched her go, certain of two things.

Men must be wary of women, regardless of age.

And Mad Moraig wasn't mad.

Though he might well be for returning to the

bedchamber when he could have fled. The penetrating sapphire gaze his foe's daughter pinned on him the instant he crossed the threshold made him feel mad indeed.

"Why was Moraig so fashed to see your thunder rod?" She sat up, the movement causing the plaid to dip dangerously. "What did she mean by saying its story is not for gentle ears?"

"The relic's past is tragic." Darroc crossed the room and poured himself a measure of *uisge beatha*, downing the fiery spirits in one quick gulp. "Moraig spoke true. You are too refined to know of such things."

Arabella bristled. "You have seen that I am not faint of heart." She rested a deliberate hand on her injured leg. "Do you think ladies know naught of sadness and hardship?"

"I would that ladies were spared the like." His eyes darkened on the words.

Arabella squelched the urge to squirm.

More than that, the ominous note in his tone made her all the more determined to find out the mystery behind his thunder rod.

So she sat up straighter against the pillows and eyed him with her best daughter-of-a-thousand-chieftains stare. It was a look she'd learned from her father though she was sure he called it by another name. Perhaps his I-am-the-mightiest-chieftain-in-the-Highlands stare. Heed me or regret it.

Either way, the look didn't seem to work well on Darroc MacConacher.

Far from telling her what she wanted, he came forward and reached to frame her face with two hands. "Calamity, heartache, and other unpleasantness should no' touch innocents," he said, his voice tight, almost bitter.

But some of the hardness left his face and he smoothed back her hair, his stroking fingers sending strings of golden warmth spooling through her. Then almost as quickly as the beautiful sensations began, he stepped back as if touching her had scorched him. Turning away, he went to an open window and stared out at the rain-swept night.

"See you, Arabella of Kintail, as leader of my people I am all too aware that ladies know tragedy." He glanced at her as if the statement should mean something to her. "MacConacher women have borne more than their share of sorrows. Moraig more than most."

The words hung between them, almost a burden.

Arabella's brow knitted. She didn't know how he did it, but she felt somehow chastened.

What she wanted to feel was him touching her again.

Even now—and despite the return of his stony-faced expression—her skin tingled where he'd caressed her. She could still feel his fingers sliding through her hair, the delicious intimacy of his touch. A strange and wondrous excitement pulsed inside her, making everything else seem unimportant.

Except the twinge of pity that nipped her when he spoke of Moraig.

Her gaze darted to the empty doorway. "You say the thunder rod is dangerous. I do not believe a piece of wood, however beautiful, can be . . . anything. But I know others who hold to such tales."

The MacConacher stiffened. "Then you are surely wise enough to stay away from the relic."

Arabella watched him closely, not liking how his hands fisted on the stone of the window splay. Nor did she think she was particularly wise.

She was nosy.

"Is Moraig afraid of the rod?" She needed to know. "Does she fear it will harm her?"

Darroc almost choked.

"The Thunder Rod doesn't harm anyone. What it does"— he whirled around, the back of his neck flaming—"is..."

He let the words tail off and started pacing. How could he tell her of the rod's powers?

He couldn't and wouldn't.

But then one of Moraig's wooden caudle cups sailed off the table and thumped across the rushes, rolling to a stop near Frang's chiefly pallet. Mina yipped and leapt to her feet, tearing for the door. Frang rose with more dignity, but even he couldn't keep his hackles from rising.

Nor was he above loping out of the bedchamber in Mina's wake.

Darroc stared after them. Then he bent to retrieve the caudle cup. If the strong burst of wind that blew the cup off the table frightened the dogs, the gust proved a blessing for him.

He now knew what he could tell Arabella about the Thunder Rod.

Crossing the room, he closed the shutters and—before he realized he'd done so—sat on the edge of the bed. Perilously near to her.

So close, in fact, that he could feel the heat of her warming him.

He shifted, highly uncomfortable. She merely peered at him, her lovely face serene and the slow rise and fall of her breasts tantalizing him.

He was a greater fool than Geordie Dhu, swayed by beard praise and the ache of a sore toe.

"Moraig surely told you that her special wine caudle is a strengthening concoction." He blurted the words, his fingers tight on the wooden cup. "That—"

"What does her caudle have to do with your thunder rod?" She blinked innocently.

He felt a burning urge to shock her.

"The Thunder Rod"—he watched her closely—"is much like Moraig's caudle. Those who trust in its powers say it strengthens men."

"*Strengthens men*?" Her eyes rounded but not a tinge of pink stained her cheeks.

Darroc's own flushed hotly.

Surely she knew what he meant.

"You mean for battle?" Her words proved she didn't.

"Some might put it that way, aye."

He set the caudle cup on the bedside table and placed both hands on her shoulders. Something drove him to touch her, to twine his fingers in the silken strands of her hair, and— saints help him—but he simply wasn't able to resist her.

"The Thunder Rod is said to make a man irresistible to women and"—he couldn't believe her was telling her— "grant him untold powers in bed."

"Oh." Now her face did turn scarlet.

Darroc felt like the world's greatest arse.

Praise God he didn't mention that in order to gain such prowess, a man must handle the rod as he would himself. Or worse, if a woman caressed the rod, she would become insatiable, burning with a fiery need that could only be quenched by the first man to cross her path after she'd touched the rod.

Even so, he'd said too much.

Arabella of Kintail was scandalized.

And—he couldn't believe his ears—she was convulsing with laughter.

"Pray forgive me." She dashed tears from her cheeks. Her beautiful eyes were streaming. "But I have never heard anything so silly. Or"—another great bout of mirth shook her—"have you tested the rod's—"

"I—Sakes!" Darroc glanced at the ceiling. How he wished the smoke-blackened rafters would crash down and bury him. Instead, one of the shutters flew open and a blast of rain-laden wind swept into the room, causing the bed curtains to swirl wildly.

Swirl, dance, and tangle around himself and the Valkyrie until they were both wrapped snugly inside the dusty, cloying swaths.

"Agggh!" He tried to fling off the heavy material, but he couldn't move his arms. Worst of all, his borrowed plaid seemed to have slipped down her shoulders. He was certain the firm roundness of her naked breasts pressed against him. Until she thrust a hand between them and yanked it up again.

"O-o-oh!" He thought he heard her gasp.

He *knew* her lips hovered but a breath from his.

Darroc groaned.

She sighed contentedly.

At least, he thought she did.

The pleased-sounding little cry hadn't seemed as close as it should, considering. Indeed, it'd sounded most distant, almost tinny.

Either way, it was more encouragement than he needed. He wanted Arabella MacKenzie. His entire body went still and he tried to squash the overwhelming urge to kiss her.

Tried, and failed.

A low moan—surely he hadn't made it—came from deep in his throat and he lowered his head, seizing her lips in a hot and furious kiss. She stiffened and arched her back, but then she clutched at him, her fingers digging into his flesh as he opened his mouth over hers, kissing her hard.

Until he deepened the kiss, thrusting his tongue into her mouth and—devil's toenails—discovering she'd never been kissed before.

The peaks of her hardened nipples brushed his chest, their heat scorching him even through the folds of his plaid. Just as the silky soft melding of her breath with his and the greedily naive slide of her tongue against his own minded him that he was playing with fire.

He had no business desiring a MacKenzie. And even less to taste the sweetness of her lips, no matter how hot, moist, and wondrously smooth.

Arabella of Kintail was an untried virgin.

And he'd just paved his way to hell.

"Damnation!" He jerked away from her, yanking down the bed curtains.

Not that there was any need, for as soon as he cried out, breaking their kiss, the heavy curtaining fell around them, pooling onto the floor in a dusty, muddled heap.

"Oh, my." Arabella pressed a hand to her plaid-covered breast. "You kissed me."

Darroc stared at her, horrified.

Words—any apologies he could have offered—lodged in his throat. His heart thundered in his chest and his blood roared in his ears.

All he knew was that he was doomed.

With one kiss, he'd ruined everything.

The die was cast.

Chapter Nine

❧

"You kissed me."

Arabella repeated the words, not sure the MacConacher heard her the first time. He *was* staring at her, clearly displeased. Indeed, if the horror on his face was any indication, she'd somehow transformed herself into some kind of fiend.

He'd paled visibly.

And he was looking at her as if her eyes blazed red and her nails flashed like flesh-ripping talons. As if her hair no longer tumbled around her shoulders but wriggled with life, a hideous tangle of writhing, shiny-scaled snakes.

Most damning of all, when he'd leapt off the bed he'd nearly tripped over the fallen drapery in his haste to get away from her. Even so, he'd quickly regained his dignity and crossed the room with long strides to take up a stern, warrior stance near the hearth.

Arabella's brow knit. He may well have been standing on the far side of a yawning abyss.

Not that it mattered.

She could still feel his mouth slanting over hers, the incredible thrill of when he'd slid his tongue between her parted lips. The way her breath hitched and her heart slammed to a sudden stunned stop and then started again, beating wildly. How a mad rush of delicious, whirling pleasure whipped through her, making her tingle clear to her toes.

She touched wondering fingers to her lips, reliving the magic.

Never would she have believed kissing could be so tantalizing.

So wondrous.

She narrowed her eyes at him, willing him to remember. She could hardly think of anything else. He had to have felt the same giddy excitement.

But his face remained cold.

"Aye, I kissed you." He made it sound as if the admission soured his tongue. "For truth, I do not know what I was thinking."

Arabella's heart dipped.

He swept his plaid over his shoulder, reminding her so much of the braw warrior she'd imagined in Dunakin's tower window. Now, as then, her breath caught at his magnificence. He could have been that man. Gelis would swear it was so. But then he glanced at the heap of tumbled bed curtains and she was sure he shuddered.

A man come to claim a maid's heart wouldn't cringe because he'd kissed her.

Arabella's face crimsoned.

Shameful heat swelled in her throat and she struggled against the urge to twist her fingers in the bed covers.

Unfortunately, although she managed to keep her hands still, she couldn't stop something inside her from spinning into a cold, hard knot.

She feared it was the tiny flicker of joy that had blazed so brightly when he'd kissed her.

Now...

She tried to pretend his rejection didn't sting like jabs of tiny, white-hot fire needles. She also ignored the awful hollowness spreading through her. Striving to appear composed, she smoothed the bed coverlet with deliberate exactness. MacKenzies didn't share their humiliations and disappointments, however lancing.

Blood tells, her father always said.

Still, the look on the MacConacher's face cut to her soul.

But then some of his fury seemed to ebb and he took a step toward her, one hand extended. "Ach, lass...."

He let the words tail off and lowered his hand. His frown returned. "See you, I ne'er meant to touch you. No' in such a way."

"I know you didn't." Arabella held his stare, her mien calm and her chin firm.

"Nae, you do not know." He shook his head. "Our kiss—"

"It was nothing." The lie sounded ridiculous, even to her. "A simple—"

"It was—" He clamped his mouth shut, ran both hands through his hair. "Something that will not happen again, I assure you."

"You needn't bother." She tried to sound worldly. "I've quite forgotten already."

His brows snapped together. "Lying is beneath you, my lady."

"Then"—she kept her voice firm—"I shall put it another way. You've made it clear that I needn't fear a repetition of your manly attentions."

"*My what*?" His eyes rounded as if she'd spoken in a foreign language. "Lass, if I'd—"

He broke off and stomped to the window. "You've spent too many long winter nights listening to bards spin tales of unrequited love and burning passion." His voice was husky, almost too low to be heard. "Such foolery had nothing to do with me kissing you."

Arabella eyed him, not believing a word. Passion had everything to do with it. He'd wakened hers—for him— and she doubted she'd ever take another breath without wanting more of his kisses.

She'd think about the love part later.

When she was alone and he wasn't standing so straight he looked as if he'd swallowed a broomstick. Or when he hadn't thrown back his shoulders with such stiff-necked male pride, she was sure he'd be wracked by muscle cramps for at least a sennight.

Men were fools.

And if she weren't so perturbed, she'd laugh. How dare he call her a liar?

He was no better.

She started to say so, but just then one of the peats in the hearth popped loudly, sending up a swirl of blue-orange sparks. They settled quickly, falling back onto the grate where they glimmered brightly before vanishing in a puff of sweetly scented smoke.

It was a dusky heathery scent, almost like a woman's perfume.

Nearby, Frang sighed heavily.

Or so she thought until she realized the shaggy beast's hearthrug was empty.

A chill slid down her spine—she was sure she'd heard a sigh—and she glanced back at Darroc, knowing he hadn't made the noise.

He had moved to the window arch where he stood with his hands braced on the broad stone splay. For a moment, he looked as if he was about to hang his head. Instead, he gave himself a shake as if to clear his thoughts and reached for the shutters, flinging them wide.

Outside, the wild weather had moved on, but a wet mist lingered. Dripping rain plopped onto the window ledge, the droplets sparkling in the glow of a nearby wall torch. The chill damp swept in, quickly filling the room and making Arabella shiver again.

She rubbed her arms, not surprised to see them covered with gooseflesh.

Darroc didn't seem fazed.

Nor did he appear to have noticed the waft of heathery fragrance or the sigh. He certainly didn't look cold. If anything, blazing heat rolled off him and even with his back to her, Arabella knew his face was stained with a dark and angry flush.

A flush noted by someone other than Arabella. Near the hearth fire, Asa Long-Legs shimmered and fumed with an annoyance all her own.

Were all MacConacher men so thrawn?

She knew well that she'd fallen for a bad one. Her MacConacher had been an ill-limmer famed for much worse than sheer knuckle-headedness. Asa peered into the peat fire, seeing again his strong, firm jaw and hearing his booming laugh. He'd been a bonny man, for all his treachery. And she'd been so certain this chieftain had all of Rhun's charm but none of his flaws.

Drifting closer to Darroc now, she peered beyond him to the blackness of the night, the thick sea-mist sliding past the window.

He didn't seem to notice her.

But then he shivered and rubbed the back of his neck.

Asa smiled.

Her heart skittered and she resisted the urge to clap her hands in glee. She didn't want to draw attention. Having spent her long centuries as she was now at Castle Bane and nowhere else, she wasn't accomplished in such dabbling. It wouldn't do if she broke some unknown charter of spirit behavior and ruined everything.

Yet there was hope if he sensed her, however faintly.

Encouraged, she reached to smooth his hair with a feather-light touch, knowing he'd think her caress was only a very cold draught of air.

Indeed, he shivered again.

Asa bit back a delighted cry.

He glanced around, his dark eyes alert. Almost as if he knew she was there. It would please her so much if he could see her. But for now, it was enough to have felt the frustration spinning inside him.

Frustration was good.

He wanted the raven-haired beauty.

Asa's heart sang with the glory of it. She twirled in a sparkly circle, wishing the young chieftain and his lady could see her rapture. Soon there'd be no need for caudle cups that sailed through the air and falling bed curtains.

No glittery showers of peat sparks to deflect words that

shouldn't be spoken. Asa tinkled a laugh as silvery as the night mist. The popping peat had been particularly clever.

And such fun!

But enough was enough.

The young chieftain was looking her way again and even the maid had cast her several thoughtful glances. It wouldn't do if they learned of her trickery, much as she wished to share in their burgeoning happiness.

So she sighed and hitched up her shimmering white skirts, not that she really needed to as—floating as she did—her feet never touched the floor.

But just as she'd once made her daily notches and now examined her legs each day, gathering up her skirts when she prepared to leave a room was tradition.

It helped her feel real.

So she tightened her fingers in the glistening folds of her gown and began twirling again, spinning faster and faster until nothing remained of her presence but a ripple in the air and a few fast-fading sparkles of her excitement, each one luminous as a star.

Across the room, Arabella blinked.

Tiny speckles of light danced at the edge of her vision and she rubbed her eyes, certain there'd been another burst of peat sparks.

But a glance at the hearth proved her wrong.

Nothing stirred there.

Nor at the window arch where Darroc still stood with his back to her, looking so tense against the dark night. He'd fisted his hands on the window splay and from the stubborn set of his shoulders it wouldn't surprise her if he remained there till morning.

Something told her he was capable of doing so.

Arabella bit her lip.

All her life she'd prided herself on mastering every situation. Regardless of what might befall her, she always knew what to do. Even some of the clan elders were wont to seek her advice. More than one called her the MacKenzie peacekeeper, a smoother of waters when times grew turbulent. Now for the first time ever, she found herself at a loss.

Until she caught the glimmer of a star just above Darroc's left shoulder. Thin drifts of clouds, gray and windtorn, stretched across the sky, blotting the other stars, but this one refused to stay hidden. It twinkled brightly, its brilliant blue-white light almost defiant.

Arabella released the breath she'd been holding.

Then she smiled.

It was time for drastic measures.

She inhaled deep, ready. But cold fear rose inside her and the blazing ache in her leg flared in protest. She winced. The hot throbbing pierced to the marrow. She might be the Black Stag's daughter, but she wasn't made of granite. Even so, she clenched her teeth against the pain and forced herself to ignore her dread.

At best, only her pride would be dinted if she fell to her knees.

At worst, her stitches would come undone.

If all went well...

Her heart swelled.

Steeling herself, she drew on all the courage of her race and threw back the covers. Quickly, before pain or fearing demons could seize her, she eased her legs off the bed and slid to her feet.

The sudden burst of agony in her leg nearly blinded

her. Once again she saw stars, but this time they were numberless and wheeled crazily before her eyes. Her knees trembled and almost buckled, but she grabbed the bedpost, clutching tight. She held on until the stars spun away and the sharp pain lessened to a dull throbbing.

Tension beaded her forehead and her palms slickened.

She *had* to do this.

Her fingers tightened on the smooth wood of the bedpost. She breathed deeply, summoning strength. At last she let go of the bed and took a step forward. Then another and another until she'd crossed the room to where Darroc still stood looking out the window.

Cold wind rushed at her, chilling the damp on her brow, the tiny rivulets that trickled between her breasts.

The MacConacher hadn't moved.

She lifted a hand, almost but not quite touching his broad, plaid-hung back. Strands of his silky black hair teased her face and his scent surrounded her, weakening her knees in a way that had nothing to do with her injured leg. He smelled of sea wind, clean wool, and a pleasing trace of wood smoke. But there was more. Something indefinably manly that set her senses to reeling.

A powerful connection pulled between them, making her heart pound.

It also made her bold.

"So-o-o!" Her voice rang clear, without a single tremor. "If it wasn't passion that made you kiss me, I would know what did?"

Darroc near jumped out of his skin.

Heart in his throat, he whirled around. Arabella of Kintail stood right behind him. Tall, erect, and looking prouder than sin.

"Saints, Maria, and Joseph!" He roared the curse, more angry that she'd left the comfort of his bed than because she'd startled him out of his wits. "You shouldn't be on your feet. Have you run mad?"

"Yes, I think I might have." A smile spread across her beautiful face. Her ebony hair spilled around her shoulders, a skein of satiny temptation, riffled by the wind and gleaming in the candlelight.

"Caught a touch of madness, that is." Her smile dimpled just a bit.

Darroc suppressed a snort.

"You don't look crazed to me." He hoped she couldn't tell how she *did* look to him.

She was pure seduction.

And—he knew—the devil was on the loose and he was the prey.

He frowned.

Her sapphire eyes lit with merriment. "Crazed or nae, I fear I might be hearing things."

"What things?" Darroc's eyes narrowed.

He flashed a glance at the bedside table and the three empty wooden cups there. It would seem Mad Moraig's wine caudle hadn't just infused her with unnatural hardiness. The concoction must've also muddled her mind.

"That curse." Her words made no sense, proving it. " 'Saints, Maria, and Joseph' is my father's favorite oath."

Darroc felt himself blanch. "Your father?"

She nodded. "He says it all the time." The pride on her face knifed him. "Saints, Maria, and Joseph. I've never heard anyone else use it."

Darroc harrumphed. It was the best he could do.

For sure, he'd never utter the curse again.

Just the thought that it'd crossed his lips now—and in the past, saints scald him—felt like someone twice as large and three times his strength had punched him in the gut.

Until Lady Arabella reached out and curled her fingers into his plaid, needing support.

Then he felt like an arse.

She tightened her grip and leaned into him. Her breasts rubbed against his chest and he could feel the thundering of her heart. And although she tried to hide it, he was sure her legs were trembling. He bit back another curse and slid his arms around her, holding her steady.

She *was* shaking.

"You haven't answered me." She proved she was also persistent.

"First we're getting you off your feet." He, too, had a stubborn streak.

Not giving her a chance to protest, he gathered her up into his arms and crossed the room. She'd already tossed back the coverlets, so he eased her onto the bed, taking care that his borrowed plaid didn't slip down her shoulders. Then he drew the covers up to her chin.

Perhaps not as gently as he should have, but Arabella of Kintail naked but for a swath of plaid and her streaming curtain of glossy raven tresses was more allure than any red-blooded male could bear.

Especially one who'd already had a very good look at her most intimate charms!

Thinking about them now—those tightly furled dark nipples and the hot, wet sleekness between her thighs—set his face to flaming. How he wished he hadn't helped Mad Moraig undress her after her rescue. But the old woman couldn't have managed alone. Not with Arabella a dead weight on the bed and her clothes a tangled, sodden mess.

So he had helped.

And he'd seen...

Darroc's loins tightened, remembering. He stepped back from the bed and set his hands on his hips, hoping she'd think he was just angry. Most of all, he hoped the fall of his plaid hid what was truly on his mind.

There could be nothing between them.

Not even a heated glance.

"I'm waiting." She fixed those maddeningly blue eyes on him.

Then she smiled sweetly. "And I'm no longer on my feet."

Devil's toenails! He muttered another favorite curse—this time under his breath.

"Why did you kiss me?" Her gaze didn't waver.

"Because—" Darroc stopped before he bellowed the truth. That he'd been consumed with the urge to taste her lips.

That he was no better than his rutting ancestor, Rhun. Builder of Castle Bane and despoiler of thousands, or so family legend claimed.

His mood worsened at the thought of his lusting for MacKenzie lips.

He shoved a hand through his hair, grasping for another explanation. "It was the Thunder Rod," he decided, half certain it was. "Such is the relic's power. Its proximity—"

"Made you...er, umm..." She flushed, unable to finish.

"Nae!" Heat shot up the back of his neck. "It wasn't what you're thinking. I—"

He was making a mess of it. "The rod has other powers. Influences, some might say."

"Influences?" Her lips twitched.

"Aye, just."

"I see." She clasped her hands on her lap. But not before he saw the spark of humor in her eyes.

She was laughing at him.

Darroc pretended he hadn't noticed.

"I've already told you that the Thunder Rod's age is beyond reckoning." He started pacing, determined to make her understand the danger. "No one knows the relic's true origins. The man who gave it to my ancestor, Rhun the Insatiable, claimed that—"

"*The Insatiable*?"

"So he was called, aye."

He now had her full attention. "The tales about him are as damning as his name. But I will tell you of him anon. First you must know that Gunnar the Strong, the rod's previous owner, believed it to hold great magic."

Darroc glanced at her as he passed the hearth. She still held her hands clasped primly in her lap, but her sooty lashes were flickering.

She was amused!

He tried not to scowl. "Gunnar the Strong was a Norse noble. Late of an e'en on dark winter nights when the winds howled and men huddled before the fire, he enjoyed boasting that one of his forebears had wrested the rod from the prow of Thor's own dragon-ship."

"Thor the Norse thunder god?"

"Aye, that one."

He knew she didn't believe a word.

"There are other tales from which to choose." He

cleared his throat, refusing to let her make him feel silly. "Some are quite romantic. One tells of a Viking raider who loved his wife so fiercely that he couldn't bear to leave her. Legend claims he carved the Thunder Rod for her to keep in his remembrance when he went warring at sea. Another story—"

"How did the rod come into the hands of your ancestor?" Her voice was low, the teasing tone gone.

She was intrigued by his mention of romance.

Darroc stopped pacing.

He'd be wise to nip such fancies before they got the better of her.

So he put back his shoulders, taking advantage of his fullest height and formidability. He also took care to stand where the glow from the hearth fire would edge him in red, making him look even more daunting.

"You mean Rhun the Insatiable?" He took some small pleasure in the way her eyes widened on the name.

She nodded.

Then pleased him further when a faint pink tinge washed across her cheeks.

When he'd finished his tale, she'd want nothing to do with him or his family. She might even try to swim back to Kintail. Though, of course, he wouldn't allow such nonsense. He'd return her himself when she was fit enough to travel. When the waters were safe enough to let her.

For the now, it served if she'd just stop piercing him with those man-melting sapphire eyes.

Looking forward to his peace, he resumed his circuit of the room. "Rhun lived in the years when the Norse ruled the Hebrides. As you can guess from his by-name, he was quite fond of women. Bold and bonny, or so say the bards, he drew them like bees to a hive. He was also a cunning chieftain, convivial and clever. Rather than fight Nordic possession of islands many Hebrideans saw as their own, he chose to make his fortune in trading with Viking merchants."

Darroc glanced at the bed, not surprised to see her hanging on his every word.

"Is that how he met Gunnar the Strong?" Her voice was soft in the quiet room.

"Aye, that was the way of it." He spoke true. "Rhun paid a visit to Gunnar at his hall at Scalloway in Shetland. It was there that he attracted the eye of the Norseman's favorite daughter, Asa Long-Legs."

"*Asa Long-Legs.*" Lady Arabella repeated the name in a dreamy voice. Her eyes went dewy. "They had a romance."

"Nae." Darroc shook his head.

He didn't care for her tone. And he disliked the soppy look on her face even more.

"What they had"—he spoke sternly—"was a tragedy."

"They fell in love but couldn't be together." She gave him the answer most innocents would.

"To be sure, the maid Asa lost her heart to Rhun. She is said to have been vivacious and lively. She would have fallen hard." Darroc started pacing again, wishing he hadn't mentioned the long-dead blackguard. "Rhun loved only himself. The thrill of conquest. He certainly didn't love his wife. I doubt Asa ever knew the poor woman existed. Leastways not until it was too late and the Thunder Rod—"

"He ruined a young girl and betrayed his lady wife?" Lady Arabella's brows drew together.

"Aye, he—"

"You cannot blame his villainies on a piece of wood!"

"Not *a piece of wood*. We speak of the Thunder Rod."

"I say we are speaking of a scoundrel." She tilted her head, her eyes taking on a glint that could only be called dangerous.

Darroc frowned.

She *was* a Valkyrie.

And this wasn't going as he'd intended.

Somewhere between "Saints, Maria, and Joseph" and Rhun the Insatiable, he'd lost control. Lady Arabella was seizing the reins and he didn't like where she was taking him. He'd meant to frighten her into having done with any romantic fancies, not turn her into an avenging angel for women who'd breathed their last centuries ago.

"I ne'er said he wasn't a scoundrel." Darroc went to stand at the window again, needing the chill night air on the back of his neck.

It was afire again.

And even worse than before.

Lady Arabella would be the end of him. He was falling apart already. Sakes, a muscle even jerked in his jaw! Hoping she hadn't seen, he leaned back against the window arch and crossed his arms.

"Rhun the Insatiable was worse than a scoundrel." He felt anger well in his chest. "Disregarding the honor he owed his host and forgetting his lady wife, he seduced young Asa behind her father's back. Unaware of Rhun's treachery, yet noting his appreciation of women, Gunnar presented him with a rare and special gift to seal their trade agreement."

Lady Arabella was sitting ramrod straight now. "The gift was the thunder rod."

"Indeed." Darroc watched her as he spoke. "As you will see, the rod does influence. Because Gunnar trusted in his daughter's virtue he sent her to retrieve the gift and present it to their guest. He surely believed her beauty would enhance the grand moment."

Darroc left out that the maid must've handled the rod in an unseemly manner in order to unleash its unholy power over women. Lady Arabella needn't know he suspected that, having tasted passion in Rhun's arms, Asa hadn't been able to resist running her fingers up and down the rod's smooth, manlike length when she'd gone to fetch it.

Sadly, caressing the rod so sinuously doomed her.

Lady Arabella glanced across the room, her gaze resting on Frang's pallet. The shaggy beast had returned. As had the wee she-dog Mina, who once again curled atop Frang's pile of tatty old plaids.

Frang sat watching them, his eyes unblinking.

Darroc lifted a hand and rubbed the back of his neck. For two pins, he'd swear the dog knew exactly what they were talking about.

"What happened then?" Lady Arabella was looking at him again, a line marring her brow. "Did Rhun"—she left off the by-name—"accept the rod?"

"You know he did." Darroc wished he could undo what came next. "But the damage was done, regardless. The Thunder Rod worked its evil on them both. Asa was so consumed by desire for Rhun that she vowed she couldn't live without him and determined to steal away on his ship when he sailed for his home."

"Which she did." The line creasing Lady Arabella's brow deepened.

"Aye." Darroc nodded. "She hid herself on Rhun's galley and didn't come out until Shetland had fallen well below the horizon. Rhun took full advantage. Asa Long-Legs, you see, was said to have been a great and alluring beauty. Few men would have been able to withstand her charms.

"Many heated nights were spent on that southbound journey. Then—"

"Rhun remembered his wife." Lady Arabella was frowning in earnest now.

Darroc made a note to never underestimate her.

She had to be the sharpest maid he'd ever met.

"You are deep-seeing, Arabella of Kintail." He gave honor where it was due. "Rhun did indeed recall his domestic duty. His earliest wealth, after all, had come with the dowry of his wife. Tradition says he remembered her—and how watchful she was—as soon as the Western Highlands loomed into view. So he took the precaution of leaving Asa with Hebridean friends, claiming he would build her a castle of her own and return for her when it was completed."

"That castle was this one, right?" Lady Arabella pulled a cushion onto her lap. She dug her elegant fingers into its plumpness. "Castle Bane."

"So it was, aye." There was no need to lie.

She didn't even blink.

"Rhun looked far and wide, finally deeming this isle remote and lonely enough for his purposes." Darroc glanced over his shoulder at the sea. The moon had risen and its silvery light gilded the night-blackened waters.

"Rhun called the isle his own and as soon as Castle Bane stood, he retrieved Asa, telling his friends he was returning her to Shetland. Instead, he settled her in their own private love lair."

"He *was* evil." That sapphire gaze still pinned him. "A true—"

"He was worse." Darroc held up a hand to silence her. "And he soon learned that the Thunder Rod held more power than simply making a man irresistible to women. Perhaps the darkness of his own soul unleashed the relic's blacker influences. Either way, the couple only enjoyed their haven for a short time."

"He tired of Asa?"

"Och, nae." Darroc looked down at the sea again, frowning. "He died. As arrogantly brazen in war as he was with women, he'd become embroiled in a friend's clan feuding and lost his life to a festered battle wound. He breathed his last far from Asa's embrace, dying beneath the cold stare of his wronged lady wife. A great tragedy for the young Norsewoman, because the need for secrecy saw the doom of the men Rhun had employed to build his hideaway keep."

Lady Arabella stared at him in horror. "What are you saying?"

"You can't guess?"

She shook her head, one hand pressed to her lips.

Near the hearth, Frang slumped down onto the rushes with a groan. Almost as if he knew what was coming.

Darroc wished he didn't. "It is said that Rhun threw the castle builders over the cliffs. The men had sworn to keep silent, but Rhun preferred certainty."

"And Asa?" The words were a shocked whisper.

"Asa…" Darroc hated this part. "No one knew of her existence."

"You mean…"

"She spent her remaining days trapped here." Darroc's heart squeezed at the thought. "The saints only know what it must've been like. I've always tried not to imagine. If she cried out to any passing galleys, trying to summon help, the men onboard might have mistaken her for a ghost. They would have feared taking a closer look."

Lady Arabella sighed. "And then she was a ghost."

"Perhaps." Darroc steeled himself against the telltale glistening in her eyes. "Clan elders claim it was her mournful wailing that assured no MacConacher would ever dwell in these sorrow-drenched walls."

Lady Arabella gasped.

Then she shivered and drew his plaid more tightly around her shoulders. Even worse, she shook her head sadly, releasing one of the tears clinging to her eyelashes. It spilled down her cheek and dripped onto Darroc's plaid.

Watching, he clenched his fists and turned back around to face the window. If he kept looking at her—seeing her sympathy—he might blurt out just why MacConachers had returned to Castle Bane.

And that was a tale he did not want to share with her.

It involved, after all, her own grandfather.

And his.

Chapter Ten

❖

Half certain he could feel the glowers of both men—MacConacher and MacKenzie—Darroc remained at the window and glared down at the sea-washed rocks beneath the tower. White with spume, they still managed to look black as death. His jaw set grimly on the thought. It was, after all, more than appropriate.

There were few men who'd brought about the ends of so many lives.

Darroc blew out a breath. Rock-glaring wasn't making him feel better. Far from it; his hands clenched and he almost wished he'd had a different grandsire. It would certainly be a boon if Arabella of Kintail did. But all the regretful musings in the world wouldn't change her blood.

Or his.

He stepped closer to the window arch, needing to put more distance between himself and her powerfully alluring presence in his bed.

As if she knew, she kept silent behind him. But he felt her stare pinning him. Not that he was about to wheel around and catch her at it. From her rustlings, she was no doubt dabbing at her eyes, still grieved over Asa Long-Legs's tragic plight.

Frowning, Darroc hunched his shoulders against the night's cold. But he straightened as quickly, too proud to show any sign of weakness.

Not before a MacKenzie.

And with surety not in front of a female of that ilk.

He did keep his gaze on the rocks, unable to look away as sea foam repeatedly wreathed the jagged crests. Again and again the glistening spume appeared and disappeared, almost seeming to mock him.

His grandfather and Lady Arabella's were long gone, but the skerries and their ever-present spray were still there and always would be. Such permanency could fill a romantic soul with yearning. Offering promises of something so tempting and so impossible to achieve, yet—just now—seeming close enough to touch.

If he was of a mind to reach for it.

Not it, but her.

Darroc's brows snapped together in a fierce scowl.

Had such a notion truly crossed his mind?

It had, and the truth of his attraction to the lass galled him to the bone. His stomach even knotted and despite the night's cold, brittle air, he could feel tiny beads of damp forming on his brow.

She slept now, he was sure. He could hear her soft, steady breaths. And—devil curse him—in his mind's eye he saw her standing beside him, her face turned to the wind and her midnight hair swirling about her hips. Moon glow would gild her smooth, creamy skin and her scent, fresh, light, and wholly her own, would enchant him. Her magnificent breasts...

"Damnation!" Pushing her from his thoughts, he stared fixedly at the rocks and willed himself to think again of Asa Long-Legs.

Doing so would keep his mind off things he had no business glomming about. Better to dwell on a tragedy no one could undo than risk unleashing a new one. He had no doubt that Arabella MacKenzie could plunge his clan into a disaster worse than any they'd yet seen.

If he heeded his damnable desires.

It would be so easy to turn around and take a step in her direction.

Forget clan honor and vengeance and...

Nae! Everything inside him—all that he was—roared denial. He could feel his mouth turning down, his face contorting with the pain of a soul rent in two. Some things mattered more than a fetching female's well-turned ankle and sparkling sapphire eyes.

And there was nothing wrong with him save how long it'd been since he'd last aired a woman's skirts. On his next supply run to Glasgow, he'd sample the charms of not one but at least three tavern wenches.

Oddly, the notion didn't bring the anticipatory twitch that it should have.

Indeed, the thought left him cold, desiring only the one maid that he couldn't possibly make his own.

So he went back to scowling at the sea, this time imagining Asa Long-Legs standing at her window centuries ago, doing the same. His innards twisted to think of her staring out at such a dark, lonely world with only the night wind to greet her.

Or perhaps the haunting song of the seals.

Darroc shuddered.

He hadn't forgotten how the seals had gathered just before the wreck of the *Merry Dancer*.

There was one down there now.

A lone seal.

The smallish creature wasn't bobbing in the waves or even sprawled across one of the skerries, but sat on a jumble of seaweed-strewn rocks on the shore.

Darroc leaned out the window to get a better look. Then he dropped his jaw when he saw that the seal's coat wasn't gray or black or even a mottled combination of the two. This animal had glossy red fur and a plumed, white-tipped tail.

The *seal* was a little red fox.

Sure he was seeing things—for he hadn't believed Mungo's tales of a fox in Castle Bane's bailey—he blinked and the creature vanished.

Or so he thought, for the wee beastie appeared again as quickly, now strutting along the boat strand. He appeared to examine the hulls of the fishing cobles and other craft beached there.

Darroc watched, his heart thundering.

The fox turned and stared back at him, the creature's handsome brush twitching proudly before he returned to sniffing the boats.

No doubt he smelled fish.

Still, there was something strange about him.

His yellow-gold eyes glowed with an otherworldly light. They also looked oddly intelligent. Darroc could tell even at a distance.

"Saints, Maria, and Joseph!" He forgot himself and used the Black Stag's oath.

The fox kept trotting down the strand, moving from boat to boat.

And then he was gone.

Disappearing as if he'd never been there, live as the day and right beneath Darroc's nose.

He shook his head, disbelieving.

He'd imagined the creature.

Or—saints forbid—he was going mad.

He shoved a hand through his hair, frowning. Next he'd see real seals wearing necklaces of ringing bells. He hadn't forgotten them either. Or perhaps the fox would return and join in the seals' eerie serenade.

He was beginning to believe anything was possible.

The only thing crazier would be to remain in Arabella of Kintail's presence a moment longer. If he did, he'd cross the room, gather her in his arms, and wake her. Then he'd kiss her again.

Kiss her in a way that would damn him more than the power of a thousand Thunder Rods.

Not wanting that to happen, he spun away from the window and strode from the room as quickly as his dignity would allow. And as he stomped down the tower stairs, bound for his makeshift bed in the hall, he knew one thing.

He wasn't mad.

He was wise.

And in his great wisdom, he'd do what he could to protect his clan from disaster. There really wasn't a choice in the matter. His hands were tied and his options limited, carved in stone many years before. It was a fate

written with the blood of his kin and—to a Highlander—
family and clan were more important than the air they
breathed.

Arabella of Kintail was the enemy.

And he meant to steer well clear of her.

Anything else was too dangerous.

A sennight later, Duncan MacKenzie swept into his wife's
ladies solar, not bothering to shut the door behind him.
His entrance made the wall tapestries flutter and almost
gutted several candles. He halted in the room's center, his
face dark and his hands fisted. His expression was fierce.
Some might even say murderous.

He didn't bother to rein in his temper.

Enough was enough.

But he did come close to roaring when his wrath pro-
voked no more than an arched brow from his lady wife,
Linnet.

She above all others should know what riled him.

For seven days three well-supplied, fully armed and
ready-to-launch galleys lay beached on his boat strand,
empty. There wasn't a man left at Eilean Creag with the
strength to shove the craft into the water. And there were
even fewer men who'd be able to hoist the sails and ply the
oars. They'd all fallen mysteriously ill.

Duncan's scowl blackened at the unfairness of it.

His patience was frayed beyond repair.

"'Fore God!" He glared at his wife, his deep voice
echoing in the tiny room. "If I hear another cough, sneeze,
or wheeze, I shall cure the fevering bastards by tossing
them into the loch. Naked!"

"Duncan..." Linnet looked at him from where she

sat on a low stool before the fire. "They cannot help that they've caught the ague."

"*The ague*?" He flashed a glance at the open door, scowling. "They're going on as if they have the poxy plague! Lying about, tossing on their pallets and moaning—"

"You shouldn't jest about the plague." Linnet pushed to her feet. "You—"

"Jest?" Duncan began to pace. "Think you I'm jesting? If it isn't that wretched malaise, why did they succumb the very night before we were to set out for MacConacher's Isle? And the whole bluidy lot of them?"

"It isn't the pox." Linnet's voice was calm as always. "They've simply—"

"Cursed is what they are!" Duncan snatched his wife's herb bag off a trestle bench and shook the bulging pouch at her. "Your wood sorrel tincture and oat gruel aren't helping them. Someone's bespelled us and is trying to keep us here. Someone who doesn't want me adding a fine row of spiked MacConacher heads to my curtain walls!"

"You don't know what you're saying." Linnet laid a hand on his arm, trying to soothe.

He jerked free. "I say it was him. Marmaduke. That's why I haven't been troubled like the rest of my men. No hacking coughs and fevering for me. The sly Sassunach wastrel wants me full by my wits so I'm aware of each day that passes. Every hour that keeps us from setting forth to rescue Arabella and—"

"Sir Marmaduke would never do such a thing. And Arabella is rescued." Linnet gripped his arm again, squeezing this time. "I've told you everything I saw. All of it, as well you know."

Duncan clamped his mouth shut. What she'd told him didn't bear dwelling on. He certainly wasn't going to discuss it. Not this night, not ever. Their last attempt to speak of Arabella in MacConacher hands had soured his mood and ruined his appetite for days.

"I told you"—his wife seemed to have forgotten—"the man and the old woman were treating her kindly. No harm has or will come to her."

"She's already been harmed!"

"You know what I meant."

Duncan pretended he didn't know. Belligerence suited him just now.

Linnet sighed and released his arm. "The gods work in strange ways. The MacConachers are the last clan we're at odds with. Perhaps it is time—"

"We're more than at odds with the hell-fiends." Duncan stalked to a window and threw open the shutters, needing air. "Every last hill in Scotland will sink into the sea before I'd allow Arabella to wed a MacConacher."

"I never said the man I saw would be her husband."

Duncan snorted. "You didn't have to." He flashed a heated glance at her. "It's writ all o'er you."

She had the good grace to flush. "The man I saw loves her."

"If he's a MacConacher, he'll regret it!" Duncan tossed back his hair, furious.

"I was born a MacDonnell." His wife's words jabbed a vulnerable place. "Our clans feuded bitterly. Truth tell, if I recall"—she joined him at the window—"that was the reason you wished to wed me. Leastways it was one of them."

She smiled up at him and something inside him softened. "I would say we've made a good match."

"The best." Duncan swallowed against a sudden and most inconvenient thickness in his throat. "Your clan were naught more than unruly cattle thieves," he argued, wishing she could see why this with Arabella was different.

"The MacConachers are shifty, fork-tongued murderers." His outrage vanquished the lump in his throat. "They—"

"They are perhaps the final clan we must seek peace with." She slid an arm around his waist, leaning into him. He scowled, trying not to notice the soft, feminine warmth of her, so familiar and dear.

"I will not argue my father's...ills." She peered up at him, her gaze unwavering. "Though I'm sure you'll agree my brothers serve you well as allies. Life has been good to us. Our children are now having their own. Would you not see those bairns born into a world without blood foes? Is not peace the greatest legacy we can give them?"

"The MacConachers will learn the peace of my steel." Duncan wouldn't concede.

Clans were made for warring.

As if she'd read his thoughts, she stepped back and returned to her stool by the fire. She clasped her hands in her lap and held her back straight. The angle of her jaw could only be called peeved.

Duncan frowned.

For some ridiculous reason, he felt chastised.

Make peace with their last feuding clan!

Hah! What he should do was throw back his head and roar with laughter. He would have, too, if he weren't so

worried about his daughter. And—he couldn't deny it—
the possibility that his wife was right.

She usually was.

Saints help him.

That same evening, Darroc flattened his back against the
cold stony curve of Castle Bane's stair tower. He stood
only a few winding steps above the arched entry to the
great hall. And he was doing his best not to inhale too
deeply. He did splay his fingers across the chill damp of
the wall. If he couldn't stop his breathing or the pounding
of his heart, he could hunker here, unmoving.

Strange things had been going on in his keep and duty
gave him no choice but to get to the bottom of it.

He resisted the urge to snort.

Nae, to laugh.

There were surely not many chieftains who'd hide in
their own turnpike stairs because the table linens in his
great hall were disappearing. But it wasn't just the missing linens that bothered him.

His men had turned sneaky of late.

And even though a fierce wind howled around the
keep, keening like a banshee, his men's gleeful voices
had carried up to him as soon as he'd set foot in the stair
tower. One hoot in particular was especially suspicious as
he was sure the gloating burst of laughter had come from
Mungo.

Everyone knew the crabbit old seneschal wasn't given
to bouts of hilarity.

If the truth were known, Darroc sometimes suspected
that Mungo had been born cranky. He'd certainly worn
dark enough scowls during the first weeks since they'd

plucked Lady Arabella from the sea. Indeed, if he cornered Darroc one more time with another outlandish suggestion as to how they could use her to knock the wind from Clan MacKenzie, he didn't want to be responsible for his reaction.

Several others had been equally annoying.

One or two, downright noxious.

Especially the first evening Mad Moraig helped the lass into the great hall for supper. Each man had slunk away, leaving empty tables and filled trenchers. Their ale cups brimming and untouched. The slight—to a lady, even of an enemy clan—had been unforgivable.

Yet now...

Darroc frowned.

Slowly, very slowly, he inched his way down onto the next step. The night wind screamed and a blast of frosty air rushed in through a narrow slit window, blowing his hair across his eyes.

He swallowed a curse.

Then he crept down one more step—the last—and edged along in the shadows, making for the arched entry into the great hall. Unfortunately, somewhere along the way he stepped on a discarded chicken bone and the ensuing *crack* sounded louder than the roar of the wind.

Inside the torchlit, smoke-hazed hall, his men's hoots and blether stopped at once.

Silence reigned.

Triumph shot through Darroc.

They *were* guilty.

Sure of it, he leapt around the corner and into the hall. At once, there came a wild scramble as his men hurried to claim seats at trestle benches or appear otherwise occupied. Only Mungo didn't move. Standing closest to the archway, he chose instead to hook his thumbs in his belt and—much to Darroc's amusement—swell his barrel chest.

"It's yourself, Darroc!" Mungo greeted him cheerily.

"Aye." Darroc lifted his hands and turned them palms up, looking down at them as if to confirm his identity. "I am myself."

Mungo slid a cagey glance at the high table. "Geordie Dhu's outdone himself this night. Fine leg o' mutton roasted all day out in the stone pit in the kitchen garden, just as you like it best. Meat's so tender it falls off the bone!"

Darroc folded his arms. "I'm no' hungry."

He *had* noticed that the high table lacked linens. It was the last table to lose its costly covering. The napery on the other two tables on the dais had gone missing three nights before.

"Where are the table linens?" Darroc looked the seneschal in the eye.

"Geordie Dhu made a grand sauce for the mutton." Mungo didn't even blink. "Wine and broth laced with just the right touch o' spices."

"And the linens?" Darroc cocked a brow.

Mungo remained where he stood, trying to appear innocent. "Linens?"

Darroc didn't bother with an answer.

He did glance around the hall, raking the other men with a narrow-eyed stare. Clearly guilty, they immediately scratched elbows, peered into ale cups, or dug energetically into their evening meat.

Darroc turned back to Mungo. "No' going to badger

me about ransoming the lass?" He tried another tactic. "No more talk of turning her over to slavering, flat-footed Campbells? Or setting her out on the Glasgow docks, abandoning her to her fate?"

Mungo coughed. "Och! That was just my tongue flapping. Though"—he exchanged a look with the men nearest to them—"I wouldn't be for shunning a bit o' sword crossing with the maid's father!"

"I seem to recall you saying we should take a blade to her." Darroc arched a brow. "What was it now? That if I wouldn't ransom her, having done with her would save us the cost of feeding her?"

Mungo clamped his jaw, silent.

He still hadn't budged. And the look in his one good eye said he wasn't going to, either. Some might even say he was deliberately blocking Darroc's way.

Having none of that—this was, after all, *his* hall— Darroc started to stomp around him. But he stopped after only two steps. There was more wrong here than he'd realized.

Sniffing the air, he knew what it was.

Mungo stank.

Or rather, he smelled like he'd been bathing in gillyflowers.

Darroc sniffed again, sure of it.

Mungo jutted his chin, defiant.

Darroc jammed his hands on his hips and stared at the old goat. He just now noticed that Mungo's salt-and-pepper hair was sleeked back, neat and shining damply. Mungo had recently washed and trimmed his usually wild mane.

His bushy gray beard glistened.

The beard had definitely seen the tines of a comb.

"What goes on here?" Darroc looked around again. He wasn't surprised when no one met his eye.

Then, from the smoky haze at the rear of the hall—just where the lighting was poor enough so that he couldn't make out faces—someone slapped a hand on the table and cleared their throat.

"Could be Mad Moraig was for boiling the linens."

Darroc scrunched his eyes. He tried to see who'd spoken. All around him, men bobbed heads and grunted in agreement with the deep voice.

"Aye," someone else called out, "that's the way of it. Mad Moraig collected the linens for washing."

Darroc grinned.

He'd never heard a greater pack of lies. Then, before he could stop himself, an always-just-below-the-surface touch of Highland mischief made him turn back to Mungo.

Still grinning, he reached to tweak a fold of the seneschal's plaid.

"And was Moraig also for boiling a few plaids?" He rubbed the squeaky clean wool between his fingers.

The sweet scent of gillyflowers was overpowering.

Equally telling, the most-times generously draped plaid now stretched tightly across Mungo's hunched but proudly held shoulders.

Mad Moraig knew better than to boil wool.

The flush on Mungo's face said he knew it.

Satisfied, Darroc let go of the shrunken plaid and stepped back. "There are extra plaids in the strongbox in my thinking room," he announced, striding toward the hall's raised dais and the now naked high table. "Anyone who might

need a better-fitting plaid can help themselves. And"—he
reached the table and dropped into his high-backed laird's
chair—"the next time you wish to make yourselves pretty, I
suggest you let Moraig do the washing."

At the other end of the high table, Conall nearly choked
on his ale. The other men crowding the long table looked
at each other.

"For sure, Mad Moraig does the laundering," two of
them said in unison. "None o' us would dare touch such
women's work."

Too bad for them, their stretched-tight plaids belied
their words.

"So I see." Darroc eyed the men until they squirmed.

Then he helped himself to several spoonfuls of green
cheese. The soft curd cheese, freshly made, and—thanks
to Geordie Dhu's mastery—delicately flavored with herbs,
was all that he could stomach.

He had a very good idea just who was behind his
men's antics and the possibility sat in his gut like a stone.
The devil was riding his back as well, so he set down his
cheese spoon and stared down the table, fixing Conall
with the most congenial look he could manage.

"And you?" His voice was surprisingly pleasant.
"Has...er, ah...Moraig been washing your plaid, too?"

Darroc smiled wickedly.

He could already see that Conall's plaid hadn't been
laundered in a while.

"Errr..." Conall busied himself tucking into the generous helping of roast mutton on his trencher. "My plaid
doesn't need cleaning."

Darroc disagreed, but now wasn't the time to argue
over clan cleanliness.

Instead, he grinned and lifted his ale cup in silent toast to his cousin. As was to be expected, the younger man's face flamed as bright as his coppery red hair.

Hair that gleamed more than usual and—Darroc couldn't help but notice—smelled distinctly of gilly-flowers.

Just to needle his cousin, Darroc wrinkled his nose.

Then he looked around the dais, taking care to keep his nose twitching. "Can it be someone has brought flowers into the hall? I'm sure I smell some . . . ?"

He let the words tail off and sat back with a look of mock confusion.

Several of his men sniggered.

Conall shifted on the trestle bench. "Goad kens!" His burr deepened in his agitation. "D'you think I'd be washing my own heid with women's soap? Moraig did it a-purpose, I swear! We asked her for some o' her sage-and-rosemary washing soap and she gave us a jar o' her own!"

"Ahhhh." Darroc sat back with a satisfied sigh. "At last, we're getting to the heart of the matter. Perhaps"—he folded his arms—"one of you will now also reveal the whereabouts of the table linens?"

Several sets of bushy gray brows drew together and more than a few bearded chins jutted stubbornly.

No one spoke.

Darroc shrugged good-naturedly. Then he leaned forward to spoon up more of Geordie Dhu's herbed green cheese.

"I'll tell you myself where the linens are." Mad Moraig appeared at his elbow, a platter of fresh-baked oatcakes clutched in her hands.

She plunked down the griddle-hot oatcakes and a waft of fine wheaten bread filled the air, the pleasing aroma rising up from her flour-dusted skirts like a cloud.

Only there wasn't a single loaf of fine wheaten bread in the entire hall.

Darroc's mood soured.

The recriminatory look Moraig shot at him as she straightened let him know he'd guessed right as to who was dining so royally.

"You haven't been to look in on the lassie in well o'er a sennight." Moraig's voice rang with disapproval. "She be up and walking more by the day. It isn't decent to have her clad in naught but your plaids and shirts. So"—she put back her bony shoulders—"I took it on myself to take her sewing linens. We're—"

"You mean the table linens." A corner of Darroc's mouth twitched despite himself.

He also felt guilty.

He should have offered her the linens. It was already clear that she could work wonders with a stitching needle. If only her name weren't such a scald on his soul, he would have thought of it himself.

As it was, he frowned.

Moraig sniffed importantly. "We're making her a few gowns, we are. Soon she'll be able to join us in the hall every night. She's making fine progress."

"Indeed." Darroc reached for his ale cup. "I am glad to hear it."

The sooner she recovered, the sooner he'd be rid of her.

Moraig glanced at him sharply, as if she'd heard. But then she preened and dusted her skirts. Little puffs of fine white wheaten flour swirled around her, making her look like a tiny, wizened sprite caught in a snowstorm.

Her blue eyes twinkled. "She's a fine lassie," she quipped, then turned and hobbled away.

"Ach, she's a fine one, right enough." Mungo took his seat at the table, the set of his hunched shoulders warning anyone who might question his changed attitude.

"Did you know"—he leaned around his bench mate to pin Darroc with an assertive stare—"word is the best man to e'er grace her father's garrison was a one-eyed Sassunach?"

Mungo looked around the table, his own single eye sparking with pride. "Sir Marmaduke is the man's name and he now lords it at his own keep, Balkenzie Castle, on the southern shores of Loch Duich!"

"Imagine that." Darroc set down his ale cup, untouched.

Now he knew why the seneschal was sporting a boiled plaid and reeked of perfumed soap.

He'd had his head turned.

Just like Moraig, Geordie Dhu, Frang, and all the rest. Flattery by a honey-tongued, sapphire-eyed she-vixen had made them forget honor and pride.

The weal of the clan.

Vengeance.

Darroc pushed aside his serving of oatcakes and green cheese.

His appetite had fled.

Mungo shoved up his sleeves and reached for the platter of roasted mutton, piling great slabs onto his trencher. "Word is"—he spooned rivers of sauce over his meat—"the lass was heading for the Seal Isles. She told Mora—"

"*The Seal Isles*?" Darroc stared at him.

The stone he'd felt in his gut was suddenly joined by several friends.

An entire rockslide was now rumbling around inside him.

Mungo stabbed a piece of mutton with his eating knife. "Aye, so I said, just." He dipped the meat into the rich gravy. "Moraig says the isles are part of the gel's dowry. She was on her way to see them when the merchant cog was attacked."

Darroc forced himself to nod pleasantly.

In truth, his world was spinning.

He'd known she had something to do with seals!

But that wasn't what made his mood go from bad to worse. It was the mention of a dowry. Heiresses had dowries for only one reason and although he knew she was bound to have one—and a right impressive one, no doubt—it didn't sit well to think of her as some man's soon-to-be bride.

In fact, the idea quite galled him.

Needing to get his mind on something else, he decided to poke a bit more fun at Conall about his flowery-scented hair. But when he drew himself up and peered down the table, he saw that his cousin was gone.

Or rather, he'd left the table.

He was still in view.

Barely, considering how he was skulking along in the shadows at the far end of the hall. And he wasn't just skulking. He was crouching over something large and unwieldy that he clutched in his arms.

Pushing to his feet, Darroc strode to the end of the dais and stood watching his cousin's awkward progress through the hall. Conall was making for the stair tower and it wasn't until he passed beneath a well-burning torch that Darroc saw what he was carrying.

It was a creel.

A laundry creel if Darroc wasn't mistaken.

And it appeared to be filled with white linen.

Darroc started to hasten after him, but stopped just a few paces beyond the dais steps. He already knew where Conall was taking the table linens and if he stopped the lad, his entire clan would make him feel like a heartless dastard.

That was the sad way of it.

So he returned to his place at the high table and pretended he'd only wished to stretch his legs.

Besides, it would have been a mistake to confront Conall. And an even worse disaster if he'd followed the lad to Arabella's room. He'd been avoiding her all these days and was doing fine without her.

But when he reached again for his wooden plate of oatcakes and green cheese, he knew that wasn't true.

He wasn't fine.

He missed her.

Chapter Eleven

✦

The wrong man loomed in the doorway when Arabella turned from the bedchamber window to see who she'd just bid welcome to enter. She stared, though she shouldn't have been surprised. In truth, she'd expected him. She certainly couldn't blame him for the squeezing pain in her chest. Or how her pulse had leapt only to slow again the instant she'd seen him. He couldn't help any of those things. Indeed, he simply hovered on the threshold, the image of innocence.

Arabella smiled at him, her heart freezing.

He grinned, his face friendly as summer sunshine. Warmth poured off him, gentle and kind.

Even so, she had to fight not to show her disappointment. She'd so hoped the knock had been Darroc. He'd been avoiding her, she knew. Each hour rode heavy on her shoulders, bearing down on her and seeping into her substance. Then the rapping on the door had sounded so strong and confident. She'd been sure it was him. But the young man with coppery red hair and lively blue eyes was Conall, his cousin.

The one with the fire-scarred arms.

Shame pinched Arabella when, seeing those arms now, she remembered how he'd frightened her when he'd helped rescue her from the barrel raft. In her dazed state, she'd thought he was a man of flame, come straight from the pits of hell to seize and take her there.

Now she knew he was one of the most gallant men at Castle Bane. One of the few who hadn't slid cold dark looks at her when she'd first started making brief visits to the hall. Ever cheerful, he'd faithfully brought her dinner trays, with Moraig often trailing on his heels, eager to help.

This time he'd come alone.

And instead of her evening meal, he clutched a large wicker creel that she knew held the table linens Moraig had promised her.

Linens she could use to make a decent gown.

"Here they are, the linen goods, fresh and laundered." He confirmed as he came into the room and plunked the creel on the floor near the window. "Moraig tucked a small bag into the basket. It holds her sewing needles and better thread. She'll surely be looking in on you later, wanting to help."

He straightened and dusted his hands. "I can find something to keep her busy until you're done," he volunteered, a pink tinge staining his cheeks. "It's no trouble if you prefer. She'd have no need to know."

"But I would." Arabella smoothed the front of Darroc's borrowed shirt and his plaid, the latter wrapped several times around her like a great tartan skirt.

An overlarge, ill-fitting skirt she'd no doubt have had to wear for weeks if not for Moraig's kindhearted suggestion that they stitch her some gowns from the keep's store of fine linens and napery.

Moraig's own prized collection of ribbons.

Arabella's stomach knotted to think how the light would fade from the old woman's eyes if she stitched the gowns without her assistance.

"I do not mind Moraig's help." She saw no point in lying. "I can fix whatever harm she does. I'll enjoy her company."

"You're sure?" He looked skeptical.

She nodded. "I'm not used to being alone. Eilean Creag— my home—is a busy place. Moraig's visits are welcome."

She didn't say that his were, too.

Young as he was, she knew he'd crimson if she did.

He did blink, looking unconvinced. Night wind pouring in the window teased his bright hair. For some reason, the effect of those dancing red-gold strands made her think of some braw Celtic god standing proud on a clifftop. She could see Conall as an avenging deity. Ancient, bold, and ready to challenge the elements and anything else in order to see the innocent protected.

Just now, she was the innocent.

But some of her thoughts about Darroc—especially his kiss—were quite wicked. So brazen and scandalous that her sister would toss back her head and laugh with glee if she knew. Their father, if he knew—saints forbid—would lose sleep for a year, she was sure.

As it was, a certain place she couldn't think about without blushing, clenched tight and began to tingle hotly. The same thing happened every time she relived Darroc's kiss and imagined what it would feel like to have him slide his mouth down her naked skin, moving slowly lower and lower.

Until...

Mortified, she gasped. Devil blast Gelis for telling her about such things. And triple damn her own self for the question burning like pepper on her tongue.

"Where is Darroc?" Her pepper-laced tongue betrayed her. "I haven't seen him in so long."

Then, a terrible thought came to her.

She stepped forward, touching light fingers to Conall's well-muscled but ravished arm. "He does know about the linens? He isn't angry at their loss?" She lowered her hand, no longer at all sure of herself. "I'll see they're replaced, you may assure him."

"Ach! He'll no' be letting you do that." He turned to face the window. The tides were running fast and a thin crescent moon rode high above the horizon. Brilliant stars glittered everywhere, dazzling against the night's blackness. "None of us will allow you to replace the linens."

He glanced at her, quickly. "Darroc knows you canna be running around as you're dressed now."

"But where is he?" She could've bit her tongue.

Instead, she continued to look out the window. The stars twinkled as brightly on the night-darkened water as they did in the heavens. Almost as if the whole of the sea sparkled with dancing fairy lights.

It was a night made for lovers.

Her face flamed and she laced her fingers together, grateful that Conall seemed as entranced by the night's beauty as she was.

Something told her he had a poet's soul.

"Darroc is...er..." His inability to finish the sentence proved his sensitivity.

But that didn't stop her from shaming herself. "I know he's avoiding me."

"Ah...." He looked down. He appeared to have a deep and sudden interest in the waves creaming over the rocks beneath the tower. "It isn't you, my lady."

"Then why hasn't he been to see me?" There was no point in backing down. "He stopped in often during my first days here."

"Aye, well." He kept his gaze on the rocks. "He has much on his mind, see you? He intends to go after the Black Vikings. There have always been tales about them, but never proof. Not until—"

"You rescued me."

"So it is, aye." He nodded grimly. "But there's more to it than that. There are men—good, strong fighting men—that we call friends and who Darroc believes will join us. Together, we can chase them from our seas. But if we wish to do so in fullest strength...."

He paused to stare up at the stars. "Such a foray will cost many sillers and"—he inhaled deeply—"Darroc is no prideless man to leave such things to others. Yet our coffers are none too full of late. Not long before we...er...found you, we fair scraped the barrel to build a new warring birlinn and Darroc has been wearing a track in the rushes of his thinking room e'er since.

"That's where he's been, my lady." He glanced at her, looking embarrassed. "More like, he's there now. Pacing and thinking, all else far from his mind."

Arabella's brow knit. "I see."

She felt a rush of guilt because her own purse had always been heavy. Her father might have ruined her chances of winning a bonny suitor's heart, but he'd been open-handed with his wealth.

Still...

Something wasn't right.

"My father has many friends in the Isles." She blurted what was puzzling her. "Some have jested about how much timber washes onto their shores. They claimed never to spend a siller on lumber for their galleys. They—"

"They weren't boasting." Conall drew himself up, the inherent pride shared by all Highlanders making him seem even taller. "We, too, have used such strand-ware. But we ne'er touch wood from a foundered ship. And we only use shore-found wood to build fishing cobles and the like."

He looked at her, his eyes glinting in the starlight. "Our new birlinn is different. It's what the early MacDonald Lords of the Isles called a *nyvaig*. Such little ships have the greatest maneuverability. They fly across the waves and can wheel about in the wink of an eye. And"—his chest swelled—"with the birlinn's high stern and raised fighting deck, we can win any sea battle. But that isn't why she was so dear. That was because we built her of wood from Nairn on the distant Moray Firth. The wood—"

"Nairn?" Arabella blinked.

Conall's head bobbed.

His confirmation confused her. She'd thought she'd misheard the name Nairn. She'd never been to the little burgh but knew it to be near the market town of Inverness. She also knew there was a deep wood at Nairn. It was called Culbin or something similar, if she recalled rightly.

Even so, Nairn was a long and difficult journey from Kintail. From MacConachers' Isle, the wee bit place might as well perch on the edge of the world.

Arabella frowned. She wouldn't have thought Darroc so unpractical. There were other, equally fine forests stretching along Scotland's mainland coast.

"I don't understand." She spoke softly, not wanting to offend. "Couldn't the wood have been bought elsewhere? Argyll's shores have many forests and—"

"Nae." Conall shook his head. "It had to be Nairn timber. Darroc would settle for no other. The trees on Nairn's coast are special."

"Special?" Arabella struggled to keep her brows from arcing.

Conall looked serious. "Aye, so many seafarers claim."

"Why?" She didn't want to pry, but growing up with a stars-in-her-eyes sister ready to swallow any tale of wonder, made her wary of anything that even smacked of magic.

She looked at Conall, waiting.

He didn't answer.

His attention was once again on the long, white-capped rollers smashing into the rocks below the window.

Arabella couldn't quite suppress a sigh.

"Please, I must know." Curiosity was one of her greatest faults. "What makes a boat built of Nairn wood different from another?"

He flushed and shuffled his feet.

She waited.

"I've already said more than I should have." He spoke at last.

"Then perhaps you shouldn't have mentioned the birlinn at all?" Was that her voice?

Arabella cringed. Faith, but she'd sounded shrewish.

Even Frang and Mina turned recriminatory stares on her. She could feel their displeasure from across the room where they reposed on the bed, their two sets of canine eyes steady and unblinking.

She ignored them and inhaled deeply.

Then she did what she had to do. "I'm sorry, Conall. I shouldn't—"

"No apologies needed. The tale does sound like a tall one, eh?" He turned to her, ever the gallant. But his face glowed brighter than ever. "Truth is"—he rushed the words—"boats made from Nairn wood never sink and no man has ever been lost from one."

"And why is that?" Arabella hoped he didn't hear the disbelief in her voice.

"Because the wood is charmed."

"By the fairies?"

"Nae, by a mermaid." Conall didn't bat an eye.

Arabella laughed outright.

"Oh, dear. A mer—" She pressed a hand to her breast, cutting off the next wave of laughter by clamping her mouth tightly shut.

"Darroc and I didn't believe it, either." Conall's gaze flickered to the door, as if he expected his cousin to appear there. "But we made enquiries and learned the tales are true. See you—" he pushed away from the window and started pacing—"the Nairn shipwright is said to have a distant forebear who once rescued a mermaid he found trapped above the tideline. She couldn't get back to the sea on her own and when he carried her into the surf, returning her to her watery home, she granted him a wish."

Arabella leaned back against the wall and folded her arms.

Her leg was beginning to pain her.

Conall stopped pacing to search her eyes. "You don't believe me."

"I want to." It was the most tactful answer she could give him.

Seeming satisfied, he resumed his circuit of the room. "The shipwright's ancestor, also being a builder of boats, asked the mermaid for the ability to build ships that would never be lost and cost no man his life."

"And the mermaid granted his wish." Arabella knew better than to make the statement a question.

Conall clearly believed every word.

His flashing smile proved it. "Aye, she did. She promised that as long as his ships were built of trees felled on that stretch of shore, the ships would always be sound and no hands lost from them."

"So Darroc wanted an unsinkable birlinn." Arabella lowered herself onto a nearby stool.

"No' for himself." Conall shook his head, vigorously. "He wanted it for his men. The graybeards and others who"—he blew out a breath, looking uncomfortable—"aren't so good in strength as they once were.

"That, my lady, is why he emptied our coffers to purchase Nairn timber."

"I see." Arabella wished the floor would open up and swallow her. It didn't matter if she didn't believe in mermaids and wishes.

She did believe in kindness and looking out for one's own.

And if she'd been half-convincing herself she was falling in love with Darroc, she knew it now.

There could be no other like him.

And her eyes were hot and stinging, her vision crazily blurred. She glanced down at the voluminous plaid she was using as her skirts, horrified when a tear plopped onto the hands she'd clasped on her lap.

To her relief, Conall was looking elsewhere.

"Darroc is like that, my lady." He turned back to her, the admiration in his eyes almost blinding. "And he'd cut out my tongue if he knew I told you. Our men, the others, know nothing about Nairn and its charmed wood. They only know the birlinn was dear and that they feel like young, fierce warriors when they're out in her."

"They will not hear otherwise from me." Arabella spared him the embarrassment of asking her not to say anything.

But the thickness of her voice embarrassed her.

She was sure he'd noticed.

He was watching her strangely. "You're fond of him, aren't you?"

"Who?" She tried to pretend she'd misunderstood.

Conall laughed. "Why, himself, of course!"

"Well...." Heat bloomed in her chest. The sensation spread until she was certain every inch of her stood aflame. She tried not to let it show. "He is caring."

"Aye!" Conall slapped his thigh. "And it would serve him well if he'd come around to admitting just who he's set his eye on!"

Arabella knew he meant her.

The truth of it made the heat inside her blaze even hotter.

Sure her face burned as well, she looked at her plaid-skirted lap again, her gaze falling on the large silver brooch at her waist. Plain, though brightly polished, the brooch belonged to Moraig.

The old woman had lent it to her as a clasp for Darroc's borrowed plaid.

"Moraig is caring, too." Arabella jumped at the chance to change the subject. But the shadow that crossed Conall's face made her regret it.

He looked pained.

"You don't think so?" She couldn't believe it.

"Och, I ken well how caring Mad Moraig is." His voice sounded distant, strained. "She's a great-hearted old woman. The best I know. Always looking out for others, she is—to her own cost."

"Do you mean me?" Arabella looked at him.

Alarm twisted her belly. He couldn't possibly have meant her.

But he'd moved away and gone over to the hearth fire. He'd turned his back to her and appeared to be looking down at the smoldering peats. Something about the way he stood there made her shiver.

"Have I upset Moraig?" She dearly hoped not.

"You?" He swung around. "She's walking on air since you've been here. Och, nae"—his usual good humor lit his face again—"I didn't mean you."

"Then who did you mean?" Arabella's curiosity bit hard again.

And once more she wished she'd held her tongue. Or could kick herself. She deserved no better for as soon she'd spoken, shadows returned to cloud Conall's eyes.

"Mad Moraig wasn't always the broken reed she is now." He went to the table and poured himself a measure of ale, downing the entire cup before he spoke again. "That was in the day when we were keepers of a small castle in Argyll. Life was good and although we weren't of such fame as your clan, we were well respected."

"You weren't always here?" Arabella felt something

cold and wet nudge her and looked down to see Frang pushing his nose against her arm.

The shaggy beast leaned into her, heavily. Mina thrust her silky head beneath the edge of Arabella's makeshift skirt and began licking her foot. She was glad for their company.

Something told her she wasn't going to like Conall's tale.

"Nae . . . ." The hesitation in his voice proved it. "Clan elders will tell you we've held MacConachers' Isle since the morning of time, but the isle stood empty for centuries. We only returned when we lost our Argyll lands and had nowhere else to go."

He paused to refill his ale cup. "It was Darroc who— years later—brought us here. Before that, we'd sheltered with allies who opened their doors to us. When Darroc came of age, he vowed it was time we left Argyll and the hearths of others. He made Castle Bane our home."

Arabella combed her fingers through Frang's rough gray coat, understanding. Mina turned three times in a circle and settled onto the rushes at her feet. "So Moraig couldn't bear to leave your earlier lands?"

It would certainly break her to see her family lose Kintail.

But Conall shook his head. "Ach, we loved Argyll. But our lands were no longer ours. We supported John Balliol as king, see you? A lost cause and, looking back, a decision that brought our doom. After . . ."

He tossed down another healthy swig of ale. "After things went badly for Balliol, and us, Robert Bruce dispersed us. Our keep was slighted and our lands were seized and divided among his favorites. So"—he looked at her, almost as if he expected some reaction other than the pity squeezing her heart—"after all we'd been through, we were well pleased to come here and start anew."

Arabella arched a brow. "Everyone except Moraig?"

"Mad Moraig, she . . ." He paused to run a hand through his hair.

Arabella guessed what he had trouble saying.

"Moraig tries to ease her distress by helping people." It was so obvious. "Doing so helps her forget how much she misses your old lands."

He blinked at her. "Once, at a tavern in Glasgow, a traveling friar spoke of your family. He said that your lady mother is a *taibhsear*. A great seeress, according to his tales of her. Do you have the sight as well?"

"Nae." Arabella smiled. "I guessed."

"Ach, well." He seemed astounded. "You were close to the truth. But it isn't so much that Mad Moraig misses the land. She feels bad about the kin she couldn't help. That's why she has a need to help people. So many of us were lost and—"

He broke off, looking stricken.

A bright pink tinge spread up his neck to blossom on his cheeks.

Arabella stared at him, puzzled.

He glanced at his feet. "Forgive me." He spoke without meeting her eye. "I've said more than I should. Darroc will flay my hide if he finds out I've talked of this."

"Talked of what?"

"The MacConacher Slau—"

He coughed. It was a poorly executed body-bent-double kind of phony hacking designed to disguise what he'd been about to say.

Arabella watched, foreboding rippling through her.

But rather than heed the chill that was beginning to seep into her marrow, she pushed to her feet and went to the table where she filled a small cup with clear, restorative spring water.

Then she crossed the room and handed the cup to Conall.

When he drank and quickly pretended a recovery, she braced herself. The ill ease prickling her nape and drying her mouth told her his *seizure* and everything else had something to do with her.

As did some vague memory flitting along the edge of her mind.

"I would hear of the people Moraig couldn't help." She stood tall and straight. "Why was that? You said she wasn't always as she is now, so—"

"She did help, but there were too many." Conall rubbed the back of his neck. "There was a raid, see you? It happened quickly. The warring party descended like a terrible racing wind. Men were cut down before they could draw swords. The raiders came on the Bruce's orders, or so we were later told. It was his vengeance because we were for Balliol. No quarter was given, though some of us escaped into the hills. Moraig stayed behind, doing what she could for those maimed but still breathing.

"By some wonder, none of the raiders slew her." He glanced aside, a faraway look in his eyes. "Perhaps they knew she'd do herself more damage than they could ever inflict on her."

Looking back at her, he sighed. "Mad Moraig accuses herself of not doing enough for the injured. She's forgotten how tirelessly she worked and refused to listen when we reminded her that no matter how valiantly she plied her healing skills, the numbers were against her. Finally, we spoke of it no more, knowing it grieves her."

"That's horrible." Arabella felt Moraig's pain like an ice-edged darkness inside her. "Surely she knows she did what she could."

Conall's face said she didn't.

"She saved as many as anyone could." He spoke slowly, as if the words came from long ago. "Yet she blames herself for the missing or crippled limbs, the lost eyes, and above all, the dead."

He lifted a hand then to shove back his hair and the fire glow shone on his arm, making his burn scars look livid and alive.

Arabella's blood chilled. "Were you burned that day?"

Conall glanced at his arm. He blinked, almost as if he'd forgotten the marks. "I..."

When he hesitated, Arabella went to him, moving as quickly as her leg allowed. She took both his hands between her own, squeezing.

The window arch loomed behind him and it didn't surprise her to see that the stars had dimmed. A thin veil of cloud now hid their glitter.

It seemed somehow fitting.

Arabella took a deep breath, wishing she could undo everything she'd heard.

"I'm so sorry." She didn't try to stop the tears misting her eyes. "I should not have pressed you to tell me. You needn't—"

"Ach!" Quick as winking, he had her hands clasped in his and lifted both for an air kiss to her knuckles. "Perhaps it is best you know—despite Darroc feeling otherwise! My mother e'er said the truth is bright enough to light the way out of any sorrow."

He released her hands, but didn't move away. "I do not

remember much of my mother, but I do recall that she was very wise. And"—his eyes glowed with pride—"she was very beautiful, too."

Arabella wiped the dampness from her face. That odd shimmer of foreboding still plagued her. "You lost her so young?"

Conall nodded. "In the raid we were speaking of, aye. Darroc calls me his cousin and I am, but many times removed. My parents had a cot-house outside the castle walls. When we were wakened by the raiders, my mother tossed me out a window and told me to run. But..."

He glanced aside, his throat working. "But," he tried again, "like Moraig, I stayed. I hid in a patch of whin bushes and watched as men torched our roof thatch. When the fire caught and they rode away, I ran back and tried to pull my parents out of the burning cottage."

"But you couldn't."

"Nae." Conall swiped a hand across his cheek. "I might have done now, but I wasn't up to the task at the wee age o' seven."

He looked at his arms again, holding them out as if for inspection. "As it was, I swatted at the flames with my hands and now"—he lowered his arms—"I have these scars to remind me."

"Of the tragedy?" Arabella could hardly speak.

"Nae." He spoke with the voice of a much older man. One who'd seen and knew much. "To make sure I never forget that nothing is more important than those we love. And that we should never let anything stand between us.

"Nothing at all, no matter how daunting, because"— he looked at her, his gaze going deep—"the regret will kill you if you do."

Arabella's heart clenched on his words.

Unfortunately, other words came to her, too. Words long forgotten and still just a low, indistinguishable mumble somewhere deep in her mind.

"You are tired and it is late." Conall glanced at the window. A thin drizzle was falling now, almost as if the heavens were weeping.

Turning back to her, he took her elbow and guided her to a chair beside the fire. "I'll leave you to your night's rest. Just..."

The familiar pink tinge stained his face again. "Don't tell—"

"Darroc will never know you told me anything." Arabella saw relief sweep him. "But I can't promise I will not speak to him of this."

She couldn't lie.

Before he could answer, a gust of damp air swept into the room, swirling his plaid around him. Again, he reminded her of some young Celtic god, broad of shoulder and blue of eye, his red-gold hair gilded by the fire glow.

As if he thought so, too, he grinned. "My lady," he said, making her a jaunty bow.

Then he was gone, his footsteps thumping down the tower stair.

But when the echoes faded and the room's quiet surrounded her, other noises rose in her memory. She recognized the sounds as the din of a crowded hall, bursting with the clamor of shouting, jesting men, barking dogs, and general mayhem. The ruckus played across the farthest reaches of her mind, vague at first and impossible to hear clearly, like the soft rumbling voice she'd heard earlier.

The voice was back again now, teasing her.

She leaned back in her chair and sighed.

The voice was so familiar.

A man's voice, deep, richly Highland, and musical. It was a voice she knew, though she hadn't heard it in many, many years. And now that she remembered, pure molten horror slid through her, damning her soul.

It was the voice of Osbald the Sombre. Long ago bard at Eilean Creag, he was so named because he frowned on singing romantic French lays and other frivolous tales. He wouldn't even recount her clan's long and illustrious string of impressive ancestors.

Osbald the Sombre only sang of battles and warring.

And his favorite tale had been one she'd heard retold this night.

Arabella began to tremble.

She even feared she might lose her supper.

Her blood roared in her ears and she dug her fingers into the nubby wool of the borrowed plaid that warmed her even now. She knew better than to try and stand, well aware her legs wouldn't support her.

And that she might splinter into a thousand pieces if she fell.

Truth was she already felt that way.

Because now she knew what dread word Conall had almost blurted before he caught himself and erupted into a fit of bogus coughing.

It was the MacConacher Slaughter.

And her own grandfather had led the raiding party.

"That one will not be leading his men anywhere!"

Well pleased that it was so, Devorgilla of Doon allowed herself a moment to roll her shawl-draped shoulders and wriggle her knotty, magic-spending fingers. She also considered enjoying a wee dollop of *uisge beatha*, the fiery Highland spirits she usually saved for esteemed visitors.

She much preferred her own specially brewed heather ale, so rich, frothy, and tasting of fine purple moors on a late summer's day.

But the little silver spirits flagon beckoned.

Indeed, she was sure she'd treat herself.

It wasn't every day, after all, that she cast her spells over someone as puissant as Duncan MacKenzie, the great Black Stag of Kintail. Conjuring a bit of ague to lay low his men was bairn's play. Thwarting the chief himself was something else entirely.

That she'd done so with such success was a grand reason to celebrate.

"Eh, Mab?" She glanced at the tri-colored cat sitting in a patch of sunlight slanting in through one of the thick-walled cottage's two windows. "Little does he know why the waves in his beloved Loch Duich have become as steep as in the cold, dark seas."

Mab ignored her.

But Devorgilla caught a malicious glint in the feline's eye.

Somerled favored that sunny patch of the stone-flagged floor. He enjoyed napping there on such cold and crisp days as this one. But the little red fox had important duties elsewhere just now. And Mab, always disdainful of him, seemed bent on taking advantage.

Still behaving as if the cottage belonged to her and no one else, Mab lifted a paw and began meticulously examining each claw.

Devorgilla started to scold her, but cackled instead.

"Never you mind," she allowed, feeling generous. "I

don't need your opinion whatever! I know fine I've done great work this day."

Sure of it, she cautiously skirted the smoke-blackened cauldron hanging on its chain above her cook fire. Strange things were known to appear in the kettle's steam and she wasn't of a mood for the like. Instead, she went to a small wooden bench against the back wall.

A basin of moon-infused water waited there.

Such water was her best means of scrying, but just now it served another purpose as well.

Very carefully, as her old bones did give the occasional creak, she lowered herself onto the bench. Then she lifted the basin onto her knees.

Scrunching her eyes, for they weren't the best anymore either, she peered hard at the edge of the bowl. She stared and concentrated until she saw not the basin's rim but the narrow shingled strand at Eilean Creag.

"Ahhhh...." She gave a satisfied sigh when three MacKenzie galleys appeared there. The ships were drawn up on the strand, unmanned and harmless. Scudding mists shrouded the shore and black waves pounded the rocks. The loch roared like a lion and endless lines of huge, white-capped rollers raced straight for the MacKenzie boat strand and nowhere else.

Most gratifying of all was the figure of a man stomping furiously up and down the length of the strand, cursing fiercely as he went.

Devorgilla almost felt sorry for him.

The Black Stag wasn't used to having things go against his plans.

"Only a bit longer..." She knew he couldn't hear her, but the assurance balmed her conscience.

She leaned forward, bringing her face closer to the basin. So near she could see his down-drawn brows and hear his outraged ranting.

"Soon you will be able to sail to her, very soon." She crooned the promise, knowing it was true. "But for now, your daughter needs more time. Days and nights, without you ruining things for her."

The nights were especially needed.

Darroc MacConacher was proving more stubborn than she would have hoped. And Arabella wasn't a born seductress like her sister.

Even so . . . .

She was sure they'd soon make good use of the hours she was determined to give them.

To that end, she drew a great breath and blew hard onto the water in the bowl. As she knew would happen, the water dimpled and danced, the sight delighting her.

But it wasn't enough.

Not by any means.

So she plunged her hand into the basin and wriggled her fingers, stirring the water round and round until it swirled crazily.

Excited, she trilled a laugh and flicked a few droplets in the air. They sparkled and glistened, then whirled around to fling themselves at the edge of the basin, just missing the tiny figure of a man still visible there.

Devorgilla cackled again, her mirth boundless.

Now she was making magic.

And there was nothing the Black Stag of Kintail could do about it.

Nothing at all.

Chapter Twelve

❧

"*Why didn't you tell me?*"

Darroc pretended not to hear the female voice behind him. Soft, lilting, and just a touch breathless, it could have been Arabella. But that was impossible. He knew she managed to move about his bedchamber these days and she'd made some visits to the hall. But the climb to his notch room, Castle Bane's uppermost tower chamber, would daunt even a Valkyrie. The steps were narrow and winding, the stone treads crumbling in places and dangerous.

Arabella couldn't possibly have mounted them.

And if anyone—or anything else—had spoken, he didn't want to know.

So he feigned indifference and stooped to pick up his special chisel. Three times now, the tool had flown out of his hands. And each time, he would've sworn he heard a woman's light, silvery laughter.

The sound echoed around the room. At times so faint the tinkling, feminine skirls were almost swallowed by the howling wind. It was a blustery morn. Full of cold and damp, with squalls of lashing rain. But whenever he decided he'd imagined the laughter, it came again.

Yet when he'd spun around, no one was there.

Darroc frowned.

This time he wasn't going to look. He did tighten his grip on the chisel, positioning it where he wanted to make a new notch in the window arch. He wouldn't allow such nonsense as flying chisels to happen again.

Yet...

The same thing had happened with his mallet, though it hadn't sailed from his grasp like the chisel. The mallet simply rolled away along the window ledge whenever he reached for it. And once—he could scarce credit it—he was half-sure the mallet deliberately leapt to the floor.

Whatever the cause, the foolery had kept him from making a single notch.

Determined to change that, he allowed himself a wickedly gratifying grin and focused on the chisel. Then, he raised the mallet for a good, stone-chipping tap. He'd make his best notch ever.

Nothing would go wrong.

"You had to know it would come to me." Arabella's voice floated to him from the door, unmistakable.

Darroc's heart stopped.

The mallet, already in full, furious swing, slammed onto his thumb.

"*Y-ooow*!" This time the mallet went flying. The chisel merely plunked onto his foot. "Saints, Maria, and—" he caught himself, cutting off the curse before its utterance could make him even more miserable.

It was bad enough that everything in the room had gone black and white.

The pain was blinding.

His humiliation was worse.

Trying to ignore the hot pulsing in his thumb, he leaned over, bracing his hands on his knees and breathing hard. He kept his head lowered, not wanting Arabella to see his face until he was no longer grimacing.

He might have made a fool of himself, but he did have his pride.

A Highlander didn't show pain.

Arabella reached a hand toward him. He felt more than saw the movement. "I remembered a tale last night," she said, her voice troubled. "One a clan bard used to sing at my father's hearth fire."

"What tale?" Darroc forgot about being a Highlander and glanced at her from under his brows.

He didn't like her tone.

How she looked really bothered him. Her hair was in disarray, with loose strands escaping the two gleaming black plaits that hung to her hips. And her borrowed clothes, his shirt and plaid, looked so rumpled that she could only have slept in them.

Worst of all, she was deathly pale and tears glittered in her sapphire eyes.

"You're crying." Darroc straightened at once.

"I am not." She raised her chin, defiant. "MacKenzies don't cry. And I'm sure you know the tale I mean. Indeed, I think"—one of the MacKenzie non-tears rolled down her cheek—"you should have told me yourself."

"Told you what?" Darroc kicked his chisel aside.

The last thing he needed was to trip over it and look like an even greater bumble arse.

"I don't know what you're so fashed about." He glared at her, finding that a safer option than letting her see how concerned he was by her distress.

The pampered and privileged daughter of one of the mightiest houses in the land shouldn't look as if all the light had gone out in her world. And he shouldn't care that she did. But he had a sinking feeling exactly what tale she meant and seeing what it'd done to her ripped him.

She was swallowing hard, pretending not to cry. But her lips trembled and her hands were making awful little fluttery gestures.

Darroc's chest squeezed.

She had to have found out about the Slaughter.

"You shouldn't be up here." He tried to sound stern, hoping he was wrong. He scowled at Frang and his wee lady-light, both sitting in the shadows behind her like twin sentinels. He'd see to them later—make sure they learned better than escorting maids to places they had no good seeking.

He shoved a hand through his hair, feeling outnumbered. "See here, Lady Arabella. You should—"

"I should not be here at all, accepting your hospitality." She looked down, plucked at his plaid. "Wearing your clothes and eating your bread. It isn't—"

"Damnation!" Darroc crossed the room in three long strides. The cold air around him vanished, replaced by a hot whirling wind.

Hell rising up to claim him.

As if she knew, Arabella swayed and leaned against the doorjamb. She looked tired, shaken, and dizzy. Darroc tried to harden his heart against her, but couldn't. It was impossible. He felt her anguish inside him, coursing through his blood and beating in his bones, his marrow, and even in the very soul of him.

He was a fool!

She touched a hand to her cheek and stared at him from eyes pooled deep with shock and sorrow. "I didn't sleep the night through. I—"

He grabbed her upper arms, gripping tight. "Who told you?"

"No one." The denial was swift. "I remembered the bard, Osbald the Sombre. He was my father's favorite when I was a child. He often sang of the raid, praising our men's triumph and valor, the deadly bite of their steel. He—"

Frang barked.

Darroc flashed the dog a narrow-eyed look, scowling until the shaggy beast lay down on the landing. Mina quickly joined him, whimpering dismally.

Satisfied, Darroc looked back at Arabella. She was staring at his hands on her arms, the beat of her pulse clearly visible at the base of her throat. She worried her lower lip, and her face had gone even whiter than before.

His was flushed red, he was sure.

"Your bard wasn't praising a raid. He sang of war. Men do terrible things when the bloodlust is upon them." Darroc couldn't believe he'd said that.

But the words had come from somewhere inside him.

A place he didn't care to examine.

War had nothing to do with the MacConacher Slaughter. There could be no excuse for such butchery. Even if the MacKenzies saw it otherwise.

He frowned.

Arabella was still staring at him, her hands clasped before her, knuckle-white.

"Those were grievous times." There he went again, traitor to his own.

"I know that, but—" She pressed her fingers against her lips.

Lips that quivered and made him feel inexplicably guilty. A lass with enough steel in her blood to stitch her own wound shouldn't shatter because of a horror that happened years before she was born.

Even more alarming, he shouldn't be so damned affected because she *was* shattered.

Darroc set his jaw, furious.

Something entirely out of his control was happening to him. It was unnatural and outrageous for him to feel any kind of affinity to a MacKenzie.

But she hiccupped then and the sound sliced into him, piercing his heart. He couldn't bear seeing her so troubled. Or so desperately in need and—saints damn him—so desirable and alluring despite everything. But watery sunlight spilled in through the notch room's east window and it shone right on her, making her glow in a room that always made him feel so cold and empty.

His fingers tensed on her arms and the blood roared in his ears. She hiccupped again and her breasts jigged beneath the soft folds of his shirt. The linen clung to her curves, so generous and enticing. She did have magnificent breasts, full and round. He could see the dark shadows of her nipples, peaked tight and pressing against the cloth.

He stared at them, unable not to. And then he did the most foolhardy thing he'd ever done.

He pulled her into his arms.

It would be so easy to yank her even closer and kiss her, deep and passionately. Slant his lips over hers in a wild open-mouthed kiss that would damn them both, together. Oh, how he wanted that. Especially when he felt her breasts crushed to his chest and those oh-so-tempting nipples seemed to burn right through his plaid, scalding his naked flesh, branding him hers. But she melted against him and when he looked down into her face, it was no longer about kisses and nipples.

It was about her.

And that awareness was like having the breath sucked right out of him.

For a moment, he couldn't breathe. He couldn't even have said where they were. He only saw her luminous blue eyes, still bright with the shimmer of tears. Holding her blotted out the terrors of the past, making everything insignificant except the feel of her pliant warmth in his arms. It was as if she ripped away a shroud of darkness, flooding him with light. A strange sense of wholeness filled him and in some terrifyingly separate part of his mind, he knew that once he released her, he'd be incomplete.

She sighed contentedly. Or so he thought until he realized the sound came from across the room. It was surely the wind again, but whatever it was, it broke the madness that had seized him.

Even so, he couldn't stop the shivers that whipped through him. They were chills that sped through his soul rather than his physical body.

She trembled, too, shaking like a leaf in the wind as he held her, loosely now. She'd slid an arm around him, clinging, and tangled a hand in his hair, holding fast as if she also felt the power beating between them.

Then she lifted her chin and met his gaze. She made no move to pull away, but something of her old fierceness burned in her eyes.

"I'd still hear why you didn't say anything." Her voice was firm now, all MacKenzie.

Darroc could have wept.

He lowered his head and touched his lips to her hair. Just once, and only lightly, but it was something that he needed to do.

"What difference would it have made?" He wished there weren't tears netting her eyelashes. The sight of them made it hard to speak. "You were here and needed our help. That is all that mattered."

"If that is so, it wouldn't have changed aught if you'd been honest."

Darroc's eyes widened. "Honest?"

She nodded.

The room was silent except for the wind and the sound of rain pelting the tower.

Darroc closed his eyes, wishing he could go back to the moment he'd become aware of her. This wasn't going how he would have wished.

"Sweet lass, honesty had nothing to do with it." He stepped back so he could see her better, but took care to keep a light grip on her elbows.

Damn him for a double-dyed fool, but he couldn't bear to let go of her.

"Truth is"—he caught a flicker of movement and wasn't surprised to find Frang had opened one eye to stare at him, piercingly—"MacConachers have never vented their grievances on women. I had no desire to be the first to start such a depraved tradition."

It was all she was getting out of him.

And it was the truth.

He just didn't add that he'd also dreaded discussing the Slaughter with her. Being a MacKenzie, she surely knew that as a staunch Balliol supporter, his grandfather had infiltrated an enemy camp for the sole purpose of gleaning information for his liege. Many MacKenzies were in that camp and it was with them that his grandfather rode when he learned of a planned surprise attack on the keep of a strong Balliol ally.

Slipping away from the MacKenzies, Darroc's grandfather had made haste to warn his friends, allowing the keep garrison to sally out and ambush the unsuspecting MacKenzies. The carnage was great, but as history showed, the MacKenzies' revenge was greater.

As though he was following his thoughts, Frang groaned as only shaggy old dogs can do and did something to express his canine opinion of the matter.

Darroc winced when the fumes hit him.

To her credit, Arabella didn't bat an eye. "It never crossed my mind that you would ill treat a woman," she said, proving her persistence. "I only wish I'd been spared the shock of remembering as I did."

"And do you know the whole story?" The words leapt from his tongue before he could stop them.

"You mean how your grandfather befriended my kinsmen, giving out that he was Bruce's man? And what happened thereafter?"

"So you do know."

"I do." She still had her arms looped around his neck,

her hands deep in his hair, fingers twined. "And I do not condone the actions of either side. It does grieve me. Especially now that I've met"—she glanced aside, blinking rapidly—"Moraig, Conall, and the others. They make the tragedy more real than listening to it recounted at my father's hearthside of a cold winter night."

"And that, my lady, is why I kept silent." He looked at her, hoping she'd believe him.

There were so many other reasons.

"I didn't want you to feel awkward or unwelcome beneath my roof." That was absolutely true.

She looked skeptical. "Is that why you've been avoiding me?"

"Nae, I—" Heat swept up the back of his neck. "I've been holding counsel with my men. And—"

"Making your notches?" She pulled out of his arms then and bent to lift his chisel off the floor. She turned it over in her hand, her face still much too pale for his liking. "Conall said—"

"He told you of my notches?" Darroc stared at her, horrified. His head began to pound. Not surprising, the strange tinkling laughter came again, this time from somewhere very close by. But he paid scarce heed.

He only wanted a piece of Conall's hide.

And to know how the chisel landed by the door. He'd kicked it in the opposite direction.

He took her by the elbows again, his need to touch her still strong. "What did he tell you?"

"Only that you were here, making them." She looked up at him, all innocence. "I told him I must speak with you. He did say"—her hands tightened on the chisel—"that you mark the days by notching the window."

"That's all he said?"

She nodded.

Darroc released the breath he'd been holding. Relief swept him. It would seem he wouldn't have to smash his cousin's nose. Even so, he burned to challenge someone—anyone—to a good round of fighting, not stopping until chests heaved and fists dripped with blood.

Lots of blood.

Darroc smiled. He couldn't help it.

Desire for Arabella still surged inside him, hot and urgent. When she'd bent to retrieve his chisel, the neck opening of her borrowed shirt gaped wide. He'd had a fine view of her lush breasts and those pert, tightly furled nipples.

It was too much.

Especially since he'd just felt her warm, womanly softness pressing so close against him. But as much as he burned for her, there were deep lines drawn between them. So he did the only thing he could do and keep his wits.

He broached a subject sure to cool his ardor.

"Why were you on the cog?" He saw her eyes widen and felt guilty at once, bringing up something that could only cause her pain.

But the thought of a betrothed and her dowry pained him also.

"Moraig told me you were on your way to see the Seal Isles." He pretended he didn't know why.

She stiffened and glanced aside. "I did want to see the Seal Isles. The *Merry Dancer* was bound for Man. Captain Arneborg agreed to stop at the isles on the way. My father paid him well to do so."

"Surely you have seals in Kintail?" Darroc released

her and folded his arms. "I see no reason to make such an arduous journey just to see seals."

"I wanted to visit the isles." She looked back at him. Her tone was cool. "They are part of my dowry."

There, she'd said what he'd wanted to hear.

And it made him feel like hell.

"Couldn't your betrothed have taken you there after your wedding?" He truly was pathetic. "Surely—"

"I do not have a betrothed." She glanced down, brushed at her plaid skirt.

Darroc's heart soared.

Arabella flushed.

She'd seen the triumph in his eyes and knew he was laughing at her. Most women her age—especially the daughters of mighty chieftains—had more than empty dowries. They had husbands and were long married, several bouncing bairns on their knees.

"I wished to visit the Seal Isles because there is a hermit's cell on the main isle." She wasn't about to tell him the rest. "It's a cave and belonged to one of St. Columba's followers. His name was St. Egbert and I want to pray at his shrine."

That much was true.

She just didn't say what she wished to ask for.

"I am no' aware of such a place on the Seal Isles." Darroc's brows drew together. "They are none too far from here, see you. I'd know if one of Columba's men had hermited close by."

She raised her chin and met his suspicion with all the dignity of her race. "He was a little known follower of Columba. Not many are aware of his connection to the

Seal Isles. A traveling minstrel who once spent time there told my family of him."

"Indeed." He didn't believe her.

She didn't care.

How could she, when all she could think about was how she'd felt when he'd held her, his arms wrapped tight around her and her cheek pressed against his shoulder. She could melt again just remembering. She'd come alive in his embrace, breathing in his scent of clean male and just a hint of wood smoke and the sea. His heart had thundered wildly, its pounding seeping into her, melding with the beats of her own racing pulse until she'd been consumed with such an intense longing she'd feared it would break her.

She was sure he'd wanted her.

Even sheltered as she was, she could tell.

His eyes had told her, too. He was looking at her that way now. It was a dark, piercing stare that sizzled right through her, making her blood leap and the heat rush to her face. She lifted a hand to her cheek, felt the burning there. Warmth curled low in her belly, tantalizing. Her mouth went dry in anticipation.

She wanted him to kiss her.

He stepped closer, as if he knew. "Why are you not betrothed?" He reached for one of her braids, smoothing his thumb over the plaited strands. "I would think all the young worthies in the land would be badgering your father for your hand."

"They have, but...." The image of her father's face flashed through her mind, purple with fury, as he glared down each suitor who'd come to call. "There hasn't been—no one has yet made a serious bid. They've all withdrawn before showing any true interest."

She hoped he'd leave it at that.

It was too humiliating to admit that her father had chased them away. There wasn't a one who'd stayed at Eilean Creag long enough to make an offer.

"I find that hard to believe." Darroc's voice deepened and his gaze went a shade darker. "Were I one of them, I would not have left until I had what I wanted. I'd never turn away from such a prize."

She lifted her chin, not caring that her face must be glowing like a balefire. "You mean my riches?"

"I mean you."

Arabella blinked. She wasn't prepared for such an answer, though she'd hoped. Hoped so much.

Prickling excitement raced through her, making her skin tingle. Her heart skittered and then slammed against her ribs, beating hard and slow.

"What do you mean, me?" Her voice hitched on the words.

"Och, lass." The look he gave her watered her knees. "You must know. I—ever since—"

He broke off and shoved a hand through his hair. Heat flared in his eyes, blazing as if he were the devil's own henchman.

Then, before she could blink, he reached for her, pulling her hard against him. She caught one quick glimpse of his eyes, saw the passion burning there. Then his mouth slanted over hers in a rough, devouring kiss that set her senses reeling and left her breathless.

She slid her arms around him and leaned close, pressing into him as he tightened his hold on her. He groaned

and deepened the kiss. She let him, savoring the intimacy, the thrill of pleasure that shot through her when his
tongue thrust into her mouth, seeking and curling around
her own. It was bliss untold. The glory of his lips moving
so masterfully over hers undid her. She was splintering
inside, aching, hungering for more.

"Ooooh...." She gasped in wonder, then shivered deliciously when he caught her sigh, drinking her breath as if
it were the sweetest nectar.

She opened her mouth wider, welcoming his essence
into her lungs, wanting to sate herself on the heady taste
and scent of him. He moaned, his tongue sliding over and
around hers in a sensual silken dance she never wanted
to end. She closed her eyes, sure that life as she'd known
it had ended, plunging her into a shining, spinning sea of
carnal delight.

She didn't care if it was wrong.

His name mattered even less.

She only knew she needed him. This blinding,
dazzling passion only he could give her. She'd yearned for
this moment since she'd first seen him. Perhaps even since
glimpsing him in the tower window at Dunakin, so long
ago in Kyleakin. She was sure now that she'd seen him
there.

Just as she knew someone was watching them.

And it wasn't Frang and Mina.

A chill raced down her spine and she opened her eyes
to slits, almost afraid to look. And with good reason, for
she saw at once that a woman stood staring at them from
the other side of the room.

Better said, the woman hovered.

Beautiful and smiling, she shimmered brilliantly near

one of the window arches, the hem of her sparkling luminously white gown at least two hand breadths above the floor.

Arabella screamed.

Darroc released her at once, panting. "Sakes!" He stared at her, his chest heaving. "I ken well I shouldn't have done that, but—"

"A ghost!" Arabella pointed. "It wasn't you. I saw a see-through blond woman in a glittering white gown. There, by that window!"

"If you did, she isn't there now." His tone was angry, his annoyed gaze on the window arch.

Something had changed.

The warmth that had been cascading through her like a golden river in spate turned cold, icing her blood and leaving her empty inside.

She took a deep breath, willing herself to appear calm, untouched by his wild kisses and how little they must have meant to him.

"There was someone here." She went across to the window and rested her hands on the cold stone of its broad, angled splay. The air felt different there, tingly, warm, and somehow charged. "I am sure of it. She had pale hair, braided like mine, and—"

She felt foolish as soon as the words left her tongue.

Then she saw the notches.

Not his. These were faint, barely there scratches that filled the entire window.

"Dear saints!" She clapped a hand to her cheek, horror sluicing her. "This was Asa Long-Legs's chamber," she cried, sure of it. "She made these marks. One for each day she was trapped here, just as you told me."

"She may have done, aye." Darroc joined her at the window. She didn't miss that he took care to stand at least an arm's length away from her. "I do believe this was her room. It follows that she'd favor this window, seeing as it looks to the north."

"The north?" Arabella blinked. She couldn't think with him standing so near.

"Shetland lies due north." Darroc was looking out into the morning, his gaze on the horizon. "Perhaps she stood here, thinking of her home at Scalloway and wishing she'd never left there."

"Then it was she I saw." Arabella touched one of the scratch marks, her heart twisting. "She was very beautiful. But she didn't look sad. She looked happy."

Darroc harrumphed. "I doubt you saw her. If she is about—which I cannot imagine—she will surely be in her beloved Shetland. She will have left here many years ago. This was no easy place for her."

"I saw something." Arabella wouldn't back down.

"You saw a beam of morning sunlight." Darroc took her gently by the shoulders, turning her to face the east window where a band of pale light slanted through that window's tall arched opening.

"This window is in shadow." Arabella broke away from him and rubbed her arms. She couldn't rid herself of the chills still sweeping her.

Darroc glanced at Asa's window and frowned. He couldn't deny the deep shadows there. The wind howled bitterly on this side of the room and cold rain still pelted the tower walls. It was a gray bleak morning, and just since they'd spoken, the watery light faded from the east window, the sun having slipped behind the clouds.

Arabella's borrowed shirt had slipped, too. Come loose during their kissing, the neck opening dipped low, revealing her breasts in near naked glory. Once more, heat scorched her cheeks.

She couldn't believe she hadn't noticed.

He surely had, if his attempts not to look there were any indication.

"I have a friend, Olaf Big Nose." He smoothed a fold of his plaid, his words making no sense. "He makes camp on a nearby isle. I shall be visiting him soon. He'll want to know of the Black Vikings that rammed the *Merry Dancer*. And"—he kept his gaze on the horizon, the dark clouds building there—"he will be eager to help me chase down the miscreants. As a peace-loving man, he'll see it in his interest to help banish them from our seas."

Arabella only half listened. It mattered more that she covered herself.

"...they will have clothes for you," Darroc was saying, now taking a brisk turn about the room.

She started. "Who will have clothes for me?"

He glanced at her, careful to keep his gaze above her shoulders. "Olaf's womenfolk. He has a whole slew of them living there on his isle. Some"—he colored a bit—"are of your size and shape. They are goodly women and will see well to you."

She lifted a brow. "What do you mean they will see to me?"

"Just that." He stopped pacing. "You can't remain clothed in table linens. However well-stitched they are, such garments are unworthy of you. Olaf's women are well-accoutered. They will be glad to share."

"I understood that part." Arabella finished fumbling at

her shirt laces. "But you speak as if you mean to take me there."

"I do."

"A sea journey?" The thought struck terror in her.

"It is a short journey of one night." He spoke as if everything was decided. "The birlinn can't offer you the comfort of the merchant cog, but I can promise she is seaworthy. Olaf must hear what happened to the *Merry Dancer.* He'll appreciate having the tale from you. And—"

He glanced at one of the room's four window arches. It was the one that held his neat rows of notches. Each mark bold and perfectly chiseled, one like the other.

His gaze remained fixed on them as if they held more meaning than simply marking days. "The journey will—"

Arabella shook her head. "I am not ready for such a—"

"You need to reacquaint yourself with sea travel." He went to stand at the notched window, lightly touching the deep scores in the stone. "We'll wait until the weather clears. Geordie Dhu is no' just a master cook, he is an unerring weather prophet. He can sniff out an approaching storm days before its coming just as he need only observe the color and quality of the sea to know danger is imminent.

"Even the feel of his fine wheaten bread dough tells him much, he says. How the seabirds fly and, believe it or not, the rising smoke from his cook fire." He glanced at her, his face hard-set. "No harm will come to you. I give you my solemn word on it."

"What of the Black Vikings?"

"My men and I will make forays beforehand to ensure they are no' about." He'd considered everything.

Arabella swallowed. "I still do not wish to go."

He came back to her then, once more taking her by the arms. But his touch was different this time. No longer caring and tender or searing with passion, the hands that held her so firmly felt cold.

It was as if their kiss had never happened.

"I will no' force you." His tone was colder than his touch. "But I hope you will deign to join me. I assure you that"—a slash of red swept across his cheekbones—"I will no' touch you again."

So he hadn't forgotten.

But he regretted it.

"I am not worried." Arabella clasped her hands. "I understand that men are sometimes overcome with animal passions," she spoke primly, not wanting him to see her hurt. "As I also know that such urges mean nothing."

For a moment, he looked as if she'd struck him.

But he recovered swiftly. "We can make a side trip to the Seal Isles on the return journey. Then, after Olaf Big Nose and I have dealt with the Black Vikings and so long as there isn't word of the English plague having reached the mainland hills, I will see you escorted back to Kintail."

"I see." Arabella lifted her chin.

He looked relieved. "Seal Isles is no great journey. But by the time we return here, you'll have lost your fear and will no longer dread the long voyage home."

Arabella's heart sank.

He wanted to be rid of her.

She broke free of his grasp and turned to the window, taking care to keep her back straight and her head high. The morning had worsened and sheets of rain blew past the tower on the rising wind. Below, the sea crashed loudly over the rocks. She welcomed the pounding roar, hoping the noise covered the disappointed hammering of her heart.

She took a deep breath of the chill, damp air and then summoned all her practiced poise. "I will think on accompanying you."

It was the most she was willing to say.

"I am glad to hear it." His voice was almost stern, as chiefly as her father's. "Now, Lady Arabella, I believe it is best if I leave you alone to consider. But I'll return shortly. I'll no' have you descending these old steps on your own." Then he nodded and strode from the room before she had a chance to argue.

Not that she would have.

She'd already made up her mind. She'd go wherever he desired to take her. And she'd put a pleasant face to it.

Her pride gave her no other option.

But when his footfalls faded and she turned back to the window to stare down at the foaming sea, one thing surprised her. Much as she loved her family, she didn't want to return home to Kintail.

She wanted to stay here.

And she wanted Darroc to love her.

Across the room, at the north-facing window arch, Asa Long-Legs dashed a glittery tear from her cheek. It was a strange sensation as she hadn't cried in so long. There'd been so many tears in the beginning, when she first learned she was trapped here. She'd wept rivers of tears then. Both in her true life and in the one she led now. Then the day came when there were no more left to shed.

These days she only wanted happiness.

And she'd felt such joy at Castle Bane since the arrival

of the raven-haired beauty. She knew the young chief wanted her. And when he'd kissed the maid—with true passion and not the brazen conquest of her own Mac-Conacher—she'd shimmered so brightly with the thrill of it that Lady Arabella had seen her.

Under different circumstances, she'd be filled with delight that it was so. She wanted so much for them to know of her. To be aware that she wished them all goodness.

But Arabella had screamed.

And her cry shattered their magic.

Asa swept away another sparkling tear as she watched Arabella staring out the window. The sadness on her face hurt her. Yet she was sure Darroc was only running scared. Soon he'd be kissing the lass again, and with even more heat. As an accomplished flirt in her own day, back at her father's court and before Rhun snatched her away, she knew how to read men.

Darroc loved Arabella.

Soon all would be well with them.

Just not for her.

And that was another reason for her tears. She knew he didn't mean to hurt her, but she wished the young chief hadn't mentioned her father and Scalloway. He'd been right. Her longing for both was why she'd chosen the north window to make her marks.

And unlike the young couple she knew would soon find such bliss, she could never return to Shetland.

Not even if she knew how to do so.

Her father would shun her if she did.

And that broke her heart.

Chapter Thirteen

⚜

Castle Bane was absolutely quiet when Arabella awoke on the morning of Geordie Dhu's final day of sea prophesying. For nearly a sennight, the magnificent-bearded cook and self-proclaimed storm wizard had sought and studied a variety of weather omens. Now, on this bitter cold morn, he'd vowed to make his final assessment as to whether the morrow would prove a propitious day for a sea journey to Olaf Big Nose's neighboring isle.

An air of excitement had been building all week and now, seized by the sense of festive anticipation, everyone had risen early to hasten down to the boat strand to hear Geordie Dhu's prediction.

Everyone, that is, except Arabella.

Her blood, too, raced with exhilaration. But it wasn't Geordie Dhu's ability to read the sea that saw her in such high spirits.

It was the castle's stillness.

She'd been waiting for such a moment and now that

it was here, she just hoped that nothing would happen to spoil it for her. Half fearing something would, she kept one ear trained on the silence as she rushed through her morning ablutions. Moraig had kindly given her a generous supply of her special gillyflower soap and Arabella now dipped her fingers in the round little jar and hurried to finish washing before ice formed on the water in her basin.

She hadn't felt such cold since arriving at Castle Bane.

Shivering, she dried as quickly as she could. She combed and braided her hair even faster. Satisfied, she grabbed one of her newly sewn table linen gowns and practically leapt into it. For good measure, she swirled Darroc's plaid around her shoulders, securing its voluminous folds with Moraig's borrowed silver brooch.

Then she stood still and listened.

Nothing stirred.

Outside, a weak sun was just rising, while a sharp wind heralded more cold yet to come. At some point before daybreak, someone had crept into the room and lit two of the hanging crusie lamps. These flickered softly, filling the air with a tinge of smoky fish oil. Several new bricks of peat smoldered in the grate, that earthy sweet smell much more pleasing than the slightly rank odor of fish oil.

Arabella angled her head, straining to catch any other noises. She heard only the rustle of the floor rushes when she shifted her feet. Except for the hiss of the crusies and the occasional popping of a peat brick, all was quiet.

Most importantly, none of the usual morning commotion rose up from the hall. Nor were there any footsteps outside her door or in the stair tower.

It was time.

Heart thumping, she flashed one last glance around

the room just to be sure she hadn't missed anyone's silent presence. Then she went purposely to the bed and slid questing fingers beneath the mattress, quickly withdrawing two neatly stitched drawstring pouches.

Her knees could have jellied as soon as she clutched them in her hands. It wasn't every day, after all, that she sewed things meant to hold pilfered goods. But she steeled herself against any twinges of guilt and shoved the pouches into a fold of her borrowed plaid.

Then she took a deep breath and slipped from the room.

She reached Castle Bane's kitchens without incident and with great speed, considering. But she hesitated on the threshold to Geordie Dhu's sacred domain. She'd never stolen anything in her life and she prayed her reasons justified doing so now.

She needed grain and honey for the Seal Isles' Giving Stone.

Hopefully she'd be able to procure a skin of the required fresh milk from one of the women at Olaf Big Nose's settlement.

For now...

She eased the two linen pouches out of her plaid and stepped into the huge vaulted kitchens. The smell of wood smoke lay heavy on the chill air, as did lingering traces of last night's roasted meats. Her mouth watered and her empty stomach gurgled loudly, but she couldn't allow time to look for a spare morsel to eat.

With Geordie Dhu down on the boat strand, the kitchens lay in deep shadow. Across the vast space, two double-arched fireplaces took up nearly one entire wall. Wood embers glowed there, the cook fires smoored but not yet

burning. And no one had bothered to light any of the wall
torches.

Even squinting, she could hardly see in the gloom.

She pushed her braids over her shoulders, letting her
eyes adjust to the darkness. The last thing she needed was
to collide with some massive oaken table or whatnot and
hurt her still recovering leg. Such would be a fitting pen-
ance for dipping into Geordie Dhu's precious stores.

So she moved forward carefully, taking light steps on
the kitchen's cold stone-flagged floor. She managed only
a few paces before almost bumping into an iron-bound
strongbox. The chest, secured with a heavy lock, surely
held Geordie Dhu's spices or perhaps the keep's supply of
beeswax and tapers. Ignoring the chest, she skirted several wicker creels brimming with onions and dried wild
carrots, the pungent smell making her nose wrinkle.

She didn't care about vegetables.

What she wanted was to find the larders.

If Geordie Dhu's kitchens were anything like those at
Eilean Creag, there'd be a walk-through somewhere. A
corridor flanked with storerooms and butteries that linked
the work areas with the great hall.

She bit her lip and looked around, straining to see in
the dimness.

Thanks to her mother's insistence that she learn every
nuance of running a large household—including the toil
of the kitchens—she quickly found the narrow stone-
walled passage she needed.

She paused at its entrance to glance over her shoulder,
then tried the first door on her right. It opened easily, so
she nipped inside, wishing she'd dared to carry a hand
torch as the icy cold larder proved darker than pitch. But

as soon as she took a deep breath, she could have wept with relief. For once, the gods were kind.

The sweet, rich scent of heather honey flooded the tiny room.

Shivering with cold and nerves, she felt along the chilly stone wall until her fingers reached the edge of shelving. Rows and rows of shelves lined with earthenware jars in every imaginable size.

They could only be filled with honey.

Conall had praised the quality of the isle's honey more than once when he'd delivered her dinner trays. Even so, she took one of the smaller jars, carefully pulled its waxed stopper, and sniffed.

Honey indeed.

Almost giddy with victory, she dropped the jar into one of her linen pouches and returned to the main area of the kitchens. Now she needed to find the meal kist, which could also be a barrel of oats, depending on how Geordie Dhu preferred to keep his stores.

Unfortunately the first barrel she peeked into held salted herring. She blinked against the stink of brine and stepped back only to stumble over a large stone quern and its protruding wooden handle.

"Gah!" She reeled and slammed into a cupboard, sending what sounded like an entire garrison of hornware clattering to the floor.

Ramshorn spoons and dippers slid in every direction across the stone flagging.

The noise was deafening.

But the silence that followed was worse.

Arabella couldn't breathe.

Her heart plummeted to her toes.

Any moment she'd be found out. The keep might be empty, but at the moment, she was sure she felt a thousand eyes staring at her. She wanted to turn and flee, but she couldn't leave without filling her second pouch with grain.

So she ignored the terror beating through her and hurriedly gathered up as many of the fallen spoons and dippers that she could. As to the rest of them, the ones that had skittered away to who knew where, she could only hope Geordie Dhu would assume one of his kitchen cats knocked down the utensils during an early morning prowl.

It was possible.

All castle kitchens had cats, even if she hadn't seen a one of them.

Feeling somewhat better—now that no one had appeared to see what caused the din—she peered through the shadows, searching for a likely repository for Geordie Dhu's stores of grain.

Fortune blessed her again.

An oat barrel stood in a dark niche just to the right of one of the massive fireplaces on the far wall. She knew the barrel contained oats this time because it was topped with a large baking board. A second baking board stood propped against the barrel's side.

Success at last!

Emboldened, she hurried over to the oat barrel and lifted its baking board lid. In addition to oats, a wooden dipping spoon winked up at her from within the barrel's grainy depths.

The gods truly were on her side.

Sure of it, she shook out her spare pouch and reached for the dipper, preparing to fill her sack with oats.

It was then that she heard a shuffling sound.

Arabella froze.

Her hand was deep inside the oat barrel, but she didn't dare move. She wished she could press her fingers to her temples for her head suddenly pounded with a vengeance. Her stomach lurched and her chilled fingers clenched around the long handle of the dipper.

Slowly, very slowly, the intense silence reassured her.

She was indeed alone.

Feeling foolish, she scooped up a large dipperful of oats and poured them into her pouch. She helped herself to a second scoop and a third, certain the Giving Stone would appreciate a generous offering.

Not that she truly believed the like.

But if she meant to bend her knees at some long-dead hermit's cell, she might as well attempt to plead her wishes to the Auld Ones.

She was desperate.

And it couldn't hurt to appease the gods of both worlds.

At best, the seabirds and island creatures would thank her for her gifts.

So she dropped the dipping spoon back into the oat barrel and carefully tied the drawstring of her pouch. Then she lifted the baking board lid back into place, only now noticing how easy it was to see where to fit the board securely across the top of the barrel.

A circle of flickering torchlight illuminated the barrel and the wall behind it. The blaze also shone on her, its heat warming her back and—dear saints—catching her out in all her thieving glory.

"O-o-oh, no!" She wheeled around, managing to hold onto her bag of oats, but dropping the jar of honey.

It landed on the floor with a loud crack, splitting into two perfect halves. The honey oozed out to spread across the stone flagging, stopping just short of a pair of small black boots, scuffed and well-worn.

"What be you doing, lassie?" Moraig held the hand torch higher. Her eyes glittered in the smoking light.

Arabella couldn't speak. Her tongue seemed stuck to the roof of her mouth and she was almost sure it would remain there forever.

She wanted to sink through the floor.

Mad Moraig hobbled around her and thrust her torch into an iron bracket on the wall. Turning back to Arabella, she dusted her hands and then set them against her narrow hips.

"If you had a need o' oats and honey, I'd have told Conall to fetch you some." She angled her gray head, peering at Arabella with bright, all-seeing eyes. "You need only to have asked."

"I couldn't." Arabella found her voice at last. It sounded rusty, mortified. "I—...I didn't want anyone to know I desired them. They're for my ablutions."

The excuse turned her cheeks crimson.

"Eh?" Moraig lifted a scraggly brow. "Be you no' pleased with my gillyflower soap?"

"Your soap is the finest I've ever used." Arabella rushed to reassure her.

Moraig's flowery scented soap *was* of superior quality.

"It is only...." She cast around for a reason. "I like to keep a small bag of oats in my cleansing ewer." It wasn't a lie. She did do this when she remembered. "The oats soften the water and soothe my skin."

Moraig nodded sagely. "Aye, I've heard the like."

"The honey . . . ." Arabella twined the oat sack's string around her fingers. "My throat has been achy since yestere'en and I wanted to keep the honey at my bedside."

That was a flat-out lie, even if honey did have restorative powers.

Her throat was fine.

And her face was burning hotter than Moraig's torch.

But the old woman merely bobbed her head again, her smile sweet. "Oh, aye. The honey be good for all manner o' ills, sure and it is."

Looking down, Moraig nudged the broken honey jar with her toe. She stared at the shards for a long moment and when she finally raised her head, she was no longer smiling.

But her expression wasn't unkind.

"Now, lass"—she pinned Arabella with a piercing gaze, her eyes deep-seeing and lucid—"I'd know the real reason you wanted the oats and honey."

Arabella swallowed.

Moraig hobbled closer and patted her arm. "I'll no' be saying anything to Himself, dinna you worry. Nor the others. I saw them eyeing you darkly at the start and we'll no' be wishing them riled again. Truth is"—she glanced again at the spilled honey—"I have a notion why you want such goods. But I'd rather hear it from you."

Arabella inhaled deeply and released a great sigh.

Shame scalded her.

And try as she might, she couldn't form the words to tell Moraig the truth. She smoothed her hands down the front of her shawl-draped plaid, her mind racing. She didn't want to lie to Moraig. The old woman had been so kind to her and deserved better.

"Ah, well...." Arabella straightened her shoulders. "You have the right of it," she admitted. "I do have other reasons for needing the oats and honey. Darroc has promised to take me to see the Seal Isles—"

She glanced aside, her face flaming again. "There's a hermit's cell on the main isle. St. Egbert was a follower of Columba and I wish to pray at his cave. I thought I'd leave victuals there in gratitude."

Moraig's brow hitched again. "Did you now?"

Arabella nodded.

"Do you ken"—Moraig looked down at her hands, worrying her gnarled fingers as she spoke—"there be folk hereabouts who pour oats and ale into the sea when the fishing's rough and times are hard. They do be hoping that such offerings might help ease their woes."

She glanced up then, the image of guilelessness. "Right enough, that's what they do."

Arabella's mouth twisted. "How did you know?"

Moraig gave a peal of fluty laughter. "Can you no' see how old I am, lassie? Besides"—her eyes twinkled as she leaned close—"so far as I ken, there's no many o' Columba's men who'd be glad of a pagan offering."

"You are most wise, Moraig." Arabella dropped onto an oaken settle against the wall. "It wasn't well done of me to try and fool you. Please forgive me."

"Whist!" Moraig cut the air with a hand. "Though I am for thinking the oats and honey aren't meant for leaving on some cushion o' heather?"

"No, they aren't." Arabella folded her hands over the

sack of oats on her lap and looked across the main body of the kitchens. "The hermit cell isn't the only shrine on the Seal Isles. There's another, much older one called the Giving Stone. I learned of it in my childhood. It's said to be on the beach of the main island. No one at Eilean Creag much speaks of the stone these days and I believe most folk who ever heard the tales have forgotten."

Moraig joined her on the settle. "And what be the stone's powers?"

"The stone blesses women." Arabella inhaled a jittery breath. She felt silly recounting such things. "The stories I recall describe it more as a strange outcropping of rock than an actual stone. Most importantly, there's a nearly perfect circular hole through its center."

"Ahhhh...." Moraig adjusted her black skirts, sending up a faint waft of gillyflowers. "Can it be the stone has something to do with love?"

Arabella dug her fingers into the pliant sides of the oat bag. "The stone serves women in three different ways, depending on their need," she explained, feeling more ridiculous with each word. "Women seeking the stone's benevolence must crawl through the hole at the moment of sunrise.

"If a woman is with child, the stone grants her an easy birth. If the woman is barren, she can be sure that she will soon ripen with child. And"—Arabella hesitated—"if a woman is unloved, the stone ensures that she will win her heart's desire."

Moraig put a hand on Arabella's arm, squeezing. "So the victuals are a thanks offering."

"They are more than that." Arabella shifted on the settle, uncomfortable. "As I understood the telling, a woman must bestow three gifts on the stone after she crawls through its hole. These offerings must be made no matter her wish. Grain represents the ripening of a child in a woman's belly. Fresh milk is required, too. It stands for an easy birth.

"Honey"—she glanced at the shattered jar—"signifies the sweetness of true love."

"And I mind that'll be what you're hoping for." Moraig slapped her knee. "I kent it, just!"

Once again Arabella wished the floor would open up and swallow her.

"That is so, aye." She spoke before she lost her nerve.

Moraig deserved the truth.

To her surprise, the old woman chortled. "There be none in these isles with more respect for the old ways than me. But—" she sprang to her feet, her eyes glinting in the torchlight—"I'm for telling you that you've no need o' such a ceremony."

Arabella stood. "I've come too great a distance not to honor the stone. And"—she smoothed her skirts—"to pray at the hermit cell."

Even if she believed neither would help, she meant to do both.

It was a chance.

Moraig raised a thin arm and clutched her hand meaningfully. "And if you kent you already have him?"

Arabella's heart jumped. "If you mean Darroc, I'm sure you mistake."

"Say you!" Moraig laughed delightedly. "Himself's besotted since the day he brought you here."

Arabella wished it were so.

Unfortunately, she didn't believe a word.

"It's true as I'm standing here." Moraig leaned close, giving her a secret smile. "I was young once, remember. I ken the signs."

Arabella laced her hands together, embarrassed. "He has shown me kindness. But if he cares for me as you say, he has an odd way of letting me know."

Moraig curled her fingers in a fold of Arabella's plaid and held tight. "The lad's ne'er been in love. All men make fools o' themselves and blunder about like dimwits when they lose their hearts."

Arabella looked down at Moraig's hand, still gripping her. She didn't want her to see her face because she was suddenly filled with so much wild giddy hope she almost feared she'd choke.

As if she knew, Moraig stepped back and hitched up her black skirts. "I'll just be fetching you another jar o' honey, though,"—her voice rose in triumph—"I'm thinking you'll be enjoying another kind o' sweetness when you visit that stretch o' beach on the Seal Isles."

Arabella's heart flipped. Moraig's prediction made her thrill with the memory of Darroc's embrace, the brief but scorching hot kisses they'd shared.

She wanted more.

And she would crawl through the Giving Stone.

She'd been raised to be content with what the saints had given her. But if there was even the slightest chance the ages-old ritual could help her achieve her dreams, she meant to risk the foolishness.

As her father and sister oft claimed, he who is bold succeeds.

So she straightened her back and gave Moraig her most

confident smile. "We shall see," she said, feeling quite daring indeed.

She just hoped she could be as brave when the time came.

Something told her it might make all the difference.

"Did you know they're calling you Darroc the Despicable?"

The words, spoken just behind Darroc's shoulder, didn't surprise him. Conall should know he made it his business to be aware of everything that went on within his walls. A mouse couldn't snag a crumb from the great hall's floor rushes without his knowledge. He certainly knew when his men turned sour and stooped to name calling.

As long as that name wasn't Darroc the Daft, it was no bother to him.

He also knew what had their dander up.

But he had good reason not to fawn over Lady Arabella like the blundering fools his men had become. Even if he did—at times—forget her name, he couldn't ignore the disaster that would befall them if he heeded temptation. His men could glare and mutter into their beards all they wished. It wouldn't change a thing.

"Do you no' care?" Conall stepped around to face him, blocking his view of Geordie Dhu's eagerly anticipated sea tasting.

They stood beneath Castle Bane's cliffs, on the narrow crescent-shaped boat strand where everyone watched the master cook brave the icy surf with long, sure strides. Seemingly unfazed by the cold, Geordie Dhu was naked save the plaid slung across one shoulder. Head high, he marched through the breakers, not stopping until the foaming water swirled around his waist. Wind screamed down from the hills behind the strand; sharp gales that tore at his plaid and whipped his curling black beard. But Geordie Dhu stood proud, the only man not stamping his feet or struggling stoically to keep his teeth from chattering. All present knew that his fiery will probed the sea's mood and kept him warm.

This was the final act of his sea prophesying ceremonies and, as such, accorded due reverence.

Even so, Darroc gave his cousin a long withering look.

"Nae, I don't care what they call me." He kept his voice suitably low as Geordie Dhu thrust his arms in the air and began chanting a prayer to the sea gods, beseeching them to share their wisdom. "So long as they refrain from bathing with Moraig's gillyflower soap and stop boiling their plaids, they can say what they please."

"Ah, well." Conall cracked his knuckles. "Could be they have the right of it. You've found an excuse to leave the hall each time Lady Arabella manages to make her way down the stairs to join us."

Darroc fixed his stare on Geordie Dhu, feigning greater interest in the cook's chant than he felt. He knew the words by heart, after all. What he didn't like was the reproach in his cousin's voice.

Conall had enough wits to know his coolness to Arabella was for her own good. And that each time he turned away from her such blinding frustration slammed through him that he could hardly see where he was going.

It was a wonder he wasn't walking around with black eyes and stubbed toes, so great was the desire inside him.

But clearly Conall's wits failed him, because he stepped closer and poked Darroc's arm. "She's a lady,

Darroc. Your treatment of her *is* despicable. Have you no' seen her face each time you push back from the table and stomp from the hall without a by-your-leave?"

Darroc folded his arms. "I haven't been in the hall of late. Or have you forgotten who gathered and raked yon pile o' seaware?"

It was the only excuse that came to him.

Seizing it, he gestured to a large mound of seaweed at the far end of the strand. Washed ashore by strong winds, the tangle was highly prized for the nourishing benefits it would bring the isle's needy soil. He and Conall had seen to its harvesting, knowing the backbreaking toil would have been too much for the others, however eager.

"Well?" Darroc arched a brow.

Conall pinned him with challenging blue eyes. "You could tell her the truth. That you're soft on her and that it scares you clear down to your stubborn toes."

"I am no' soft on her. I—" Darroc's jaw slipped when the little red dog fox he'd seen before crept around the corner of the seaweed pile.

The creature stared at him with piercing yellow-gold eyes, twitched its plush tail, and then darted back behind the seaweed before Darroc could blink.

He grabbed Conall's arm. "Yon fox! Did you see him?"

Conall shook free. "I see naught but our pile o' tangle and your fool kist o' plaids."

"The plaids are for Lady Arabella's comfort." Darroc's gaze flicked to a travel chest not far from the seaweed mound. The beached birlinn loomed only a few feet away. "It'll be bitter cold on the water. The extra plaids will keep her warm through the night."

Conall snorted. "I can think of better ways to warm a lass! Especially one I'm sweet on."

"Your tongue's flapping worse than a woman's." Darroc shoved a hand through his hair. "I feel responsible for her well-being. Honor-bound as chief to ensure—"

A great roar went up from the others.

Geordie Dhu was just plunging his drinking horn into the sea. Freezing mist swirled low across the water, cloaking him in a mantle of white as he raised the ram's horn for his testing sip. A sharp intake of breath went through the onlookers and even Darroc felt gooseflesh prickle his nape. With his black-bearded chin tilted heavenward and the curved drinking horn poised at his lips, Geordie Dhu could have been Manannan himself, pagan god of the sea.

For a long moment, he swished the sea water in his mouth, eyes closed as he communed with whatever powers gave him the answers he sought. Then he swallowed deeply and tipped the remaining contents of the horn back into the surf.

"Ho!" He pumped the horn in the air, grinning. "The wind and waves are kind! Clear skies and no storms shall greet the morrow!"

He began stamping back through the surf and another rousing cheer went up from the men on the strand. They surged to the water's edge, Mungo running at the fore with a dry plaid draped over his arm, the rest jostling and shouting, their excitement thick in the air.

Until Geordie Dhu reached the shore and tossed aside his wet plaid, then shook his great girth like a dog coming in from the rain. Mungo threw the dry plaid across the cook's wet glistening shoulders and gave him a hearty congratulatory slap on the back, but a change rippled through the others.

Everywhere men smoothed hands down the fronts of their plaids or raked fingers through their wind-tossed hair. Many coughed and cleared their throats noisily. All drew themselves up as straight as they could. Some shuffled feet and swelled their chests. They all seemed to have forgotten Geordie Dhu. And they also seemed determined not to look in Darroc's direction.

He had a sinking feeling he knew why.

Conall's grin proved it.

As did the way the entire morn suddenly shone brighter. In a blink, the day felt warm and almost golden, as if the sun had burst through the clouds, banishing the mist and even the cold, sleety wind.

There could be only one reason for the world to feel as if spring had arrived early.

The same reason his heart betrayed him with its rapid hammering.

Knowing he shouldn't, he turned to follow his men's moony-eyed stares. The sight that greeted him chilled his blood. Arabella and Mad Moraig were picking their way down the precarious stone steps cut into the sheer side of the cliff, Frang and Mina trotting happily in front of them.

"Damnation!" Darroc's eyes rounded. He flashed a furious glance at Conall. "One misstep and they'll both tumble into the sea!"

"Ach, they're stepping careful enough." Conall eyed them, still beaming. He clearly underestimated the danger of the slippery, zigzagging steps.

"Careful, my arse!" Darroc roared, then pounded

across the shingle to where the two women were just taking the last dozen or so steps.

Mad Moraig's hand was clenched tight on Arabella's elbow and he knew the old woman made her way up and down the cliff path several times or more a day, surefooted for all her tottering gait.

It didn't matter.

The image of Arabella soft and pliant in his arms flashed across his mind, her hair spilling around her shoulders and her eyes full of wonder and innocence. Her lips parted for his kiss, her breath sweet. Life's breath that could so easily be snatched from her if she slipped on the narrow steps to plunge into the churning surf below.

Terror as he'd never known gripped him. He could almost see her falling, her body still and broken on the terrible, jagged rocks.

"No-o-o!" He ran faster, willing her to tread with care.

Behind him men cheered and hooted and from somewhere outside the red haze blurring his vision, Frang and Mina's barks nearly split his ears. Then the dogs were racing circles around him, romping and leaping at his legs.

A small hand grabbed his arm, squeezing hard, and chasing the horror from his mind. "Yourself didnae think I'd be for letting her fall, did you?"

Darroc jerked free of Mad Moraig's grasp. "You could have both plunged to your deaths."

The crone had the cheek to cackle. "Aye, well, we didn't then, did we?"

Darroc glared at her.

She thrust out a bristly chin, her eyes alight with triumph. "We came to see Geordie Dhu taste the sea."

Lady Arabella peered down the strand to where some

of his men were slapping Geordie Dhu on the back and plying him with *uisge beatha*. Others gallivanted about like a pack of preening peacocks.

"It would seem we came too late." Her voice was cool as spring rain.

"Aye, and I'll just see you back to the keep." It crossed Darroc's mind to lie about Geordie Dhu's predictions. "You are too late, so—"

"No' too late for the two o' you to share a kiss to thank Manannan!" Geordie Dhu cut him off. Striding up to them, he clamped a strong hand on Darroc's shoulder.

Darroc felt the wet sand shift beneath his feet.

Now it truly was too late.

His men pressed near, the whole prancing lot of them, circling round and chanting in unison. "A kiss! A kiss for the god o' the sea!"

Blessedly they didn't shout that Manannan was also a fertility god. But the mischievous glints in their eyes said they knew it well.

Darroc's face flamed.

Lady Arabella smiled sweetly.

"So the sea tasting was propitious for our journey?" Her words made him regret he'd suggested the voyage.

He nodded, feeling doomed.

"Aye, just!" Geordie Dhu grinned at her. "There'll be naught but high winds and clear skies, though the cold might freeze your gizzards!"

"I never feel the cold." She spoke like a true Valkyrie.

Darroc swallowed a groan.

He flashed a glance at his kist of plaids, his mood worsening. He'd hoped she'd pass the journey bundled inside them, her charms well hidden from view. Her lush curves and tempting womanliness buried within a lumpy bulk of chin-high tartaned wool.

"A kiss for Manannan!" His men took up the cry again.

Darroc could've sworn.

But the excitement on their faces gave him little choice but to join in their antics. And even if he'd denied them, Lady Arabella had stepped forward and tilted up her chin, her eyes closed and her lips proffered.

Not to kiss her would be to shame her.

Yet doing so would seal his fate.

Furious, he bracketed her face with his hands and leaned down to let his lips brush hers. Only lightly, a kiss as fleeting as possible, though even that brief contact seared him to the marrow.

Somewhere—at a great distance it seemed—his men roared their approval. Once again Frang's and Mina's barks added to the clamor. But he took little heed of any of them. Not even the beauty in his arms who somehow managed to twine her fingers in his hair and deepen the kiss before he could honorably break away from her.

Worse yet, he pulled her closer, happily obliging.

All around them time seemed to slow and one truth beat hotly in his breast, damning him with its scalding message. Somehow things had changed since he'd first suggested they make the voyage to Olaf Big Nose's isle.

Arabella no longer dreaded the journey.

It was him.

The thought of a night spent at sea with her jellied his knees. And, saints help him, but he knew he'd be a different man when they returned to Castle Bane.

He'd be in love with a woman he couldn't have.

And he didn't know if he was man enough to bear it.

Chapter Fourteen

❦

He who is bold succeeds.

Arabella repeated the words like a silent chant, timing them to match Conall's rhythmic beating of the birlinn's gong. She slid a look at him, taking comfort in his confident stance and the way his smile flashed each time he caught her glance. He made a fine helmsman, his baton strokes steady and sure, the repetitive clangs in perfect harmony with the oarsmen as they dipped and pulled the craft's long sweeps through the smooth, dark-glistening water.

The Hebridean Sea stretched around them, empty of danger and benign.

Everything Geordie Dhu had prophesied proved true.

A brisk wind filled the birlinn's single square sail and Conall's gong-beating and the oarsmen's strength kept them flying over the waves at speed. MacConacher's Isle lay far behind them, its cliff-girt silhouette having slipped below the horizon several hours before. Night was closing in now, the sky turning a deep, dark blue with the first stars just beginning to twinkle high above them.

Every once in a while strange shapes loomed out of the darkness, black and silent against the encroaching night. Jagged skerries and tall, fingerlike protrusions of rock, they vanished almost as quickly as they'd appeared. Even so, Arabella couldn't keep from shuddering whenever they sped past one of the eerie sentinels.

She didn't want to be afraid.

Darroc stood at the stern and she trusted him. His grip on the long, broad-bladed steering oar looked firm and he seemed to anticipate the shockingly sudden appearance of each death-bringing cluster of rocks or reef before they rose in terrifying challenge.

Nowhere were there signs of sea raiders.

No black-painted dragon-ships, nor even a shred of mist to hide such jackels if they were about.

Indeed, the night was beautiful.

And so cold she was sure her feet had turned to blocks of ice.

She'd long since lost feeling in her fingers. It cost all her will to keep from thrusting her hands beneath her arms to warm them. Her nose and cars were beyond such repair. It wouldn't surprise her if they snapped off any moment. And even though she sat near Darroc, well sheltered from wind and flying spray by the extra sail screen he'd hoisted for her privacy, she couldn't feel the sturdy oaken planks of the stern platform beneath her.

Her buttocks were surely frozen to the wood!

Geordie Dhu had predicted—correctly—that the cold would freeze her gizzards.

But her MacKenzie pride wouldn't let her admit it.

Especially when the racing wind and splashing waves made Darroc seem more alive and vivid than she'd ever seen him. His eyes held a gleam of excitement and each time the flashing oars sent up more clouds of icy spume to douse him she would've sworn he smothered a grin. Never had she seen a man so at one with the rolling sea.

Arabella hugged herself in an attempt not to shiver. But it was so hard when just looking at him made her believe that the world was meant to be untamed and wild.

"Still no' feeling the cold?" He tossed a sidelong look at her. "I've brought along a kist filled with extra plaids just for you."

"I do not need them." She lifted her chin to the bracing air. "This is nothing to winters in Kintail," she lied. "I'm enjoying the night wind."

It was a wonder her teeth didn't clatter on the words.

"Cold is good for the lungs." She sat up straighter, feeling a need to prove herself.

"It's also turning your lips blue." He returned his gaze to the glassy black troughs before them. "When we lie-to for the night, you'll see that the roaring traveler hasn't yet shown us his worst. Once we drop anchor—"

"Roaring traveler?" Arabella blinked.

"That's one of the names Vikings gave the wind." Darroc lifted a hand to dash droplets of glittering spray from his cheek. "Once you've heard its shrieking when all else is still and feel its chill slicing through the birlinn's hull, you'll understand why. Yon sail screen"—he glanced at the makeshift partition, flapping crazily even now—"and one plaid won't be enough to keep you warm."

He who is bold succeeds.

The chant marched across her mind again, persistent and encouraging.

Her chin came up a bit higher. "My father once told me men didn't just wrap themselves in their plaids for warmth at sea." She spoke quickly, before her daring failed her. "He said they slept huddled together."

Laughs rose from the men on the rowing benches.

"Aye, and so we do." Darroc glanced at her, his hair streaming in the wind. "That's why I brought the chest of plaids. They'll give you the same extra warmth."

Arabella bit back the urge to purse her lips.

That wasn't the answer she'd wanted.

It would seem that *bold* didn't work as well for her as it did for her father and sister.

"Tell me of Olaf Big Nose," she said, changing the subject. "From his name, he's of Viking blood."

She hoped only she heard the tremor in her voice.

The birlinn plunged into a deep trough and rose again before Darroc spoke. "Olaf is a Norseman and he lives by the old ways. But you needn't fear him. He's a big man as fierce-looking and shaggy as a Highland stirk, yet I've seen him shed tears o'er ancient harp songs and shake with laughter at the antics of a puppy.

"He is a good friend and trusted ally with no time for outlawry." Darroc glanced at her, his smile widening into a grin. "Once he hears the fate of the *Merry Dancer*, you will see the strength of his hand and why—"

"You sound sure he'll join you against the Black Vikings." Arabella had trouble believing it. "In Kintail we say that blood tells."

"And so it does." He didn't disagree. "But when blood is tainted, honor speaks louder."

"A Viking's honor." Arabella couldn't keep the skepticism out of her voice.

Darroc threw back his head and laughed. "Olaf Big Nose is no marauding sea pirate. He loves his wee isle as much as I do my own. And"—he ducked when a shower of spume crashed over the stern platform—"his family's called the isle theirs since before Rhun set the cornerstone for Castle Bane. Olaf's great-great-great grandsire was one Einar Ironhand, a merchant who served the sea routes from Norway. When other merchants grew envious of his success and tried to damage his trade by blackening his good name, Einar left his home for Iceland, settling there only to run into the same problems he'd had in Trondheim.

"Disillusioned and with his fortune already made, he gathered his friends and womenfolk and sailed for the Hebrides. That was in the day these isles were still in Norse hands and called the Sudreys. Einar claimed an isle that pleased him and found the peace and good life he craved."

"Olaf is no different," Conall tossed in, raising his voice above the clangs of his gong. "He will tell you his greatest joy is watching the wind chase clouds across his hills."

"Or"—one of the oarsmen twisted around with a grin—"learning that one o' his women is swelling with a new bairn!"

Arabella's face flamed despite the cold. "One of his women?"

Darroc coughed and beat his chest with a fist. "I told you," he said at last, ignoring his men's sniggers, "Olaf honors the old ways. Norsewomen are strong free-thinking females. There are many women in his camp who enjoy being the wife of their leader. Even if—" he cleared his throat—"other women share the privilege."

"I see." Arabella huddled deeper into her plaid.

She was sure her jaw was hanging open but with her face feeling frozen, she couldn't tell for certain.

She also knew Gelis would've split a gut laughing to hear such wickedness.

That the notion sent scorching heat racing to her cheeks made her wish she hadn't crept out from behind the protective screen of the sailcloth. Her questions about the Norseman had ruined the night's air of adventure. Conall's face blazed as red as his hair, the oarsmen had gone embarrassingly quiet, and Darroc was scowling at them all.

But then he brightened and flung out an arm. "There are your Seal Isles!" He grinned at her, and the awkward moment passed. "You can just see them way off to the right."

Arabella looked to where he pointed and her breath caught. Her eyes flew wide. And she was sure her heart stopped beating in her chest. She opened her mouth to cry out, but her throat had closed. Worse, for one terrible moment, hot tears blurred her vision and she couldn't see a thing. But she pressed a hand to her cheek and blinked hard until the isles swam into view once again.

The Seal Isles were more beautiful than her dreams.

Little more than low humps on the horizon, they glowed silver in the moonlight. The sea glittered around them, sheened like liquid glass while the surrounding waters stretched cold and dark, the contrast making the Seal Isles seem all the more wondrous.

It was a world beyond.

And the end of a journey that now seemed to wrap around her like a cloak, immersing her in beauty, warmth, and comfort.

"Oh!" She found her voice at last. "Th-th-they're even more l-l-l-ovely than I'd expected."

She clapped a hand over her mouth, realizing too late that she'd let her teeth chatter.

"I mean they're—"

"God in His Heaven!" Darroc stared at her, only now seeing that her lips *were* blue. "You are cold!"

He'd been jesting earlier, believing that the bluish tinge was only a trick of the silvery moonlight. And like the bampot he always seemed to be around her, he'd taken her on her word that the freezing wind didn't faze her.

Now....

"*Conall*!" He flashed a look at his cousin, signaling him to slow the gong beats. "Hugh—take the steering oar!" he shouted to the nearest oarsman as he sprinted down the narrow aisle between the rowing benches. "Men, ship the oars! We halt here for the night."

He reached the bow just as his men raised the dripping sweeps out of the water and the birlinn began to lose its spanking pace and glide.

"Damnation!" He didn't care who heard him curse as he scrambled over the swords, axes, and other weapons wedged into the small space between the front rowing bench and the edge of the bow platform.

He needed the kist of plaids that some fool had buried beneath two grappling hooks and a jumble of horn lanterns. Bow and stern lanterns he didn't dare light lest he wished to trumpet their position to any passing galleys that could prove unfriendly.

They might not have seen Black Vikings on their scouting forays, but that didn't mean they weren't there. Hoping it wasn't so, he dropped to his knees and swept aside the clutter on top of the chest.

Then he threw open the lid and reached in to grab as many plaids as he could carry.

He pulled out handfuls of seaweed.

"*Yaaaaw*!" He leapt to feet, flinging the stinking tangle into the water. "What devilry is this?"

He stared down at the chest, disbelief beating through him. But there could be no mistake. It was the plaid kist. And it was filled with dead and reeking seaweed with nary a single plaid in sight.

For one crazy mad moment, he saw again the little red fox on the boat strand, remembering how the wee beastie had crept around the harvested sea tangle. The chest of plaiding had stood only a few paces away.

He frowned.

To even consider that the fox had anything to do with switching the plaids for seaweed made him madder than Moraig. Furious that the possibility even crossed his mind, he spun around to glare at his men.

"Who did this?" He jammed his hands on his hips. "Speak now or you'll find no bolthole to escape my wrath!"

Silence answered him.

His men stared at him with rounded eyes. Their bearded jaws hung open, their amazement as great as his own.

They were innocent.

And he was doomed.

There was now only one way to keep Arabella warm.

As if his men knew it—and that he wouldn't be after their hides—chuckles began rising from the rowing benches.

"Damnation!" he growled again, whipping around to seize the kist and hurl it into the sea.

When he turned back to face his men, one of them slid a pointed glance at the birlinn's center aisle where they'd all soon stretch out for the night. Plaid-wrapped and packed tightly together, the closeness of their bodies would keep them as warm as if they sat round a hearth fire.

Darroc frowned again.

The cheeky bastard who'd glanced at the aisle wriggled his eyebrows. "You told the lass how we stay warm of a night," he reminded, grinning. "If she settles down in the middle of us, we can—"

"And I say you give me your plaid, each of your plaids." Darroc enjoyed how the grins slid from his men's faces. "We sleep naked and Lady Arabella can sleep beneath our plaiding, behind her sail screen."

"Nae." Arabella pushed to her feet. "I cannot allow that," she argued, wishing she could control her shivering. But the instant she'd stood, the full wind hit her, cold and wet and too much even for a MacKenzie.

"I'll b-b-be fine behind the screen." Her teeth chattering proved the lie.

"You can sit up through the night and hold her." Conall stamped down the aisle and clapped a hand on Darroc's shoulder. "We kept her warm that way when we fetched her off the barrel raft."

Darroc glared at his cousin. "She was unconscious."

"And this night she'd be asleep." Conall grinned.

So did the oarsmen.

Arabella bit her lip, seeing her chance.

If she were bold.

"He's right." She whipped back the sail screen, challenging him to join her. "Come, please, and we shall keep each other warm. Anything else is simply foolish."

He cocked a brow and for one frightening moment she thought he'd refuse. But then his eyes darkened with a look that sent hot shivers racing through her and he strode forward, climbing up onto the stern platform and yanking the sail screen into place behind them so quickly, she was in his arms before she could blink.

Arabella sucked in a breath and felt a rush of heat stain her cheeks.

He pulled her even closer and turned that *look* on her again. "For a maid who doesn't want to be foolish, you are quite daring," he said, his voice deeper than usual. So smooth and husky that the words curled right through her to settle low in her belly and make her tingle in ways that should send her dashing right back outside the sail screen to where his men had gone suspiciously quiet.

"My sister is daring." She couldn't think of anything else to say. Not when she felt so strangely breathless and he was looking at her with such smoldering intensity. "I am—"

"You are"—he lowered his head toward hers—"a great temptation."

"Me?" Arabella took a deep breath. It was hard to think of herself as anything but a quiet and dutiful daughter. She certainly couldn't see herself tempting anyone. Yet he made her wish that she could. He also made her realize how empty and meaningless her life had been until now. And how much she hoped that would soon change.

He was still looking at her in a way that made it seem

possible. Indeed, his lips were just a few breaths away from hers and they were curving in a smile that did funny things to her knees.

She was trembling, too.

But this time her shivers had nothing to do with the cold.

"I'm sure you're mistaken." The possibility pinched her heart. "I've told you that no suitor was ever serious enough about me to even make a bid. It truly is my sister who turns heads and bedazzles men. She—"

"She is not here." He lifted a hand to capture her chin and hold her face so that she couldn't glance aside. "And if by some witchery she were, I would still see only you."

Arabella swallowed. "I think you are a great flatterer. Or, perhaps, you are being kind because of the history between our families."

He shook his head slowly. "It is because of the past that I would never lie to you, Arabella."

"Then what you are saying is…" She couldn't finish the sentence.

He began tracing the line of her jaw with his thumb. "I believe you know. My feelings have been strong enough to make me forget my honor more than once. To forget many things! So…" He paused and the only sound was the creaking of the birlinn and the snapping of the sail screen in the wind. "You, lass, are a maid like no other. I find myself fascinated by you. Ever since the moment I first saw you. You must have sensed…"

He paused again and closed his eyes. Almost as if the words cost him as much to speak as it did her to believe they were true.

"I have never felt this way before." He looked at her,

the heat in his eyes stroking her soul, making her melt in his arms. "Not for any woman. Only you!"

Arabella bit her lip. All the boldness inside her—every shred she could summon—screamed for her to throw her arms around his neck and shout that she was falling in love with him. That, truth be told, she might already be, despite his name and hers, the past, and all that had gone before. She drew a breath, wanting to tell him that only the future mattered. But her heart seemed somehow lodged in her throat, thundering wildly, and making it impossible to speak.

This was everything she'd dreamed.

Her dearest hopes come true.

Yet inexplicable fear paralyzed her.

As if he knew, he caught her hand and pressed her fingers to his chest. She could feel the strength of him, his warmth, through the rough wool of his plaid. His heart hammered against her fingertips, the beat as fierce and rapid as her own. And, heaven help her, but the moonlight streamed down on him, picking out blue-black highlights in his glossy raven hair and making her want to thrust her fingers into the strands and pull his mouth down to hers so he could kiss her as he'd done before, the wonder of his lips making her forget everything except the burning desire she felt for him.

"Arabella, I know you are no' ready for this." His voice held a rough edge, silky deep and seductive. "I would never rush you, or hurt you."

"I know." Was that shaky whisper her voice? "And I—I have feelings for you, too."

Dear saints, she'd admitted it!

"Lass..." He tightened his arms around her and

brought his mouth down over hers. She gasped, but then the world spun and somehow her fingers *were* in his hair, digging deep and pulling him nearer as he slanted his lips over hers, kissing her thoroughly until pleasure spilled through her. Nothing mattered except his tongue tangling with hers, his warm breath sweeter than wine and so much headier. But then he broke away and stepped back, the sudden end to their kiss almost a physical wrench.

"You see what you do to me." He shoved a hand through his hair and glanced aside, staring out at the glittering night sea. "If you do have feelings for me, Arabella, and doubts, this is your chance. Tell me now and we shall end it here. I swear to you on my dead mother's soul that I will no' touch you ever again."

He looked back at her. "Tell me, lass. Before it is too late."

Arabella pressed a hand to her breast. She was shaking. "I have already told you what is in my heart," she said, feeling both hot and cold inside. "I do not have any doubts. I've never been more certain."

"Then"—He slid his arms around her again—"because I have doubts that this is happening, I shall have to kiss you one more time. Just to be sure that I am no' dreaming and that the gods are truly smiling on me at last."

Arabella swallowed hard. She could see the passion in his eyes. Her fears spiraled away and something seemed to split within her, allowing a wild yearning to beat through her veins, heating her blood and making places that should shame her quiver with excitement.

She wanted the kiss he'd promised.

She ached for more.

And then he was kissing her. It was a kiss so wondrous

that she was lost as soon he slanted his lips over hers. She lifted up on her toes and leaned into him, opening her mouth freely beneath his, needing him to deepen the kiss. And he did, letting his tongue slide over and around hers, plundering her mouth and tantalizing her with the deliciousness of such startling intimacy.

His tongue kept stroking, slow and deep. Then somehow he lowered them both to the planking of the stern platform, cradling her against him and using his body to cushion her against the wood's hardness. They were lying side by side and through the sensual haze of their kisses, Arabella felt the long hard ridge of his manhood pressing against her hip. She gasped and stiffened, her sudden cry causing him to release her at once and pull away.

"I'm sorry, sweetness." He kept his arms banded loosely around her. The bright gleam of desire in his eyes said he knew exactly what had startled her. "There are some things a man can't always control."

Arabella nodded, wishing she were as worldly as Gelis.

A part of her was terrified and yet another newly awakening place inside her thrilled to know that he wanted her so much to have such a reaction.

Indeed, she was almost dying with longing herself, so badly did she want him.

But her surprise had damped his ardor. She didn't need carnal knowledge to see that the heated look in his eyes was now a look of tenderness. And the arms still encircling her were holding her gently. The hungry, almost desperate way he'd clutched her to him moments ago had vanished like mist before the morning sun.

"You should sleep now, precious," he said then, his

words proving it. "I will keep you warm till morning and then we shall speak when we reach Olaf's isle."

"I am not tired." She doubted she'd sleep the entire night. Not with such awareness crackling between them. He'd slid his hands down her back and then smoothed her hair away from her face, cradling her cheek against his shoulder. Simple touches but so weighted with meaning, each caress sending tingles of golden warmth spilling through her.

Each moment spun with promise, making it impossible to close her eyes. But it was so easy to relax against him. She could hear the steady beat of his heart and feel the hard planes and ridges of his muscled chest. Succumbing would be so sweet. Her eyelids did seem heavy and the rocking of the birlinn was soothing. Even the wind lulled her, its gusting roar somehow softer now, gently keening and oddly melodic.

Almost like a song....

She sighed and snuggled closer to his warmth. He was stroking her hair now, his touch feather light as if he were lifting single strands and letting them glide through his fingers. Astonishingly pleasurable shivers prickled her scalp and the sensitive skin of her nape. Beautiful sensations that made her want to purr but the effort was too great.

Her eyes did drift shut then, her long and sooty eyelashes giving her an innocence that both pierced Darroc's heart and jabbed him with a pang of guilt.

Arabella of Kintail was innocent.

And the twitches he still couldn't stop from stirring at his loins made him the most despicable sort of beast he'd e'er condemned for their callousness.

A state he only worsened when he dipped his head and kissed her hair. She made a soft little mewling sound in response and seemed to melt even more sweetly against him, her reaction making his pulse jump and *that* part of him tighten and pull with even more insistence.

Scowling fiercely, he slid a discreet hand down between them and squeezed hard until the throbbing abated. Then, because he was a greater fool than he would have ever believed, he lowered his lips to the crown of her head again and kissed her softly. Her hair felt silky and cool and smelled faintly of gillyflowers, entirely beguiling.

The subtle contact made him ache for more. He knew from caring for her that her skin felt even silkier. Smooth, unmarred, and whiter than the creamiest milk, her limbs would glow so sinuously in the moonlight were she naked in his arms. Her breasts...

He groaned and closed his eyes. But that, too, only brought torment when he rubbed his cheek against her hair and her delicate scent flooded his senses. Unable to resist, he dropped another soft kiss to her temple, then along her brow, her cheekbones, and even those lovely eyelashes.

Blessedly she didn't stir. At least she didn't until she splayed her fingers across his chest and slid her hands up to his shoulders, gripping tight.

"Darroc..." Her voice was husky.

He tightened his arms around her, no longer caring if he was callous or not. She was so soft, rounded, and warm against him. His need for her consumed him and he wanted her now, without shame and regret. Somewhere he imagined a buzz of activity, his men's laughter and the clanging of the gong, the sounds breaking rudely into his dreams of sinking into Arabella's silken, womanly heat.

He frowned, trying to ignore them.

"Darroc." The voice came even deeper. Grasping fingers dug into his shoulders, shaking him much harder than Arabella had the strength to do. "Wake up, you oaf. You slept soundly and warm I see!"

"Damnation!" Darroc's eyes snapped open.

Conall's hairy legs came into frightening focus. The bastard loomed above him, grinning like a fool. Behind him, Hugh, one of the oarsmen, beat the gong, and it took Darroc all of a blink to note that they were flying across the waves. And that the weak, watery sun had made its appearance more than a few hours before.

He sat up and rubbed his eyes, amazed that Arabella still slumbered deeply. "Why didn't you wake me?" He glared at Conall, grudgingly accepting the oatcakes and cup of morning ale his cousin offered him.

"What?" Conall laughed. "Wake you and ruin what looks to have been a most *warm* night?"

"We'll have words later, whatever." Darroc took a deliberate munch out of his oatcake. "Dinna think I'll forget."

Conall grinned again and sketched a mocking bow.

"Darroc…" This time it was Arabella. She tugged on his arm, looking so delectable in her disarray that his heart twisted despite his cousin's gawking presence. "Look! There is land," she said, pointing.

"Sakes!" Darroc leapt to his feet, pulling her up with him. "That's Olaf Big Nose's isle."

"Indeed." Conall punched him in the arm, beaming. "Now you see why I wakened you. We've made good time while you've entertained us with your snores."

Scarce believing his eyes, Darroc stared at his friend's isle. They were so close he could make out its jagged cliffs, cut into so many small headlands and sweet narrow bays. Already small fishermen's huts could be seen dotting one of the larger sea lochs. Cook smoke rose in blue threads above the huts' thatched roofs and several beached longships were pulled up on the golden sand. A thickly wooded defile stretched behind the settlement and thin morning mist still wreathed the tops of the trees.

Somewhere a dog barked, the sound carrying on the wind. But what caught everyone's eye and brought a cheer from the men on the rowing benches was the single-sailed, low-slung galley that swept around the loch-head and raced toward them. Moving at speed, the galley's double banks of flashing long oars sent up great clouds of spume as the craft flew across the water.

"Ho, MacConacher—welcome!" A huge bear of a man bellowed the greeting as the galley swept up with a grand flourish, the oarsmen only back-watering the sweeps when they were well within shouting distance. "You come timely!" Olaf Big Nose grinned even more broadly than Darroc's men. "I have great tidings! News we have waited long to hear!"

"And I have news for you," Darroc called to his friend, signaling his men to lower their oars as the galley drew near. "Grim tidings, Olaf, but a stroke of fate we can turn to our advantage."

Jumping down from the stern platform, he ran forward, leaping onto the bow platform even as the two prows bumped together.

"I've brought a maid." He flung out an arm to indicate Arabella, still standing beside her sail screen. "She survived a Black Viking attack. The dastards rammed the merchant cog she was traveling on and—"

Olaf Big Nose threw back his head and laughed. "Can I ne'er outdo you?" He sprang across the narrow space separating them, grabbing Darroc's arms when he landed on the bow platform. "You've stolen my news."

Darroc stared at him. "You heard of the *Merry Dancer*?"

Olaf nodded. "The whole sorry tale, just!" He stepped back and folded his arms. "I've a bedbound survivor we found just days ago, clinging to a skerry. The man has a fever, but he'll pull through. The Black Vikings meant to ransom him, but"—he cast a glance at Arabella and lowered his voice—"when they discovered he'd lied about his connections, they set him out on the reef to drown."

Darroc felt his jaw slip. "And who is he?"

Olaf Big Nose's chest swelled. "A Norseman," he boasted, his voice ringing with pride. "You know it's nigh impossible to have done with us."

"And his name?" Arabella was suddenly at Darroc's side. She slipped a hand through his arm and he could tell that she was trembling. "Who is this man?"

"One who will be right happy to see you, lass." Olaf Big Nose turned to her, grinning. "He's the cog's shipmaster. Captain Arnkel Arneborg."

Chapter Fifteen

✤

Lady Arabella!" Arnkel Arneborg's voice was a raspy croak. "God be praised it is you."

"Captain Arneborg." Arabella looked down at the man in the narrow bed, buried to his chin beneath linens and fur coverings. Sweat beaded his brow and his blue eyes glittered feverishly. He'd lost his ruddy coloring and his cheeks were sunken, his jaw beneath the bushy blond beard jutting like a blade. Everywhere in the dimly lit room braziers glowed softly, giving off warmth and scenting the air with aromatic herbs.

A heavy wax candle burned on an iron wall pricket near the bed and in its flickering light, the shipmaster looked almost cadaverous. Of the laughing-eyed sea captain with his bluster and plague bells was nary a trace.

Arabella forced a smile. "It would seem the saints cast their eye on us both."

She hoped the words didn't sound as hollow as they felt. Truth was she could clench her fists and rail at the saints for not treating him as kindly as they had her. Before Olaf Big Nose had ushered her toward the heavy woolen hanging that separated the sickroom from the rest of his longhouse, he'd sworn that his women were seeing to the captain's every need. He'd also declared that he was sure Arneborg would regain his strength and recover fully.

Seeing him now, Arabella wasn't so sure.

She took his hand, trying not to show her dismay when she found his fingers clammy and limp. "I have Mina." She struggled for something to say. "I tied her in a length of blanketing and kept her bundled in my cloak. She is well and has charmed everyone at Castle Bane."

Captain Arneborg's eyelids flickered and he gave a terrible rattling cough. "I've heard that you have charmed someone, too, my lady."

Arabella flushed. Before she could reply, there was a soft clacking of curtain rings and the *swooshing* of the wool room divider being drawn aside. An attractive blond woman with large breasts, dressed in a colorful full-skirted gown, swept in, carrying a copper laving bowl and an armful of linen cloths. She set the bowl, filled with steaming water, on a small table beside the bed and turned to smile at Arabella.

"It is time that one was charmed," she said, her voice low-pitched, almost smoky. "Darroc MacConacher has needed a good woman for long."

Arabella's face flamed hotter. But she managed to return the Norsewoman's smile, recognizing her as Jutta Manslayer, Olaf Big Nose's favorite concubine. Darroc had pointed her out when they'd first passed through the busy settlement on their way to Olaf's longhouse.

"I think you're mistaken." Arabella watched the

woman dip a cloth into her bowl and begin dabbing Captain Arneborg's brow. She couldn't admit to a stranger that charming Darroc was her heart's greatest desire.

Or that, after the voyage to Olaf's isle, she believed she'd actually done so.

"Darroc will be returning me to Kintail after we leave your isle." Her stomach fluttered against the possibility. "He knows my father will be beside himself worrying about me."

Jutta Manslayer's lips curved in another smile. "Your father will joy to see a man as fine as Darroc at your side. There are few men so worthy."

"I know, but"—Arabella glanced back at the half-open woolen curtain. The main room of the longhouse loomed dark beyond, but the smell of wood smoke drifted into the sickroom and she heard the low murmur of men's voices as they sat gathered around the central fire. Darroc's voice was one of them, and just hearing him speak made her heart flip.

"He's already made firm plans to escort me home." She turned back to the other woman, wishing it wasn't so. She also wished she wasn't worried about what her father would do when he learned Darroc's name. "One of the reasons he brought me here was to help me prepare for the long voyage."

"Ahhh, but everything's changed now, hasn't it?" Jutta Manslayer plunged her cloth into the bowl, wringing out the excess water. "There will be much to do when you leave here. Men's business. He will scarce have time to think of journeying north to your distant Kintail."

Arabella felt her heart skip again. "I know he hopes that he and Olaf Big Nose can find the Black Vikings."

"Hah! They *will* find them." Captain Arneborg pushed

himself up against the bed bolsters, his eyes lighting with a trace of his old spirit. "I've told them where the blackguards make their camp. Their leader, Svend Skull-Splitter, is a snake but his greed is greater than his wits. Olaf and MacConacher mean to—" He broke off in a wheeze, followed by another burst of coughing.

Jutta hurried to fill an ale cup and tipped it to his lips. "You must rest now." She placed a gentle hand on his shoulder as she helped him drink. "I will tell the lady of the men's plans to banish Svend Skull-Splitter."

"He should be sent to hell and nowhere else." Captain Arneborg coughed after she set aside the cup and wiped his chin with a cloth.

Jutta waited until he slumped back against the pillows. When his chest heaves subsided and his eyes drifted shut again, she smoothed the bed coverings and then took Arabella's arm, drawing her aside.

"When Arnora Ship-Breast and the other women took you away to see to your clothes, I heard the men speaking as I served them meat and broth." She spoke softly, the words meant not to carry beyond the wool partition. "Olaf has ever desired a charter for this isle but the Scottish crown has always refused to acknowledge Olaf's rights. His wishes are well known in these isles. Now"—she cast a glance at the bed and the sleeping shipmaster—"we shall put word out that the crown has accepted Olaf's offer, but only in exchange for much silver.

"Olaf means to send out a galley that he hopes Svend Skull-Splitter will mistake for the ship carrying Olaf's payment to the crown. Then—"

"He hopes the Black Vikings will attack so Olaf and Darroc can ambush them at sea," Arabella finished for her, all too familiar with her father's warring strategies. "It could work. If they plan well and—"

"It will work." Jutta's eyes sparkled. "Olaf is a peace-loving man but his blood runs hot with the fire of his grandfathers. And Darroc"—her smile widened—"has good reason to see justice served. He wishes to avenge you!"

Arabella looked down at her hands, now clenched into her new brightly colored skirts. "I would not wish either of them or their men to suffer injuries. I have seen the Black Vikings' dragon-ship and what they can do."

The other woman laughed. "Then you know what Olaf and his men are capable of when they desire it. They, too, are Viking! But first"—she stepped back and turned a critical eye on Arabella—"we must find you some adornments for tonight's feasting."

"Feasting?" It was the first Arabella heard the like.

"So I say!" Jutta shoved back the woolen hanging and led Arabella back into the smoky darkness of the long-house's main room. They moved slowly, slipping past the empty sleeping benches lining the walls and taking care to avoid the men still huddled around the fire, talking.

When they stepped outside, the Norsewoman released Arabella's arm. She smiled at a group of children play-ing noisily in front of one of the fishermen's huts. "There will be a celebratory feasting with much merrymaking." She indicated a clearing where men were setting up great sailcloth awnings and preparing two whole bullocks to be roasted over open fires. "It is not often that we can enter-tain visitors."

Arabella's pulse jumped. Already there was an air of excitement in the camp. A sense of anticipation that made her belly all fluttery again, this time in a good way. Merrymaking meant music and dance. And that meant...

She felt herself color again. She knew well enough from her father's hall the kinds of things that could happen when ale flowed freely and spirits were high. Her sister wasn't the only one who'd crept out of bed and hidden in the stair tower to watch the raucous revelry.

"Yes, there will be dancing." Jutta Manslayer spoke as if she'd read Arabella's mind. "Later, it could be that Darroc will take you to admire the moon from our boat strand." She leaned close and winked. "It shines there most invitingly."

"We shall see." Arabella wondered if she could be so bold.

Deep inside she knew she had to be.

Her happiness depended on it.

"I'm worried about Captain Arneborg."

Arabella raised her voice above the sound of music and laughter coming from the center of the clearing. She and Darroc sat at a well-laden trestle table beneath one of the sailcloth awnings, a good distance away from the whirling, stamping dancers. But even here the wild skirl of the pipes was earsplitting. Bonfires and flaming resin torches turned night to day, casting all in a weaving, ruddy glow. Including the dark forms of couples who, tired of jigs and reels, hastened away to disappear into the quiet behind the fishermen's huts and bunkhouses.

Arabella knew why they were leaving.

Seeing the excitement on their faces as they rushed past did funny things to her stomach and made her mouth dry. So far Darroc had given no indication of wishing to take her to see the moonlight as Jutta Manslayer had predicted.

Quite the opposite, he applied his enthusiasm to digging in to the roasted beef rib the huge-bosomed Arnora Ship-Breast had plunked down on his trencher. He ate with gusto and showed no sign of sharing her concern for the shipmaster. Indeed, Arabella doubted he'd even heard her.

But guilt pinched her, so she curled her fingers around his arm, stilling his hand just as he reached again for the beef rib. "Do you not think the noise is keeping him awake? Or"—she hated this possibility—"that he hears the music and is sad he can't join us?"

"Who?" He jerked around to face her, a speck of rib juice glistening on his chin.

"Captain Arneborg." Arabella reached to dab away the grease, then gasped when he seized her hand and kissed the tips of her fingers.

"Arneborg?" He turned her hand over and dropped a kiss on her palm, his gaze not leaving hers. "He will no' be sad to hear the din. He—"

"It has to be ruining his sleep."

"To be sure!" Darroc grinned. "And he will be glad for each burst of laughter and song. He knows we're celebrating the banishment of his foes and that"—he leaned forward and gave her a swift kiss on the mouth—"is sweeter than any dreams he might have in his sleep."

"He wants worse than banishment for the Black Vikings." Arabella fingered the carnelian and rock crystal beaded necklace Jutta had given her. "He said this afternoon that he wished to see them in hell."

"And so they will be—as Arneborg knows."

"But you just said they are to be banished."

Humor sparked in Darroc's eyes. "That is the way of it, aye. See you"—he sat back, his lips twitching—"there are places one such as Svend Skull-Splitter will find more terrible than hell. After we capture him, we shall give him a choice. Either we consign him to Valhalla then and there or Olaf will see him escorted to Greenland."

"Greenland?" Arabella blinked.

"There are few places more distant." Darroc lifted the silver-gilt goblet they were sharing and took a long drink of spiced wine. "Or more forbidding. The land is rocky and frozen and the seas are so shrouded with impenetrable mist that many give them the name Ocean Called Dark."

"He would never stay there." Arabella couldn't believe the men had overlooked something so simple. "As soon as Olaf's men sailed away, he'd leave."

Darroc shook his head. "Many of Olaf's men have family in Brattahlid. Men as fierce and unforgiving as the icebound world they call their home. They will be glad for extra labor to help work their farms. And"—he grinned again—"they will ensure that not a single Black Viking escapes."

"You have thought of everything." Arabella's heart swelled with pride.

"It was Arneborg who gave us the idea." Darroc glanced back toward the darkened longhouse where the shipmaster rested. "Olaf told me Arneborg had mentioned settling in Brattahlid upon his recovery. He—"

"Why would he want to go there if it's such a cold wilderness?" Arabella rubbed the rock crystal pendant of her necklace. Shaped like a large disc and polished smooth, it was carved with an image of Thor's hammer. "It seems the last place he'd find welcoming."

"Nae. He'd find it ideal because"—he looked around the trestle table, then lowered his voice—"he was deeply in debt. Arneborg lost everything with the *Merry Dancer*. He was a broken man. In such straits even a desolation like the Ocean Called Dark sounds good to a man."

"But he's an Orkneyman." A frown creased Arabella's brow. "Surely he has family there."

"He has no one." Darroc paused when a group of dancers returned to a nearby table, their laughter and chattering voices loud on the night air. "Yet"—he shook his head again—"in the end his very loneliness is what saved him. Apparently he'd spent a lifetime boasting about a nonexistent family, claiming royal Norse blood.

"He told Olaf that's why the *Merry Dancer* was attacked. Svend Skull-Splitter believed Arneborg's tales of illustrious connections in Norway and meant to ransom him."

"And when they discovered the truth, they set him out on the skerry." Arabella repeated what she'd heard earlier. "How heartbreaking. But"—she blinked, confused—"you said Captain Arneborg *was* a broken man. It seems to me that he still is, considering."

To her surprise, Darroc grinned. "He isn't now." He cut a look toward the clearing where couples whirled in a blur of flying heels and arms. "Do you see Arnora Ship-Breast?"

Arabella followed his stare, her own falling at once on the dancing Norsewoman. Her gown's bodice was cut precariously low and her huge breasts bounced wildly as she jigged, their generous swells glowing white in the moonlight.

Arabella's gaze snapped back to Darroc. "Don't tell me there's something between her and the shipmaster?"

Darroc's grin said there was. "So it is claimed. And apparently it's serious. They were sweethearts once, in their youth in Orkney. When Arneborg went to sea, they never saw each other again until Olaf found the captain on the skerry. Word is Arnora never loved another." Darroc glanced at her, still dancing. "Olaf offered them one of the fishermen's huts. The pair plans to wed as soon as Arneborg recovers."

"You mean Captain Arneborg will be staying here?" Arabella's throat began to thicken. "Olaf Big Nose has welcomed him into his settlement?"

"Now you see why I said Arneborg *was* a broken man." Darroc reached for the wine goblet and took another healthy sip. "He is no more. Some"—he set down the goblet and wiped his mouth with his sleeve—"might even say he's damned lucky."

"But his debts..."

Darroc cocked a brow. "Are unfortunate, but do you really think anyone will bother him here?"

"Nae, but—"

"You needn't fash yourself o'er him." Darroc slid an arm around her and drew her close. "He plans to save and eventually buy another cog. He'll go merchanting again someday and then he'll be able to repay his moneylenders."

Arabella nodded, horrified to feel a tear slide down her cheek. She dashed it aside before anyone could notice.

Or so she hoped.

"I am so glad everything has worked out so well for him." She helped herself to the spiced wine, needing something to wash down the lump in her throat. "It would seem things are tying up nicely for everyone."

Darroc's arm tightened around her. "Aye, so it does.

It lifts my heart to know Arneborg has a good future ahead of him." He looked at her, his eyes darkening with an expression that made her breath catch. "Had he not thought quickly when the Black Vikings attacked his ship, I would never have found you."

"Yet you are going to return me to Kintail when we leave here." The words escaped before she could stop them. "You have made your plans. You said—"

"Aye, I have plans." He touched quieting fingers to her lips. "You have just no' heard them yet. We shall both journey to Kintail. I intend to ask your father for your hand when we get there."

"Oh!" Arabella's heart stopped. The tears that had been misting her eyes now filled them, the stinging heat blurring her vision. "What are you saying?"

Darroc smoothed her hair back and leaned close to kiss her brow. "Things I'd rather discuss with you without so many prying ears."

He sat back and slid a telling look down the table. Arabella blinked, seeing at once that everyone present was watching them, their faces split in grins. Even those at neighboring tables were craning necks and jabbing each other with elbows.

"Oh, dear." Arabella felt her face flame.

"Come, let us dance." Darroc sprang to his feet and—to the cheers of those around him—pulled Arabella up with him, dragging her into the midst of the leaping, whirling dancers in the clearing. "No one will notice now when we slip away," he promised, already spinning her in a lively circle. "There is an empty hut on the far side of the boat strand. We can be alone there."

"Alone...." Everything Arabella had ever believed—

the imagined horror on her father's face—made her start
to object, but her heart wouldn't let her say no.

Moonlight spilled down into the clearing and all
around them the torches crackled and blazed, making
the night shimmer with color and excitement. The other
dancers wheeled and leapt, their faces bright with joy and
a wild, fiercely tempting abandonment that heated her
blood and set her pulse to racing in ways that had nothing
to do with the vigorous dance.

It was the magic of the night.

And Darroc.

The love shining in his eyes.

The ground seemed to tilt beneath Arabella's feet and
the stars, so many of them, twinkled as if they were winking at her. She felt herself melting and couldn't remember
having ever been happier. And she wanted this man.

"I will no' force you, lass." Darroc grasped her waist
then and lifted her high as they spun, whirling ever closer
to the edge of the dancers and the dark woods beyond.
"We can speak of this at Castle Bane when we—"

"Nae, I do want to be alone with you," Arabella panted,
breathless from the dance. "Now, tonight."

He who is bold succeeds.

The familiar chant beat in her mind, loud and thrilling as the screaming pipes and cries of the dancers. But
something else thrilled her, too. It was the surety that once
they closed the door of the fishermen's hut, they would do
more than talking. Darroc would take her into his arms
and kiss her again. Quite possibly he'd do more. Perhaps
even some of the wickedly delicious things Gelis had told
her men and women did when they were in love.

And she did love Darroc MacConacher.

He touched her cheek then, his fingers smoothing back her hair as he looked down at her. She blinked, only now realizing they were inside the wood. Thick trees separated them from the clearing with its blazing, smoking torchlight and blur of colorfully clad dancers. She hadn't even noticed he'd maneuvered them away.

"You must know"—he gripped her shoulders, his voice husky—"if you come with me now, I'll ne'er let you go."

He couldn't lie to her.

Not when she'd slid her arms around his neck and tangled her fingers in his hair, her whole face shining with the same love and passion that was filling him so completely he was sure he'd soon burst from the glory of it.

"I do not want to leave you." She rose up on her toes and kissed him, even sliding the tip of her tongue across his lips. "Not this night or ever."

"Arabella...." He pulled her tight, slanting his mouth over hers in a furious kiss, hungry and demanding. "Then let us be away!" He broke the kiss and grabbed her hand, pulling her through the trees toward the boat strand and the fishermen's hut where their fate awaited them.

Rustling noises rose behind them then, quickly followed by a woman's peal of laughter. Darroc glanced over his shoulder and quickened their pace until they burst out of the wood and onto the moon-shadowed strand. Candlelight flickered in the windows of one or two of the huts and smoke rose, thin and high, from the thatched roofs. But each dwelling stood quiet and the curving shore stretched empty save for the dark shapes of the beached galleys and a thick line of seaweed washed ashore by the rolling waves.

"There!" Darroc pointed to the last hut, set a bit apart

from the others. It, too, had peat smoke curling from the center hole in its thatch and the door stood ajar, spilling golden light into the darkness. "That has to be the one Jutta prepared for us."

Then they were there, slipping into the cozy little cottage and pulling the door shut behind them. No less than three tiny braziers crackled softly, filling the single room with the earthy rich scent of peat and a welcoming orange-red glow. A large soot-blackened cauldron hung on a chain over a well-going wood fire and a tantalizing aroma rose from the bubbling venison stew someone had thoughtfully prepared for them.

Whoever it'd been, no doubt Jutta Manslayer, she'd also dressed the single sleeping pallet with stacks of brightly colored blankets.

Arabella's eyes flew wide and she flushed crimson when she saw them. Darroc reached for her, drawing her to him before she could panic.

"You know nothing will happen that you do not desire." He rubbed her back as he spoke, hoping to soothe her. "There's no reason for you to be fearful, you have my word. But"—he gave her his most reassuring smile—"I think we've reached a point where only honesty can stand between us."

"I trust you already. I would not be here if I did not." She'd stiffened a bit in his arms, but she made no move to pull away.

It was a start.

And it gave him the courage to tell her something that sounded fantastical even to him.

"Sweet lass," he began, encouraged by the unmistakable longing in her eyes. "I know it sounds crazy, but

I am convinced we were meant to find each other. I've felt it since the moment I first saw you and"—he drew a breath—"I believe I knew it even before then."

"But how could you?" She pulled back to look at him, her face luminous in the fire glow. "We never met before the sinking of the *Merry Dancer*."

"Nae, but I believe I was given a sign." Darroc released her and went to a tiny oaken table to pour them each a cup of spiced wine. "The night of the tragedy a great many seals gathered beneath Castle Bane's tower. They were everywhere on the rocks and bobbing in the water. I'd never in my life seen so many."

Arabella accepted the wine cup he handed her and took a sip. "There must've been herring swarming," she said, smiling. She clearly wasn't following him. "We have seals in Kintail, too. They always follow the herring."

"Nae, lass, this was different." He shook his head slowly. "The seals were singing. They do, you know, though to hear them is a rare and eerie thing. Some say"—he forced himself to speak, feeling silly—"their song is a portent of disaster. Others claim to hear them herald a coming of great wonders and blessings.

"I believe, now, that the seals came to let me know that you were coming into my life." He set his hands on her shoulders, willing her to believe. "When you told me of your Seal Isles, I was convinced that was the reason."

"And so you feel we were meant to meet?" She placed a hand to her cheek. He could see the pulse leaping at the base of her throat.

"Aye, I do." He tightened his grip on her, his gaze holding hers. "And I believe more. I am certain we were meant to fall in love."

She gasped. "Are you saying you love me?"

"I am." He swept his arms around her and pulled her close. "More than I would ever have believed possible."

"O-o-oh, Darroc!" She leaned into him, the entire length of her trembling. "I love you, too. So much!"

Darroc's heart jumped to hear her say the words. They held so much warmth and feeling, certainly her trust. That trust shone in her eyes as well, and he didn't think he'd ever seen anything as lovely. Or that moved him more deeply. Whatever hardships stood before them, they'd have done with them, together. Sure of it, he bent his head to kiss the soft place beneath her ear, nuzzling her neck as she eased her shawl off her shoulders.

It slipped to the earthen floor, one barrier between them gone. Although she trembled, she didn't pull away and gave no sign of maidenly fear. Not even when his lips brushed her hair and, unable to stop himself, he stroked one finger across the bared swells of her breasts.

"I will no' touch you if you tell me to stop." He had to give her one last chance to end this. "Say when and—"

"I know what we are doing." She stepped back, her hands going to the laces of her bodice. "And"—she began undoing them, her chin boldly raised but her fingers shaking—"I want this very much."

Darroc swallowed hard and lifted one of her braids, drawn by its sheen and silky smooth feel beneath his fingers. He lifted the ebony plait to his lips, knowing a chaste kiss would never satisfy him.

Heat pulsed through his groin and his heart hammered against his ribs, reminding him of how fiercely he wanted her, his need almost a physical pain. An urgency that ripped him, racing out of control as she finished undoing the stays of her gown and it slid down her arms, freeing her thrusting breasts and exposing her nakedness.

"Lass...." He groaned and cupped her fullness, plumping and weighing her firm, pleasing roundness and seeking the taut peaks of her nipples with his thumbs, circling and rubbing until she moaned her pleasure.

He looked down at her, wanting her desperately.

It wasn't enough to hear her whimpering in need; he wanted her gasping in pleasure. He burned to feel her sliding hot and sleek against him, skin to skin and with their mouths clinging in an all-slaking, ravenous kiss. He ached to take her at last, joining their flesh as he knew their hearts already beat in steady, loving rhythm.

"I want you naked." His voice was deep, pure desire streaking clear to his toes, banishing reason and everything but his urgent need to possess her.

"Then take me." She wriggled out of her gown, kicking it aside when it slithered down her legs to pool in a froth of colored silk at her feet. "I am yours to do with as you will and"—she shivered in the cold air—"I yearn to be one with you."

She leaned into him, arching and rubbing against him in ways that would have brought a lesser man to his knees. The cool smoothness of her thighs sent flaming heat pouring into his loins and the soft brush of her maiden hair threatened to steal his wits if he couldn't soon claim her.

"Christ Jesu!" He stared at her bounty, sure he'd spill before he even savored her slippery, molten-hot charms. She locked her gaze on his and the passion simmering in those sapphire depths fired his blood. Her womanhood pulsed against him, damp with her arousal.

"I think you would unman me!" His voice was stran-
gled, his own desire almost a torment.

"I would be bold!" She sounded breathless, her hands
sliding beneath his plaid to find and caress his skin.
"We have both waited long, I'm thinking. Now"—she
smoothed her hands up and down the sides of his ribs,
then reached down to cup his buttocks, digging her fingers
into his flesh and pulling him near as she thrust her hips
against him—"now, it is time for us to seal our destiny."

"Arabella...." Darroc threw off his plaid, biting hard
into the side of his cheek lest he toss her down onto the
hard-packed dirt floor and thrust into her.

The saints knew he was ready!

Instead, he held back and stifled the burning rush of
his release. But he did groan as he swept his hands up and
down her tempting, silky smooth curves. He wanted so
much of her. There wasn't an inch of her lusciousness he
didn't burn to explore, gentling her first with his hands
and then using his tongue to bring her ecstasy.

"You take my breath." He twined his fingers in her
hair, lifting a handful of glossy, ebony strands to his lips.

"You *are* my breath." Arabella seized his face with her
hands and drew him to her for a searing kiss. She drank
greedily of him, needing his taste and essence as fiercely
as she needed air.

She drew back to peer at him. Her heart thundered at
her daring, but even as her palms dampened and her belly
quivered, cascades of delicious shivers rippled through
her. It excited her to see how eager he was to claim her.
Desire twisted inside her and her female place clenched
hotly when he stood back and held his arms out to his
sides as if he understood her need to look. He was magnif-

icent in his nakedness, all male hardness and perfection. The fire bathed him in shades of red and gold, making him seem like a pagan god striding forth from some passionate fiery realm to possess her.

And she wanted to be his.

So much that she felt her herself growing hot and tingly between her legs. She became aware of dampness misting her thighs and a strange insistent throbbing that both frightened and exhilarated her. It was a wondrously delicious weightiness her sister had told her to expect. Feeling it now, and knowing its meaning, was a miracle, a woman's triumph that she'd never thought to experience.

As if he knew, he gathered her in his arms and lowered her onto the pallet, following her down onto the soft mound of colorful blankets.

He stretched out beside her, their bodies closer than a hand's breadth. "You are the most beautiful woman I've ever seen, Arabella."

The words made her heart jump and he slid an arm around her waist, drawing closer still. "I do not want you to feel shame or fear." He spoke against her breasts and the warmth of his breath on her bared flesh made her shiver again.

Something inside her was splintering, splitting wide open to let tantalizing molten heat fill her. She was melting, burning with such tingling anticipation she could hardly bear the pleasure. Even her skin tingled and she felt caught in a whirlwind of sensation so intense she feared each shuddering breath might be her last.

"I am not ashamed." A voice much stronger than her own startled her.

The voice of a woman about to give herself to the man she loves.

"But"—her own voice spoke up, too—"I am—you know that I have never—"

"I will be gentle with you." He began kissing her breasts and then his mouth was at her nipple, his tongue swirling around the tightly puckered furls. "But I will no' lie to you. There will be pain, though"—he smoothed one hand along her curves, then down across her stomach, his fingers lightly brushing her maiden hair—"there are ways to prepare you so that the hurt isn't so great."

"Then"—Arabella couldn't believe she was saying this—"tell me what to do."

"You must let me touch you, sweetness." His voice was rough, deep and rusty as if it pained him to speak. "You must open your legs for me."

"Open my legs?" Her eyes flew wide. She wasn't ignorant of how couples mated, yet the thought of parting her thighs suddenly terrified her.

It would mean he'd see everything.

Her most secret parts and—she flushed—she was wet!

"You are as good as my wife now, Arabella." He was rubbing her breasts, kneading and caressing them. "You know that in olden times a man and woman need only declare their desire to be one and they were wed." He leaned close and kissed her, gentle and sweet. "Here on Olaf's isle the ancient ways are honored. There is no reason we shouldn't seal our love."

"And if my father refuses you?" She had to ask.

Darroc pushed up on an elbow. "Then I shall feel most sorry for him," he vowed, hoping it wouldn't come to that. "Because, lass, I meant what I told you at the feasting. Now that you've told me you love me, I shall never let you go."

"Oh, Darroc . . . . Then make me yours! Let us be joined

in the old ways and with the blessing of the ancients." She reached down to touch him, her fingers light and questing as she slid them along his length.

"Lass!" He jerked and grabbed her wrist, pulling her hand away just as she circled her fingers around him. "You mustn't touch me. No' yet. If you do, I'll shame myself."

"But I want you to have pleasure. I—"

Darroc almost choked. "You are my pleasure. My entire joy."

And she was. It was a truth powerful enough to bring him to his knees. She wasn't the only one trembling. And when she shifted against him and he felt her honeyed warmth slide across his hip, he nearly spilled himself from that brief, tantalizing contact.

He'd never wanted a woman more.

And never had he taken a virgin.

Humbled that he was about to, he began murmuring Gaelic love words to her. He gently stroked the soft skin of her thighs, hoping to soothe her into relaxing. When she did, parting her legs just enough to allow him to slip his hand between, he found the hot moist center of her slick and slippery, her silken heat filling him with a fierce, primordial need greater than any he'd ever known.

As if she sensed his urgency, she rubbed herself against him and opened herself to him, letting him stroke her. She glided her hands down his sides, then to the small of his back and his buttocks, her fingers grasping, digging into his flesh and holding him tight.

"Och, lass, you shouldn't have done that." He groaned and rolled on top of her, urging her legs farther apart. "I can wait no longer." Careful to keep his hand on her heat, he let his fingers circle and flick across her most sensitive spot. She cried out and pressed herself into his hand, her desperation letting him know she was ready.

His heart squeezed and he raised his head to look at her, but she'd closed her eyes. "I am sorry for the pain," he breathed, grasping her hips. He reached down to take a hold of himself, nudging her softness until he could hold back no more and thrust inside her, wishing he could block his ears to her sharp cry of pain. It was a cry that soon quelled to a soft accepting sigh.

Exaltation filled him, almost splitting him with the wonder of her. "The next time will be different," he promised, lifting a hand to smooth the dampness from her face. He rubbed his lips against her hair, gentling feather kisses across her brow, her tear-stained cheeks. "You'll never feel pain again, I swear it."

"I know...." Looking very brave, she bracketed his head with her hands and kissed him, slowly rocking her hips as she did. "But I would suffer the hurt again gladly if it meant being one with you."

"Arabella." Darroc's world upended, all the sorrow and anger he'd ever known spinning away as if it'd never been. "Saints, but I love you."

He began to move again, as slowly and carefully as he could, but the exquisite pleasure was almost killing him. The urge to plunge deeper and faster made his pulse roar and his heart race with such savage need that sweat beaded his brow. It dripped into his eyes, stinging, but he scarce noticed.

Arabella was kissing him passionately, her lips and tongue scorching his soul. The wonder of it caught him by the throat, her tempestuous kiss blotting everything but the astonishing intimacy of their joining, the melding of their hearts.

Then, as if she'd been born to love him, she tangled her fingers in his hair, deepening their kiss and wrapping her legs around his hips.

It was too much.

"Mother of God!" He stiffened, his seed pouring into her. He shuddered with indescribable sensation, the little room going dark around him, then bursting with brilliant light as if every star in the heavens swept down to blind him.

Arabella lifted her hips and arched into him. She kissed him still, making soft little mewling sounds as he collapsed on top of her, spent and consumed, the aftershocks of his release still coursing through him.

He broke her kiss at last and pressed his cheek against her temple, panting. "I can ne'er live without you," he swore, knowing it was true.

Through his bliss he thought he heard her murmur something about someone being bold and succeeding, but then she was kissing him again and nothing else mattered.

Only the knowledge that he could walk through life forever with her and it would never be enough.

Chapter Sixteen

❖

It took a full sennight for a day of dark drifting mist to descend on Olaf Big Nose's Isle. Seven bright, crisp days and frosty, passion-filled nights, but now—at last—the Hebridean Sea was a deep, inky black. Even the foaming white crests of the waves were tinged a steely gray, each steep trough and long, fast-moving roller more uninviting than many had ever seen. It was a day of biting wind and cold. A morn that broke for good and ill and that would end in joy or sorrow.

Darroc released a tense breath, watching Conall leap nimbly from one beached galley to the other. The younger man's face shone with excitement as he ensured that each craft was ready to be launched. Dense, icy mist swirled everywhere, but other men were equally engaged. Olaf Big Nose stood in the midst of them all, shouting orders and looking keen to be away.

Bloodlust glittered in the Norseman's eye and Darroc didn't miss that his friend had thrust not one but two

Viking war axes beneath his belt. The handle of an extra dirk peeped up from his boot and everyone who'd been in his longhouse the previous night knew he'd spent hours sharpening his sword.

A blade he'd vowed would run red before another night passed.

The brilliant steel sullied with the spent blood of Black Vikings.

Curling his fingers around the hilt of his own sword, Darroc prayed for victory. Anything else was unthinkable. Especially now. Unfortunately, the place in his heart that should have blazed with confidence proved dimmed by the unshakable dread of what would happen if they failed.

Though Arabella was still abed, he could almost feel her beside him. Her scent, so clean and fresh, seemed to fill the cold air, teasing and tempting him. And he could almost imagine her hand slipping through his arm. The soft, warm press of her as she'd leaned into him, her cool, silky hair brushing his arm and her breath so welcome against his cheek as she reassured him of her love and wished him well in battle.

She'd done so in the small hours, before they'd slept. Then when she'd caressed the lines of his old warring scars, nipping and lighting her tongue along each one until he could take it no more and had seized her, kissing her hard. He'd thrust his hands into her unbound hair, wrapping the glistening strands around his fingers as he'd ravished her mouth and plunged into her, his thrusts as hot and demanding as his kiss.

She'd arched into him, clinging and matching his pace, her cries echoing in the little fisherman's hut they shared.

They'd shattered together, both panting with the powerful force of their passion.

Darroc swallowed, his gut twisting.

One false move this day—one fleeting moment judged or timed in error—and Svend Skull-Splitter and his band of cutthroats would unleash the furies of hell onto Arabella and Olaf's womenfolk.

The possibility sliced through Darroc like a frigid wind, stealing his breath and almost laming him. He tightened his grip on his sword hilt, bile rising hot and fast in his throat. Tossing back his hair, he shoved aside the thought, the ghastly images.

He opened his mouth to grind out a curse, but a hand, large and grasping, closed around his elbow. "A favor, MacConacher—asked by an auld, ill man."

Captain Arneborg.

Darroc whipped around, surprised to see the shipmaster out of his bed. "Whate'er I can do for you, aye," he agreed, alarmed by the shadows beneath the older man's eyes. His frailty and pallor. "But you are no' auld. You're only recovering from an ordeal that would've been the sure end of a less stout-hearted man."

The captain nodded, looking pleased. "I've something for you." He let go of Darroc's arm to fumble at the folds of his cloak. A fur-lined bedrobe that wasn't a match for the driving wind and freezing mist, though the morning's chill didn't seem to faze him.

Even so, Darroc frowned. "Whate'er it is, I'd rather you give it to me after we've had our way with Svend Skull-Splitter. You should be abed—"

"I should be going with you is what I should be doing." Captain Arneborg's voice was strong. "As is"—he glanced at the bay, the war galleys men were just beginning to slide into the water—"I'm asking you to take this plague bell with you in my place."

He plucked a bell from inside his bedrobe, proffering it with pride.

"*Plague bell*?" Darroc blinked at the dented, tarnished bell. He hadn't forgotten the bells that had caught on the rocks after the wreck of the *Merry Dancer*.

Still...

"There isn't any plague in these waters." His brow furrowed. "None that—"

"Svend Skull-Splitter is plague enough." Arneborg's blue eyes flashed with spirit. "His men are the scourge of this earth. When they took me, I snuck one of my bells into my cloak. The bells kept my ship free of the pox and"—he stepped back, standing tall—"who's to say it wasn't this bell that kept me alive?"

Darroc nodded, understanding.

He'd thought the bells on the rocks were charmed. He surely didn't blame Arneborg for holding on to one of them.

He'd capture and defeat the Black Vikings using wits and steel, the help of his good friends and their own cunning and prowess at arms. But if taking along the shipmaster's bell was important to the man, he'd gladly oblige.

Though he would secure its clapper!

"I thank you, sir." He opted for tact and kept the notion to himself.

Captain Arneborg's smile rewarded him. "I promised Lady Arabella that I'd look after her. Now that she's lost her heart to you, I'll not see her widowed before she becomes a proper bride."

Darroc started to assure him that he had no intention of failing. And that—in his eyes—Arabella already was his bride. But before he could open his mouth, the captain slipped away to head slowly but purposefully back up the strand, toward the path to the longhouse.

Then the whirling mist swept around him and he was gone.

Darroc looked down at the bell in his hands and his heart squeezed as he remembered once more when he'd first heard and seen the bells.

It was the day that had changed his life forever.

Hours later, Darroc stood on the stern platform of his birlinn, free now of Arabella's sail screen. Blessedly, the day's dark, freezing mist hadn't lessened. A superstitious corner of his mind wondered if Captain Arneborg's bell—rendered silent and tied to his steering oar—wasn't charmed indeed. The day could not be more perfect.

Grateful, he stroked his chin, ignoring the knife-sharp wind and keeping his eyes on the fog-shrouded sea. A score of Olaf's galleys rocked in the waves nearby, the ships' rowing benches manned double.

Beyond the sheltering cliffs of the narrow inlet where they hid—a bay far distant from Olaf's isle and so remote Darroc hadn't known of its existence—Olaf's dragon-ship beat past them, the clanging of the gong sounding eerie in the near impenetrable mist.

"How many times has he gone past?" Conall stood beside the birlinn's gong, the baton clutched in his hands, waiting.

"No' so loud." Darroc cut the air with his hand, not taking his gaze off the sea. "You know sound carries on water. Svend Skull-Splitter could be anywhere. Just because we think he'll come from the east doesn't mean he will."

"My balls are freezing." Conall scowled. "The bastard may not even know Olaf is about."

"He knows." Darroc was sure of it. He could almost taste the blackguard's stink in the air. "Word has been passed by signal fires all through the Isles. Friends and allies who've agreed to our ploy and are acting as if they'd welcome Olaf on his way to claim his charter."

Conall snorted. "Snakes like the Black Vikings will suspect the deception."

"What if they saw us leave Olaf's isle? They could attack the settlement." Hugh, one of the oarsmen, spoke from his rowing bench. "If the Black Vikings suspect Olaf is bluffing, they might think his supposed coffers of silver are on the isle, with the women."

Darroc pulled a hand down over his face. "Hugh...."

The large, broad-faced man was strong as an ox, but didn't quite have all his sillers.

"Why do you think we spent the last few days ranging every spare vessel Olaf had in his bay?" Darroc reminded him, secretly proud that the idea had been his own.

They'd even rounded up old and rotting fishing cobles and erected extra masts in the galleys, all in the hope of making the bay look crowded with a fleet of moored long-ships. Anyone spotting the clustered vessels would think a great party of men had gathered on Olaf's isle.

The womenfolk were as safe as if it were so.

Or so Darroc hoped!

But Hugh was worrying his lip, doubt all over him. "In

this fog, the Black Vikings might not see the false fleet we built in the bay!"

Darroc clamped his jaw in annoyance.

Hapless Hugh had a point.

And it was a consideration that could make his head pound if he thought too long on it. So he scowled at the hulking oarsman until the wretch shrugged and resumed peering into the mist, just as all of them were doing.

"Here comes Olaf again." Conall set down his baton and raked both hands through his hair. "I swear that's the twentieth time he's gone past."

"Have patience." Darroc's own was waning, but he refused to show it.

"Patience when my fingers are about to snap off." Conall spat over the side of the birlinn into the water. "I swear if the Black Vikings do appear, I won't be able to beat the gong. The baton will slip from my—"

A sharp trilling cry like a curlew rose from one of the other galleys.

The signal that the Black Vikings had been sighted.

"A dark sail to the west!" The call came from the nearest galley, the men at the bow pointing to the mouth of the bay.

Darroc saw the black-painted dragon-ship at once. Darker than the mist, it flashed past at speed, the lashing oars sending up great clouds of spume as it sped after Olaf.

For one sickening moment, Darroc's gaze flew to Arneborg's bell, fury tightening his chest. His pulse roared in his ears, almost blotting all else. To think that a small, dented bell was all that remained of the large, sturdy cog. A ship filled with living, breathing men. The woman who'd come to mean the world to him.

Rage shot through him and the day's blackness seemed to pour into him, chilling him to the bone.

In his soul, he knew he could so easily forget his and Olaf's carefully laid plans and tear apart Svend Skull-Splitter limb by limb. He'd use nothing but his bare hands and gleefully damn the devil to die a death as horrible as he'd inflicted on innocents.

Instead, he sucked in a hot breath, ready.

Throughout the inlet, men sprang to action. They raised the oars, their eyes fixed on Darroc, waiting. High on the cliffs, lookouts returned the curlew cries. One of them, a man deemed with the best eyes, stood and waved a torch. Hidden in a crevice unseen save by those inside the sheltered bay, his signal was their final assurance that the dark-sailed dragon-ship that had sped past had indeed been the Black Vikings.

It was all they needed to know.

Darroc's blood heated. Exhilaration whipped through him, hot and sweet.

"Now! Pull the oars!" He roared the order, the air ringing with the beat of a dozen gongs before he even closed his hand over the steering oar.

As one, the galleys shot from the bay, flying past the soaring cliffs and into the open water, moving as fast as if not swifter than their prey. As planned, Olaf slued his dragon-ship around in an explosive burst of spray and bore down on his pursuer the instant Darroc's birlinn and the other galleys flashed into view.

Seeing them, Svend Skull-Splitter swung his own dragon-ship in a wide arc, the flourish sending up an impressive brace of spray. Far from fleeing, the Black Vikings drove straight for Olaf, clearly intent on ramming him in the side before Darroc and the other galleys could reach them.

"Nae!" Darroc slued the steering oar, hoping to cut off the enemy dragonship. "Men! Pull harder!"

Conall's gong clanged louder, faster. "They'll no' be veering off this time," he yelled, grinning as the oarsmen matched his beats.

The birlinn shot forward, flying spume blurring everything but the flashing oars and, just ahead, the black-painted dragon-ship, turning at last, seeking flight.

"Faster!" Darroc pumped a fist in the air, assured by the churning, boiling water that the other galleys were keeping pace. "*Pull, men, pull*! Don't let them raise the oars!"

In a blink they had the rogue ship surrounded, Darroc and another birlinn shooting forward with incredible speed to shear off the black dragon-ship's oars. They snapped with amazing ease, spinning away into the sea or, much worse, flying back onto the rowing benches to skewer any oarsman who had the misfortune of being in the way. Crippled, the huge galley swayed in the water. Men not maimed or killed by the splintered oars leapt to their feet, swords rattling and shouting, even though their doom was sealed.

With a well-practiced flourish, Darroc whipped the birlinn around, following Olaf's lead to shoot back to the wounded dragon-ship and draw themselves up on either side of the enemy vessel.

"Svend Skull-Splitter—I greet you!" Darroc called, jumping up on the bow platform. "I am Darroc MacConacher, chief of that noble race!"

"You are a dead man!" The Black Viking leader

whipped out a war ax, his eyes hot with fury. "Svend Skull-Splitter cowers for no man and leaves no enemy alive."

Darroc laughed and jammed his hands on his hips, not bothering to reach for his sword. "My good friend, Olaf Big Nose and I"—he flashed a grin in Olaf's direction—"are here to consign you to Valhalla!"

Svend Skull-Splitter glowered at him. "I will get there on my own and send you to hell in the by-doing." He was a huge man not unlike Olaf in his blond shagginess, and a jagged scar bisected his left brow and disappeared into his beard, the puckered gash giving him a perpetual sneer.

"Come then, Hebridean!" He tossed his ax from one hand to the other and back repeatedly. "Fight me like a man and see how quickly your toes get roasted."

"It is you who will roast in hell, Skull-Splitter!" Olaf leapt onto the black dragon-ship and, brushing aside sword swipes and swinging fists, crossed the deck to vault himself over the side and up on Darroc's birlinn.

Joining Darroc at the bow, he unfastened his hip flask and took a long swig. "There are men who say you are a clever and prudent man." His voice rang out, deep and clear. "You can see there is little point in sword clashing." He flung an arm at the score or more galleys circling them, the well-armed longships drawing ever closer in a tight, inescapable net.

He didn't bother to indicate the men slumped wounded or dead across the dragonship's rowing benches.

Nor was it necessary to point out the shattered long oars bobbing on the waves.

That Svend Skull-Splitter was aware of them showed in the hatred rolling off him.

"So-o-o, Skull-Splitter! Even if you slew a handful of us"—Olaf shot a glance at Darroc and laughed—"what men you have left are sorely outnumbered. For each one of us you bring down, ten will rise up to put an end to you."

The Black Viking's face darkened and his chest swelled beneath his rust-grimed scale armor. Gold bracelets glittered on his arms and a wide golden torque, jewel-crusted and gaudy, winked from his large, bull-like neck, the flashy jewelry at stark contrast to his dirty, unkempt appearance.

He said nothing.

"Well?" Darroc spoke easily, glad he was not downwind of the man. "What shall it be?" Now he did unsheathe his blade, pleased when its appearance deepened the other's frown. "Your choice, Skull-Splitter. Death or hell?"

"That is no choice, Hebridean simpleton." Svend Skull-Splitter's eyes narrowed with scorn. "You are as soft-headed as your landsmen. I have nothing to say to you. I speak with my blood ax and my sword, not with foolish words."

"And if those words had a deal for you?"

"I would rather fight you."

"Then so be it." Darroc nodded to his men, his earlier grin disappearing as they whipped out their swords. "It would suit me well to see these waters redden with your blood."

The Black Viking shrugged. "Your glory will be dim if that is the style of you—slaying men who are wounded and outnumbered."

"It does not have to be that way." Darroc looked down at his sword, pretending to consider. "If you have no wish to leave this earth today, I would be as pleased to see you banished from these waters."

A murmur went through the men on the black-painted dragon-ship.

Bristling with swords, daggers, axes and other wicked-looking weaponry, many of them now shoved their dirks and maces back beneath their belts or simply threw down their steel, one even hurling his sword into the sea.

Those bearing oar wounds moaned pitifully.

Svend Skull-Splitter glared at them all. "Women!"

Turning back to Darroc and Olaf, he kept a demonstrative grip on his own blade, clearly not ready to sheathe it. "I am accustomed to being paid handsomely to take my leave," he declared, pride edging the words. "The king of Man filled my coffers with two thousand pounds of silver for the privilege of seeing my back."

"I am no king, but I'm offering you your life." Darroc was tempted to smile. He could see interest beginning to kindle in the Black Viking's eyes, however much the man grumbled and glowered. "There are many who would prize such a bargain higher than a few chests of silver."

"Humph." Svend Skull-Splitter threw another angry look at his men. "You offer what I already have. That is no great bargain, Scotsman."

Olaf Big Nose went to the low-slung side of the birlinn and, leaning down, snatched a broken sweep from the water. "How long do you think your life would last if we snapped it like this oar?" he called, brandishing the shattered wood. "In hell"—he tossed the oar back onto the waves—"you can live to fight and raid another day."

"Just no' here in our domains." Darroc joined Olaf at the rail.

Neither one of them bothered to mention that the men of Brattahlid would ensure the Black Vikings never set foot on another ship again.

They'd spend their days picking rocks from fields and sowing corn.

If they were truly unfortunate, the women of Brattahlid might even set them to spinning wool.

The thought made Darroc grin.

He slid a glance at Olaf, who looked ready to convulse with laughter.

"O-o-oh, aye, Skull-Splitter, hell is where you'll soon be." Darroc's lips twitched on the words. "You and your remaining crew, escorted there by our men. Or"—he jerked his head at the circling galleys—"do you think we brought so many men just to gawp at you?"

"You're both full addled." Svend Skull-Splitter continued to scowl. "Speaking of hell as if it were a place on this earth!"

"Ah, but it is." Darroc was enjoying this. "Have you ne'er heard of Brattahlid? It's a fine frozen village on the iciest edge of the Ocean Called Dark."

Wind was beating the Black Viking's hair about his face, but Darroc was sure he blanched.

"You think to take us to Greenland?" His voice dripped derision.

His men exchanged looks.

They began to mumble and mutter again. Those few still gripping their swords now cast them aside, cursing. But it was clear they preferred Brattahlid to Valhalla.

Seeing himself alone, Svend Skull-Splitter threw down his own blade. "How do I know your men won't cut our throats when we sleep?"

Darroc turned to Olaf and plucked his hip flask from his belt. Lifting it to his lips, he quaffed a quick gulp of the fiery spirits and then tossed the flask to the Black Viking. "Let us share a drink to prove my word!"

"The word of a trickster, I'm thinking!" But Svend Skull-Splitter caught the flask with ease and tipped its contents down his throat, sending the empty flask sailing back through the air to Darroc.

"So be it!" Darroc caught the flask with equal ease. "Our men will now board your dragon-ship to strip you of your weapons. You can sleep on your decks, untroubled by us. But"—he flashed another grin—"at first light your ship will be torched and you'll be split up onto three galleys for the voyage to Greenland."

"Curse you, Hebridean!" Svend Skull-Splitter raised a balled fist.

"Too late, my friend." Darroc laughed. "I've been cursed all my days."

He didn't add that he wasn't any longer. But that sweet knowledge made his triumph all the sweeter.

Indeed, he was powerfully pleased.

Chapter Seventeen

❧

Three days later, after many hearty embraces, shouted well wishes, and some tears, Darroc and Arabella bid farewell to Olaf Big Nose and his friends. Another full day and one bliss-filled night spent at sea, once again behind Arabella's sail screen, and finally the Seal Isles loomed into view. At first little more than a blue smudge on the horizon, the long serrated line of them soon stretched like glittering jewels set on the very edge of the world.

"They look like Tir nan Og!" Arabella caught Darroc's arm as she stared, her heart thumping. To her, the sparkling isles, each fringed by white cockleshell beaches and ranging in color from palest lavender to deep blue-black, could well be the mythical Land of the Ever-Young, a magical place said to hover beyond the western horizon.

She refused to think about the isles being part of her marriage portion. Now wasn't the time to worry about home and—saints help her—her father. This was a moment to savor fully, to toss aside caution and sail close to the wind.

So close that every memory made here would be forever branded on her heart.

Willing it so, she lifted her face to the wind, excitement beating all through her. It was a wild, giddy kind of exhilaration that increased when Darroc threw back his head and laughed, his grin matching her own.

"If these isles are Tir nan Og"—he leaned close to kiss her cheek—"the only inhabitants are seabirds and seals. You'll no' find a fair race of tall, blond Valkyries waiting to greet us with honey and mead."

"I know what I'll find there." She kept her gaze on the fast-approaching isles as she spoke, certain the sky above them appeared wider and more open than anywhere else and that even the air smelled different, more clean and brisk. "You know I want to pray at St. Egbert's shrine."

Darroc arched a brow. "I still don't understand why you wished to journey so far to kneel before moldering bones. Like as not, they're long gone. Seabirds or rats will have carried them away."

"It doesn't matter if his remains are in the cave or not. The shrine is still there and it's a holy place." Arabella fingered the Thor's Hammer pendant that Jutta Manslayer had insisted she keep.

No doubt St. Egbert would go cross-eyed if he saw her wearing the pagan necklace.

But the Giving Stone might look in favor on her.

At the thought, she flashed a glance at her traveling pouch, guilt nipping her. What would Darroc think when she unpacked her honey, oats, and the skin of sweet milk Arnora Ship-Breast had given her?

She'd soon find out because already they were sweeping around the jutting sea cliffs of the Seal Isles' main

island and beating into a deep U-shaped bay lined with a
broad shell-sanded beach. Machair-covered dunes backed
the strand and beyond that, grassy hills rolled away into
the distance, the highest peaks cloaked with clouds and a
thin misty drizzle.

The isle's beauty took her breath.

And the seals bobbing in the water delighted her. They
were everywhere, their gleaming wet heads bobbing up
and down as they peered at her with curious, doglike eyes.
Others basked on rocky offshore islets or swam around
the birlinn, playfully following their race to the shore.

Then they were there, Conall slowing the beats of his
gong and the oarsmen taking his cue. The birlinn dropped
speed and they began to glide, the bow running up on to
the sand. A great cheer rose from the rowing benches and
the oarsmen raised their sweeps.

Laughing, Darroc leapt onto the strand. He opened his
arms to Arabella, catching her around the waist and lifting her down to join him.

"Your isles, my lady." He sketched a bow. "And that"—
he pointed to a steep and twisting goat track that led up
the cliff face on the far side of the bay—"will surely be
the way to your hermit's cell."

Arabella looked to where he indicated and her heart
clenched.

The path was worse than the one that climbed from
Darroc's boat strand to Castle Bane, not to mention that
the cliffs were white with seabird droppings.

A fool would know how slick the track would be and
she was anything but a dimwit.

"Oh, dear." She saw no reason to hide her dismay.

"I will no' let you fall." Darroc didn't tell her he was

equally concerned about slipping. But he couldn't bear to see her disappointment.

If it'd please her, he'd crawl up the track on his hands and knees, letting her ride on his shoulders. After all, compared to facing her father and demanding her hand when they journeyed to Kintail, a wee thread of a goat track was nothing. The steep cliff it crept up was even less significant.

A dust mote held more importance.

Only she mattered.

And she was looking again at the cliff, frowning. "I don't know...."

"Come, lass." He set his hands on her shoulders. "Have I ever let you down?"

"Nae, but—"

"The men will be putting up the sail screen for us." He glanced to where they were already busy erecting the small, tentlike shelter. "Now is as good a time as any to visit St. Egbert."

He took her hand, pulling her down the strand before she could protest. Something told him she had more reasons to wish to visit the Seal Isles than a hermit's cell. And he hoped her prayers at the shrine, if she spoke them aloud, would shed some light on the mystery.

But the saint's cave proved more difficult to find than he'd hoped. And the track up the cliffside was so dizzy-making, he wasn't sure they'd find it before good sense made them turn back. Especially when they rounded a sharp turn and were faced with retreat or a mad scramble across a steep crevice filled with jagged, loose rocks and gravel.

"Lass." He gripped her elbow. Below them, the cliffs

fell sheer to sea and heavy swells crashed over the reefs, and the white-crested waves glistened in the afternoon sun, cold and windy as it was.

Winds gusty enough to pluck them right off their feet and send them hurtling down into those shifting, glittery waves.

Darroc frowned, his decision made.

"I say we go back." He placed his fingers against her lips when she started to protest. "I'd ne'er forgive myself if you fell and"—he forced a smile—"I'm no' of a mind to make you a widow, either."

Her eyes flared on the word *widow* and he knew she was thinking of his avowals that—since their promises to each other on Olaf's isle—they were as good as wed. In his eyes they certainly were, by God. And he'd not tolerate anyone saying otherwise.

A muscle in his jaw twitched.

The tales of her father were as black as the man's by-name, the Black Stag. Darroc checked the urge to curse. He might not have a by-name, but men would speak of him with even greater dread if Duncan MacKenzie refused to see reason.

Arabella was his now and he wasn't about to let her go.

Nor would he allow her to plunge down a cliff.

"Come, sweet." He tugged on her arm, pulling her away from the treacherous spill of broken rocks. "You can pray to St. Egbert on the strand. He'll no' mind."

"But I will! And we're almost there." She bit her lip and looked around, the stubborn set of her jaw not surprising Darroc at all. "I can feel it. Here"—she pressed a hand to her breast, her gaze still darting about—"and because I heard the seals singing the night we sailed to Olaf's isle. I know—"

"There wasn't a single seal near us on the voyage." Darroc's brow knit, trying to remember. But he was sure. "You must have heard the wind."

She shook her head. "I know what wind sounds like. But I did think it was the wind at the time. Then"—she glanced down at the water, the hundreds of small dark shapes swimming there—"when we reached the bay here and I heard the seals' calls, I recognized the sound. It wasn't quite what I heard the night of our voyage, but the sounds were close enough for me to be sure that's what it was.

"And so I'm certain that I was meant to come here." She pulled him out onto the scree with her, stepping lightly over the broken rubble. "I believe we were both meant to make this trip, together."

"Even so, I'm for returning to the strand. We can—"

"There!" She smiled, her gaze on a spring pouring from the rocks on the far side of the crevice. Several feet away, a dark vertical opening yawned in the cliff face. "That has to be the cave. And St. Egbert's holy well."

Darroc tried not to groan.

She slipped from his grasp and hurried forward, nipping into the cave before he could stop her. "Damnation!" He sprinted across the rocks, following her into the hermit's dank, foul-smelling sanctuary.

"It is the shrine!" She whirled to face him, her eyes bright. "See, there's the altar." She pointed to a low stone slab, incised with a Celtic cross and covered with bird droppings and what could only be splatters of centuries-old candle wax.

A narrow ledge nearby was surely the hermit's sleeping bench. Formed naturally by the rock of the cave, the ledge now held nothing but a scatter of pebbles and a smear of mold. But even in the dimness, it was clear to see where St. Egbert made his fire, the roof above still blackened with soot.

"I—do you mind if I say my prayer now?" Her voice cracked on the words and she brought a hand to her mouth, biting her forefinger.

"Sweetness, what is it?" Darroc slid his arms around her, pulling her close. "Do you want me to leave? I can wait outside."

"Nae." Arabella shook her head, embarrassment scalding her. "I want you here with me, but..."

She glanced aside, blinking hard to keep her eyes from misting. "Now that I have you, my reason for beseeching St. Egbert's benevolence no longer exists. And now"—for someone who didn't believe in magic and superstition, she feared to tell him what was bothering her—"I am worried that I might jinx us if I ask for something more."

She was especially concerned about performing the Giving Stone ritual. But having come so far, she also feared she'd anger the old gods—if there were any—if she didn't pay homage to the stone.

Darroc was staring at her, his fingers stroking her hair. "Perhaps you should tell me what you wished to pray for."

"A man." She blurted the answer before she could bite her tongue.

"A man?" Now he was really staring at her.

She nodded. "But not just any man." She rushed on, sure her face glowed crimson. "I didn't tell you, but the reason my suitors all left without making an offer was because my father chased them away. He—"

"Your father?" Darroc's brows snapped together. "What do you mean he chased them away?"

"He didn't want me to wed." She forced the words, knowing the truth sounded awful. "Or perhaps it is more that he can't bear to think of me married. But I so wished for a husband and family. I"—she slipped out of his arms and went to stand before the little altar—"knew of this shrine and wanted to come here and beg the saint to send me my true love."

"And now you have him." Darroc joined her at the altar. "You will always have me, Arabella." He rested his hands on her shoulders and dipped his head to nuzzle her neck. "You did not need prayers to find me and you do not need them to keep me. Your father will no' scare me away and neither will I allow him to tear us apart. That I swear to you."

She reached up and placed her hands over his, needing the contact. She so wanted to believe him. "I couldn't bear to lose you." She spoke past the swelling in her throat. The strange little cave with its stone-carved cross and musty smell made it seem so possible that some vengeful saint or god might spring from the shadows and snatch away her happiness.

She couldn't voice her fears.

But Darroc seemed to guess because he turned her in his arms and kissed her, claiming her lips with a slow and gentle sweetness that curled straight through her soul, warming her to her toes and banishing her doubts.

"You will no' lose me, Arabella." He broke the kiss and rested his forehead against hers. "I told you once that I'd never walk away from a prize like you and I meant that. My word is my honor.

"And"—he stepped back and grinned—"I say we head

back down to the strand now and I shall show you exactly how much I love you."

But when they reached the beach a short while later, a score of beaming faces greeted them, each man's eyes ale-bright and his spirits high. They'd also used their time alone to fill the sail screen tent with every comfort and amenity. Thick woolen plaids carpeted the sand and a tiny brazier glowed red in a corner. Someone, likely Conall, had dug a pit and built a cook fire, its crackling flames already roasting a side of beef ribs and what looked to be at least six freshly caught herring.

A fiddle was propped against a rock and a few feet away stood a small ale cask, several battered tin cups sitting in the sand beside it.

There could be no mistake that the men were looking forward to a long and raucous evening.

Conall strode up to them, his mile-wide grin proving it. "So-o-o!" He looked from one to the other. "Did you find the hermit's cave?"

"We did." Darroc reached for Arabella's hand. "Though"—he laced their fingers, squeezing—"I wouldn't recommend the trek up there."

Conall laughed. "No worries. I'm a seaman, not a mountain goat!"

He was also a great cloven-footed loon who, at times, couldn't hold his ale, Darroc decided hours later when his cousin started retelling the same no-longer-amusing tale he'd been regaling them with all evening.

Every other man had long since returned to the birlinn.

Most were snoring deeply, the flutey rumbles carrying on the wind.

Conall showed no signs of tiredness.

Until—Darroc could have killed him—Arabella gave her third voluptuous yawn and, pleading exhaustion, slipped inside the sail cloth tent.

"I'd best hie myself back to the birlinn." Conall pushed unsteadily to his feet. "Sleep well, cousin!" He gave Darroc a lopsided grin and then took off, weaving down the strand to seek his bed at last.

Furious, Darroc watched him go, only turning away to enter the tent when Conall scrambled over the side of the birlinn without mishap.

As he'd dreaded, Arabella slept deeply.

But she'd stripped naked and her skin gleamed softly in the moonlight seeping in through the open edges of the sail screen. Even worse, depending, she'd rolled onto her stomach and the twin rounds of her buttocks proved so tantalizing that it was all he could do not to drop to his knees and straddle her, taking her from behind as he'd been burning to do but hadn't quite had the courage to suggest.

"Damnation." He growled the word, his frustration deepening when she shifted on the pallet, drawing up one knee so that the sweetness between her thighs was exposed to him in all its sleek, raven-curled glory.

Darroc's heart slammed against his ribs and he rammed both hands through his hair. Need, sharp and urgent, flamed through him, unbearable heat pouring into his loins as he stared at her. He was unable to look away.

His manhood ran granite hard.

He wanted to lick her. Throw himself upon her and bury his face in all that dark, musky-scented sleekness. He ached to drink his fill of her essence until the taste of her was forever branded on the back of his tongue.

But she slept so soundly.

He frowned, knowing he couldn't disturb her.

"Odin's balls!"

He whipped around and flung back the tent flap, letting the frosty night air cool his ardor. Only when his hardness diminished, did he turn back and lower himself onto the pallet beside her.

He eased his arms around her, drawing her close so that she lay along the naked length of him. Not for his passion, sadly, but because he wished to keep her warm. But he could feel her every soft breath and the slow, rhythmic beating of her heart. Privileges that filled him with such wonder and love that he soon forgot his frustration.

They had a lifetime to love each other.

And he'd use the advantage of the morning, taking her slow and sweet when she awakened. Kissing her endlessly and letting his fingers tease and tempt her until she writhed and moaned for him, begging him to claim her.

But when at last the first gray light of morning began slipping into the tent, pulling him from his dreams, he found the pallet cold.

Arabella was gone.

The sail screen tent was empty.

"Damnation!" He leapt to his feet, wide awake.

He dashed outside, naked and uncaring.

Arabella was nowhere to be seen.

He looked about, frantic. Cold panic seized him and, he wouldn't have ever believed it, but his damnable knees were knocking!

He ran around to the other side of the tent and stared down the strand at the beached birlinn. But all was still there and a chorus of assorted snores and other bodily noises came from the ship, assuring him that his men still slumbered deeply.

Arabella would never have gone there.

Desperate now, he began to run, making for the goat track to the hermit's cell. He couldn't think of anywhere else she might have gone. The thought of her picking her way up the treacherous path curdled his blood.

He ran faster, his gaze searching everywhere. He scanned the beach and the dunes, the weird clusters of glistening black outcroppings of rock that broke the monotony of the broad, white-sanded beach.

She had to be somewhere.

And then he saw her.

Or rather he saw her naked buttocks.

Darroc froze, staring. She was on all fours, her delectable arse bobbing in the air. Disbelief slammed through him, making his jaw slip as he watched her disappear into a round hole that appeared to be a tunnel through one of the strange rock formations.

"By the Rood!" He blinked, then knuckled his eyes.

It could be he was dreaming.

But then she emerged from the other side of the tunnel and he knew he wasn't.

He was wide awake and not believing his eyes.

She hadn't yet seen him. Indeed, she seemed intent on fumbling in her travel pouch, which Darroc only now noticed sitting on the sand near the rocks. He looked on as she withdrew a skin of something—milk, he quickly saw—and poured the liquid onto the sand in front of the tunnel entrance. Not yet finished, she produced a small linen sack and, walking naked along the edge of the outcropping, began shaking oats on the rocks.

Finally, she bent to retrieve a small earthen jar from her pouch. Darroc recognized it immediately as one of the honey jars from Geordie Dhu's larder. Still unaware she was being watched, she removed the waxed stopper and, dipping her fingers into the jar, began dabbing the rocks with honey.

It was more than Darroc could bear.

Naked as he was, he strode forward, not stopping until he was right behind her. "Lass!" He put a hand on her shoulder. "What in God's name are you doing?"

"Oh, no-o-o!" She spun around, the honey jar flying from her fingers. "I thought you were asleep!"

"And I thought you were." He looked at her, sure he'd never seen anyone turn so many varied shades of red.

"I—" She flipped back her hair then and gave a great sigh. "Ah, well, you deserve the truth. This is another reason I wished to come here."

"Indeed?" Darroc arched a brow and tried to keep his lips from twitching.

Now that he'd found her, the hilarity of the situation was taking its toll. As was her nakedness, which was causing twitching of an entirely different sort.

"This"—she indicated the outcropping and its tunnel—"is the Giving Stone, a pagan shrine dedicated to women and—"

"A pagan shrine?"

She nodded. "Legend claims that any woman who crawls through the stone at the moment of sunrise will be granted her heart's desire."

She looked down at the fallen honey jar. "The honey and oats and milk were offerings. It's said—"

"Ahhh...." Darroc rubbed his chin. "Yestere'en it was St. Egbert and this morn the Auld Ones."

She clasped her hands before her, twining her fingers. "I forgot to pray at the hermit's shrine. I don't really believe in pagan magic, but since I came this far and always planned to do this, I worried that if there is any truth to the stone's powers, I might anger the rock spirits if I ignored them."

"And was your wish the same as yester'en?"

"It was."

"And if I offered again to show you why you have no need for such prayers and charms?" He slid his arms around her, drawing her close. So close that the round fullness of her breasts were crushed against him and the tantalizing softness of her nether curls meshed with the black hair springing thickly at his own sex.

He kissed her, his lips cold and tasting of the clean, brisk air. "What if I show you now how very much I love and desire you?"

"I think I already know." But she let herself melt into him. Delicious shivers rippled down her spine when he slipped a hand between them to cup her breast, his fingers toying with her nipple.

"Och, nae, minx." He lowered his head to nip the lobe of her ear and then nibbled his way down the side of her throat, his fingers still plucking and rubbing the crested peak of her breast. "You might know fine that I love and desire you, but there are many ways I'd like to prove it to you."

He dropped to his knees before her then and she suddenly knew.

He meant to do something Gelis loved.

Something very, very wicked that she didn't think she could bear. He grasped her hips and looked up her, the glint in his dark eyes saying she'd guessed rightly.

"Oh, no." She tried to jerk free. "You can't do *that*."

His lips curved into a roguish smile. "Ah, but I can and shall," he purred, rubbing his cheek against her belly. "Again and again"—he kissed her maiden hair—"until I've sated myself on you."

"But you can't—aaagh!" Arabella threw her head back when he parted her thighs and licked her.

It felt so good!

She began to tremble, sure she'd fall if he wasn't holding her. Proving his word, he kept licking her, stopping only to drag hot kisses over her hips, belly, and thighs. He smoothed his hands up and down her legs as he pleasured her and she thrust her fingers into his hair, holding him close as he kissed and teased his way back to where she burned the hottest.

"Darroc, please . . . ." She clutched at him as he spread her legs wider, licking her more slowly and thoroughly now. He caught her gaze, his own eyes flashing with an expression that made her insides quiver.

"I want to please you." Still watching her, he slid one finger slowly down the center of her, then back up again. "I do not want you to ever doubt me," he vowed, using his tongue to circle her most sensitive place as he slipped one finger inside her. "Not now"—he began suckling that special little nub—"and not e'er."

"I won't. I mean I don't—aieeeee!" She tossed her head again, crying out this time as astonishing pleasure streaked through her. Maddeningly delicious waves of tingly heat streamed out from that one tiny spot he was still flicking with his tongue.

"That's my lass." He opened his mouth over her, sucking hard on the whole of her.

It was too much.

Her knees buckled and she sank onto the sand, breathless and spent. "Oh, dear saints." She could barely speak, the words a mere gasp. "I have never...."

"No' like that, I know." Darroc grinned at her.

She smiled back, sure she'd never be able to get to her feet again.

As if he knew, he leaned down and scooped her up in his arms. He carried her to the little sail screen tent, his own strides sure and steady.

"No more doubts?" He threw back the tent flap and shouldered his way inside. "Not a one?"

"Not even half a one." The truth of it spooled through her, heady and sweet, as he crossed the small space and lowered her down onto the blankets.

"Then rest if you can." He drew a coverlet over her, gently smoothed her hair.

"We sail for home as soon as the men have slept off last night's ale."

Arabella blinked up at him, still too limp from what he'd done to her to do much more. But his words circled in her mind, pleasing her heart as much as his lovemaking had pleasured her body.

We sail for home....

He meant Castle Bane.

Arabella sighed with happiness. She couldn't think of anything sweeter.

Chapter Eighteen

✣

The first thing Darroc did upon returning to Castle Bane was visit his notch room. To his surprise, or perhaps not, someone had made changes to the bleak little chamber in his absence. Strewing herbs, fragrant and sweet, covered the floor's sturdy wooden planking and colorful tapestries graced cold stone walls bare of decoration for centuries. Someone had tended the hearth as well, sweeping out years of cobwebs and ash.

A fire didn't burn there, but a new grate stood at the ready and a wicker basket waited close by, brimming with kindling and peat.

Only the room's four tall windows were the same, the stone splays still cut deeply into the tower wall and the notches there as always.

His marks jumped out at him. Bold and exact, they ran up and down the window arch in neat, orderly rows. Those made by Asa Long-Legs, saints grace her soul, also remained as they'd ever been. The scratches were still faint and barely visible, their number greater than his own but the lines painfully crooked.

Looking at Asa Long-Legs's notches, Darroc's own words came back to him. *MacConacher's Isle wasn't made for women.* But he knew now that he'd been mistaken. The isle was made for women, leastways a very special one that he meant to marry as soon as arrangements could be made.

With or without her father's blessing.

But first he had other business to attend to. Something he never thought he'd do but that filled him with bright hope and exaltation.

It felt good to put the past behind him.

Especially knowing his future held such unexpected happiness and bliss.

Taking a deep breath, he cast a glance at the room's open door and the only other thing that hadn't changed while he was away at Olaf Big Nose's settlement, banishing Black Vikings and winning his lady's heart.

Frang lay flopped on the floor of the landing, just outside the notch room's threshold. The dog's eyes were ever watchful and he swished a dutiful tail, perhaps thinking a show of some loyalty or affection might make up for his refusal to enter the notch room.

Mina was there, too.

Like Frang, she wouldn't enter the room, preferring to huddle behind the larger dog's shaggy bulk. But her bright tufted head peeped over Frang's shoulder, her ears perked and curious.

Looking away before he went misty-eyed—he'd missed them both fiercely—Darroc crossed the room to his own notch window and reached for his special chisel and mallet. He turned them over in his hands, remembering how he'd bought them in Glasgow as a lad. He'd used his last coin to make the purchase and he took such good care of them that both could still be passed off for new.

They'd served him well.

But now...

Darroc heard a sigh, the sound soft and sweet. It was a sigh of great contentment. And—he knew—a sigh that he hadn't made.

He frowned and pulled a hand down over his face.

As always, the notch room worked on him in strange ways at times. Imagining a sigh when there hadn't been one shouldn't surprise him. But it was odd that the noise had sounded so feminine.

Almost like the breath of an angel.

He decided he'd only heard the soughing of wind and returned his attention to the tools in his hands. They'd grown warm from his touch and he almost felt sorry for them, knowing what he was about to do.

Then, before sentiment got the better of him and spoiled an act he'd been planning for days, he pressed them once against his chest, just over his heart. That last nod to olden times behind him, he drew a deep, fortifying breath and stepped closer to his window. He pitched the tools through the arch, leaning forward to watch them spin their way down to the sea where they vanished beneath the waves, gone before he even realized he no longer held them.

"Live well," he said, feeling foolish, but knowing he had to say something.

The chisel and mallet had been his companions for long.

Now he was glad to be rid of them.

Wanting to return to his bedchamber and slip beneath the covers with Arabella, if only to hold her as she slept, he dashed a hand across his eyes and strode from the room, taking the tower stairs two at a time.

His thumping footsteps echoed loudly in the turnpike stair, the noise carrying into the notch room and drowning out the soft, satisfied sigh anyone might have heard if they'd only bothered to listen.

But the little room was empty again.

Cold and lonely as had been its fate for so many long years.

Though this morn the room had borne witness to something new.

Something so wondrous and exciting—who would have thought that the young chief would throw away his notch-making tools?—that Asa Long-Legs could contain herself no longer. It was just such a shame that he'd heard her sigh and, as always, dismissed her as the wind.

She was bursting with happiness for the young pair and wished she could share her joy with someone.

She'd tried to speak with the old woman, the one they called Mad Moraig, when she'd hobbled abovestairs to put the notch room in order. Not mad at all: the crone knew before the return of the couple that things had finally turned good for them.

Asa had seen that in Moraig's eyes.

But the old woman had never guessed that she wasn't alone each time she'd scurried about, dusting and tacking her tapestries on the wall. Wishing it were otherwise, Asa closed her eyes and began to spin and shimmer, glowing ever brighter until she wasn't just a thought but a true presence in the little room.

She drifted about, trailing shining hands along the newly hung tapestries, remembering how the silken threads would have felt beneath her fingers if only she could still touch them for real.

Her home in Scalloway had been decorated with many such hangings, each one more exquisite than the other. Asa's heart hurt to think of them. But then it always pained her to remember her home.

She lifted a hand to her cheek, dashing away tears that sparkled like the jewels her father had once showered on her. But those memories, too, were bittersweet. So she tried again to focus on the young couple, wishing she could make them something special for their wedding.

She so wished she, too, could have enjoyed such a gloriously happy ending.

Then perhaps it is time.

The deep voice came from right behind her and she jumped, whirling around so fast that she would've made herself dizzy if she'd done so in her true life. She peered around the familiar little room, but no one was there. It was just as empty as before, and just as cold.

She sighed again and started to glide toward her special window—the north one because it looked to Shetland—but she froze in the middle of the room when she saw that one of the new tapestries was shimmering and shining, turning bright and luminous just like her.

"Oh, dear." She hovered where she was, fear gripping her.

Nothing like this had ever happened.

But then something else startled her.

Something so astonishing, she had to blink three times to be sure she was seeing it. The new tapestry was *open-*

ing now and the gay woodland scene she'd come used to seeing every day had disappeared. Only the edges of the tapestry remained and as she stared they rippled and glowed, letting her peer deep into a new landscape that was slowly replacing the old one that had vanished.

Asa shimmied closer, wanting to see more.

"Aggggh!" She reeled backward, almost tripping on her luminous, flowing skirts when she saw her old home. It was Scalloway, there could be no mistake. The bright blue bay was there and her family castle, the stout keep's familiar walls bringing crystal tears to her eyes again.

Swiping at them, she kept staring at the tapestry, now noting the low rolling hills where she'd tumbled and played as a child. They were green with spring grasses and dotted with yellow buttercups and red and blue primroses as if whoever was making such magic knew that spring was her favorite time of year.

Do you think I'd forget?

The booming voice came again and this time she recognized it as her father's.

"O-o-oh!" She clapped her hands to her face, too frightened—and hopeful—to believe it.

Her heart, such as was left of it, beat fiercely. And although her tears were spilling badly now, she was shimmying too much to lift a hand to brush them away.

So that is how you greet me after all these years? With tears, girl? I'd at least expected you to run into my arms!

"O-o-oh!" Asa shimmied even more, the whole glittering length of her rippling uncontrollably. "Father! Oh, please, where are you?"

Here where I've always been—if you'd have had the sense to come home.

Asa saw him then. Big and bold as she remembered, he was inside the tapestry, standing beside his favorite deerskin-covered couch. The hall fire burned cheerily behind him and Asa couldn't imagine how he'd managed to come to her through the wall hanging, but he was there all the same.

And he was reaching for her, his powerful arms open wide and his eyes twinkling in welcome. Though, as Asa cried out and went to him, she saw as she drifted nearer that his eyes weren't twinkling after all.

They were bright with the sheen of tears, just like her own eyes.

"Oh, Father!" Her voice cracked on the words as she felt his arms band around her, pulling her tight against him. "I have missed you so!"

Still shimmying madly, Asa threw a look over her shoulder at the notch room. But it was no longer there. She turned back to her father and clung to him, holding fast to his strength as the tapestry closed around them, taking them home.

And then they were gone.

But the bleak little notch room would never be called bleak again.

The woodland tapestry would always glow with rich light and color when the sun caught it just so. And sometimes when Frang and Mina, who claimed the room for their own, stood peering hard at the fanciful hanging, there were some who claimed the tapestry didn't show a sylvan setting at all.

Those folk insisted the scene was Nordic, a seaside village in a distant place where the spring grass is especially green and buttercups and primroses thrive.

*   *   *

Darroc opened the bedchamber door as quietly as he could.

He crept inside, wishing the room let in more sunlight. Or, at the very least, that someone had left the night candle burning. But the heavy wax candle sat cold and unlit on the night table. And not one of the hanging cresset lamps or the wall torches burned. Even the hearth fire had dwindled to a softly glowing clump of blackened peat and gray ash. There wasn't the spark of a single orangered ember.

Most annoying of all, the bed curtains were drawn tight.

He'd hoped to catch a glimpse of his sleeping lady, naked as was her wont and—he couldn't deny—his greatest delight. Truth was he doubted he'd ever tire of gazing upon her.

It didn't matter if she was sleeping or awake.

He simply couldn't get enough of her.

Needing her now, he strode across the room and hooked his fingers in the bed's heavy brocade hangings. He waited a moment before drawing them, savoring the anticipation. With luck, he'd be treated to a tempting view of her naked breasts. Or, if the saints were kind, he'd be able to feast his gaze on the sooty-black silken heat between her shapely thighs.

If her legs were parted enough, he might even lean down and drop a kiss right in the middle of her sweetness.

O-o-oh, the joys of a woman who slept unclothed!

Feeling blessed, he drew a deep breath and yanked back the bed curtains.

Arabella wasn't there.

Frowning, he started to turn away, but something caught his eye. He stepped closer, peering down at the mussed furs and linens. Nothing looked amiss, but he was sure he'd seen something.

Something glittery.

Perhaps it was Arabella's rock crystal and carnelian necklace. The one with the Thor hammer etched on the disc-shaped pendant. She loved the necklace, claiming it reminded her of their days—and nights—on Olaf Big Nose's isle.

Like as not, she didn't know the necklace was here and had gone searching for it.

Sure that was it, Darroc shoved back the bed curtains a bit more and started looking through the coverlets and beneath pillows.

He didn't have to look far.

What he'd seen rested smack in the center of the bed.

And it hit him like a hammer blow to the gut.

It was the Thunder Rod.

"*Nae!*" He stared at the hoary relic, his stomach heaving. "Nae!" he cried again, clutching his middle and bending double, the pain agonizing. "It canna be...."

But the truth winked up at him.

Brilliantly colored, glistening, and ripping the soul right out of him.

"Ach, God!" Darroc dropped to his knees and pressed his forehead against the edge of the bed. He dug his fingers into the mattress, sure he'd fall flat on his face if he didn't. The floor kept threatening to fly right up at him and he wasn't sure, but he'd almost swear someone had sucked all the air out of the room.

He knew there wasn't any left in his lungs.

Breathing was impossible.

And he couldn't see anything either.

Only the damnable shining piece of wood that Arabella had to have caressed in a dangerous way. He should have told her how the wretched relic works on women. How its magic possesses them, filling them with insatiable desire; unquenchable lust for the first man to cross their path after they've touched the rod, fondling its length as they would a man.

Fury and bitterness welled up in Darroc, an agony so thick and damning he almost choked. Aye, he should have told her, warned her. But he'd never dreamed the relic would fall into her hands.

Now he knew why she'd capitulated so easily.

It wasn't him at all.

She didn't love him, either.

Their entire happiness was only the false passion conjured by the Thunder Rod. And the knowledge gutted him. Burning emptiness flooded his heart, scalding his soul and snatching away every shred of hope, joy, and happiness he'd found with her. Wondrous beauty he should have known would not last. Perhaps even punishment for having fallen so deeply in love with a woman he should never have touched.

Darroc groaned, his world crumbling around him.

"Dear saints!" A light hand touched his shoulder. *Arabella*. "Are you ill? Tell me, what is it? I'll go back to the kitchens and—"

"Nae! I'm no' ill." Darroc sprang to his feet. "I am fine. I was—er... praying," he lied, unable to think of anything else. "Thanking the saints for bringing us safely back here. And"—he hated what he was about to say,

but the sooner she was gone, the better for them both—
"asking them to see you well to Kintail when you go."

She blinked. "But we're going together. You said—"

"A man says much when he's tempted by a beautiful
woman." He shoved a hand through his hair, shamed to
note that his fingers trembled. "What happened between
us came about because of the excitement of the feast at
Olaf's. It was wrong and I cannot take further advantage
of you."

"Dear God—Darroc!" She blanched, her eyes round
in her face. "What are you doing? Are you"—she glanced
around the room—"drink-taken?"

"Nae." He shook his head. "I've ne'er been more by
my wits."

And much as it pierced him, his honor *did* forbid him
to take advantage of her. He started pacing, almost wishing he were a man with lesser morals. But he'd spent his
life struggling to rebuild his family's reputation and he
just couldn't blacken the name MacConacher any further
by keeping a woman at his side who'd only fallen in love
with him because of a bespelled piece of wood.

It was absolutely unthinkable.

Beyond unfair to Arabella. She deserved a chance
to marry a man she loved truly. A husband chosen by a
father who adored her and—despite his own feelings
about the man and what she'd said of his stance against
her suitors—would surely see her settled with a worthy
consort she could come to care for deeply.

A man whose very name wouldn't cause a rift in her
clan.

It was just a damned shame the notion made him want
to wring the bastard's neck.

And it was an even greater tragedy that—despite everything—he still wanted to sweep her into his arms and kiss her fiercely, binding her to him. It would be so easy to let the wonder of her make him forget how wrong it was to love and keep her.

He had to let her go.

"Do you not care what I think of this?" She was staring at him, hurt all over her. "What it will do to me?"

"I am thinking of you. Only you." He thrust a hand through his hair, wishing she didn't look so miserable. "It's for the best, lass."

"Whose best?" She came after him, two bright spots of red flaming on her cheeks. Her eyes glittered hotly, sparking such fury that she looked like one of the Valkryies he always thought of her as.

She certainly looked as dangerous.

And he'd never seen her more beautiful than now, in such a temper.

"*Tell me! Whose best*?" She railed again, grabbing his arms. "Not mine, surely! I will die without you. Perish cold, alone, and bereft, aching for you—as I've told you often enough!"

"That's no' true." He broke away from her, needing distance. "You'll forget me once you're safely returned to Kintail. You deserve a good life with a man you love and who is worthy of—"

"I love you!" She flew at him, tears tracking her face. "There is no man more worthy. No man I want but you. Please"—she started to fall to her knees, but he caught her, pulling her up—"don't do this, I beg you."

"Sweet lass, you don't know what you're saying."

Darroc couldn't believe his voice was so steady. But he had to fool her.

She'd never go if she knew the truth.

He turned away from her and went to stand at the window, keeping his back to her. "There will be another man you desire. A good one with no bad history between your families and who will—"

"No other man will have me now." She stayed across the room this time, her voice sounding oddly broken. "And I do not care. If I can't have you, I—"

Your passion for me isn't real!

It doesn't exist except inside that unholy piece of wood lying on the bed!

Darroc's heart screamed the words. But of course she didn't hear them.

He clenched his fists, hating that it'd come to this. "There is no man under the heavens who can resist you, Arabella." That much was true. "It will no' matter to your future husband that—"

"You are my husband!" She ran at him again, digging her fingers into his arms and yanking him around to face her. "You said so in the fisherman's hut, telling me the old ways were honored on Olaf's isle and that we were as good as wed. You said that you loved me.

"Are you telling me now that those were lies?"

Darroc closed his eyes and drew a ragged breath. The agony inside him was so great, so soul ripping, he wondered he was still standing.

His heart was broken.

"Answer me!" She shook him, her voice breaking on a sob. "You owe me the truth. Were you lying to me all along?"

Darroc opened his eyes and looked at her, immediately wishing he hadn't.

The misery on her face split him.

He couldn't bear it.

"Well?" Her nails sank into his arms, drawing blood. "What was true and what wasn't?"

"Ach, lass..." He heaved a great sigh, feeling suddenly ancient. "Everything I ever said to you was true. I've ne'er lied to you."

She stepped back, her eyes rounding again. "Then why?" She shook her head. "If you love me, then—"

"It is because I love you that I'm sending you away." He put his hands on her shoulders. He knew he shouldn't, but he was unable to see her pain without trying to offer her some small solace. "It will hurt me much more to see you sail away. And know this"—he spoke slowly, willing her to listen—"I will never love another. Indeed, I'm sure I'll never even look at another woman. My heart will always belong to you and I'll keep you with me in my memories."

"No-o-o!" She knocked his hands from her shoulders and spun away, pressing her fist against her lips. "I won't let you do this. I don't want to be a memory! I want—"

You want something false.

The truth sliced through him again, cutting him off at the knees and—praise God—giving him the strength to do what honor deemed he must.

Somehow he managed to walk past her to the door. "I'll have Geordie Dhu test the sea and weather. If the signs are propitious, you can be away on the morrow. Conall will escort you. He—"

"No-o-o! *Please....*" Her sob slammed into him, breaking him.

"Someday you will thank me, Arabella." He spoke before the scalding thickness in his throat made speech impossible. "I wouldn't send you away otherwise."

The words spoken, he stepped from the room, closing the door behind him. But the look of horror on her face, her misery, followed him as he lurched away, almost stumbling down the stairs.

At the first landing, he paused to slump against the wall. Hot tears blinded him and he pressed a hand to his mouth, stifling an anguished roar.

He should be feeling gladness.

He'd done right by her. Someday she *would* thank him.

Darroc pulled a hand down over his face, despair crushing him. Who would ever have thought a man's honor could bring him so low?

He certainly hadn't, but now he knew.

Saints pity him.

Chapter Nineteen

✤

*H*ow *can you do this?"*

Arabella regretted the words as soon as she spoke them. She'd vowed to leave with grace. But she'd been searching Darroc's face ever since she'd stepped onto the boat strand. She'd hoped to see some small flicker of emotion, a shred she could cling to in days to come when she'd wonder if he'd ever truly loved her.

Unfortunately, his expression revealed nothing except a cold stoniness that cut her to the quick.

She stared at him, fearing her knees would buckle any moment, but doing her best to stand tall. "I know you love me. Th-this"—her voice broke—"is madness. Please, I beg you to reconsider. One last time, I'm asking you, pleading—"

"Do not make it worse, lass." He glanced at the cluster of solemn-faced men a bit farther down the strand, the birlinn so close to the water's edge, poised for launch. When he looked back at her, his eyes were still shuttered, his jaw tighter than ever. "Conall is returning you to Kintail and the life you deserve. Be well and know that—"

Frang whined beside him. The shaggy beast pressed into him, looking morose.

"Know what?" Arabella's stomach knotted at the dog's whimpering, the pitiful way he stared at the wicker basket she clutched in her arms. Frang, too, was losing his heart's joy this day.

As was Mina, who fretted and howled inside her covered basket.

"I won't leave until you tell me," Arabella prompted, starting to feel belligerent. The morning's brittle air and the dark, freezing mist swirling down the hills and along the strand made her stubborn.

The choppy seas, so cold and forbidding, squeezed at her chest, reminding her she wasn't as courageous as she was so desperately trying to be.

This was no day to begin a sea journey—despite Geordie Dhu's assurances.

Icy wind blew her hair into her face, but she hardly noticed. What did such a little thing matter when the man she loved so fiercely was turning his back on her? So she shifted Mina's basket on her hip and lifted her chin. "What should I know?"

Darroc frowned. "That it is best you forget me."

Arabella blinked, a sick feeling washing over her. He truly was letting her go. Until this moment, she'd hoped he'd relent. That something unexpected would happen and he'd realize what a terrible mistake he was making.

A grave error every taut line of him said he chose to ignore.

Seeing that finality, she summoned the steel she knew flowed in her veins, even now. "Is that what you want?"

"It is." His voice was hard.

"Then so be it." She spoke as a MacKenzie, her tone now as emotionless as his.

He nodded. "It is time, lass. Conall will wish to catch the tide."

Arabella returned his nod, even managing not to cry out when he strode away from her, making for the men gathered near the birlinn.

She did cast a longing glance at Castle Bane, looking so stern on its cliff above the sea. Drifting mist hid the parapet walk from view, but torchlight flickered in some of the narrow slit windows. For one brief, tempting moment, she almost hitched up her skirts to run back up the steep flight of steps in the cliffside to the door she knew waited at the top of that precarious, stony stair.

Instead, she tightened her grip on Mina's basket and let her gaze take in every black-glistening fissure in the cliff, each ancient rough-hewn step, and every stone in the castle walls and the harsh, yet oh-so-dear keep. She stared long, not even looking away when her vision began to blur and her eyes stung with hot, blinding tears.

Castle Bane and its rugged, windswept isle had become home and the thought of leaving filled her with a wrenching pain she knew would stain her soul forever.

The thought of leaving Darroc...

"*Dear God!*" The cry escaped her and she pressed a trembling hand to her lips, hoping he hadn't heard. But a glance showed he couldn't have. He was at the birlinn, pacing and shouting orders for its imminent launch, his actions proving he'd already dismissed her.

Only Frang lingered. He sat a few paces away, watching her with great, mournful eyes. His tail lay unmoving on the cold, wet sand and his ears drooped so pathetically that Arabella could scarce bear to look at him.

His whines made her heart contract.

"Oh, Frang!" She blinked hard. She would not board the birlinn crying.

She would go with a raised head and no backward glances.

Or memories that would crush her.

Steeling herself, she lifted a hand to her necklace. The carnelian and rock crystal beaded one Jutta Manslayer had given her. The instant her fingers closed on its round rock crystal pendant, a thousand bittersweet images swept across her mind, each one powerful enough to steal her breath and bring her to her knees.

Tears pricked her eyes again. She couldn't keep the necklace. Doing so would only intensify the sorrow she knew she wouldn't be able to fully banish.

Jutta Manslayer would understand.

So she set down Mina's basket and reached to undo the necklace's clasp. Then she put back her shoulders and walked over to the only other person on the strand whose face wasn't set in hard, grim lines.

Mad Moraig stood apart from the rest, wringing her hands as she watched the men slide the birlinn into the water.

"Moraig!" Arabella reached her. "I want you to have this," she said, fastening the necklace around the old woman's neck. "A token of thanks for all you've done for me and to keep in my memory."

"Eh?" Moraig glanced at her chest, the Thor's hammer

pendant resting there. When she looked up again, it was to thrust her bristly chin. "I'd no' be needing baubles to remember you by if you'd stay."

She peered at Arabella, her blue gaze sharp. " 'Tis here with us you be belonging now. Everyone knows it!"

"Not everyone." Arabella glanced at Darroc. The birlinn was already in the water, Conall holding the steering oar and the giant called Hugh at the gong. "Darroc—"

"Is being an arse as all men tend to be at times!" The old woman glared at him.

"He's doing what he feels he must. He says his honor—"

"Honor a pig's eye!" Moraig spat on the sand. "Once you're gone, he'll soon see how warm honor keeps him of a night. Then"—she lifted a bent finger, her eyes narrowing—"he'll be wishing you back. Men always realize what they've lost when it's too late."

Arabella's heart pounded on the words. "Oh, Moraig, how I wish that were true."

"It is. Dinnae you be forgetting it." Moraig shot another glance down the beach.

Following her gaze, Arabella saw that the day's mist appeared to be lightening and the choppy, white-capped waters of the bay were settling. The seas were turning glassy and calm, just as Geordie Dhu had prophesied.

Arabella's heart sank.

She'd so wished for a tempest.

Now...

Even the weather gods were readying the way for her departure.

And Darroc was heading toward her, clearly intent on escorting her to the birlinn. Honorable to the last, he surely meant to carry her through the surf, setting her dry into the vessel that would bear her away, breaking her heart.

Knowing it would undo her if he touched her again, she threw her arms around Moraig, squeezing her in farewell. Then before tears could spill anew, she spun around and ran back to Mina, snatching up her wicker basket.

Quickly, she raced across the sand, sprinting for the birlinn.

"Arabella—wait!" Darroc shouted behind her, his pounding footsteps almost shaking the strand.

"No." She didn't care if he heard.

She did yank up her skirts and plunge into the surf, reaching the birlinn in three splashing strides. A score of hands stretched out to help her board, but she only shoved Mina's basket at them and leaped into the craft on her own, a feat that amazed even herself.

Then, before anyone could stop her, she seized the baton from Hugh's hand and banged it hard against the gong. "Away!" she cried, raising her arm in the command she knew would see the oarsmen lowering the sweeps into the water.

Conall blinked, but thrust up his own arm—surely thinking the men might not heed her.

But they did, Hugh beating his gong and chanting loudly, the oarsmen pulling so hard that the birlinn shot forward in a cloud of spray.

On the strand, Darroc cursed.

But as the birlinn flew across the water, Arabella kept her gaze on the mouth of the bay and the open seas beyond. Looking back would do her no good.

Truth be told, it would break her.

*   *   *

Two days later, just as the birlinn rounded yet another nameless cluster of jagged, protruding rock and skerries, one of the oarsmen leapt to his feet, pointing.

"Three sails on the horizon!" he called, lifting his voice above the beats of Hugh's gong and the other men's steady, rhythmic chanting. "War galleys."

At once, all heads swiveled, everyone seeing the three galleys swinging round in their direction. Three galleys that flashed forward in style, cutting swiftly across the long, westerly swells, each craft with a proudly rearing stag painted on its single, square-cut sail.

Arabella stared, her heart hammering wildly. She clapped a hand to her breast and squinted, straining her eyes to see better.

It couldn't be, but it was.

Her father.

She sprang to her feet, grabbing Conall's arm. "It's my father! Those are Kintail galleys!"

"Aye." Conall pulled on the steering oar, causing the birlinn to slue around to face the approaching galleys, now almost upon them. "Raise the sweeps, men! Let's show them we're friendly."

Arabella almost choked at his unconcerned tone.

It wasn't the MacConachers who'd cause havoc.

It was her father.

She'd spotted him even before the galley glided to a slow, rocking halt. He stood at the prow of the middle galley, staring right at her. Wind whipped his plaid and tore at his raven hair. His hands were fisted on the rail and even at this distance, his knuckles gleamed whitely.

Wishing she hadn't noticed, Arabella swallowed. But

he *was* her father and she loved him so powerfully that seeing him now, even furious as he appeared, brought hot tears to her eyes and made her tremble. A strange mixture of dread, relief, and joy swept her, making her pulse quicken and her blood roar in her ears.

She dashed a hand across her cheek, not taking her gaze off him.

Never had he looked more magnificent or—her mouth went dry—so utterly terrifying.

"He will have heard of the *Merry Dancer*." Conall lowered his voice, speaking only for her. "He'll be coming to fetch you, is all. You've no need to fear him. He'll be hearing naught o' Darroc. No' from us."

"He'll know." Arabella could see in his eyes that he did. "And—I mean to tell him anyway as I'll not be wed to another. Not ever."

In her basket, Mina barked.

Arabella bent to soothe her and when she straightened, it was to see her mother and Sir Marmaduke join her father at the bow. Her uncle looked as calm and untroubled as ever, a state that clearly irritated her father for his scowl deepened when Sir Marmaduke leaned close to say something in his ear. But her mother beamed and lifted a hand, her bright, red-gold braids streaming in the wind.

Then, with deliberate flourish, her father's galley sped forward in a burst of spume, the rowers only backwatering and raising the sweeps in the last seconds before the galley bumped alongside the birlinn.

"MacConacher!" Her father glared across the few feet between them. "I've come for my girl. Hand her over lest you wish to lose your life! Truth is"—he gripped his sword hilt meaningfully—"I'm of a mind to take it anyway."

"Good sir—I greet you! I am Conall, cousin to my chief." Conall's tone was courteous. "The MacConacher is not with us. But"—he glanced at Arabella—"he charged us with seeing your daughter safely returned to you in Kintail. We were taking her there now."

Arabella stepped forward, her chin high. "I am well, Father. These men have shown me naught but kindness. If you've heard—"

"I know everything!" Her father shot a dark look at her mother. "All of it. We'll have words later when we're—"

"The MacLeans sent a courier to us, dear." Her mother lifted her voice above the wind. "We came as soon as we could and"—she glanced at her husband, sharply—"I believe your father has more to say to Conall."

Her father apparently disagreed because he clamped his jaw and said nothing.

Sir Marmaduke sidled closer to him and—Arabella was sure—must've tramped on her father's foot because his eyes suddenly flared with annoyance.

"I—" He blew out a gusty breath, shoved a hand through his hair. "I thank you for rescuing my daughter at sea." He spoke quickly, his gaze fixed on a spot somewhere just to the left of Conall's head. "We"—he flashed another heated glance at his wife—"are beholden."

"And do we not have other thanks?" She lifted a delicate brow, prompting.

Duncan scowled at her. "I've said my appreciation."

"Indeed?" Sir Marmaduke braced a hip against the side of the bow platform and crossed his arms. "What of the MacDonalds?"

"I am no lackey to John of Islay!" Duncan turned

crimson. "Clan Donald is well able to spread their tidings without my help."

"Father!" Arabella gripped the rail. "What tidings?"

"None that concern you," he snapped, his soured expression saying they did.

Linnet slid an arm around him, but kept her gaze on Arabella. "We encountered a MacDonald galley several days ago. They were John of Islay's men on their way to Darroc MacConacher and a Norseman named Olaf—"

"Big Nose," Arabella finished for her, flashing a glance at Conall.

But he only shrugged. "We have no strife with the Lords of the Isles, sir." He addressed her father. "Or can it be the MacDonalds heard—"

"Of you and your Norse friend banishing the Black Vikings?" Sir Marmaduke smiled at him from where he still leaned against the stern platform.

The smile earned him a scowl from Duncan. "Aye, that was their tidings!" Duncan glowered at Arabella as well. "Now that you've heard, I'm fetching you onto this galley and—"

"Duncan, you cannot leave it at that." Linnet's voice held reproach.

He spluttered, turning a deeper shade of red. "What? Would you have me tell her the rest?"

Her silent stare said yes.

Sir Marmaduke rejoined them at the rail, lending her his support.

Duncan frowned at them both. "Young man," he began, fixing his scowl on Conall, "John of Islay was pleased by this with the sea raiders. We were told"—he paused, his annoyance palpable—"that he's sent men to the crown bearing recommendation that Clan MacConacher and the Norseman be duly rewarded."

Cheers rose from the MacConacher rowing benches.

Conall stared. "Rewarded how, sir? Did anyone say?"

"They spoke of pardons for previous...ills against the realm. And coin." Duncan made each word sound as if it pained him. "For the Norseman, coin as well and a charter for the island he calls his own."

The oarsmen went wild.

Mina joined in, barking madly.

Arabella's heart seemed to stop, then thundered against her ribs. Dear saints, this was everything Darroc had dreamed of. The goal he'd worked toward for years. A lifetime. Forgetting herself, Arabella threw her arms around Conall, hugging him tight.

"Did you hear?" she cried, gladness welling inside her.

"I did, but I can scarce reckon it." He shook his head, his eyes bright. But then he pulled away from her and smoothed his plaid.

Clearing his throat, he called to her father. "Good sir! These are glad tidings. Will you not return with us to Castle Bane and celebrate? You would be"—he glanced at his men—"most welcome!"

Arabella started to decline, but her father's booming voice spared her the embarrassment. "Nae, we cannot. We're heading back to Kintail now, this very hour."

"But we wish you well." Linnet smiled at Conall. "Please give our felicitations to your chief. Tell him"—she raised her voice over the wind and Mina's barking—"he is always welcome at our hearth."

"I shall, my lady." Conall inclined his head respectfully.

"Are you ready?" Sir Marmaduke spoke at her elbow.

Arabella started. She hadn't seen him jump across to the birlinn. And, she saw with equal surprise, Mina's basket had already been reached over to her father's galley. One of his men was just lowering it carefully to the deck.

An awkward silence fell over the birlinn.

Men looked down at their feet or out at the water, their closed faces speaking volumes. Only Conall met her eyes, his own mirroring her sadness.

"I'm so sorry, lass." He spoke low, for her ears alone. "I know he'll always love you."

Arabella nodded, grateful. Her throat was too thick for words. She pressed a hand to her breast and drew a great breath. Any moment she'd sink to her knees. She'd dreaded this final parting and now it was upon her, swooping down to shatter her world.

"Conall..." She couldn't finish, couldn't even see him through the stinging haze of tears.

Then, as if he sensed her pain, Sir Marmaduke swept her up and handed her into her father's galley, giving her into his outstretched arms.

"Lass!" Duncan crushed her to him, reaching to pull Linnet into their embrace. "If you ever speak of another adventure, I swear I'll—"

"You needn't worry, Father." Arabella slipped away from them and went to the rail. "There will be no more adventures. I have had my fill of them."

But that wasn't true. She'd only had a taste and it'd been far too brief.

Now she was going home.

How sad that her father's galley was carrying her in the wrong direction.

Chapter Twenty

❖

Several nights later, Darroc sat alone in his thinking room, his glare pinned on the Thunder Rod. Once more, the clan's supposed treasure hung innocently on the wall, secured by its frayed and faded tartan ribbon. And—to torment him, he was sure—the rod's gleaming black wood and bits of brilliant color repeatedly snagged his gaze.

All evening, he'd tried to force his attention elsewhere.

And each time he'd failed.

He knew why.

The damnable relic was his last tie to Arabella. And even if it gutted him to know it was the Thunder Rod that had ultimately torn her from him, he couldn't bear to do what he knew he should. Namely, snatch the vile length of wood off the wall and toss it into the hearth fire.

Cast it to the flames where it could do no more damage.

Truth was, powerful as the relic was known to be, he doubted it could be destroyed. Like as not any attempt to do so would circle around and bite the *attempter* in the arse. Or worse, the smoke formed by the burning wood would turn into the avenging souls of every life the Thunder Rod had ruined, each wretched spirit haunting him all his days.

Darroc shuddered. He was half certain such horrors were possible.

His life was haunted enough as it was. Especially since he'd sent Arabella away.

Scowling, he reached to refill his ale cup only to drop both cup and ewer when the door flew open and slammed against the wall in an ear-splitting bang.

"Saints!" He leapt to his feet, spinning around to see who'd dared to breach his sanctuary.

He'd given strict orders to be left alone.

Even Frang gave him wide berth these days. And when the dog deigned to come near, it was only to stand and pierce him with accusatory stares.

Or the beast came when he wanted food, which wasn't particularly flattering.

Just now it was Conall eyeing him. Only his cousin's stare wasn't recriminatory. Far from it, he looked like he hadn't slept or bathed in a fortnight. His bright red hair stood up in tufts. His walk was an odd, lurching gait that was surely from being at sea. But most annoying of all, he was grinning like a loon.

He clearly didn't know Darroc was in mourning.

Loping across the room, he grabbed Darroc's arms and shook him. "Have you heard? John of Islay has sent men to the crown! They will—"

"To be sure I know." Darroc jerked free and brushed at his sleeves. "MacDonald's men were here days ago, full of tidings and goodwill." He bent to snatch up the ewer and ale cup, returning them to the table. "Every tongue-wagger in the Isles will be speaking of—"

"You aren't pleased?" Conall's brows lifted. "Don't you understand? This means—"

"I know what it means." Darroc turned away, misery slicing through him. "But"—he wheeled back around—"what does it matter when all the light and joy has been ripped out of my life? Now that—"

He broke off, a horrible suspicion jellying his knees. "Why are you returned so soon? You haven't brought her back, have you?"

Darroc would kill him if he had.

He didn't have the strength to send her away again. Indeed, one reason he'd been hiding away in his thinking room was because if he went anywhere near the boat strand, he'd hop into the first fishing coble he stumbled upon and set off to fetch her, honor be damned.

Indeed, before he'd so wisely sequestered himself in here, he'd spent days prowling her bedchamber, hoping to catch some lingering waft of her scent in the air. For the same reason, he'd forbid Mad Moraig to strip and wash the bed linens.

He was that pathetic.

And he didn't think he could get through another day without her. The cold and empty nights were a trial that would soon put him in his grave.

So he funneled all his frustration into a scowl and glared at his still-grinning cousin. "Well?" He resisted the urge to cuff the lad. For two pins, he'd do that and worse. "Where is she?"

"Halfway to Kintail, I'd imagine."

Darroc's eyes rounded. "How can that be with you here?"

"Her father intercepted us two days out." Conall spoke as if that was nothing. "Three galleys, manned for war. But—"

"She's with her father?" Darroc pressed his hands to his temples. His head was beginning to ache. "How did he know to come looking for her? We hadn't yet sent word to him."

Conall shrugged. "He seemed to know everything. Apparently the MacLeans heard of the *Merry Dancer* and dispatched a courier to Kintail."

Darroc sank back onto his chair, all his hopes of Conall coming back with her—and of himself fetching her—evaporating like mist before the sun.

If her father had her...

"We can still go after her." Conall made it sound so simple.

"I sent her away for a reason." Darroc glared at him. "It was a very good one."

"But it's making you miserable." Conall spoke the obvious.

Darroc clenched his jaw, unwilling to admit it.

Especially when a whine sounded from the doorway where Frang stood pinning him with another of his mournful stares.

"He is making me miserable." Darroc jerked his head at the dog. "Otherwise, I am—"

"She loves you."

"Aye, I know." Darroc's gaze flashed to the Thunder Rod. "She loves me because—"

"She's told her father." Conall leaned close. "She's

sworn never to marry another. Only you. Do you no' see? You've ruined her for life."

Darroc shot to his feet. "Havers! It's my own sorry self I've ruined."

"Then do something about it." Conall flicked a speck of lint off his plaid. "I would if she were mine."

If she were his.

The words echoed in Darroc's head long after Conall strode from the room. Arabella *had* been his, regardless of why she'd fallen in love with him. And unless he wished to live the rest of his life in darkness, he really had no choice but go after her.

As for the Thunder Rod...

He pushed the hoary relic from his mind. In time, he was sure he could make her love him for himself, winning her heart without the help of his ancestor's wretched seduction tool.

Eager to begin, he glanced at the darkened windows, willing the morn to come quickly.

He had much to do, after all.

And he hadn't felt so good in days.

"Sail on the horizon!"

The cry came not long after sunrise, the MacKenzie oarsman who'd spotted the vessel pointing at the sleek birlinn cutting a furious swath toward them. Moving at tremendous speed, the craft flew across the waves, its long, lashing sweeps churning the sea and leaving a boiling wake.

It also looked familiar.

So much so that Arabella's breath caught in her throat and she bit down hard on her lower lip. Still, she feared to hope. But when the birlinn sped closer and a large dog's excited barks rose above the beats of the gong, she knew.

Especially when Mina jumped up in her basket, returning Frang's barks so enthusiastically that Arabella almost feared the tiny dog would harm herself.

"Dear saints, it's Darroc!" She ran down the galley's center aisle to where her parents and Sir Marmaduke stood on the bow platform. "He's come for me!"

"He'll be disappointed." Her father was already scowling daggers at the fast approaching birlinn. "You'll not be going anywhere with him."

Her mother and Sir Marmaduke said nothing. But they did exchange glances, the look letting Arabella know they were on her side.

The birlinn was almost upon them, and on seeing Darroc her heart galloped so fast it hurt her ribs. He stood at the steering oar as always. But his gaze was steady on her, the look on his face making her forget everything except that he was racing toward her.

That could only mean one thing.

And the truth of it sent joy spiraling through her.

She wanted to shout, whirl, and dance. She would have, too, if she didn't wish to risk making things worse between her father and Darroc.

Then he was there, the birlinn shooting past to whip around in a tight circle of lashing spray before gliding to a smooth, backwatering halt alongside the galley without even a single, jarring bump.

"MacKenzie—I greet you!" Darroc jumped into the galley without invitation. "I, Darroc MacConacher, chief of my race, have come to ask for your daughter's hand."

"You are a mad man." Duncan bristled. "And you shall not have Arabella."

"Then, sir, I will take her." On the birlinn, Frang barked agreement.

Duncan glared at the dog and leapt down from the bow platform, going toe-to-toe with Darroc. "Over my dead body, you will!"

"I should hope that it will not come to that." Darroc put a hand to his sword hilt, gripping it loosely. "But if you give me no choice…"

Duncan roared.

Then he leapt backward and reached for his own steel, yanking it halfway out of its scabbard before a strong hand gripped his wrist and forced the blade back into its sheath.

"Have done, Duncan." Sir Marmaduke waited a few moments before releasing his grip. "Let us hear what the man has to say. There can be no harm—"

"You stay out of this!" Duncan twisted around to glare at him. "Arabella is my daughter, not yours."

"She's my niece and"—he slid an arm around her when she ran up to them, pulling her close—"I, for one, have grown weary of watching her pine for this man."

"She hasn't been pining." Duncan waved an agitated hand. "She—"

"No, Father, you're wrong." Arabella broke away from her uncle and went to stand next to Darroc, demonstratively reaching for his hand. "I have been pining for Darroc and"—she laced their fingers—"I do want to be his wife."

"By the Rood!" Her father's face turned purple. "He's a bleeding MacConacher!"

"And you, sir, are a MacKenzie." Darroc smiled at him. "As is the woman I love more than my own life. There cannot be another man in all broad Scotland who could want her more. Or"—he squeezed her hand—"who will worship the very ground she walks on and make her wishes come true before she even knows she has them."

A muscle beneath Duncan's left eye began twitching. "What are you, MacConacher? A poet?"

"He is the man who loves me." Arabella lifted her chin, her heart swelling on the words. "And he is the man I love. The only man I shall ever want."

Duncan glared at her, his eye twitch worsening.

He said nothing.

"Is silence your consent?" Darroc spoke into the sudden quiet.

"My daughter will never marry a MacConacher." Duncan snorted. "I'd sooner see her paired with a four-eyed toad!"

"Father, please!" Arabella's face flamed, shame scalding her.

"She's my daughter, too." Linnet joined them, hooking her arm through her husband's. "I would know her happy. And"—she looked up at him, catching his gaze—"if not for this MacConacher, she wouldn't be here with us now."

"So what would you have me do?" He broke away from her and began pacing the galley's single aisle. "Marry her to the enemy?"

"Oh, yes. . . ." Linnet studied her fingernails. "The man who not only plucked her from the sea, but served vengeance on the men who would have killed her, not to mention ridding our seas of—"

"Enough!" Duncan threw up his hands. "I will... consider the match."

"Considering isn't good enough." Darroc pressed him. This time he was the one who went toe-to-toe. "I'd have your answer now."

"Saints, Maria, and Joseph!" Duncan rammed his fingers through his hair. "What if I'm not of a mood to give it?"

Arabella spoke before Darroc could answer. "Did you know, Father, that 'Saints, Maria, and Joseph' is one of Darroc's favorite curses?"

She smiled sweetly, waiting for the explosion.

When none came and he only stared at her, almost cross-eyed in his annoyance, she decided to press her advantage.

Quickly, before anyone could stop her, she bent to seize Mina's basket and thrust it to the MacConacher oarsmen looking on with interest from the birlinn. Then, as soon as Hugh had the basket, she winked at the man beside him.

Understanding, he stretched out his arms and caught her about the waist, lifting her into the birlinn.

Behind her, Darroc laughed, joining her in a wink.

Her father bellowed his outrage. "MacConacher! Dinna think to steal her away!"

"He doesn't have to, Father." Arabella gripped the birlinn's rail, standing tall. "I am going with him whether it pleases you or nae. But"—she leaned forward, not wanting to hurt him—"it would mean so much to me if you'll be happy for us. You know how much I love you."

To her amazement, a smile flickered across his face.

It was gone in an instant, but it gave her hope.

"I saw that!" She beamed back at him, her heart flipping. "Does this mean you'll come with us to Castle Bane? Stay there long enough to get to know Darroc and then see us wed. Our union properly blessed and feasted?"

The smile didn't return, but he jerked a nod. "Where did you learn to be so brazen?"

Arabella laughed. "If you don't know, perhaps you should ask Mother."

"Oh, he knows." Linnet smiled across at them. "He just isn't fond of owning to things that displease him."

"I can sympathize." Darroc returned her smile, willing to come halfway.

"I'm sure you can." Linnet's eyes twinkled.

The rowers on each craft exchanged commiserating glances, clearly of a like mind. Some even chuckled. Those married for many years nodded sagely.

Duncan scowled at them all. Then, almost as an afterthought, he offered a grudging *humph*.

Then, before he could voice a more unpleasant protest, Linnet drew him from the rail.

As soon as they moved away, Darroc swept Arabella into his arms and kissed her deeply. Again and again until they broke apart, gasping for air.

Darroc slid a glance at the galley, already pulling away. "I wouldn't say we've won him over, but—"

"It's a fair start, I agree." Arabella could hardly believe it. "Considering how he is...."

"You know what this means, don't you?" He smoothed back her hair, the love in his eyes melting her. "You are mine now, Arabella. All mine, praise every saint in heaven! And, by God"—he cradled her face as if she were the most precious thing in the world—"I'll never ever let you go."

"You won't have to. I've been yours forever, I'm thinking." She slid her arms around his neck, twining her fingers in his hair. "But if ever you do wish to be rid of me, you'll be very sorry."

"Ach, sweetness, I was sorry this time." He kissed her, lightly now. "I didn't last an hour before I wanted you back in my arms. I paced the battlements and prowled about your bedchamber, aching for you."

"Aching?" Arabella leaned into him, letting her body press against his.

"Aching terribly." He brushed the hair from her face again, his gaze going to her father's galley. The other craft beat along beside them, but at a courteously discreet distance. "When night falls, I will show you how much."

Arabella's eyes flew wide. "But we can't—not this trip."

Scandalized, her gaze flitted to the crowded rowing benches. The narrow center aisle and stern-and-bow platforms, both glaringly bare of a sailcloth awning.

When she looked back at him, she knew her cheeks were tinged pink. "Your men would see us."

To her surprise, Darroc laughed. "Sweet lass, I thought you were bold?"

Arabella swallowed. "Not that bold."

"I am glad to hear it!" He laughed again and gave her another fast, hard kiss.

Then he slid a pointed glance at the prow. "But if you're inclined to change your mind and be daring, perhaps it will please you to know there's a new plaid kist tucked away near the bow."

"A new plaid kist?" Arabella blinked.

He nodded. "To replace the one I pitched into the sea on our way to Olaf's isle."

"What's in the new chest?" She had a good notion.

"Ach, just an armful of plaids to make a comfortable pallet and"—he grinned—"our own special sailcloth screen, brought along just for you."

"You were that sure of me?" Her pulse quickened at the thought.

"Nae." He shook his head. "I was that sure of us."

"Oh, Darroc!" She flung herself at him, her heart bursting. "I love you so!"

"Not as much as I love you." He leaned down to nibble her ear.

Arabella shivered. "Perhaps we can decide tonight who loves who the most?"

He arched a brow. "Are you feeling bold, my lady?"

"I am." She cupped his face in her hands and kissed him. "Most bold, indeed."

Epilogue

OLAF BIG NOSE'S ISLE

A CELEBRATION IN THE CLEARING

SPRING 1351

I ask you, did you e'er see anything sweeter?"

Olaf Big Nose waved a parchment scroll in the air, laughing heartily when the dangling wax seals swung on their bright red ribbons.

"This is my island!" He jumped to his feet, looking down the festively dressed table, and at other tables ranged close by. He didn't, after all, want anyone to forget the reason for this gathering.

It was to give thanks for the charter granting him rights to his beloved little isle.

So he began marching to and fro, proudly thrusting the parchment beneath the nose of anyone he could corner and, hopefully, impress.

Truth be told, there was much to wonder at this fine spring e'en on Olaf Big Nose's newly acquired isle.

Newly—*officially*—acquired isle.

No less than six whole bullocks roasted over open fires, the mouth-watering aroma drifting on the air, tempting palates young and old. And every lavishly set table held not only a wealth of savories and jugs of tasty honey mead, but was illuminated by candle braces cast of pure, gleaming silver.

The guests were no less fine.

And so numerous that extra trestle tables had to be brought from Castle Bane on nearby MacConacher's Isle. Equally astounding, the MacConacher's new lady wife— it was rumored—had spent months stitching additional sailcloth awnings to accommodate the expected crush of well-wishers.

The most splendid sailcloths gracing the fest were believed to be her work, though the lady herself was too modest to claim the glory.

So it was only right and good that she and Darroc were seated at one of the best-placed feasting tables lining the clearing. They had a splendid view of the grassy area where musicians would soon be playing and those merrymakers so inclined could whirl and jig to screaming pipes and lively fiddles.

Bonfires and resin torches waited to be set ablaze at dusk and already a sense of anticipation and excitement filled the air. Everywhere people milled and conversed, many laughing. Some, perhaps, were enjoying a bit too much heather ale. But on such a grand day, no one minded.

Indulgences were expected and welcome at Norse feastings.

Even so, Arabella declined the potent brew, a sweet secret making her wary of partaking. But she enjoyed watching the revelries. She especially thrilled to see Olaf Big Nose's swell-chested joy in his land charter and the great pleasure of Captain Arneborg and his new wife, Arnora Ship-Breast, in the captain's newly built merchant cog, a gift from her father, in gratitude.

Arabella's heart squeezed thinking about her father.

She missed him so much and wished that he—and all her family—could be here, but Gelis was about to give birth to her first child. A wee laddie, if her mother and Devorgilla had the right of it. So Clan MacKenzie was away in distant Kintail, though Devorgilla and her little helpmate, Somerled, were in happy attendance.

Holding court at the next table, Devorgilla exchanged herbal remedies and spelling charms with Mad Moraig. The two women seemed to get on well, although Devorgilla clearly took it badly each time Somerled accepted a treat from Moraig.

She was quite possessive of her little friend's favor.

"*Do you truly think the wee fox put seaweed in the plaid kist?*"

Arabella started at Darroc's question. She'd been so lost in watching the clearing fill with late-coming arrivals. But now, she turned to him, pleased when he leaned close to nuzzle her neck.

"That's what Devorgilla said." She glanced at the cailleach, unable to suppress a shiver. "She isn't one to tell tall tales."

Darroc lifted a brow. "And the strange mist?" He nipped his way up her neck to her ear, giving her shivers of an entirely different sort. "I know Geordie Dhu can taste the seas and predict weather, but to summon it?"

"My sister would say suchlike is possible." Arabella

angled her head, giving him greater access to the sensitive area beneath her chin. "Gelis believes in all magic. She would love your Thunder Rod." She glanced down the table to where the relic held pride of place near a softly glowing silver candelabrum.

"*The Thunder Rod!*" Darroc blanched. "How did that thing get here?"

"I brought it. I thought you'd be pleased because this feast is also to celebrate us." She glanced at the rod. "A bit of family tradition."

"I'd sooner have none." Darroc reached for his ale cup and drained it in one gulp.

Arabella's face heated. She didn't understand his displeasure.

Truth was, she'd hoped to surprise him by sewing a new tartan band for the rod. The old ribbon was in tatters and Jutta Manslayer and Arnora Ship-Breast had promised her several colorful ells of cloth.

Now it would seem her surprise might ruin their only night of true revelry since their first visit to this isle.

Hoping it wasn't so, Arabella flashed another glance at the rod and—suddenly—all the hushed murmurings and whispers she'd ever heard about the relic's powers came rushing back to her. Every one, including what the supposedly magical relic purportedly did to unsuspecting females.

How could she have forgotten?

But she answered her own question when she slipped her hand to her slender waist and her heart flipped on the possibility that there might be a new life quickening beneath her breast.

She hadn't thought of anything else in two moon cycles.

Now horror washed over her.

"Merciful saints!" She stared at Darroc, comprehension sweeping her.

He looked even more miserable than she felt.

Only a man who loved deeply and saw his world shattering could appear so lost.

So empty and glum.

Suspicion high, she reached along the table to retrieve the Thunder Rod.

"Is this why you're staring at me as if I've grown two heads?" She waved the rod at him. "Because I've touched the fabled Thunder Rod?"

His expression said it was.

"Why did you take it again?" His voice sounded choked, not his at all. "I know you had it once before. I found it in your bed."

Arabella stared at him. "Of course it was in my bed. I was working on it."

"But why?" He still looked as if he expected the relic to turn into a fire-breathing dragon and gobble them both. "You should never have touched it. It's—"

"It's a piece of wood." Arabella couldn't believe he saw it as anything else.

He clearly did.

She couldn't possibly. So she slid her arms around him and leaned close to brush soft kisses across his lips and cheeks and his brow. "There was nothing wrong with me touching it, I swear to you."

He pulled back from her, his gaze going to the relic. "When did you touch it the first time?"

"Ages ago." She smoothed her hands up his back and over his shoulders, lacing her fingers behind his neck. "I think when I was able to walk after the *Merry Dancer* wreck. I'd taken it to my room one night and Mungo—"

"*Mungo!*" Darroc's brows shot up. "You spoke with Mungo after holding the Thunder Rod?"

Arabella nodded. "Of course, but it was Moraig I'd wanted. When I couldn't find her, I went to Mungo. I needed stitching thread and needles."

"I'm no' following you." He did sound confused.

"Have you never noticed how tatty the rod's ribbon has become?" It made perfect sense to her. "I wanted to surprise you by making a new band for the relic. But I didn't have the right kind of tartan cloth, so—"

"But you saw Mungo *after* you'd touched the rod?" His eyes were still round. "And"—he pulled a hand down over his face—"nothing happened?"

"What should have happened?" She pretended innocence.

She'd been at Castle Bane long enough to have learned its secrets.

"If you mean the Thunder Rod's magic, you should know by now that I don't believe in such nonsense." She kissed him, breathing the words against his lips.

"But—"

"Stop *butting* and kiss me back."

"Och, my sweet bold lassie." He gathered her close, almost crushing her. "You must know that's why I sent you away. I'd found the rod in your room and thought its damnable power was the reason you fell in love with me. I wanted you to—"

"Have a chance to *truly* fall in love?" She shook her head. "Oh, Darroc, I can't believe we almost lost each other over such silliness."

"Can you forgive me?" He looked stricken.

"I already have!" She tightened her arms around him. "But you should have known the truth all along."

"The truth?" He blinked.

"That the Thunder Rod"—she kissed him, pressing a new kiss to his lips between each word—"had nothing to do with my falling in love with you. It was you and you alone that won my heart."

"Oh, how I love you!" He kissed her hard. And it was the kind of kiss that went straight to her toes.

And, perhaps, spoke of wickedly delicious things to come later.

She sighed, melting. "Then don't ever doubt it again."

"Doubt what?"

She lifted her chin so that she could look into his beloved face. "That there isn't a greater magic on earth than the power of a heart that loves."

With the words spoken, a deep peace settled over them both.

And had either of them glanced heavenward, they just might have seen a shooting star.

A wee bit of magic sent from a very happy, bright-shimmering soul in Shetland who wished them well.

THE DISH

Where authors give you the inside scoop!

♥ ♥ ♥ ♥ ♥ ♥ ♥ ♥ ♥ ♥ ♥ ♥ ♥ ♥ ♥ ♥ ♥

From the desk of Shannon K. Butcher

Dear Reader,

For thirty days, I lurked inside the mind of a deranged serial killer. And let me tell you, it may be an interesting place to visit, but I'm glad I don't have to live there. Thirty days was long enough, and I spent every one of them looking over my shoulder, in the backseat of my car, and under my bed. Just in case.

Luckily, I had some professional help with the profile for the killer in LOVE YOU TO DEATH, but little did I know how much more it would creep me out when I realized I was creating this character from bits and pieces of *real* people and *real* crimes. In fact, it creeped me out so much that the security system and our dog were no longer enough. I went out, bought a gun, and learned how to use it, just in case someone like Gary decided to come calling.

Ridiculous? Probably. But my Sig Sauer, its magazines holding eighty bullets, and I all feel much better.

This book opened my eyes to a world that I'd never really thought about before. Sure, we see reports on the news about murder and abduction, but there's always a kind of distance to those stories. This project forced me to put myself inside the heads of both the victims and the killer, and after doing so, every story I've seen on the news has suddenly become real—a waking-up-with-nightmares, buying-a-gun kind of real.

Being able to write about two people who fall in love during such a difficult time was something I wasn't sure I could do, but I hope I pulled it off. Elise and Trent and their love for each other brighten up the darker parts of this book, and their relationship highlights just how important it is to have someone to lean on when things become impossible.

I won't spoil the end of LOVE YOU TO DEATH, but I can confidently say that I've never felt more satisfied with the justice I've inflicted on my deserving characters than I did with Gary. I hope you agree. And if you do decide to crawl inside the mind of a serial killer by reading this book, I recommend doing so with the lights on and the doors locked.

Enjoy!

Shannon K Butcher

http://www.shannonkbutcher.com/

♥ ♥ ♥ ♥ ♥ ♥ ♥ ♥ ♥ ♥ ♥ ♥ ♥ ♥ ♥

From the desk of Kate Perry

Dear Readers,

Hot naked men!

An unorthodox beginning, I know, but you have to admit it caught your attention. Also, it's vastly more interesting to talk about hot naked men than it is to discuss, say, tutus. Not to mention that hot naked men and my Guardians of Destiny series go hand in hand. Tutus? Not so much.

For instance, in the first book, MARKED BY PASSION, we have Rhys, the British bad boy who's got it all—except the woman who sets him on fire. Rhys is hot on so many levels, and when he strips down...I'd suggest keeping an extinguisher on hand.

And then there's Max, the hero of CHOSEN BY DESIRE, the second Guardians of Destiny novel. A past betrayal has Max closed off—until he meets the right woman, who makes him want to bare it all. Naked, he's a sight to behold. Plus, he's got a big sword, and he knows how to use it.

Unclothed, finely chiseled men. Sassy heroines who tame them. Kick-ass kung fu scenes. Much more exciting than tutus, don't you think?

Happy Reading!

Kate Perry

www.kateperry.com

♥ ♥ ♥ ♥ ♥ ♥ ♥ ♥ ♥ ♥ ♥ ♥ ♥ ♥ ♥ ♥

From the desk of Sue-Ellen Welfonder

Dear Reader,

Sometimes people ask me why I set my books in Scotland. My reaction is always bafflement. I'm amazed that anyone would wonder. Aside from my own ancestral ties—I was born loving Scotland—I can't imagine a place better suited to inspire romance.

Rich in legend and lore, steeped in history, and blessed with incredible natural beauty, Scotland offers everything a romantic heart could desire. Mist-hung hills, castle ruins, and dark glens abound, recalling the great days of the clans and a time when heroism, loyalty, and honor meant everything. In A HIGHLANDER'S TEMPTATION, Darroc MacConacher and Arabella MacKenzie live by these values—until they are swept into a tempestuous passion that is not only irresistible but forbidden, and acknowledging their love could destroy everything they hold dear.

In writing their tale, I knew I needed something very special—and powerful—to help them push past the long-simmering feud that could so easily rip them apart. With such fierce clan history between them, I wanted something imbued with Highland magic that would lend a dash of Celtic whimsy and lightness to the story.

Fortunately, I didn't have to look far.

One of my favorite haunts in Scotland had just the special something I needed.

It was the Thunder Stone, an innocuous-looking stone displayed on the soot-stained wall of a very atmospheric drovers' inn on the northwestern shore of Loch Lomond. Said to possess magical powers I won't describe, the stone is often borrowed by local clansmen. I've eyed the stone each time I've stopped at the inn and always thought to someday include it in a book. A HIGHLANDER'S TEMPTATION gave me that opportunity.

Changed into a prized clan heirloom and called the Thunder Rod in A HIGHLANDER'S TEMPTA-TION, the relic provided just the bit of intrigue and lore I love weaving into my stories. I hope you'll enjoy discovering whether its magic worked. *Hint:* Darroc and Arabella do have a happy ending!

With all good wishes,

Sue-Ellen Welfonder

www.welfonder.com

**Sue-Ellen Welfonder also writes as
national bestselling author**

ALLIE MACKAY

Tall,
Dark, and
Kilted

"Allie Mackay pens
stories that sparkle"
—Angela Knight

ALLIE MACKAY
Author of *Highlander in Her Dreams*

"ALLIE MACKAY PENS STORIES THAT SPARKLE"
—Angela Knight

Highlander
in Her
Dreams

**ALLIE
MACKAY**
Author of *Highlander in Her Bed*

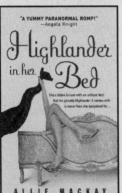

"A YUMMY PARANORMAL ROMP!"
—Angela Knight

Highlander
in her
Bed

She's fallen in love with an antique bed.
But the ghostly Highlander it comes with
is more than she bargained for...

ALLIE MACKAY

**Look for her sexy
paranormal romances
featuring ruggedly
handsome Scottish
highlanders**

**"Allie Mackay pens
stories that sparkle."**
—*USA Today* bestselling
author Angela Knight

SIGNET ECLIPSE
Member of Penguin Group (USA) • penguin.com

Want to know more about romances at Grand Central Publishing and Forever? Get the scoop online!

GRAND CENTRAL PUBLISHING'S ROMANCE HOMEPAGE

Visit us at www.hachettebookgroup.com/romance for all the latest news, reviews, and chapter excerpts!

NEW AND UPCOMING TITLES

Each month we feature our new titles and reader favorites.

CONTESTS AND GIVEAWAYS

We give away galleys, autographed copies, and all kinds of fun stuff.

AUTHOR INFO

You'll find bios, articles, and links to personal websites for all your favorite authors—and so much more!

THE BUZZ

Sign up for our monthly romance newsletter, and be the first to read all about it!